SMEARED

LAVENDER

First Edition

ISBN 9798990869004 (print)
ISBN 9798990869011 (ebook)

Smeared Lavender

The first novel in the
Smeared Lavender series
by the writing brand

Characters

Nexxa Davoren

Employed with
Kuretz Investments,
lavender glow

Iliada Ballou

Nexxa's younger sister

Sergei Kozlov

Russian entrepreneur
and suitor of Nexxa

Quinn Osian Kane

Irish entrepreneur, UVF Party member, and suitor of Nexxa

Klarin D. Maoilriain

Irish assassin for hire, former RIRA member, sky-blue accessories

Kilmer Davoren

Ex-husband to Nexxa and former IRA member,

"Charming Kilmer"

Diane Soo Hoo

China Black Road V.P.

Faroud Abboud

General Manager for the
National Lebanese Bank,
Nexxa's client

Tarek
Head of Finance for
Hezbollah controlled entity

Medan Muran

Agent for General
Directorate Lebanon,
acquaintance of Nexxa

Zarian "Zarry"
Medan's friend and
Iliada's love interest

Sal
Nahil's husband,
Medan's cousin, and
Hezbollah member

Nahil
Nahil's Fashions shop
owner, Sal's wife

Bogdan
Sergei's Head of
Security

Mr. Albert

Chinese entrepreneur from
NYC and Nexxa's mentor

Ankica
Sergei's babushka

Philip
Nexxa's married colleague

Natina
Sergei's baby niece

Dan Kuretz
President Kuretz Investments,
Nexxa's boss

Demo/Donat
Sergei's actor brother
and Natina's father

Hoolihane "Hooli"
Sergei's employed IT specialist,
hacker

Rosha
Sergei's babushka's
cousin

Mikhail
Sergei's business partner in
restaurant Vogue, brother
to Ella

Rochelle
Sergei's stalker
ex-girlfriend

Prologue

Sky Blue

IRELAND — LATE SEPTEMBER 2013

Klarin always dressed in a sky-blue something. Today she tied a sky-blue silk scarf around her angular neck. Drinking her morning cup of PG Tips tea, she signed into one of the many darknet sites she used for work—KosmicMarket.onion. User CrownofJools had a message from the username KitchenGod; KitchenGod's message was vague, saying only that there was a job to "remove something that doesn't belong" in New York City. She initiated the conversation with a request for more details. It became clear that there was a possibility to take care of the job in Beirut.

She wrote the details on a dry-erase board: blonde woman, thirty years old, broker-dealer, New York. Then she wrote dates in October. She doodled a woman's face with flowing hair beside the notes on the board. Stepping back to look at her drawing, she smiled, then went to her bedroom.

The room was simple with sky-blue curtains, an off-white armchair in the corner, a wardrobe, and one nightstand by the impeccably made bed. She took off her skirt and laid it carefully to prevent it from wrinkling, removing a strand of her long black hair. Beside the bed, she had a framed photo. In the nightstand was a blonde wig perfectly brushed, neatly placed. With care, she placed the frame photo side down and withdrew the wig, draping it across the panties she still had on. Sliding her hand down, she massaged her clitoris with her left hand and stroked the hair on the wig with her right hand. Climaxing, she cackled. The right hand lifted the blonde wig. Finished, she went to the dry-erase board and smeared her creamy fluid across the woman's face she had drawn.

It was almost hard to take the petite, feminine-looking man from the Far East seriously. To look at him, KitchenGod, you wouldn't think he was the type to troll the dark web. Once in Beirut, Klarin purposely arranged to meet him in the hotel's restaurant between lunch and dinner, knowing this would provide the necessary seclusion. His English was battered, not broken, she decided as she sat properly whilst drinking her afternoon tea. He clumsily drank tap water, even missing his sip once, letting water drip down his chin. She almost felt sorry for the poor bloke; eliminating him too crossed her mind. When they parted, she returned to her room in the InterContinental Le Vendôme Beirut. She obsessively brushed her silky black hair and lint rolled her cream cashmere jacket, which she had already done before meeting the Asian for tea. On-time, he delivered the rest of the details and the second installment.

Her next step, after she wrapped her sky-blue Loro Piana scarf over her head, was to meet up with an old friend. Klarin wanted to let him, and in turn his organization with ties to Iran, know she was in Beirut. Sal gave her an address: a home with a fountain outside, guarded, of course. Emerging from the car, her timid nature shrouded her like a proper Muslim woman. Hezbollah guards escorted her inside to see the one in charge, Sal's uncle. She intended on a simple cross-organization conversation, out of courtesy. As a rogue IRA member, she needed to get paid to buy sky-blue things; she didn't mention that detail. She did mention an American woman; she didn't mention the sloppy man from the Far East. Should anything go wrong, she might need safe passage to leave Lebanon, for she would never intend on spilling a drop of her icy, sky-blue blood.

55TH ST., THE ST. REGIS NEW YORK

3 WEEKS EARLIER

Philip imagined sliding his hands down Nexxa's black Wolford lace thigh highs, following with his eyes from her ankles to where the lace ended and her toned upper thighs were visible. Standing against the chaise lounge in the ladies' room of The St. Regis hotel, Nexxa recited, *"Cogito ergo sum, sed ante futuis me—Ya dumayu, poetomu ya est'. No snachala trahny menya."*

Philip had bought her the black lace panties she was wearing. He imagined pulling them slowly down around her ankles. "These are new?" Philip reached out, running a finger over her knee as Nexxa was now seated, legs crossed on the chaise lounge. Nexxa reached for her phone after it pinged, glancing at a text from her sister Iliada before acknowledging his question.

"No." She shrugged a shoulder then changed the song playing on her phone to a song by Thievery Corporation. Nexxa enlarged the pic of the nail lacquer color, Glittery Black, which Iliada sent in her text. If it had a speck of black, it excited Nexxa. She purposely bought anything black that was by the Austrian brand Wolford. A black long sleeve bodysuit, black Fatal dress, everything from The Ready to Wear to tights. She could still taste the Lambrusco Rosé she had drunk at the hotel bar, King Cole, when she swallowed. She didn't want to admit to Philip that she was tipsy; instead, she turned the conversation to her personal investment account, which had produced a nice profit thanks to him.

"My account is up," Nexxa barely got out before Philip pushed her back on the lounger.

"I want you," Philip said as he lay on top of her kissing her. The ladies' room smelled fragrant like sugar water, and Philip's breath was minty cold with his lips moving to her breasts. The music stopped—Nexxa turned her head toward the noise from the passersby on the street.

"I can't right now. I need another song to play," Nexxa exhaled, reaching for her phone. "Or I'll lose my rosé high."

"Just the tip, darling," Philip whispered, moving his hand down between her legs.

Nexxa fumbled for her phone, reaching behind her back where it had fallen from the top of the chaise lounge. Philip stopped kissing her, pushing himself upon his knees still over her body. Nexxa selected her Vampy playlist, then laid her phone back down and smiled up at Philip.

Philip leaned, kissing the part of her thigh that was exposed between her panties and thigh highs. "Mmm," he breathed into her body as he used one hand to tug at her panties gently.

Nexxa pulled up her lace thong from his hand. "I can't do this here."

"Can't do what?" Philip managed sarcastically in his subdued European accent.

Nexxa laughed. "Uh, fuck in the lobby bathroom." Nexxa caressed Philip's hair. "This isn't the Milano suite."

Philip pushed himself up and huffed, "I'm going away for a week. Work." His eyes were a mix of irritation and intense desire for her.

"I'm sure you can make it for one week." Nexxa's feelings of resentment always crept in when she least expected them to. "Next time," Nexxa sat up as Philip stood from the chaise, "the Milano suite, unless you don't want me again."

"Want you again?" Philip scrunched his forehead.

Nexxa extended her arm; Philip grasped her hand, helping her to stand. He knew he would miss her, miss fucking her while he was away. Partly, he worried he wouldn't be able to focus on his work, wondering if she was going on a date. He would never admit that to her. Philip stepped toward Nexxa and, before she was able to slip on her bra, kissed her perfect breasts. "This is very ambiguous of us," Philip said, between kissing her décolletage. "It's not like we can go to a movie or a play. We could bump into someone from the office."

"You could get divorced again," Nexxa responded. Philip and Nexxa began seeing each other almost immediately after she started working with him at Kuretz Investments, a broker-dealer specializing in the Fixed Income bond market. An innocent kiss on the cheek on Nexxa's part led Philip to kiss her one night after a work dinner. From then on, they met discreetly after work under the guise that Philip would teach her Latin. He was in yet another unhappy marriage, his second, and Nexxa had just left her ex-husband. "*Aut habet ille gustum meliorem quam meum. Ily na vkus ona luchshe menya?*"

"Or does she taste better than me?" Philip translated from Latin and Russian, eyeing Nexxa in the mirror while she blotted her face with a tissue. "*You* taste the best." His eyes were still on her. "And your Russian tutor," Philip's tone changed, "how's that going?"

"Uh-huh, good." Looking away from the mirror, she smiled. "He's good." Nexxa knew what Philip meant. He wanted to know if she fucked her Russian tutor. At least she knew he was jealous, even if it came from him wanting to see if she slept around.

Nexxa applied her Dior lip balm and repositioned her hair into a ponytail. "So, I um." She fiddled with the lip balm container, sliding it apart and back together again, and turned to face Philip.

"You want to tell me something?" Philip raised his eyebrows.

"I just—I keep having dreams that I really feel are warnings."

"I'm quite sure most dreams have a meaning of some sort."

"I keep having the same lucid dream." Nexxa paused, pulling her hand along her ponytail. "A snake keeps coming up to me, then a strange man; it's disturbing."

Philip positioned himself against the wall, crossing his feet and folding his arms. On the weekends, he volunteered as a counselor to troubled teens. A licensed social worker, *The pay is not realistic to the lifestyle*, he would say, which is why he continued to work in finance. "I think you've got to discern what could have influenced your dreams, something that happened during your day, from what could actually be an indication of a warning."

"Yeah, I guess." Nexxa suspected she was experiencing a psychic attack causing repetitive dreams. She wouldn't mention this to him, though.

Philip gave her a stern look. "*That* is the real question," he said, before he lifted the glass of white wine he had carried from the bar, taking a sip.

Nexxa took Philip's glass from his hand, also taking a sip. Then she took his hand in hers and kissed it. She respected him, and although they weren't in love, she knew she could be if given a chance. Philip was only about five foot ten with dark, receding hair, but his dark eyes and sophisticated accent attracted Nexxa along with his five o'clock shadow.

Philip leaned over, lifting a shopping bag he had brought with him. He pulled out a split of champagne and slipped some folded cash. "Something for you," he said as he kissed her on the cheek.

In Nexxa's world, everything needed to have a benefit. Philip's purpose was evident, but cash and prizes, as she called it, were her way of feeling empowered. Being a blonde, elegant, well-spoken thirty-year-old woman attracted plenty of attention. However, she was more than that. Kind, she told herself; most women from the tri-state area aren't kind. She liked to joke that she was a luxury import.

Nexxa put the money in her purse and picked up the shopping bag, placing the champagne back in the bag. "I'm going shopping with my sister in Takashima this week." Groping Philip's penis through his pants, she sighed seductively. "Thank you for your financial backing."

Philip folded his arms again, grasping his chin, "One thought—before you go."

"Yeah?" Nexxa asked as her stomach rolled. She liked to leave their Latin lessons, personal time, on a casual level. Things could get messy if she didn't. *Thank you for your financial backing*, was brilliant. All she wanted to do was slip across the street to the Peninsula and text her co-worker that she was now at the gym since her appointment ran late.

"I was thinking. How about we—" Philip was stopped by Nexxa looking at her phone. She had a text from her co-worker; if one was out, the other one had to be on the desk, that she would leave to run an errand. Nexxa knew her co-worker was probably irritated because Nexxa had left the office during the day for what Nexxa referred to as a "doctor's appointment." *White lie*, Nexxa reminded herself of her "appointment" with Philip.

"How am I going to get back now?" Nexxa shook her head, assuming Philip would know what she meant.

"Get back to?"

"She just texted me that she is leaving to run an errand. I mean, what if she walks this way, down 55th Street? I have no idea what direction she will go in."

"Take an Uber." Philip removed his phone from his pocket.

"Yeah, and if she sees me walk out of the hotel?"

"So, I was thinking…" Philip tapped on his Uber app.

Nexxa slipped two freshmint Tic Tacs in her mouth and threw her YSL purse over her shoulder. She kissed Philip on the cheek. "I need to go," she said, thinking *something needs to change* before she briskly exited the hotel, eager to be in the company of the Ukrainian women that worked in the spa across from her office.

55TH ST., THE PENINSULA NEW YORK

SEPTEMBER 2013

"You look like the film actress Kim Novak." Nexxa had to hold on to each word through the heavy Eastern European accent the ladies' room attendant spoke with.

"Oh, okay." Nexxa replied with a smile but really was thinking, *Who is Kim Novak?* She stashed her toiletries in her make-up bag and stowed away her gym bag in one of the wooden lockers. Nexxa Googled an image of the actress. There was a striking resemblance. They were blonde and had perfectly shaped almond eyes, high cheekbones, and softly shaped lips that lent to a seductive face.

Nexxa climbed the curved staircase, and with each step, she could see the dusk sky through the skylights revealing smeared clouds looking like potions brewing over Manhattan. The stairs led to the hotel's rooftop bar, Salon de Ning, and out to the bar's terrace. This was one of Nexxa's 3: the three spots she graced within her triangle of coveted spots in Manhattan.

"Nex, how are you?" asked Viraj as he and Nexxa embraced. Viraj and Nexxa had become friends since Nexxa joined the "spa," as Viraj referred to it. The Peninsula Hotel had a gym with a pool, a sundeck, and a spa, of which anyone who could afford to join could become a member. She once met Ozzy Osbourne. She thought he was just some white trash from New Jersey; only later did she realize who he was. His long, ridiculous pink and blue hair tied back in a low ponytail was deceiving. John Travolta was another A-list celebrity she encountered. He had asked her where the pool was. He had an impeccable disposition about him. Ozzy seemed gracious, as well.

"Such a beautiful sky tonight, kind of sexy," Viraj said.

"Yes, it is." Nexxa looked over her shoulder. "I have that feeling I get before a premonition."

"Oh, do tell," Viraj inquired with sex in his eyes.

"No, not that, my dear friend." Nexxa reached out, touching his arm. "More like a chance encounter," she said, fluttering her hand in the air, "or should I say the next twist of fate?" Just as the word *fate* left Nexxa's mouth, a gentleman approached them and asked to borrow a light. Viraj blew from his cigarette and held out his lighter, engraved with his initials, VD, to the man.

"Mmm, look at him," Viraj gushed. As the man went farther out onto the terrace for a smoke, Nexxa turned to watch him. He was attractive for his age, she guessed about mid to late fifties, and his darker skin muted the gray in his dark hair. By his accent, she assumed he was Middle Eastern. She wasn't surprised Viraj had eyes on the man since Viraj himself was attractive and armed with a South African accent, which paired well with his dark East Indian skin. It wasn't long, just long enough to size him up, then the man returned from his smoke and graciously returned Viraj's lighter.

"May I buy you a drink?" he politely asked them.

"Please sit. I'm Viraj, and this is Nexxa."

"Nice to meet you. I am Faroud Abboud."

"So, you are staying in the hotel, I presume," Nexxa said. Usually, Viraj would ask guests questions, but this time was different.

"Yes, I am. I am here on business."

"Ah, okay. We are members of the spa, but my office is right across the street," Nexxa turned her upper body looking over her shoulder, "Kuretz Investments."

"The spa?" questioned Faroud.

"Oh, well, that is what Viraj calls it. We are members of the gym, which has a spa with access to the pool and sundeck for members."

"Ah, very nice," said Faroud.

"So, how long are you in New York?"

"Well, I am here for a few more days. I work for the National Lebanese Bank."

"My firm, Kuretz Investments, is a broker-dealer." Nexxa turned her body into Faroud. "Fixed Income, that is our area of the market."

"Ah, very good." Faroud's response mimicked his first. "We are trying to raise capital to rebuild our infrastructure so that we may increase tourism in Beirut and the rest of our country."

"I would love to introduce you to my firm." Nexxa figured he would take this as a come-on. Most men did. But his demeanor was different. She could tell. Nexxa couldn't help but feel that this may be just what she was looking for. If only it hadn't been for her recurring lucid dream with an unknown man and the snake that appeared before her, she would definitely feel excited. But then again, she usually attributed her dreams to warnings about dating. Like the loser she once fell for from Long Island that she dubbed a *Long Island Lolito.*

"Tell me," Faroud paused, "have you been to my country before?"

"No, I haven't, but I would love to. I would love to travel more. I've only really been to Europe. But I would love to go to the Middle East and Russia."

"Can we get another round?" Viraj said to the waiter. Sparkling water for him as Viraj's only vices were men and smokes.

"The sea and the mountains are all there together. You won't see any country as beautiful as mine. We are the most religiously diverse country in the Middle East. We all exist together now. After the war, everyone is happy," continued Faroud as the waiter served a new round of drinks. Nexxa lightly nodded.

"You must come and see my country. My personal guest!" Faroud appeared just as sincere as he was jubilant.

"Why don't we meet here for brunch tomorrow? They will serve us on the sundeck. I'll bring my boss. I know he would love to meet you."

"I would love to."

"Wonderful. It will be so nice. I find that brunch time is a great time of day in the city."

"Nex, *any* time is a great time in New York. I love this city."

"I know, Viraj."

"So, you must come," Faroud continued with his excitement.

"To Beirut?"

"Yes, it is settled; you are coming!"

"Well, I have to have a reason, for work," Nexxa countered, motioning with hands palms up. She wasn't holding back. Not this time.

Viraj took a call, a gentleman calling—stepping away with a cigarette in hand—and Faroud leaned in closer to Nexxa.

"I am the *General Manager* of my bank."

"I see." Nexxa shook her head in acknowledgment.

"Well, my firm is small, but I tend to work closely with my boss."

Viraj returned from smoking and announced, "I need to go check on my poodle baby."

"Ah, you have a poodle. I have a dog; you call it a Schnoodle. Her name is Jasmine."

"Well, why don't we have one last drink, and then I should go home as well. I don't have a dog, but I do have a sister to check on." Nexxa looked at her phone: no new text messages. "She was supposed to join us, but I guess she had to work late."

Nexxa kissed Viraj on the cheek and wished him a good night. As he made his way inside from the terrace, he found Iliada making her way toward them. "Iliada!" Viraj embraced her with a kiss on her glimmering cheeks. "Come." He led her by the hand to Nexxa.

"This must be your sister," Faroud announced, spotting

Iliada as she approached them. "A stunning blonde like your sister," Faroud continued, standing to greet her. Iliada was often mistaken for being older than Nexxa since she was taller.

"Hi." Iliada was gracious.

"Come, come sit." Faroud moved a chair for her. Iliada sat and positioned her purse on the chair. "Your sister tells me she works in finance. Do you as well?"

"No, no, I work for the Namaguto family. I just moved here from Canada to live with Nexxa."

A waiter approached, and Iliada ordered a glass of red wine. "The same as my sister," she told the waiter. "It's a Japanese firm called Namaguto." Iliada had befriended Sufu, the daughter of Mr. Namaguto, who was like an adorable puppy with the attitude of an Irish gnome. Sufu was Iliada's only friend, and they were never more than a fairy wing's length apart in the office.

"So, what is it that you do there?" asked Faroud before motioning to the waiter for another drink.

"Well, while my sister has private," Iliada used air marks, "'Latin lessons' in The St. Regis hotel, I have lessons in painting nails with Sufu in the rooftop garden of Namaguto." Iliada laughed. Nexxa turned her head to the side, a slight flush, before laughing. She knew Iliada wanted to be like her—live in a big city, date, shop, have a career, and *apparently* be facetious.

The three of them chatted more about everything from dating to shows on Netflix while they had yet another round of drinks. Inside, Nexxa couldn't wait to text her boss Dan after she concluded her evening with Faroud. She knew he would be up late, probably trolling something sordid online, trying to *quietly* swipe on his Tinder app as he lay in bed next to his snoring wife.

With the evening sky gone and the next day's gray skies arriving, Nexxa waited with Dan to greet Faroud on the sundeck by the pool for a brunch meeting. She wore her professional face. This meant subdued red, dabbing on a little red lipstick, and her hair in a French twist. She kept telling herself that she was fifty-fifty—fifty percent confident and fifty percent okay with the meeting not going well. No, that wasn't true. She had already Googled Beirut and mind fucked the hell out of the satisfaction that could come from putting a deal together, getting a huge commission, and traveling to the Middle East, one of the places in the world she most desired to visit.

Dan looked good as usual in a greige cashmere sweater he had recently acquired on a trip to Italy, and she smelled his optimism.

"So, I guess this turned out to be the spot, huh," Dan said.

"It's been fantastic all around. This hotel, or spa, is my home away from home."

"I need a girlfriend to bring here," Dan joked, appeasing the little devil on his shoulder.

Nexxa shook her head, showing moderate disapproval.

"So, tell me what you think. Should we go for it?"

"I want to go—all the way." Nexxa stood and said, "Faroud," as he approached the table.

"Lovely to see you again."

"This is Dan, my boss." Dan shook Faroud's hand with enthusiasm. He had a way of being genuinely interested in anything that Nexxa touched. While watching Dan converse with Faroud, Nexxa's confidence rose. So did her desire to stay in that four-star hotel, Gray something, she had found in Beirut.

As Faroud effortlessly began telling them about his modern Lebanon, a small peek in the clouds let in just a tad of sunlight. Dan noticed something; the tad—of sun—looked unusual on Nexxa. It was plausible the mimosas were affecting him. Nexxa saw Dan's perplexed face and discreetly put her hand on his thigh, and suddenly, the sunlight was gone. Dan smiled at Nexxa and took a drink of his mimosa while the sound of ice from the waiter grabbing the champagne bottle was a perfectly timed distraction. Nexxa knew Dan wasn't an enlightened soul and had many lessons to learn in this incarnation; therefore, he wouldn't be able to see her lavender glow. For now, her lavender glow which made her recognizable to other enlightened souls in each incarnation and provided protection from spiritual attacks would remain her secret.

"Isn't this all wonderful?" Dan was spry again.

"It has been a most enchanting time in New York. I had great luck, it seems, by meeting Nexxa."

"I'm intrigued, but we primarily focus on Latin America."

"Ah, I see," Faroud said with a smile.

"Lebanon doesn't have a desert," Nexxa noted while turning her head to Dan, looking him in the eyes. "But, they have beautiful women." Nexxa looked from Dan to Faroud, winking.

"We are like the Phoenix." Faroud paused. "Beirut," he continued with a solemn voice.

Nexxa put her hand on Dan's; she nodded, indicating she agreed with Faroud.

"So, I think after hearing about Beirut and how far you've come, we should do this. I think a private placement is a good option all around. We have accounts already interested in emerging markets, and our fee will be competitive. This will be a far less exhaustive process. You know we'll have to file Form D with the SEC after each round of securities is sold. Let's start our due diligence." Dan's face softened. "Don't want to get into any trouble," he finished with a chuckle as he turned to Nexxa with his captivating smile.

"I have to get back to the office. Faroud, it's been great meeting you." Dan stood and shook Faroud's hand. "Nexxa, why don't you spend some time with Faroud? I have to get over to see my client. I need to coddle him a little," he stated with a snicker. Dan tugged at his jeans and left. Nexxa knew she could handle Faroud alone. Thinking quickly as always, she showed Faroud around the sundeck—from the side where they were dining to the side where guests could lounge in the sun or swim.

"Over there is my office." Nexxa pointed to the building across Fifth Avenue, directly across from the hotel.

"Aw, so you can be on the sundeck sunbathing and see your co-workers!"

"Yeah, pretty much," Nexxa replied, laughing along with Faroud. A woman emerged from one of the loungers (this side of the sundeck was reserved for bathers) and managed to position herself in their sightline. Noticing the unfortunate—the woman's pubic hair peeking out from her one-piece swimsuit—Nexxa wished she had been standing in front of Faroud, blocking his view.

"Nexxa, it has been most wonderful meeting you and your

boss Dan."

"Oh, thank you."

"I look forward to talking with you and Dan more."

"I'm confident we can collaborate."

"I want you to talk with me more on Bloomberg."

"Yes, I will be working with Dan on putting together a proposal. I want to get something to you by early next week."

"I am ready to chat anytime. You can do the instant email with me."

"Oh, oh, you mean the IB, Instant Bloomberg." Nexxa tried to hold in her amusement.

"Yes, yes, you type to me, I type to you. I talk to my friends all over the world that way."

"Yes, Faroud, we can talk that way," Nexxa confirmed with a smile.

"Okay, Nexxa, it is time I return to my room for a rest."

"Sure, sure. I must get back to my office."

With utmost politeness, Faroud saw Nexxa down to the hotel lobby. He reminded her to stay in touch with the "instant email"; Nexxa promised. Deciding to check the time on her phone before making her way down the steps to exit the hotel, Nexxa noticed she already had a text message from Faroud. A smile emoji. And an emoji of a woman in a bathing suit. As Faroud stood waiting for the elevator, Nexxa heard him say under his breath, "The lady with the bush, bushy pussy," obviously amused by what they had witnessed on the sundeck.

IRELAND, 10 YEARS EARLIER — 2003

It was harder to leave home than Nexxa had anticipated. She told everyone she would be studying abroad in Europe as if she were privileged.

In the small town where Nexxa was from in Canada, she met a man in a café where she worked part-time. Patrick was old enough to be her grandfather, but she considered him attractive even with his gray hair. He was having coffee and reading *The Irish Times*. As she would later learn, he passed through to deliver needed money to smuggle into Ireland in support of the IRA, the Irish Republican Army. He smiled at her a few times in an authentic grandfatherly way, eventually asking her if she would like to sit with him. Patrick looked like a successful businessman, but he had a sordid side. When Nexxa talked with him, she told him about her desire to travel. Nexxa mentioned that a Native American man, Thomas, raised her along with her mom, and through this, Patrick learned that she was the young girl come woman that Thomas had spoken about over the years.

Patrick and Thomas had been friends since their younger days, both growing up poor. Moving to Ireland as a young adult, Patrick now split his time between Ireland and Canada, managing his many established businesses. He would occasionally see Thomas over the years but only by chance. At the time, he was aware that Thomas trained a young Caucasian girl with fair skin and blonde hair. Thomas taught Nexxa how to raise her vibration, balance her polarity, and guided her on developing her innate gifts passed down in her ancestral line, nothing like what Patrick's organization did.

Patrick, a sympathizer of the "Ra," IRA in its short form, glorified the idea of traveling during his informal proposal to recruit Nexxa. He knew she would be an unsuspecting addition to the organization. Nexxa was intrigued by the idea of training in tactical skills on a fundamental level different than her supernatural training. Thomas had tried to discourage her, but she was eager to travel and live abroad, eventually going against Thomas' wishes.

"It's a cold summer," Kilmer said as he retrieved Nexxa's suitcase, plopping it into the boot of the car at the Dublin Airport. Nexxa wasn't sure what to make of Kilmer except that he had strikingly dark wavy hair and that she was to train with *and* take orders from him. Kilmer spoke fast as he showed her a few things in the apartment like the kettle and how to turn on the shower. Watching him move around, Nexxa determined he was a skillfully-crafted human. After a few days, they relocated to the countryside, where the days seemed chillier and the nights even colder. Nexxa found herself precariously drawn to him—perhaps because he was cocky, different than any guy she had ever been around or dated, and was the leader of his faction within the Ra.

Daily, Nexxa would wake early—part of keeping her vibration raised—and take walks before training started. She found that the fog and green balanced each other in the mythical landscape. She heard them around her. It was raining, misting as some called it; still, she stopped and bent down. She knew she was alone. She reminded herself that only humans with a specific vibration could listen to the music surrounding the fairies' existence.

"They like you." Kilmer had a passionate accent and a way of suddenly appearing.

"How—"

"Look." He knelt beside her. Kilmer took her hand, holding it out so a fairy could grasp it. The fairy pulled itself onto her hand as Nexxa tried to hold it steady. The dainty creature was about an inch and a half high and translucent with a silver brilliance. It pranced around a bit, then fluttered its wings before jumping down from her hand.

Nexxa watched as Kilmer smiled for the first time. She had questions. Many. Was he like her? Like Thomas? How could he see the fairies?

"I'll walk you back." Kilmer helped her up. "We'll start soon."

That day during training, Kilmer taught her how to use a handgun. Nexxa had never held a gun. It was exciting, yet the physical training part was intense; it required perseverance. She did enjoy the faster pace, and as the intensity grew, she became different. It was as if an armored exterior had attached to her lovely lavender glow. She wasn't able to look in on the inner of people yet as her mother could, so she had to wonder if maybe Kilmer was enlightened—could see her lavender glow.

Kilmer trained the faction during the day and brilliantly managed to prepare a meal every evening for them all. That was his "masterly humanness"—training, cooking, noticing Nexxa's gracefulness in every task she was given. Kilmer also noticed how lovely her brown eyes looked with her high cheek bones and blonde hair. She was the first woman, first-ever outsider, Kilmer trained. He decided, yes, she was ready; Kilmer took her on outings with him, teaching her how to watch people inconspicuously. It worked for him, being a mentor, teaching a graceful blonde what he had learned.

They were supposed to be watching the opposition, those loyal to the crown believing Northern Ireland should remain part of the United Kingdom; however, their excursions morphed into lessons about food and culture. He also held open doors for her, refilled her wine, usually a Côtes du Rhône, his preference, and sometimes checked in on her in the wee hours of the night. He observed her; he was kindly instrumental. Some would say he was sly. After a few months, Kilmer decided Nexxa was ready for their first mission.

They were to pose as a couple at a private club in Dublin. On a Thursday, Kilmer took Nexxa shopping for a luxury rigout for the assignment. She chose a black Prada jumpsuit, her first garment by a luxury brand. Kilmer paid. She wore it well. The plan was for Kilmer to engage Nexxa in a tiff to garner the attention of a powerful man from the Ulster Volunteer Force, a Loyalist. Upon gaining entrance using false identities, they were seated at the bar. Kilmer ordered Nexxa a white wine spritzer, a pint of Guinness for himself. Kilmer took a few gulps of his beer and then started their fabricated argument. Although he naturally had a temper, he had a pain in his stomach when he got up and stormed out of the club.

Nexxa was on her own now. The moment felt different than she had expected. Kilmer had been at her side since arriving at the airport in Dublin. Nexxa had always been independent; Thomas had always emphasized never relying on anyone, yet something inside her knew she would need to compartmentalize her feelings.

The minder from the table nearby approached her. "I think you should join our table."

She was in; she had captured the attention of the powerful man from the UVF.

"And why is it that a lovely lady like yourself is alone?" Well-dressed and better than Nexxa could have described, the man sitting at the table was unexpected.

A chair was pulled out for her.

"We had a—"

"I don't miss anything." He leaned back in his armchair.

"Okay," Nexxa smiled, glancing over her shoulder. Kilmer was for sure gone. The waiter promptly served her a new white wine spritzer.

"I'm having an end-of-summer party. Would you like to come? Three weeks from now."

Her mind told her to imagine that Kilmer was standing in the corner, nodding, encouraging her.

"Um…" *Say yes, Nexxa, say yes, and thank him.* "Yes, yes, that would be nice." *They are all just staring at me.* Nexxa lifted her wine and drank. *Should I say something else?* With relief, the waiter came around and asked if she wanted another glass of wine. "Oh no, thank you, it's been a long night. I should get home." Nexxa knew she was to meet Kilmer one block down the street and around the corner by Spar.

Moving her chair to stand, the men at the table also stood; the good-looking subject asked, "Can we drive you somewhere?"

Think quickly! "I want to walk—let me write down my number." She could tell this wasn't what he would like, but she stepped over to the end of the bar, grabbed a cocktail napkin, and asked the bartender for a pen. The subject's minder stepped forward; she handed him the napkin. He folded it and gave it to the well-presented man: Quinn.

Nexxa felt she had earned a place in Kilmer's world. She had proven she had the natural magnetism to attract the subject's attention, but she still lacked the skill of manipulation. Nexxa worked primarily with the Feminine Principle of mind, which is always in the direction of receiving impressions. She would learn from Kilmer to use the *Masculine* Principle. Kilmer utilized his Masculine Principle of mind to dominate the minds of others, and his magnetic personality was different from Nexxa's because he could impress his ideas upon other people.

After returning to the North, Nexxa's training focused on the subject, Quinn, with her and Kilmer working assiduously in mock scenarios over the next week. One evening Kilmer had Nexxa do her hair and dress in any sexy rigout she had. He poured her some wine; he encouraged her to drink; he moved in close to her. "If he—and he will—places his hand on your lower back as he introduces you to his guests," Kilmer imitated his words, gliding his hand along Nexxa's back, "stay composed. Never let him see you are nervous. Never let him know you are flattered by his words." Kilmer continued, "Remain an anomaly to him."

Nexxa poured herself some more wine.

Kilmer gently removed the glass from her hand. "You'll want to watch how much you drink," he cautioned, taking a swig.

"I thought you, I mean you were just insisting I drink." Nexxa sat down and huffed.

"When alcohol and emotions are involved, you have to be careful." Kilmer refilled her glass. "You can't refuse a drink. And you'll be offered more." He handed her back the wine glass. "You'll have to drink, but drink slowly, carefully. Watch yourself."

Nexxa nodded; she understood. It was her first espionage experience and her first attempt at manipulating anyone.

"Your job is to get information." Kilmer sat in the chair opposite her, scooting it closer, looking her in the eyes. "Don't be direct but find his weakness. Use that."

Recruiting an asset was hard, so this was the first attempt by those within the Nationalist Party to place an operative amongst the Unionist Party to garner intelligence on potential attacks and bribes paid to those in the government, but mainly on the inner workings of Quinn's business.

Kilmer's next scenario was to show Nexxa how to assess the environment around her. He called it "storytelling."

"Define their story. Note their body language and how they are interacting," Kilmer explained to Nexxa as they were watching people in the North, Northern Ireland, at a restaurant. He pointed out whether patrons were using cash, credit cards, ate alone, ordered only a drink, how they were dressed, if they were likely tourists or locals. Leaving the restaurant, Nexxa pulled out her Canon camera.

"Do you fuckin' want to draw attention to us?" Nexxa hadn't quite pressed the button in her attempt to take a picture of the British military watchtowers dispersed around the city when Kilmer asked this.

"I'm Canadian." She lowered her camera. "They can't do anything if I want to take a picture."

"For fuck's sake. Let's get out of here; it's time to get back to Dublin."

Nexxa was set up in a flat used as a safe house and directed on the identity she would continue to portray. The apartment was scarce, so she decided to put up a few personal belongings she had brought from home, suggesting to Kilmer that it would look odd if nothing personal—girlie—were visible. Nexxa stayed there alone for a few weeks before attending the party she had been invited to by the opposition leader, Paddy, as Kilmer referred to him. "Paddy's men will most likely be watching you. And he will send one of his men, a driver, to drive you to the party. So don't be alarmed but act surprised when one of them arrives unannounced to take you to his home for the party,"

Kilmer had told her.

Nexxa had become accustomed to Kilmer being by her side, always, but Kilmer couldn't come around to her flat since it would indeed be monitored. So, she practiced having conversations with Quinn while making tea in the mornings, while making tea again in the evenings, and while taking mostly hot baths in the evenings. For the first time in her life, she was alone. She missed Iliada, but Kilmer had suggested she not call her, not yet anyway. She could know how her sister was through telepathy; she didn't mention this to Kilmer.

Iliada was still in high school, living at home, and somewhat harnessing her natural abilities. She was stubborn but willing to practice with their mom. Then there was Thomas. Iliada loved to be around him. Thomas had trained Nexxa, teaching her about the spirits amongst the living since she was about six years old. With Nexxa gone and Iliada maturing, he was now working with her.

During one of her evening baths, Nexxa sensed that Iliada was very emotional, crying because of Thomas. It felt to Nexxa that Thomas might have been tired, run-down. Nexxa told Iliada that all would be okay and not to be sad. Nexxa knew he was most likely resting more to receive guidance from his spirit guide during his astral travels. Connecting with Nexxa helped Iliada since they had fought before Nexxa left for Ireland.

Nexxa's telepathic concentration extinguished when a knock came at the bedroom window. Abruptly sitting up, the water suddenly felt cold; Nexxa grabbed a towel. She stood, listening for a second knock, before walking into the bedroom.

"Open up. I brought you more milk. Tea." Kilmer had an

anxious tone as he held up the shopping bag to show her. "I wanted to make sure you had plenty of tea."

Nexxa unlatched the lock; her hair was dripping water down her back. Kilmer hesitated once he climbed in the window. The space between them was awkward—*he* trying not to look directly at her, *she* trying not to notice.

"Okay, I can put it in the kitchen."

"No, don't be silly." Kilmer seemed giddy. "I'll take care of it."

Nexxa followed him to the kitchen and watched him put away the milk and tea. Kilmer quickly grabbed the tea kettle. "Tea?" he asked. Nexxa nodded. "You should put something on before you catch a cold."

She was sure he watched her while she walked away with wet footsteps.

"Have you chosen a dress for the evening? The party," he shouted from the kitchen.

Nexxa shook her head. Then, realizing he couldn't see her, she said, "Um, yes. Yes, I did."

"Good." Kilmer cleared his throat. "Good, let's have a look."

Nexxa slipped on her new dress, twisted up her wet hair, and walked into the kitchen. Her nipples were showing through the fabric of the dress.

Kilmer stood up from his chair and walked over to examine her. He shook his head. "Gorgeous, gorgeous. I made you a cup of tea."

"Okay." Nexxa pulled at the neckline of the dress. "I'm going to change now."

Nexxa returned to the bedroom, sliding on lounge pants under her dress, looking over her shoulder before she slipped the dress over her head and pulled on a sweater. Her hair was still wet; she wanted to blow-dry it.

She heard Kilmer say, "Your tea is getting cold."

In a hurry, she tangled her hair.

Kilmer appeared in the bedroom doorway. "Let me do it." His voice sounded irritated. "You're tangling it." Taking the brush from her hand, for he wouldn't want her beautiful blonde locks tangled, he tenderly brushed her hair.

Nexxa shivered; she clutched her hands together.

He continued brushing her hair. "Ya right now?" Kilmer put the brush down.

They sat at the small, scratched kitchen table, sipping the tea Kilmer had brewed. Nexxa couldn't help but wonder if he imagined what she looked like with her clothes off.

Kilmer lit a cigarette and squinted his eyes. "Ya think you're ready?"

MOSCOW — SEPTEMBER 2013

Sergei sat at his desk, sipping his Mortlach 25 Year Old Scotch whisky. He lifted a framed photo of him with his parents. His dad was an attractive man, tall with dark hair, while his mother was reminiscent of a Siberian princess with fair skin flanked by long blonde hair. In the photo, his mom held Sergei when he was about two years old while his dad stood along her side, looking adoringly at her. Sergei was a perfect blend of his attractive parents, six feet tall with short dark hair and a perfectly chiseled face, practically a mirror image of Max Ryan, the British actor with a bit of modern James Bond—Russian, of course—mixed in. His Russian accent was not detectable when Sergei spoke English, attributed to his private tutoring and time spent in the UK and Canada. His parents had passed away when he was in his early twenties from a car accident while driving through the Balkan Mountains. His father, like Sergei, was always seeking out investment opportunities abroad.

"Dinner is ready," Ankica, his babushka, announced as she walked into Sergei's office. He took the last sip of his Scotch whisky while putting on his black Canali wool sport coat before walking over to her and kissing her on each cheek.

"You aren't hungry?"

"I'll eat later; I need to go to the restaurant."

Outside in the dusk, the lights on the Italian cypresses lining his home's perimeter began illuminating his mini château. The pinkish sky cast a perfect glow on the flurry of white butterflies that fluttered around him as he stopped to check his phone before getting into his car. The drive into Moscow was about thirty minutes without traffic from his home. Because Sergei trained as a race car driver during his time abroad in Canada, he arrived in half that time, with strategic Muscovite maneuvering. Sergei had invested in several businesses, one of which was Vogue, a cosmopolitan restaurant frequented by Moscow's elite. Arriving in front of Vogue, Sergei illegally parked his white Jaguar—typical of the privileged.

The over-accentuated women dining in the restaurant eyed Sergei like it was a Spartan sport, each hoping to draw attention to herself as he walked through the restaurant. Knowing that women were gawking at him gave him zero pleasure. He concluded that all these women were the same as he headed upstairs to the office to meet with his partner Mikhail.

Sergei had barely stepped into the office when he heard Mikhail holler, "Sergei!" as he was watching a clip of *Moscow Fashion Week*. Mikhail jumped up from the office chair he was sitting in.

"I wanted to speak to you. Ella's brand is becoming popular, but she needs more money." Mikhail's sister, Ella, was a famous fashion designer, but given the nature of Russia's economic system, it was hard to be an entrepreneur. Sergei happened to be fond of fashion and liked supporting the Arts. The sentiment in Russia was to have everything "Russian-made" from clothing to cheese, yet fashion designers, artists, and craftsmen alike were thriving only through private financial support.

"So, can we help her? Business is good, and I promised my mother I would take care of her."

"Of course!" Sergei motioned with a raised hand. "You know I would do anything for your mother *and* Mother Russia."

Possibly prematurely elated, Mikhail whisked a bottle of Beluga from a shelf above the desk and poured them shots. Swallowing, Mikhail suggested, "Let's go out. You need a woman."

"I have one—my babushka."

"C'mon." Mikhail patted Sergei's shoulder. "A real woman."

"You know I cannot find a woman here. I love my country, but she's not here." Sergei motioned for another shot. "I'm going to Beirut in a few days."

"What's in Beirut?" Mikhail tucked his chin in before laughing. "Your girl?" He should have known better.

"A property." Sergei wiped his mouth. "I have a friend from Cyprus, and he tells me that there are a few buildings that would be good investments in Beirut. I want to establish a foothold in the short-term rental industry there. Now is the time while property is still cheap. Tourism is increasing there a few percent each year."

"Okay, yeah, you have my support," Mikhail spat off, pouring more vodka. In his mind, Mikhail considered himself to be a big shot.

Sergei eyed him as he threw back his third shot. With his hand on Mikhail's shoulder, he said, "You are my friend, and we are partners." What Sergei didn't say was, *We are only partners in this restaurant because that is all you could ever handle. My father was right when he told me always to have fifty-one percent.* Sergei had opted not to have the same investor or partner across his financial ventures. That was a lesson from his babushka.

Her advice for him always came in the form of a metaphor. "A foe can be a friendly bear." Sergei understood this to mean that anyone can become your enemy. And that an enemy can also serve a purpose.

"I must go; my babushka will be upset that I rushed off. We'll talk about Ella when I get back," Sergei informed him. Mikhail tapped his tablet to replay a clip from *Moscow Fashion Week* earlier in the year.

Sergei nodded. "Later."

"She was crying, but she sleeps now." Ankica cleaned up some baby bottles while Sergei sat at the kitchen island, pulling apart a piece of bread. Sergei and his babushka cared for Natina, his brother's baby girl. His brother Donat, a gay man—not openly—had a one-off relationship with a woman. She was a young actress who worked with Donat on a TV series but became addicted to drugs. Ankica had already convinced the woman to let her take the baby once she was born. Shortly after Natina's christening, her mother died from an overdose. Adopting the stage name Demo, Donat had decided to take a gig with a theater troupe, leaving his baby. Sergei had been happy to provide financially for the baby while his babushka took care of her.

Sergei looked in on baby Natina in her room. He gently rubbed her back, wondering what it would be like to meet a woman and have a child. Down the hall, his babushka sat in the sitting room. She was a petite woman with short grayish-brown hair and liked to wear black pants and floral print tops; she was traditional, wise, and had unexpected moments of humor.

"I'm going to go to Beirut for a few days."

"Let me see," she muttered as she moved her hand across a piece of cloth lying on her sitting table, while sipping her nightly tonic, a cherry brandy, which she claimed helped her decipher her nightly visions. "Blonde, maybe Irish."

"Who, babushka?" Sergei's eyes were curious. "Who is blonde?"

"Your girlfriend."

"I don't have a—"

"She is," his babushka continued, moving her hand over her cloth, "coming to me." She took the last sip of her brandy and tilted the glass to the side in the light of the table lamp. "She has a special gift."

As he heard her words, Sergei's mind raced. *What is this about a blonde woman? The woman in my fantasies is blonde.* He lowered his head, touching his forehead.

With her eyes closed, Ankica reached for Sergei's hand.

For a moment, he shut his eyes. Exhaling, he stood. "*Loku*

notch, babushka."

Sergei retired to his room and poured another Mortlach Scotch whisky. He undressed to his underwear, lying down on his massive bed. He switched on RuskiPorn, a popular porn channel in Russia. Each month he told himself he would cancel his subscription. Sergei took another sip of his Scotch then exhaled. A video of a threesome, the girls moderately attractive, came on. The man began penetrating one woman while the other woman caressed the man's testicles. Sergei became aroused; he pulled his growing penis from his underwear. The threesome continued; the man withdrew his little penis from girl number one and started for the woman with clearly fake boobs. Sergei shouted in Russian, throwing the remote across his room toward the TV.

He rose from lying to sit on the edge, moving his hand across his head. He screamed, then laughed, then screamed again. *I can't even get hard looking at porn anymore.* He thought about his babushka, her spiritual ways. Could she really be seeing a blonde, a foreign blonde woman that would be for him? His babushka had been right in the past. She predicted his tumultuous dating, or lack thereof, reminding him that he was picky. She predicted his successful venture into the restaurant industry. When he sought advice for another venture, she drank her cherry brandy and moved her hand along her cloth as she had done this evening; what she saw manifested.

Yet what Sergei wanted, craved, was intimacy. Or to at least stop having the dream. The dream about the intellectually arousing blonde woman. He knew she wasn't speaking Russian to him in his dream, but he couldn't quite tell what she was saying either. Each time he would reach out for her, touching her blonde hair, she would tell him she had to go. *Mmm, I want to see her breasts. I want to kiss her breasts*, he would think. Sergei's erection grew strong as he thought about the woman from his dream. He lifted his Scotch, took a sip, then slammed the glass against the wall. Glass everywhere, he began to pick up most of it. A shard penetrated his foot.

Sergei hobbled to the bathroom. Standing with his hands on the shower wall, he bowed his head as the rain shower poured on him, rushing the blood from his foot down the drain. *I'll know her when I see her.*

TAKASHIMA BLDG., NYC — SEPTEMBER 2013

Nexxa turned off the alarm on her phone and glanced at the site she still had open for hotels in Beirut. This week would be different. Focusing on a proposal for Faroud would give her much more to do than just shop, go to the spa, and be irritated with Philip.

The morning was usual—log in to everything and order breakfast for the traders. She wanted to be excited about working with Faroud, but it was a slow day, which afforded her time to obsess and stress over meeting *Charming Kilmer*, her ex-husband, for a drink later in the week. Luckily one of the traders was a distraction. Annoying, but a distraction. He was always trying to find a reason to talk to her. He was intrigued by her and suspected something was going on with her and another trader.

As she checked her email, she sensed his corduroy pants

closing in on her from behind. With his hand on her shoulder, he said, "I know your secret."

"Suspecting something is different from knowing something," Nexxa asserted keeping her eyes on her monitor.

He caressed her from her shoulder down to her hand and patted her. She peered up at him. "Do you want to come into my world?"

He took a deep breath, sighed, and just stood there.

Typical, typical—nothing to say, like always. No wonder your wife treats you the way she does. Nexxa smiled. *Damn Nexxa, your thoughts are harsh. Well, if he won't say anything, that's the first thought that comes to mind.*

With the awkward co-worker encounter over, Nexxa started working on the proposal for Faroud. One version for GO bonds, general obligation bonds where no assets are used as collateral, and the other for Revenue bonds, a type of municipal bond supported by an income-producing project. Each plan had the same executive summary, with differences highlighted in the schedules and legal matters. She wanted to get as much done as possible to have the proposals reviewed by their legal team before meeting Dan to go over them.

It took her only two days of turnaround time. Since fall tended to be a slow time of year, (people in the industry managed to take vacations in late summer and early fall) and the fiscal year-end is typically months away, everyone was eager for a project. Dan reviewed the two proposals, and everything was approved.

The week was finally ending, so Nexxa emailed Faroud. She wanted to give him a teaser that they would be presenting him with an initial proposal soon and obviously that she would be taking that much-desired trip to Beirut to make a formal presentation in person. Nexxa kept her enthusiasm at a modest level; she thought so, at least.

After emailing Faroud, she resumed her due diligence on China Black Road. Nexxa had been tasked by the compliance officer with aiding in the vetting process of CBR, providing her findings to her compliance officer to vet further. Dan knew it was a necessary part of the Private Placement process to conduct due diligence on the potential general contractor that their client, the National Lebanese Bank, would secure a contract with for construction services. Lastly, Nexxa re-read the obscure profile on CBR's website of Diane Soo Hoo, the VP of Project Management. "Photo coming soon," it read in place of a profile picture.

She minimized her email and stood to make eye contact with Dan. He was in the all-glass conference room, which overlooked Fifth Avenue, and had just ended his call. She slid open the glass door and approached him where he was sitting. Slowly, she pushed away his cell phone and sat on the table. She crossed her legs as she touched her eyelashes before looking him in the eyes.

Dan smiled, leaning back in his chair. "I think you are great. How about this? You're going to Beirut."

Nexxa knew she was in a great place with this opportunity to execute a proposal on a private placement with a client. And, it helped that the client, Faroud, was fond of her. She was natural at attracting positive energy.

"Dan, I'm reminded of the Hermetic axiom, 'The wise ones

serve on the higher, but rule on the lower.'"

"And that is why I hired you! You have everything in order?"

Nexxa nodded. "Yes, our security officer has briefed me." She pushed her hair behind her shoulder. "He went over the areas of Beirut and has briefed me on our company's policies."

"Abduction has become a billion-dollar industry, and abductors are much more sophisticated than you think." Dan furrowed his brow. "Going to an unsafe neighborhood and not having an escape plan is dangerous. So, we have a number, and I will tell you that before you leave."

"Well, we could always start a GoFundMe page if our company number is too low."

"GoFundMe!" Dan laughed then stood up and moved closer to Nexxa, rubbing her shoulders. Nexxa closed her eyes, leaning her head to the side. She could feel jealous eyes penetrating through the glass walls of the conference room from the trading desk.

The same kind of envious eyes that watched her every move the night before when the company took a training course that, among other things, discussed how to spot potential kidnapping threats. It was cloudy and warm, the type of weather that might precede a storm, when Nexxa and her colleagues had met in New Jersey for the session on abduction and recovery. Nexxa wore her "assassin" leggings, as she referred to them, and her APL sneakers. Her co-worker showed up in the same outfit. Nexxa knew imitation was the sincerest form of flattery, which she found ironic since she and her co-worker had a tumultuous work relationship.

"So that was something, huh?" Dan moved over to the

window. "Going through a mock abduction. I think you handled it the best out of anyone in the office." Nexxa knew her training with Kilmer was why she could remain calm as she portrayed an abduction victim. Charming Kilmer could box the head off any man and was an anomaly, according to himself. Men like him only existed in movies. Nexxa remembered how she felt when she first saw Kilmer a decade ago when she arrived in Ireland. She was intimidated by his good looks and charm, yet unbeknownst to Nexxa, he was intimidated by her. She had always credited him with teaching her proper etiquette about wine, cuisine, luxury cigarettes, and how to speak to people. Even though their relationship began with him mentoring her, her becoming his protégé, she eventually became his wife. Kilmer had made for a perfect teacher with his impeccable balance of street smarts and higher education.

"Yeah, I feel like yoga and meditation had something to do with it." Inside her mind, Nexxa was rolling her eyes at her response.

"Yoga is great." Dan toggled his eyes and head, laughing. "If only I could get my legs in some of those positions."

Nexxa considered suggesting she show him a yoga move to get a rise out of her colleagues. Instead, she decided that going back to her desk and announcing that Dan told her to take the rest of the day off would be better. She also knew if she went back to her desk and complained to her co-worker that she had to leave soon to meet her ex-husband for a drink, and gave her the usual story that, unfortunately, she couldn't meet any suitable suitors, her co-worker would feel better. She would feel just a bit better knowing Nexxa was no better off than her in the dating world with an eight-to-one ratio of women to men in Manhattan. It was like feeding a puppy a treat.

IRELAND, 10 YEARS EARLIER — 2003

Nexxa waited patiently, trying to focus on a book on astrology and chart interpretation. Closing the book, she plopped it down on the couch and slipped on her stilettos. "I should practice a little, maybe sitting and standing to maintain my balance." She heard two knocks on the apartment door. *Here we go. That must be Quinn's driver.* A tall, rough-looking man, who managed to fit into a suit, was standing on the other side of the door when Nexxa opened it.

"I'll be driving ya to the party," the man announced in a rough Irish accent.

"I just need my purse."

He stood in the doorway while Nexxa stepped away. Walking to the kitchen and through the scent of her perfume, she decided she felt relief and apprehension that the evening was commencing.

"I'm gettin' the door." He meant he would *lock* the door for her.

"Oh, sure." Nexxa handed him her key to the door. *So, he's a minder and a driver.* Kilmer had used the word minder before. Now Nexxa knew what a minder was.

The driver opened the door. Nexxa positioned herself in the backseat; she felt the supple leather of the car against her exposed back. Kilmer had chosen a few dresses for her to choose from for the event. The one she was wearing he described as "graceful" when they had gone shopping.

She was supposed to be Claire for the mission, the daughter of a well-to-do American businessman studying at the university in Dublin. Winding through the streets further from her flat, Nexxa thought about Claire, her cover identity; Claire was everything she was in looks, yet nothing like her. The only thing they really had in common was that they were both leaving Kilmer. The car moved fast, probably seventy miles an hour on some roads, yet it was a smooth ride. Nexxa, undisturbed by the speed, looked at herself once more in her compact mirror to check her makeup.

"Two minutes."

"Oh," Nexxa acknowledged, quickly closing her compact.

"Ya look right, ma'am."

Nexxa exhaled. "Okay." *So what? He saw me primping.* She looked out of the car window for the rest of the ride.

The home was reminiscent of a French château with tall outdoor flamed heaters flanking the pathway and front entrance. Nexxa felt the subtle heat from the flames, just enough to warm her skin as she walked the path, just enough to calm her beating heart as she saw the other guests through the windows.

In her naïveté, she expected to see Quinn answer the door, not his proper British butler. The foyer was grand, and she followed the butler, keeping a poised smile, wondering if something important was left out of her training. A server attending to the guests offered her a glass of champagne. She contemplated; she stopped herself from telling him she was nervous.

Quinn was conversing with a few guests when he noticed the room now consisted of a graceful blonde. He watched Nexxa, chatting with his guests, then blatantly ignoring those dispersed around him. Lighting a cigar—he puffed—he observed.

Nexxa stood in front of a painting. The smoke from Quinn's cigar carried itself across the room; it told her she was being watched. She should have known the art that flanked the walls of Quinn's home. Maybe that's where her training had failed. Inhaling the smoke mixed with a side of Quinn's scent, she gracefully glanced over her shoulder. *This is it*, she told herself.

"I see you have an interest in art. You're studying European art at the university." Quinn pulled from his cigar. "Tell me, what is your favorite?"

"I love," Nexxa began, keeping her eyes on the painting, "Gothic art."

"Why choose to study here?" he persisted. Nexxa looked at him. She already knew he was older, wiser, and could more than likely see through her.

"I've always been independent. I wanted to see something more."

With a smile, he said, "Come." Quinn placed his hand on her lower back and ushered her over to some guests. With each step, Nexxa heard Kilmer's words, *If he places his hand, and he will, on your lower back...*

"I want you to meet the exquisite Nexxa."

"Hello, I'm Nexxa." She made eye contact with each guest.

"She came across the pond to study European art. I had the pleasure of meeting her at my club."

"I—"

"She was with an eejit," Quinn emphasized with his hands raised. "The bloke is an eejit." Quinn laughed, his guests chuckled, Quinn laughed louder. "Right, Nexxa?"

"Yes, yes he was. He is."

Nexxa took the last sip of her champagne and twisted, looking for the server. Quinn motioned for him to come around. While the server replenished several of their drinks, Quinn told his guests how happy he was to cross paths with Nexxa.

"You see, she was with a man who I'd say wasn't the best bloke," he reiterated more astutely.

"And Quinn was gracious enough to, well—"

Quinn winked at her. "I invited her to join me."

"Yes, he was so gracious to me. Being that I am here alone and I haven't made any friends yet..." Nexxa slightly toggled her champagne flute before continuing, "It was nice to meet someone like Quinn."

"So, this *bloke*, the man you were with, where ever did you meet him?" questioned the woman with her blouse buttoned to her neck.

"Oh, well, in a café."

"Ah." The woman lifted her chin.

"Well, I was studying. Needed a change of environment from

my flat."

"And how long have you been in Dublin?"

"Only a semester."

Thankfully, the rigid, unfuckable-looking woman turned her attention to another guest. She asked him about his wife and kids. His response showed his disinterest in conversing with her.

Nexxa grasped her champagne flute tighter; the champagne was all she had in her system. "Excuse me; I need to visit the ladies' room." She remembered the special mint in her purse.

"I'll have one of my men show you." Quinn gestured for one of his minders.

Walking toward the minder, she wished she could just poof and be in the bathroom.

"Ma'am." The man motioned for her to follow him, leading her upstairs to the toilet.

When he closed the bathroom door, Nexxa turned the lock. She quickly turned on the sink faucet and removed a small tin from her purse. Kilmer had given her some mints saying, *You should only need one for the evening.* Nexxa put the lid down on the toilet and sat down. She placed the mint on her tongue. It tasted like a fragrant herb, invigorating like a shot of vitamin C. *Okay, only time to freshen up, quick pee maybe.* She took out her lipstick; it was more blue-red than orange-red. She had asked Kilmer to buy it for her when they went shopping. "A rigout isn't complete without a new lipstick." Nexxa dropped it in the sink, and it made a clinking sound, rolling around before she could grab it. She picked it up, top lip was done, then bottom; the minder knocked on the door.

"You right, ma'am?"

Nexxa opened the door, and he extended his arm, directing her back down the staircase. Walking down, she saw Quinn waiting for her at the bottom of the stairs. *Six, then three, four sitting, plus the butler, four minders inside.* She knew more were in another room. *Crap, not sure how many in there. Plus the kitchen and wait staff.* She guessed forty in total, trying to get a headcount. Some alone time with Quinn was what she needed; the night was going by so fast.

"Join me outside." Quinn winked at Nexxa, reaching for her hand. "I want to show you something." Quinn raised a hand; minder number two backed off. They were finally alone, out on the terrace. "You see that building there." Quinn pointed with his free hand. "That is full of oysters. Oysters, Ostrea edulis, have been growing off the coast of Ireland for centuries. Our business has flourished and allowed me an attractive lifestyle."

"Okay." Nexxa had never eaten oysters, and silly her, she expected him to show her or tell her about a building full of guns or weapons.

"My family was the first to harvest oysters in Ireland. Our oysters are finished in France and sold in the finest restaurants in Europe. Have you been to Paris?" Quinn asked without pausing.

"I've made plans to go someday soon," Nexxa lied. She impressed herself. But she was lying; she hadn't any plans of going to Paris.

"I'm going to take you to Paris." Quinn waved his hand with the cigar. "To a grand place, Hôtel Costes."

Nexxa adjusted the strap on her left shoulder. "That sounds

nice," she responded, not believing him.

Quinn was definitely the older, wiser man Nexxa had surmised him to be. Did Nexxa capture his attention? Sure. Was she going to be his weakness? At fifteen years her senior, with barely detectable spots of gray in his hair, he wore his tailored clothes well. It wasn't his style to go after younger women; it wasn't his style to explain himself either. Yet here he was with a college-age blonde from across the pond. He saw only what he desired. They chatted more. Nexxa smiled.

"Come, I'll have Kieran drive you home. I'll have him come around for you in the morning—for Paris." Quinn kissed her on the cheek. "Pack light."

Kieran emerged. "Come, we'll be gettin' off in the wee morning." Nexxa closed her eyes. She worried Kilmer would be angry with her.

In the car Nexxa fumbled with her seat belt. "Kieran, um, could you take me to a store for cigarettes?" That she had called him by his name instead of "driver," seemed weird, but yet maybe like she had a part in Quinn's life now.

"Then straight to your flat," he answered, sounding less irritable than when he picked her up earlier.

Kieran walked Nexxa to her door, unlocked it, and waited as she entered. He nodded and handed her the key before closing the door after she stepped into the flat.

"Okay, goodnight," Nexxa whispered with her hand on the closed door. *Time to call Kilmer. Maybe light a cigarette first. Isn't that when people smoke? When they are nervous about something?*

Nexxa only heard one ring. "Kilmer."

"I'll be round in a few minutes."

He was around in *less* than a few minutes.

"You're smoking? Give me a fag."

"A what?"

"A cigarette," he said, as he reached for the pack on the kitchen table. "So, how did it go? Did he ask to see you again?"

Nexxa took a drag from her cigarette, then another. She didn't mention to Kilmer that because she had given her real name the night she met Quinn, that she had no choice but to forgo the identity of Claire. At least the name, anyway.

"He is sending his driver for me in the morning."

"The morning?"

"Yes, he wants to take me to Paris."

"For fuck's sake! I'll have to take the boys with me." His eyes pierced hers as he took a drag from his cigarette. "We can't be too sure what he's up to." Kilmer suspected Quinn used his business to help fund the UVF party. Who were his associates in France for his oysters? Could his business be sabotaged? Could they follow the money and cut it off? "What will yous be doing there?"

"I'm not sure—he mentioned oysters and a hotel."

With a smirk, Kilmer huffed, shaking his head before standing up. He paced a bit before smashing his cigarette.

"If you're in trouble, text, *he gave me a gold rose, but I prefer red roses*, to my number. Keep your phone on so we can reach you."

"Okay." Nexxa looked to her cigarette; it was burned down. "Anything else I should know? Kilmer?"

Kilmer took two cigarettes out of the box and patted her on

the head.

"Lock the door behind me." Kilmer pulled up his hood and left her flat.

Kieran promptly arrived at Nexxa's flat at nine a.m. She was ready since seven a.m., even though she tossed most of the night, getting little sleep. Kieran carried her bag and opened the car door for her. Sitting on the supple leather again, she grasped her abdomen. *Not now, my stomach can't do this. Like, potty again?* Dare she tell him she needed to go back into her flat?

"Soda?" Kieran asked as he held up a diet coke. "Me stomach always bothers me before I fly."

"Oh." Nexxa hesitated before reaching for the drink. "Thank you."

When they approached the airport, Kieran drove past it, turning down a side road that led to a large gate. Nexxa's stomach had just settled, but that nauseating feeling returned. Kieran stopped at the entrance and typed a code on the digital screen. The gate opened, and he drove in. Nexxa saw jets and realized all was okay.

"Let's go." Kieran briskly walked her toward a Learjet. Nexxa held onto the railing with one hand, using her other to tame her hair as the wind blew while climbing the stairs into the plane. A stewardess greeted them and showed her to her seat.

"What can I offer you to drink?"

"A soda," Nexxa replied eagerly.

"How about sparkling water? Pellegrino."

"Yes, thank you. I always forget about sparkling water." Nexxa sighed as she settled into her seat.

Kieran gestured for her to buckle her seat belt. "Quinn will meet us there. He flew out last night."

"Oh—okay."

Nexxa missed Kilmer. She was nervous. No—excited. She was nervous and excited. She sipped her sparkling water and looked out at the clouds. And voilà—they were in Paris.

"Paris," Kieran said, clapping his hands during landing.

"Already?" Nexxa leaned closer, looking for anything recognizable on the ground. Once they landed and deplaned, a car was waiting for them on the tarmac. Kieran held Nexxa's hand, escorting her off the plane and into an Obsidian Black Mercedes S-Class Sedan. The vehicle smelled of Quinn.

The drive to the hotel looked like most highways until they reached the city centre. The entrance to the hotel was obscure. A doorman held open her door, and Kieran exited the car, escorting Nexxa inside. If she had blinked, she would have missed Kieran's nod at a poised lady at the front desk while making their way to the elevator. Like magic, Kieran withdrew a room key card from his pocket and opened her room. "Your gear will be brought up. Be in the lobby at noon," he grumbled.

"Noon," she repeated, thinking how his mood had changed. *He's probably tired and needs a fag.*

Nexxa put down her purse. "Wow, sexy." She panned the hotel room, which had muted red walls and patterned tapestries. "Fuck, this is nuts. Beautiful!" Nexxa took her phone out of her purse; Kilmer more than likely had texted or called her. She saw that her phone was still off before putting it back. A knock came at the door, and a porter was there with her luggage. Staying there was her first experience in a cosmopolitan hotel; Kilmer had prepped her on etiquette. She *knew* to tip the porter.

Music emanated in each guest room unless you turned it off manually, encouraging your devilish side. Nexxa brushed her teeth and primped, applying more lipstick while doing a happy dance. She grabbed her purse and opened her room door, looking down the corridor each way. No minder. She was hungry, but it subsided on the ride down in the elevator. The door opened, she stepped out, and the ambiance gave her the whimsical imaginary wings she wished she had. Nexxa glided through, taking in the conversations in diverse languages, understanding each as she had never before. (Her mother had told her she would start developing her innate ability with spoken dialects in her twenties.)

Standing before the Roses Costes, a boutique just for roses, Nexxa only had the fifty quid that Kilmer had given her; she went in anyway. The boutique walls were covered in tiny silver tiles flanked by mirrored tiles with reddish antique glass wall sconces illuminating the shop.

"Lavender…" Nexxa held a hand to her chest. "Roses!"

"You like?" The florist took notice of Nexxa. "Yes?" he asked as he lifted the arrangement, a mix of old lavender, lavender mist, and pink lavender roses in a white and gold porcelain flower pot.

"Oh, yes… it's just I've never seen lavender roses."

"Oh, but you must have this."

"I—" Nexxa paused, clutching her purse. "I can't buy it."

"Here." He took a lavender mist rose from the pot and handed it to Nexxa. "For you."

"*Merci!*" Nexxa held the rose against her chest and kissed the man on the cheek. Smiling, her smile was different in France, she inhaled her newfound *lavender*, a lavender rose. Wishing she had money to shop *for real*, she decided window shopping or "just looking" would have to do.

With rose in hand, Nexxa perused the Costes Parfum boutique. She learned from the lady in the shop what "home fragrance" was as she lifted a bottle, attempting to apply some to her wrist. Kieran appeared standing with his arms folded, looking through the shop's glass. He motioned with his hand. Nexxa acknowledged him; she began to thank the shop lady. Kieran stepped into the shop. "Ya got to be gettin' on." Kieran walked her to the elevator. "Noon," he said as he pushed the button to request one.

On the dresser in her room were two bouquets of roses. Nexxa assumed they were courtesy of the hotel. Hanging on the closet door was a garment bag. Nexxa unzipped it to find a white lace and tulle dress and a white underwire bra with delicate lace detail. On the floor by the closet was a shoebox. She lifted the box, placing it on the dresser. Inside, there was a pair of white Balenciaga stiletto sandals. "So, this is *definitely* not from the hotel." Nexxa held the dress against her body. "I'm guessing from Quinn," she said, looking in the mirror.

On the bathroom vanity, she found a bottle of Hôtel Costes *parfum*. Nexxa leaned her head, checking the time on the clock by the bed; she had enough for a quick shower. The water was hot when it first came out, then just a tad warmer than the water in Ireland. Halfway dried off, she slipped on the bra, securing the clasp, and shimmied on the dress before spritzing on the *parfum.*

Nexxa twisted, looking at herself in the mirror. Iliada came to her mind. This was the sort of thing she would love to call back home to tell her sister about, lavender roses and a trip to Paris. She knew it was a risk to call her. Could she even make an international call? Nexxa looked to the stationery on the desk. Realizing it was time to meet Quinn for brunch, she sealed the envelope and quickly put on her new stiletto sandals. She put the letter to Iliada in her purse and made a kiss with her lips as she checked herself in the mirror.

Nexxa stopped by the reception, waiting as the man behind the desk finished his call before asking if they could mail her letter. Kieran was again in the lobby to escort her, and Quinn was waiting outside in a car. Kieran handed her a wrap. "There's a chill in the air." She draped it over her shoulders. Just when she had the feeling he didn't like her, he did something charming.

"I'm happy to see the dress fits."

"Yes, thank you." Nexxa scooted in next to Quinn. "And thank you for the perfume and roses too."

Quinn's eyes moved from her chest to her legs. "Gorgeous! Just gorgeous." Quinn patted the driver's seat, and Kieran pulled away from the hotel. "I'm taking you to Le Marche du Lucas for brunch."

When they arrived, Quinn emerged from the car and adjusted his jacket. He took a deep breath before holding his arm out for Nexxa to take hold. Like a celebrity couple, they glided through a discreet door into the restaurant. The wait staff was waiting for them and directed them to a table filled with mirrored vases that flickered with lavender and rosemary-scented tea lights. Nexxa sat poised with her hands in her lap as Quinn ordered drinks for them. She watched him conversing with the waiter, him sitting there in his jacket and collared shirt; she realized she had a crush on him, like the mature hot businessman she once desired to meet.

"This, my dear, is a Kir Royale."

"It's so pink," Nexxa announced, delighted as she held up her glass.

"It's an apéritif, a drink before you eat."

Minutes later, with drink in hand, Quinn stood as a couple approached their table. "This is my good friend Seamus and his wife, Klarin." He held his hand on Nexxa's upper back. "I want you to meet Nexxa."

"Hi, hello." Nexxa stood, holding out her hand.

"You're from America?"

"Oh, no, I'm Canadian."

"Ah, she's just gorgeous, Quinn," admired Klarin.

Klarin was petite with lovely black hair and dressed mostly in black but with a powder blue pashmina wrap over her shoulders. Nexxa later learned the color was referred to as *sky-blue*. Nexxa adjusted the top of her white lace dress, noticing the neckline of Klarin's black sweater was a trendy style she had just seen in a magazine ad.

"I love your outfit." Nexxa corrected, "I mean rigout," hoping to impress Klarin. Nexxa had never met a woman to emulate, and the small town she grew up in didn't offer many places to shop, especially with her lack of money.

"Kieran will take you girls around for some shopping later,"

Quinn announced over Nexxa and Klarin chatting.

"Oh, yes, okay," Nexxa said, astutely nodding. She knew she was there with Quinn to find out anything she could to report back to Kilmer, but pink libations, shopping, and a new friend were taking over along with the oysters Quinn ordered, which were devoured as quickly as they were brought.

Seamus seemed hyper and eagerly motioned for the waiter. "A round for the road! I want to be at me best when we go gambling," Seamus bellowed while shaking his closed hand, mimicking throwing dice. The waiter brought a round of drinks, and the men each drank theirs in one mouthful. Klarin barely sipped her drink; Nexxa noticed and did the same.

Seamus reached for the bottom of Klarin's drink. "Bottoms up!"

"Go on, Seamus!" Klarin muttered, twisting her body away from him.

Quinn moved his hand onto Nexxa's thigh. Her eyes met his; he reached across her lap for her purse. He moved her purse onto her lap, unzipped it, and put in one thousand euros. He pushed her hair behind her shoulder and took her hand to help her up from the table.

"Kieran," Klarin started, "we're going to the 15th *arrondissement*." She settled back in her seat, crossing her legs. "I know a gorgeous Italian *atelier*."

"What is that?"

"A shop." Klarin kept her face turned to the window.

"Oh." Nexxa unzipped her purse, reaching in to feel the cash.

"It's *très*—" Klarin couldn't cover her thick Irish accent, "—

chic."

"I went once to a gorgeous store in—" Nexxa realized she was about to recount when Kilmer took her shopping. Klarin huffed. Nexxa watched her as she sat straight, shoulders back, adjusting her sky-blue pashmina.

Finally, with a smile, Klarin stood as she waited for the doorman to open the door. Inside the *atelier*, she was quick to suggest Nexxa try on a pair of black pants, and she selected a sky-blue jacket for herself.

"You have to check the label. Cashmere and wool, these are the best for clothes," Klarin directed while examining the inside of the jacket.

"Oh, okay." Nexxa searched for the label in the pants thinking that Klarin seemed like Kilmer; she knew how to shop properly. With Klarin opting for the jacket and insisting Nexxa take the pants, they paid, and Klarin had Kieran drive them to the next stop.

"Now," Klarin said, as she pulled out her compact and applied her mauve lipstick, "Guerlain, for some gorgeous cosmetics."

Nexxa wanted to enjoy her shopping time with Klarin, but she reminded her of Kilmer with the way she carried herself and spoke to people. And, how would the rest of the night go with Quinn?

"Try this," Klarin said as she handed Nexxa a round box covered in pastel colors.

A sales lady came over. "This is from our Meteorites collection." She offered to apply some of the pastel mix of powder pearls onto Nexxa's cheeks. "Our secret Stardust technology." She stood in front of Nexxa, holding the makeup brush. "Would you like me to wrap this up for you?"

"Yes," Klarin answered for Nexxa. "And one of those," she added, pointing to one of the mascaras. "We've got to go now; the boys will be ready for dinner."

In the car, Klarin opened two splits of champagne, handing one to Nexxa. Nexxa glanced down at Klarin's noticeable diamond band and wondered if she would ever wear one of those.

"How did yous meet Quinn?" Klarin asked as she lit a cigarette.

"A young Irish man."

"Is this your boyfriend?"

"No, we broke up. We had a bad fight one night in a restaurant. Then that's when I met Quinn."

"Quinn likes pretty girls," Klarin breathed, blowing smoke out of the window.

Keiran maneuvered the Mercedes so that they were directly in front of the hotel's entrance, where Hôtel Costes music was playing outside, signifying the beginning of the evening soirées.

"The music is amazing," Nexxa said. She might have been tipsy, hoping Klarin would agree and smile again. That didn't happen. Klarin stepped out of the car and handed Kieran her cigarette, which he put out using his fingers. Then he went around to Nexxa's door, opened it, and escorted them into the hotel lounge, where Quinn and Seamus were already entertaining themselves with drinks. Quinn stood from the sofa as Nexxa approached, extending his hand to her. She lost her balance as she moved into the tight space and fell into him, practically sitting in his lap. For a few seconds, she closed her eyes, inhaling his cologne. The thought of being intimate with him crossed her mind, excited her. She wanted to melt into his muscular arms.

Quinn ran his hand along her arm. "Darling, your skin, mmm."

"I'm sorry."

"Me bullocks, you're sorry," his slang came out when he drank. "I would give me right arm to have you." Strong as he looked, he lifted her a bit. "Let's dance." Nexxa felt his groin pressed against her. Kieran swiftly moved the table so they could step aside. Quinn put his hand on the back of Nexxa's neck, touching her hair, and with his other hand on her abdomen, he swayed them together slowly. Hôtel Costes music played at the right decibel, just loud enough to drown out Klarin and Seamus chatting in the background. Quinn turned Nexxa around, kissing her slowly; his lips moved down, tasting the side of her neck, as he confessed, "I want you. I want to take you to me room."

Nexxa had her left hand on her clavicle bone, and her right hand was in the air as she danced close to Quinn. "We can go."

Quinn reached for his drink; he took a sip. "What's that?"

Nexxa leaned into him. "To your room. We can go to your room."

Quinn moved his hand along his jaw. "Love, I would in a heartbeat. But not tonight." Quinn grasped her, dancing slowly. He whispered something. Nexxa smiled.

Then, looking past Quinn, she saw a man with strikingly dark wavy hair enter the lounge.

Charming Kilmer approached the bar; he ordered a drink. He withdrew his smokes, lighting one. A gulp, a drag, watching Quinn. A gulp, a drag, watching Nexxa.

"Ya fucking bollox!" Kilmer shouted from across the lounge.

Quinn turned, and Kilmer charged, slogging him. Unfazed by

Kilmer's punch, Quinn put an arm out in front of Nexxa. A tear slid down her cheek. She looked to Kilmer, attempting to step toward him; Quinn held his stance, holding her back. Kieran reached in his jacket for his gun. Quinn shook his head; Kieran pushed his gun back in.

"I'll fuckin' bollox your head off too," Kilmer spat with a raised chin to Kieran.

Keiran stepped toward him. Quinn looked Kilmer in his piercing eyes. Kilmer's strikingly dark hair was perfectly coiffed, black Irish some called it. He turned his head; he looked to his friends Klarin and Seamus. Klarin had strikingly dark hair.

Kilmer grabbed Nexxa by the arm. Nexxa looked to Quinn, lowering her head, her hand to her brow. Kilmer flashed Klarin the evil eye before taking Nexxa by her hair and dragging her out of the lounge. The doormen attempted to intercept; one of Kilmer's boys by the waiting vehicle opened his jacket, exposing his gun. Kilmer shoved one of the doormen, pushed Nexxa in the car, and his driver sped off.

Nexxa held her chest, taking deep breaths. Did Quinn understand who she really was? Why didn't he stop Kilmer? "Did I do something wrong?" Nexxa looked out of the window. "I was just doing," she said through tears, "what you told me to do." Nexxa wiped her nose and eyes.

Kilmer put his hand over his mouth. "Quinn was trying to take advantage of you," he said with his voice cracking. "He was trying to get into your panties!" Kilmer hit the dash. "Ya fuckin' prick, Quinn!"

Nexxa flinched, covering her face.

"You have to be more careful!" Kilmer turned to the backseat. "This isn't a woman's game."

KILMER'S WIFE

2003

Kilmer had sold Nexxa on the idea of going to America with him after the botched Paris operation, promising more Prada rigouts and red lipstick. She would never again have to think about weapons or missions. More promises—a future trip to Russia, he remembered she mentioned wanting to go there, maybe a side trip to seek out more fairies. Kilmer was confident he would be accepted to join the FBI since the U.S. government accepted Irish nationals into the military and specific government organizations. Nexxa was impressed with his confidence and promises. That opportunity failed when they discovered his alleged IRA involvement. Nexxa began a career in finance, which came upon her by happenstance, whereas Kilmer ventured into the restaurant industry. Twice, he sought to start up a restaurant, but he became indignant when financing fell through time after time. Always believing in him,

Nexxa found opportunities for him, such as Head of Security for wealthy expats in Bahrain. She was willing to relocate to the Middle East, learn Arabic, and even dye her hair brown.

Nexxa would have moved anywhere and done anything for Kilmer to succeed. She continued with her persistence in applying for positions for him abroad. When nothing came to fruition, they remained in Brooklyn. Yet slowly, he changed. He became jealous of her success and envious of the family she had back home in Canada. Kilmer was not accustomed to seeing affection within a family, and he had been vague with Nexxa about his harsh upbringing.

His jealousy was exacerbated whenever they were out together, as men frequently looked Nexxa's way. She wasn't a flirt or promiscuous, merely blossoming into her beauty and allure. It became a positive nightmare. He was clever; he began to degrade her, then would remind her how he was the luckiest Irishman to have his "brown-eyed girl" while kissing her tenderly on the side of her neck. Twelve months in a year came many times over, and then Nexxa knew that she would be without him someday through a premonition she had. (Nexxa hadn't fully mastered her inherited gifts of premonitions, telepathy, and looking in on people that her mother had; she could use them just enough though to interpret signs when they manifested.) The confidence that had once attracted Nexxa to her mentor come husband had left him and was now hers. When she left him without notice, he became even angrier. How dare she? I mean, he was *Charming Kilmer.*

IRISH BAR, MIDTOWN NYC, SEPTEMBER — 2013

One night, a few years after they were divorced, Kilmer spotted Nexxa getting into a taxi in midtown. Dressed in a sleek black dress with her hair in a French twist, he could smell her beauty from afar. Kilmer's dejection rekindled. He decided to call her, suggested they meet for a drink. He told her that their old friends had been asking about her.

"There's my brown-eyed girl." Kilmer greeted her with a huge smile. "This is my wife, Nexxa," he bragged to the bartender. The bartender greeted Nexxa. Nexxa wished she was back in her office on the trading desk with her jealous co-worker.

"What?" Nexxa asked as she placed her purse on a barstool. "We are divorced. Why would you introduce me as your wi—"

Kilmer motioned with his eyes to the glass of wine he had waiting for her. "I like your hair this way; it's lovely on you."

Nexxa took a sip of the wine Kilmer had so graciously ordered for her. *He seems so sincere, but I just can't trust him. Either way, he no longer controls me.*

"So, how are ya?"

"Well, I'm okay."

"Yeah, yeah, I'm okay, too," he said with an air of innocence.

"So, how are our, well, your friends?" Nexxa asked.

"Good, good. They're *gas*."

"Ah, okay. Well, that's cool."

"So, I saw ya the other night. You were all dressed up."

Nexxa tilted her head to the side. "Sooo, like when did you see me?" she asked, trying to think of when he could have seen her.

"You were probably going on a date."

"No, I don't think so, probably a work dinner." Nexxa took a swallow of her wine. "Yeah, I actually—I have an opportunity to go to Beirut."

"Ya do now?" Kilmer tucked his chin in, burping. And within an instant, his demeanor changed, and he became the Kilmer Nexxa had always known.

"Yes, just for work." Nexxa regretted her words. She flipped her hand in the air, trying to downplay her enthusiasm. "It's nothing really."

Kilmer took a sip of his beer, turned into the bar, and started chatting with the bartender. *How could she be surpassing the mentor? Fucking unbelievable*, his mind raged.

The bartender paused, asking Nexxa if she wanted another drink. "I have to go, no." Nexxa smiled. "My friend is waiting for me outside."

"Don't you want to know how I've been? I'm dating this girl from Columbia." Kilmer turned to Nexxa, leaning in, and said, "It's the best sex I've ever had."

Nexxa took a twenty-dollar bill from her purse and handed it to the bartender. He put a hand up. She returned it to her handbag and thanked him. *Still trying to get a rise out of me.* Nexxa made her way toward the end of the bar.

"Go on now, ya cunt!" Kilmer shouted.

Nexxa moved through the crowd and out of the bar's entrance. *And that will be the last time I hear that. It's almost enjoyable, laughable.* Kilmer repositioned his stance at the bar with a huff, and while he had a pint or two for the road, he texted his friend Sal.

Kilmer: *The cunt is going to Beirut. Can you believe that?*

Sal: *Who?*

Kilmer: *Who? Who do you fucking think?*

Sal: *Man, I thought you divorced.*

Kilmer: *Yeah, but I saw her and called her up for a drink. You know, for ole time's sake.*

Sal: *Maaan.*

Kilmer: *It's for work, she said.*

Sal: *Maaan, it's late here. Hit me up on the instant message tomorrow.*

Kilmer couldn't handle his newfound agitation, so he went out for a smoke. He paced, taking a few long drags from his cigarette, then started to text Nexxa.

Kilmer: *How the fuck are you going to Beirut?*

Kilmer: *I listened to you moaning for years, and you were moaning tonight about your job.*

Kilmer: *I put up with you for years. If it weren't for me, you wouldn't even be here.*

What? Nexxa questioned as she read Kilmer's string of text messages. *Oh my god, he's gone crazy again.*

Nexxa: *Kilmer*

Nexxa deleted the text she began to him and turned off her phone. Just for now. She knew she might look at his texts again later in the night. She hated that she was disappointed, how he fooled her, how he treated her again. Nexxa hated to admit that he would forever have some sort of impact on her life going forward. She struggled to answer the biggest question she had ever had for herself: Why did she have a soft spot for him?

BEIRUT — SEPTEMBER 29, 2013

The waiter looked like someone who was more on the nerdy side and probably had been shy until taking a job working around tourists. He seemed so genuine and captivating, telling them the history of hookah. While Nexxa decided the young waiter had such a sweet disposition about him and was a natural storyteller, Iliada remembered how Nexxa told her she was excited to experience some "Mid-East pleasures" while in Beirut.

"So, are you going to college, university?" Nexxa asked.

"I go for one year but had to stop to help my mother with my brothers and sisters," the waiter answered in broken English.

"What did you study?"

"I studied writing." He blinked, and his smile widened; someone had taken an interest in him. "I wrote stories for my younger sister and brother. I would love to go to school again, and I am saving so that I may someday." He continued with his friendly rapport. "I will leave you now; please enjoy your hookah. I hope to see you again during your stay here."

Nexxa delicately held her hookah mouth tip between her breasts. "Hookah is also called shisha or hubbly bubbly. I love seeing the smoke billow when you exhale."

"I like hubbly bubbly; that's cool," Iliada gushed, moving her shoulders in a table-dancing way. The city's elite was filling in the vaulted restaurant, it's red walls bejeweled with gold. Beirut's energy made it possible for alter egos to exist, like fragrances in a perfumery, kind of like dirty sex amid beautiful creatures. The satisfaction amongst the stunning people was so transparent you could see it naturally occurring. Nexxa was in mid-draw from her hookah when Medan walked into the lounge. *He looks hot in that button-down blue shirt and jeans. I bet he's hella sexy with his clothes off. Shit, stop. Now take a draw and smile at him.*

The tempting Arab man in his early forties did a double take as he passed Nexxa. *Where did she come from? A beautiful blonde right here in Beirut.* He was aware he had provoking eyes while moving across the hookah lounge to the end section of the couch where he was seated. While the waiter was preparing hookahs for him and his friend, Medan couldn't stop glancing at Nexxa.

"You want to talk to her, eh," Zarian teased, hoping to ruffle Medan's nerves.

"I'm smoking, don't bother me," laughed Medan.

But really, for a blonde, Medan didn't hesitate to leave his hookah.

He had a boyish grin when he asked, "May I sit? I am Medan."

"Yes. I'm Nexxa." Nexxa adjusted her legs as Medan sat

beside her on the couch. The seating left little space between them, allowing Nexxa to feel his warmth as her arm grazed his.

"I am so surprised to see you here. How did you come to be here?"

"In this hookah lounge—or Beirut?"

"It's just that I've never met anyone like you here."

"Well, I'm here for work and used to have Palestinian friends. That's how I started smoking hookah."

"Really? I would love to know more about the Palestinian friends you have."

"Well, I knew them when I was married. They were friends of ours. Sheba taught me how to cook some dishes, the one with stuffed squash."

"Oh yes, yes, I love this one." Medan shifted his body closer. "You know how to prepare that?"

"Yeah, I do. My friend, she taught me about Middle Eastern spices and introduced me to date cups."

"I am impressed." Medan lifted her hand. "Your hands are beautiful."

"So… you're not married?"

"I had a business in the United States selling cars. My wife did not like it there and came back here to live with our kids."

"Okay." Nexxa shook her head. "I see." Her eyes might have shown her skepticism.

"We are divorced now," Medan quickly offered to clarify. "So, how is it that you are divorced?"

"I've been busy with work. It just didn't work out." Nexxa handed Medan her hookah, offering to share with him, then clarified, "My marriage." Medan took a draw and gave her the hookah, placing his hand on her thigh. The smoke from the hookahs twirled around Nexxa. *This is so intimate without being intimate; he looks so sexy when smoking.* He held her hostage to the moment.

Zarian, Medan's friend, was in his early thirties and the same height as Iliada with a slender build. He picked up his tea and brought it over to Iliada, introducing himself as Zarry.

"I'm Zarian," he corrected himself. "You're so beautiful; you could be my girlfriend."

Iliada's eyes widened at his forward remark. She immediately determined he wasn't sleazy like a lot of men in New York City. Even though he seemed to come on strong, he was different.

"I'm Iliada," she replied, putting a hand to her chest. "We are from New York City," she said proudly.

"You want more tea?" Zarian asked, motioning for the waiter. Her glass was full.

"What are you here for? Two girls like you."

"My sister is here for work."

"Yeah, she seems busy working now," he joked as he looked over at Medan with Nexxa.

Nexxa found that it was easy to talk to Medan. It was enjoyable to converse with him. Or... maybe the smoke was going to her head. So, she asked Iliada to go to the bathroom with her. Iliada agreed. Turning to Zarian, she said, "I'll be right back." Nexxa's peripheral vision took account of the curious eyes as they maneuvered to the ladies' room. For a moment, she detected something, but the scent dropped, and she assumed it was only smoke from the plethora of flavored hookahs. Sighing, putting her hand over her chest, she asked, "What is his name?"

"Zarry, well, he said Zarian, but his friends call him Zarry. Oh my god, he's so hot!"

"Yeah." Nexxa entered the stall to pee. "I don't know what it is about Medan."

Looking up at the intricate ceiling, she took mental notes. *He's mesmerizingly hot, Arab, a little Americanized but probably Muslim.* A proper assessment, but what was the risk factor? That, she still needed to determine. Looking down, she admired the woman's suede sky-blue heels in the next stall. She had assumed they were alone in the women's room.

Iliada didn't even need to say what her face was already saying. "Well, I *really* like Zarian."

Nexxa washed her hands. "Yeah, but he lives here—we live in New York."

Drying her hands, Nexxa looked over her shoulder to the stall occupied by the woman with sky-blue heels. Iliada started to speak but was interrupted by a group of ladies that quickly ascended into the room and the stalls. Nexxa shook her head, indicating that Iliada should not. Nexxa wanted to lecture Iliada, worrying that she was delving too deep too fast, but now was not the time.

Sergei watched her drawing from her hookah pipe, the way she exhaled the smoke. His table offered a view just right, inconspicuously right. He was already seated, perusing the menu, when she—Nexxa—and her sister, entered and were seated in Beirut's most coveted hookah lounge. Of course, she was unexpected, but it was even more so unexpected when two locals, Arab men, approached her and her sister. He had been enjoying watching her, even more so than the music and the dancers, even more so than his trip intended. Usually, he would have checked his watch and phone messages, taken the last sip of his libation, and left. He wasn't the type to be interested in a woman who was actively being pursued. And then, when she made her way past him to and from the ladies' room, he noticed how the air that carried her smell was intoxicating.

Zarian jumped right back into canoodling with Iliada, continuing to whisper to her playfully. Even though she could be shy, she knew there was something about him. She liked the attention, and he was her type. Medan left just enough space for Nexxa to sit back down, forcing her to cross over him. Yet there wasn't any space between her and the smell of the cologne doused on his desirable skin. It might've been a bad idea, (she at least wanted to have a risk level properly assigned to Medan— separated from her lust level for him,) but she hoped to see him again.

"Would you join me for dinner tomorrow?" he asked as if he could hear her thoughts.

KLARIN

BEIRUT — SEPTEMBER 30, 2013

Klarin retrieved her sky-blue suede stilettos from the bottom of the wardrobe. She noticed a minuscule scuff on the toe of the right shoe. As she stood in her heels, feet together, in her room in the InterContinental Le Vendôme, she looked out over the city of Beirut. She thought about Nexxa and the day they had spent together shopping and dining a decade ago in Paris. She had managed to keep a blonde hair of Nexxa's that had fallen on her lap in the car ride as Kieran, Quinn's minder, had driven them around the various *arrondissements*. Tucked away went the blonde hair into her double-strap black leather purse.

Last night was eventful as she usually only ventured out, when at home in Ireland, to restock her tea. But here in Beirut, it was to follow Nexxa. She deemed Medan "Middle East-Fuckable". But then again, Klarin never really fucked anyone. Seeing Medan and Nexxa interact in the hookah lounge, she became aroused—which enraged her—and fed her icy sky-blue blood. Klarin ordered a pot of tea from room service and tapped on her iPod to play her Hôtel Costes playlist. That was the only playlist she had. Standing with her sky-blue heels on and nothing else, she moved her petite body awkwardly to the music. Mouthing words to her fave on the playlist, she moved to the mirror and lifted her tweezers from the dresser to pluck a chin hair. Staring at her bare self, she moved her hand between her legs. She regretted not bringing her blonde wig—the one she liked to drape over her when touching herself. The wig was left at home in Ireland, safely tucked away in the nightstand in her bedroom. Only when the job was done, when there was a pool of blood around Nexxa's head, would she reward herself with the touch of the blonde wig again.

Scrolling through KosmicMarket.onion, looking for her next job, she noticed on KitchenGod's profile how he had changed his avatar to a female and the color to sky-blue. "Hmm, imitation is the sincerest form of flattery," she said in her undeniable Irish accent as she looked down to her sky-blue heels. She wondered if KitchenGod was back in the Far East or if they were still in Beirut. When she first accepted the assignment, a contract for murder, she didn't recognize the woman in the photo. Sure, a pretty blonde, something to think about when masturbating, someone to imagine stealing her man's affection, all that was there. It wasn't until she saw Nexxa with her blonde hair flanking her poised smile that she realized who she was—the same young, pretty, graceful blonde from America—no, from Canada, she remembered being told.

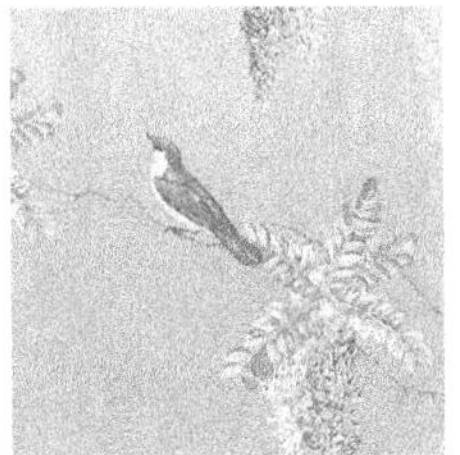

BEIRUT — SEPTEMBER 30, 2013

Iliada flipped through the pages of the hotel binder on the desk. She ran her finger across the listing, then shouted, "They have Lucas Carton Rosé on the menu!"

"Really?" Nexxa tapped the pen she was holding against her hand. "Well, that makes sense since this is the Paris of the Middle East."

Iliada perused the rest of the menu, having no problem taking charge of ordering champagne and treats from room service, while Nexxa decided to put her mental notes down on paper, just in case she needed to be reminded. Previously lived in the U. S. with business selling cars. Divorced, kids, Muslim, Hot. Nexxa folded the paper, put it in her purse, and walked to the mirror above the dresser. Putting her hands on her cheeks, sliding her hands down to her neck, she exhaled and closed her eyes.

Turning, gazing at the illuminated city through the window, she said, "You can't deny Beirut's alluring effect. I think my perfume even smells better here."

"What are you going to wear?" Iliada asked as she sprinted to greet room service.

"I would think that in Beirut, I would know what I want to wear. Good," Nexxa said as she watched the waiter open the bottle. "I need some champagne to calm my nerves."

"Yeah, I can't wait to see Zarian." Iliada poured two glasses.

Nexxa walked over to the crisp, white, modern wardrobe, which flawlessly displayed her mostly black ensembles and stared at her hanging clothes. She lightly stroked her midnight blue velvet jumpsuit, which looked almost black but with a slight glimmer.

"I know I wear black a lot," started Nexxa, making an apologetic face, "but I love this jumpsuit since it's *almost* black."

"Oh, I understand. Just do you." Iliada was supportive of anything black. "I'm just going to wear my new outfit," Iliada said as she pulled on her new black leggings. "My orchid spaghetti strap tank you got me from Barneys." Iliada slipped on her emerald ring, and her phone pinged as she sprayed on her delicate perfume. "Zarian just texted me that they could pick us up."

"Hmm, no, I wouldn't feel comfortable with that. I *already* had the hotel arrange a driver for us, and we can meet them there. Medan gave me the name of the restaurant."

"Uh…" Iliada stood straight with her arms by her side. "Well, I think it will be okay." Lifting her arm, holding her cell phone, she said, "I'll text him back." Zarian and Iliada had been texting each other since their first meeting. He had been incredibly flirtatious. One text had an emoji of a man and woman holding hands, where he wrote, "This is me and my new girlfriend."

"I'm going to go downstairs to have a look around the hotel while you finish." Iliada drank the last sip of her champagne and then made a pout with her lips, looking in the mirror by the door. She looked ambrosial with her softly curled shoulder-length blonde hair that fell lovely on her collarbone.

"Oh." Nexxa glanced at Iliada as she looked through her purse. "Okay." Having taken Medan's business card that he gave her out of her handbag—Medan Muran Enterprises Imports and Exports—she tapped it on the dresser, then took a sip of her champagne. *What does he really do?* Her phone buzzed with a text.

Medan: *Looking forward to a beautiful evening.*

Nexxa fluffed her hair, then held her hair behind her head with one hand and moved her other hand onto her chest. Looking at herself in the mirror, she imagined Medan touching her as she moved her hand over her left breast, sliding her hand down her body, reaching into her panties.

Her phone buzzed again. It was a text from her boss. "Fuck!" Nexxa lifted her phone again: *Hey, how is the trip going?* Nexxa tossed her phone then went to the champagne bottle, pouring another glass. Between sips, she brushed on her silver iridescent Chanel eyeshadow, applied mascara, and put on her Bloody Snowflake lip stain. *Yep, look hot; he'll want to fuck me.*

While checking for her room key in her purse, she felt her velvet pouch. Nexxa always carried quartz, rose, obsidian, and amethyst stones. She took out the obsidian, warming the stone in her hands. Sitting on the bench at the end of the bed, she had the feeling of being with a man she didn't know yet and a baby that seemed familiar. She wondered if somehow this was related to her dream with the snake. Disrupted by the phone ringing, she answered; the hotel concierge informed her their car was ready. Nexxa stowed her stones away in their velvet pouch and put on her stilettos.

Downstairs, it wasn't hard for Nexxa to spot Iliada in the hotel bar; she was flanked by two Arab men. Medan turned, grinning as Nexxa walked toward them. Glad to see him, her smile expressed, but caught off guard, her mind hid.

"I didn't want you to travel alone," he explained as he kissed her on each cheek. Unsurprisingly, Iliada was engaged with Zarian. Medan reached for Nexxa's hand; she liked his forwardness. Medan looked to Zarian, motioning it was time to go; Zarian prepared Iliada with his arm to leave. The four of them walked outside, where Medan waved over the taxi he had waiting for them.

"So, how was your first day in Beirut?" Medan asked.

"We really just rested, adjusting to the time change. Tomorrow we will venture out, though."

"Beirut is a wonderful city; I love my country so much." Driving through the city streets, Medan pointed out the window, showing Nexxa prominent buildings mixed with Parisian and Ottoman influence. She heard his words, going on about Beirut, and she felt his hand moving against her thigh—that's when she remembered her mom's warning, *I see two men who will approach you when you are together with Iliada. They intend to do you harm.* Nexxa never mentioned their mom's warning to Iliada. Now, she wished she had, at least sometime after Iliada had moved to live with her in New York.

DAHLIA FLOWER RESTAURANT

Medan fell silent, no more about Beirut, only checking his phone a few times while still en route to dinner. Nexxa presumed it was either a woman contacting him or something with his work. When they arrived at the restaurant, he put his phone in his jeans' front pocket and took her hand to help her out of the car.

"Come, I want to show you." He brought Nexxa up a staircase, which led to a terrace filled with fragrant dahlia flowers and fig trees. Zarian whisked Iliada to the side of the restaurant, where a few locals were dancing to traditional music. The terrace overlooked the sea. Medan pointed in the direction of Cyprus. A waiter brought up some wine, poured some into the glasses, and swiftly went back down the stairs.

"This is my uncle's restaurant," Medan explained as he handed Nexxa a glass of wine. "My father met my mother here many, many years ago, before they were married. Have you ever been with a man like me? An Arab?" Medan added.

"I—have not. Did you date any American women? Right—you were married."

"I met my wife when we were teenagers."

"Oh, okay." Nexxa realized he had most likely not been with many women, let alone a blonde Western woman.

"You can hear the music and the sea at the same time." Medan leaned his head back as he stretched his arms out along the edge of the terrace wall. Nexxa observed his heavy face, his stance that looked as if the Arab were trying to escape himself. *Change the direction* came to mind, so Nexxa walked away from the Arab. Standing in-between the rows of dahlia plants, she caressed the blooms of the flowers.

Medan came up behind her. "They are beautiful," he said in a low voice while running his fingers under her hand. "My uncle grows them." Medan grasped her hand. "Let's go down to them."

Medan guided Nexxa to a table where a waiter stood ready to seat them. With a pause in the music, Zarian and Iliada joined them at the table.

"Some wine for my girl," charmed Zarian while reaching for the wine, pouring some for Iliada.

"Were you guys dancing this entire time?"

"Yeah, I show her how to shake her hips."

"Zarry can dance."

"Medan, you should show her to dance."

"Here, do you want some more wine?" he asked Nexxa, seemingly ignoring Zarian.

"This man is shy," snickered Zarian.

"Medan showed me the terrace; it is lovely," Nexxa interjected while trying to get Iliada's attention. "The terrace was amazing. You can see all the way to Cyprus from up there."

"Excuse me," Medan said as he stood from the table. He tore a piece of pita bread, ate it, and wiped his mouth with his cloth napkin. "I'll be right back." Like a puppy following his master, Zarian rose, jetting after Medan over to a man standing in the doorway to the restaurant's kitchen.

"So… the terrace had tons of dahlia flowers planted."

"I'm in love." Iliada moved her shoulders to the music. "He's so hot!"

Nexxa heard her sister but kept her attention on Medan and the man he was talking with. Medan was speaking into the man's ear. Because of the music? Or was it something else? The man seemed to be looking to Nexxa as Medan talked to him.

Medan returned to the table. "This is my uncle." Nexxa started to stand to greet him. "Sit, sit," he insisted.

Nexxa extended her hand. "*Salam alaikum.* I'm Nexxa."

"*Salam alaikum.* Lovely to make your acquaintance." He poetically put his hands around hers, gently clutching. "How are you enjoying your stay in Beirut?"

"It's lovely. A little serendipitous." Nexxa moved her eyes to Medan.

"What has brought you to Beirut?"

"I am here for work. To meet a prospective client."

"Ah, well, very good then. Please enjoy your dinner."

"Thank you."

Medan's uncle embraced him, saying, "*Salam alaikum.*"

"Come on, let's dance." Iliada pulled on Nexxa's hand. Zarian stayed at the table and clapped along to the music. Medan took his seat, poured himself some wine, then turned his chair to keep his eyes on Nexxa. When a slower song started playing, Zarian stood up and approached Iliada, pulling her toward him. Nexxa made her way back to their table. She turned her chair to face Medan and scooted closer, her legs between his.

He leaned in and took her hand. "I just can't believe I have met you.”

“I’m glad I met *you*.”

The waiter came to the table with more pita bread and another bottle of wine. Medan let go of Nexxa’s hand and turned to grab a piece of bread. “I’ll fill your glass for you.”

Nexxa turned her chair back to face the table. “Thank you.” She adjusted herself in the chair. “So, how long have you and Zarian been friends?”

“Zarian was going to marry my cousin.”

“Oh, okay.”

“She left to study. University in London.”

“Ah, okay, well, that sounds awesome. I mean for your cousin.”

“Yes, she is doing very well. I am proud of her.” Medan stuffed another piece of bread in his mouth. “So tell me, what is it again that you do?”

“Well, I work in finance, and I am here, in Beirut, to meet a prospective client.”

“So, what did you study?”

“Oh, I—didn’t. I did not go to college.”

“Really? You must be smart. I, I like smart women.”

Nexxa nodded and sipped her wine but wondered if he did, in fact, like intelligent women. Iliada was hot from dancing; with one hand, she fanned herself as she returned to the table for a drink. Nexxa took the opportunity to suggest they go to the ladies’ room.

“I like Medan,” Nexxa began telling her once they were in the bathroom. “It’s just something seems off.”

“Oh, *he* likes you. And Zarian is *so* hot.”

"Yeah, yeah, you told me that," Nexxa remarked.

Iliada huffed, rolling her eyes.

"I'm sorry. It's just that I'm not sure." Nexxa tilted her head. "Something is askew."

"Did you say anything to him?"

"Like what? I find you attractive, but I haven't assessed your risk factor yet."

"Well, no, but…"

"Yep, there's not much I can say."

"You ladies always go together," Medan stated as they returned. Adjusting in his chair, he continued, "You had something important to discuss?"

"No, no," Nexxa laughed, fluffing her hair. Could he detect her apprehensions? "I can't drink too much since I have a meeting tomorrow," Nexxa continued as she swirled the wine in her glass.

Medan unexpectedly put his hand on Nexxa's upper back, rubbing her gently. "Have your wine," he insisted.

Nexxa sensed a yawn coming on; she didn't want to be tired—she didn't want to drink any more wine either. "Excuse me," she said, yawning and setting her glass back down. "Sorry, guess I am more tired than I realized."

"Come, we will take you back in a taxi."

"Okay, thank you."

Medan excused himself and walked over to his uncle. He spoke to him briefly before returning to their table.

"Thank you for waiting for me."

"Oh, sure."

Zarian and Iliada walked ahead of Nexxa and Medan, flirting as they walked toward the door. Part of Nexxa wanted to return to the hotel, and part of her couldn't help but wonder if she would or should see Medan again. Maybe the excitement was wearing off. Yes, he was sexy, but something didn't feel right; Nexxa swirled around in her mind the notes she had taken on Medan while they waited outside for a taxi.

Medan grasped her hand; he looked up at the night sky. "You know the Arabic name for Lebanon is *Lubnan,* which means white like the color of the snow-covered Lebanese mountains." Nexxa looked down at their hands; her thoughts stopped. A taxi pulled up to the curb, and Nexxa felt Medan's lips upon each cheek.

The car door was opened for her, and as Nexxa started getting into the backseat, a dahlia flower fell to the ground, landing on her foot.

BEIRUT — OCTOBER 1, 2013

The next afternoon while walking up the three flights of stairs to visit his friend Tarek, the lights went out in the building. "How can this still happen?" Medan gestured with his hand in the air. "Isn't *Lubnan* coming into the modern-day?" Climbing the last few steps, he could see the door to Tarek's apartment was open, and two scantily clad women inside the apartment were flanking his cousin Sal. Turning his back to the doorway, Medan withdrew his phone, checking for updates on the city's power outage. After some time, the lights flickered; Medan looked up from his phone, seeing the electricity had been restored.

Medan coughed, covering his mouth as he entered the apartment. "What are you doing?" he shouted to Sal as he entered.

"Come on." Sal fanned the smoke from a candle. "I can share."

"I'm only here to talk." Medan looked from one side of the

room to the other. "We need to speak alone."

Sal motioned with his eyes to Shula. She sauntered over to Medan. Grabbing his hand, she slowly moved it into her bra. Medan sighed before yanking her hand away, causing Shula to lose her balance. "Come on, she like—you," Sal slurred.

"We need to speak!" Medan slammed his hand down on the kitchen table. The women scattered about the apartment, snickering. "The March 8 want more."

"Relaaax," Sal managed with more coherence. "We have set everything in place for our deal."

Medan's eyes burned into Sal, and Tarek emerged from the back bedroom carrying his prayer beads. "We are to meet with the representatives from China Black Road this week to discuss their proposal. They can provide financing as well. This deal could be very good for everyone."

Shula stood from her crouch, taking a step toward Medan; he put his hand up to her, "*Sharmuta*, shhh, shhh."

"I was appointed head of finance for a reason," continued Tarek, unfazed by Medan's interruption. "Do you think the National Lebanese Bank is thinking about who is in control in Lebanon? We can get cheaper financing with China Black Road and control the funds ourselves. The bank will pay more doing it their way, and it is a betrayal to work with the Americans!" Tarek started again louder, "The United States has always supported Israel. They consider Hezbollah a terrorist organization. The sanctions! Iran provides support!"

"What are you talking about? The bank?" Medan raised his hands. "What are they doing?"

"They are trying to make a deal with an American broker-dealer." Tarek motioned with his head. "Here, in Beirut. They have sent a woman."

"How did you come to know this?" Medan asked, furrowing his brow.

"I invited the men from China Black Road to meet some of the girls," Tarek responded while he fluttered his hands around, motioning to the girls disbursed around his apartment.

Medan shook his head. *What the fuck? He should have told me about his plans.* Medan cocked his head. "You said *they sent a woman.*"

"*Yes*," Tarek huffed, swaying his head, "they have sent a woman."

Medan walked over to the window in the kitchen; he watched kids down below playing. *She said she was here for work. To meet a client this week. Could she be the same American woman?* Music began booming; he turned from looking out of the kitchen window. Sal shimmied with a girl while Tarek cavorted with two girls.

Medan made his way past Sal, Tarek, and the women; no *salam alaikum.*

He tapped the steering wheel incessantly on the drive home. In his living room, he rolled out his prayer mat, knelt, and prayed. After praying, he decided to go to the neighborhood shop and buy a beer. The closer it got to Ramadan, the guiltier he felt for drinking alcohol. Whatever, he wanted a drink.

Back in his apartment, he looked at a picture he had framed of him and his family on a trip they had taken to NYC. His kids looked happy, and his wife was smiling. He remembered that day well because he and his ex-wife had fought about returning to Lebanon. It wasn't so much that he didn't want to move back from the U.S. to Beirut; it was more that she made him feel he wasn't as successful as she expected in the States. He assumed taking her on one last trip before they moved home would show her that he was capable of giving her everything. Medan smashed his fist against the picture. "That's it!"

Taking a drink from his beer, he powered up his laptop and typed "Nexxa NYC finance" into Google. He didn't get any results. Then he typed in "Iliada NYC" and found her sister on Facebook. Using his son's saved account information, he was able to sign into Facebook. From there, he found Nexxa under Iliada's friends. Nexxa's Facebook profile was scarce.

She didn't list where she worked or any other pertinent personal information, only a few old posts from when she first created her account. Her page did confirm her last name, Davoren. *Okay, found her.* Searching using Nexxa's first and last name, he pulled up her profile on her company's website.

"She does work in finance." Medan nodded. "Let me see what she does." Her profile wasn't all-encompassing, but he had enough information to confirm his suspicion. *What else about her?* He scrolled down and saw a result of an Instagram profile. Medan clicked on the link for the Instagram profile and saw: "This Account is Private, Follow to see their photos and videos."

"*El'ama!* I have to join Instagram so that I can look at her pictures!" Nexxa's profile picture was the only viewable photo on Instagram. Medan opened another browser. Finding Iliada's account, he could see several of her posts without joining. He took the last sip of his beer and enlarged a picture of Nexxa wearing a revealing black dress that Iliada had posted on her account. Medan stood up and unzipped his jeans. Leaning over to adjust the screen, his erect penis brushed against the picture. He spat in his hand and started to stroke his penis. Medan glanced at his phone as it pinged, ignoring it. Realizing he hadn't been this hard in a long time, he moaned, *"Badde nikek!"* He grabbed his laptop and laid it down on the couch, standing over it. Climaxing, he squirted his cum all over Nexxa's photo. Medan leaned back and roared before touching her face.

His phone pinged again. He looked at the text: *Shula says you are sexy.* *"El'ama!* That *sharmuta* can't make me hard like Nexxa." He pushed his phone away. Before pulling up his pants, he slowly stroked his penis some more. "I want to fuck her so bad." He cleared his throat. "I want my dick so far in her mouth." Medan put his hand to his face, rubbing his stubble. *This is a problem. I have to take care of this.* He slammed the laptop shut and went to his kitchen, retrieving a towel. It had embroidery on it and was from his mother. Medan opened the computer and wiped his semen from the screen. Nexxa's picture was still enlarged; he minimized it, then expanded it again. Lastly, he closed the browser and shut the laptop again. Medan sat on the couch and picked up his beer for a taste. *"El'ama,* it's empty!"

Lying in bed, he reflected on how Tarek had been strategically placed in his role just as Medan had been. (Medan had been approached and recruited by his friend Tarek upon returning to Lebanon.) He was in a position with resources, working as an agent within the General Directorate of State Security Missions, and could provide information on foreigners and foreign entities. Medan was mainly motivated by money and now found himself in a predicament where he was conflicted. He knew that this new revenue stream that Tarek was working on would be lucrative for Hezbollah. (Tarek's organization, a shell company fronting as a charitable organization for the betterment of Lebanon, would funnel some of the funds to Hezbollah.)

Something else was bothering him: the assassination of a fellow agent. Was it that the assassinated agent didn't follow orders from Hezbollah or something else? It still seemed foreign to him to be in business with the Chinese, taking a loan from them. Earlier that night, in the neighborhood shop, while buying a beer, he had examined a toy, a remote control car; the box said "Made in China." Never before had that bothered him—but it did now. And, was the American company even a threat? Medan tossed, finally turning on his stomach to sleep.

Around eleven p.m., he awoke. Nexxa was the first thing that came to mind, an image of her with a bullet in her head—blood streaming from her face—flashed in his mind. He lay awake for about half an hour before finally getting out of bed to take a piss. After using the toilet, he plopped down on his bed and picked up his phone. What had Nexxa been doing all day? He tossed the phone down, lifted it again, and headed back to the bathroom, stepping into the shower.

BEIRUT — OCTOBER 1, 2013

Faroud reminded Nexxa of her boss Dan. He was boyishly spirited. Since their meeting in NYC, he liked to keep in constant contact through Bloomberg. He regularly sent emails; most were silly jokes. Some included "online stickers," as Nexxa called them. It was her co-worker who snidely informed her that online stickers were called memes.

Nexxa decided to introduce Faroud to celebrity gossip blogs such as Dlisted, thinking that this would be a better source of entertainment for him. This action led to Faroud wanting to chat via Bloomberg messenger every time he read a post about a celebrity that he deemed hilarious. He even went as far as to read archived posts about certain celebrities. He would then chat to Nexxa things like, "Hey, they call Brad Pitt and Angelina Jolie 'Brangelina,' can you believe that LOL LOL LOL?"

Nexxa debated whether to bring Iliada to her meeting with Faroud since the meeting would be held at Faroud's home. She expected Faroud's reaction would be excited, borderline smitten when she arrived with her sister.

Faroud's housekeeper greeted Nexxa and Iliada when they arrived. She told them he was still getting ready.

"Getting ready?" Nexxa laughed under her breath.

"Come, I'll take you to the courtyard."

"Yeah, what man has to finish," Iliada used air quotes when the housekeeper turned, "'getting ready?'"

"Faroud has asked me to prepare Bellinis for you."

"Okay." Nexxa smiled, assuring the housekeeper. "Thank you."

She served the drinks. "I will tell Faroud you are ready for him."

Waiting until the housekeeper walked away, Nexxa pulled Iliada close to her. "I can't believe we are starting with Bellinis. I should be drinking tea or coffee. I don't want to be rude, though."

"Oh no, I like Bellinis," Iliada confirmed.

Nexxa held her chest, sighed, and took a sip of her Bellini.

"Hello!" Faroud announced with arms wide, entering the courtyard. "I'm so happy to finally have you in my country."

"Hello, Faroud." Nexxa embraced him for a hug.

"And who is this?" Faroud laughed and winked before he gave Iliada the traditional kiss on each cheek. Iliada delighted in the attention.

"How has your stay been so far? How are your accommodations? How is Dan? I must send him this funny joke."

"Oh um, good, and hotel, yes, is good; Dan is also good." *Oh my—he is hyper*; Nexxa maintained her professional face.

"Sit, sit," Faroud insisted with his arms extended.

"Thank you."

"How do you like your Bellinis?"

"Very good, yes." Nexxa touched the base of her glass.

"Excellent. So Faroud," Nexxa started, moving her eyes around the courtyard, "your home is lovely."

"Thank you; it has been in my family for many generations. My father's father's father built this house. How do you say?"

"So, your great-grandfather," Nexxa said as she followed how many fathers Faroud had said.

"Yes, yes, that is it."

"Well, Dan is excited for us to work together. I have our proposal for you to look over." Nexxa touched the folder she had on the table. "We also need to discuss specifics for the prospectus."

"Very well," Faroud said with one nod of his head while looking over at Iliada and smiling.

"Can you excuse me? I need to use your bathroom."

"Yes, yes, let me get my housekeeper to show you."

Faroud proceeded to call his housekeeper on his phone. Nexxa and Iliada met eyes. *Don't laugh, don't laugh.* Neither laughed out loud.

"Faroud, I thought you would call her out loud, like, not on your cell phone. I don't want you to have to bother her."

"It is no problem; sometimes I send her a picture of what I want that I see on Instagram." Faroud held up his phone, showing a post of a cup of tea. "You know, instead of a boring text, I send her a pic of a post," he assured them, drowning them with his laughter. Nexxa held her face; she laughed, and Iliada laughed.

The housekeeper approached the table and motioned for Nexxa to follow her. Nexxa used the toilet and practiced her composure. When the housekeeper didn't return to accompany Nexxa back to the courtyard, Nexxa wandered. She ventured to the main living room and decided to pop in for a peek. Nexxa touched a picture frame; *wow, she's pretty, must be his daughter.* Looking around, she saw several more framed photos of more beautiful women. "Ooh, these probably aren't all his daughters, hmm," she whispered to herself as Iliada came to her mind. "I definitely should check on them." Nearing the garden, she heard music and the banter of Faroud and her sister. Faroud had insisted that Iliada dance and that his housekeeper join them for drinks. Nexxa told herself to resist, only to self-correct and oblige. She glanced at the table, wondering if Faroud had looked at the documents she had brought with her. *Been here before. Better enjoy myself and appease the client.*

"So Faroud, I am meeting with China Black Road."

"Good, good, you can advise me on a deal with them."

"We've done our due diligence on China Black Road." Nexxa danced to the surprisingly good electronic dance music, maintaining her professional composure. "I just need to speak with Dan to finalize some things." It was in her favor that Faroud wanted Nexxa's firm to be part of the negotiations for securing a general contractor. *Okay, so maybe this is going well.* "We can discuss that more in detail after I meet with CBR." Nexxa made her way back to the table, taking a sip of water. She lifted her phone. Time had flown by; it was evening already.

"Are you waiting for a boy to call?" joked Faroud, multitasking his ladies.

"Oh—no." But as she held her phone in her hand, she realized that yes, yes, actually, it would be nice if there had been a missed call from Medan.

On the drive from the hotel to Faroud's house, Nexxa had noticed that the driver kept looking in the rearview mirror. Now on the way back to the hotel, she saw him doing it again. When he made an abrupt turn and sped up, she caught eyes with him in the rearview mirror. But then, all of a sudden, they were back at the hotel, and she considered that it might just be all the Bellinis she drank affecting her mind.

"I had a good time! What do we do now?"

"Yeah." Nexxa could tell Iliada was in the party mood. "Faroud is fun. I need some tea, and then I need to video chat with Dan. Can you order some from room service? I need to splash some water on me to wake up."

Nexxa twisted her hair up in a clip and stepped into the shower. She held her shoulder, tilting her head with the hot water flowing. Nexxa wished Medan would kiss her body, starting from her neck.

In another part of Beirut, Medan stepped into the shower and adjusted the water to be warmer. He thought about kissing Nexxa, reminiscing about masturbating to her picture earlier that night. While still in the water, he reached for his phone, typed a text to her, and then deleted it.

THE HARET HREIK

BEIRUT — OCTOBER 2, 2013

When their waiter from their first night in Beirut told them where he lived, Nexxa knew she would have to see for herself, take Iliada. Walking around the dahiyeh—Haret Hreik—Hezbollah's de facto capital, they followed the power lines that decorated the streets from side to side.

"Someone always has less than you have, and somebody will always have more. I think it is good to see it both ways. Maybe it keeps you balanced, seeing both ends of the poles," Nexxa explained.

"Yeah." Iliada watched an elderly man. "I mean this is definitely different from New York." She noticed how he sat in a chair by a store front watching people passing by. With narrow walkways, they were forced to pass closely. The man spoke a few words with a smile; Iliada and Nexxa paused to listen. "I don't know what he is saying." Iliada looked to Nexxa.

"He said he hopes God will bless you."

"What should I say back?"

"Just say thank you."

"But he probably doesn't know English," Iliada whispered before she smiled and thanked the older man. Nexxa pulled out some money and handed it to him. He thanked her in Arabic.

"That was strange. But nice that you gave him some money." Nexxa put her arm through Iliada's, pulling her closer as they walked away, each turning to look back at the older man.

Iliada lifted her phone, snapping a picture. A stern look came from a woman passing in a hijab. Iliada quickly lowered her phone.

"Look, we are moving through here the same as in a forest with predators," Nexxa explained.

"Kind of like no matter where you are," Iliada paused, "you will use and need the same survival skills."

"Yeah." Nexxa smiled, grabbing Iliada's hand, patting it. "Exactly." Nexxa had been taught some survival skills by Thomas, such as using her keen sense of smell, the ability to track scents on a higher level, similar to the Canis lupus species, which she referred to as her "wolfness."

It wasn't long before another woman passed wearing a hijab, clearly showing her disapproval. "I'm putting this on." Iliada took the scarf out of her purse that she had bought in the hotel gift shop. "Did you bring a scarf to wear?"

"I should buy one." Nexxa adjusted Iliada's scarf. "Good reason to shop."

Something colorful and a smell caught Nexxa's attention, causing her to change direction. Down this particular street were several boutiques for women. Some shops were dim, so when they looked inside, it was hard to tell if they were open even in the daytime.

"I didn't expect to see shops like this selling lingerie. I figured only chain stores near the hotel would sell risqué clothing." Nexxa stopped in front of a shop that had a rendering of a pink bra as part of the signage. The shop had pink roses in a vase in the window, which immediately reminded her of Paris.

"Come, come inside," insisted an attractive woman with short dark hair and Kelly-green eyes. "How are you ladies today?"

"Good," Iliada let out, pulling down her headscarf.

"Are you married?" she promptly asked them.

"No, no," they said in unison, laughing.

"You are such pretty ladies. I am Nahil; this is *my* shop," she said, tilting her head when she said "my."

"*Salam*," replied Nexxa.

"*Salam*." Nahil gave a slight nod. "In my culture, it is important to wear lingerie for your husband. To look sexy for him when in the bedroom."

"Really? I didn't know or expect that."

"Yes, yes, once you are married, every wife will choose lingerie that she thinks her husband will like." Nahil pulled a fuchsia chemise from a rack and held it up. "You like this?"

"Oh, well, it's, um, bright."

"Yes, the men in my culture like these colors."

"Okay, well, I'm from New York, and I just wear so much black."

"She does," Iliada confirmed while sifting through a clothing rack. Amusing, yet she doubted Nahil would be able to convince

Nexxa to wear something that colorful.

"You know I did meet a good-looking man from here on our first night here in Beirut. He has some sort of import and export business. He took me to dinner in his uncle's restaurant. Well, all four of us, my sister and his friend."

"Imports and exports. This man must do very well."

"Nexxa, why don't you try this," Iliada suggested as she held up a dark red teddy.

Nexxa looked over to see what Iliada was holding up. "Sure, let me see it." Nexxa moved across the shop to Iliada and separated the crotch part of the teddy. Iliada's eyes widened; she put her hand to her mouth as she gasped. *Thought so*, Nexxa laughed.

Nahil sifted through a box of lingerie that had just arrived, not yet on the floor, when she noticed some men lingering across the street. She knew most of the shop owners on her street, and most of the customers in her area were residents and usually women. "Are you ladies," Nahil began, pretending to search through new garments, "traveling with someone?" Nexxa's eyes met Nahil's. Nahil smiled.

"How about these?" Nexxa held up a few chemises, handing them to Iliada. With Iliada occupied, Nexxa looked to Nahil then moved closer to the shop window so she could get a look outside. Across the street, and determined to stare her down, were two men. *Abduction?*

Nexxa picked up a scarf from a selection on a table in the front of the store. "You know, I believe I'll take this scarf." She looked at Iliada until she caught her attention. Iliada faintly nodded.

"We should use your toilet before we leave, yes?"

"Yes, yes." Nahil quickly folded the scarf and placed it in a shopping bag. She waved off Nexxa pulling money from her purse. "Come," Nahil said, moving from behind the register. "You can leave through the back." She moved briskly, urging them to follow her. Standing at the back door to the shop, Iliada struggled with her head scarf; Nexxa assisted her before pushing open the door, leading them onto the street. Nexxa quickly wrapped the scarf she had just bought around her head, then stuffed the bag in her purse. She spotted the two men from the other end of the street coming in their direction. They abruptly stopped when two young boys approached Nexxa and Iliada, begging. Their hands and fingernails were dirty, and they looked like they might be brothers. Nexxa orchestrated a way out in her mind while Iliada took out some money, her hand shaking as she handed it to them.

A tattered taxi turned onto the street, and Nexxa waved to the driver to get his attention. The car sounded as if it could barely change gears, but as long as it could drive, it was all they needed. A few of the roads were full of potholes, and with every hole the car hit, Nexxa and Iliada clenched each other's hands. Iliada held her purse tightly in her lap; Nexxa desperately followed each street name.

"Okay, Hadi Hassan Nassrallah Road," Nexxa said under her breath. When Nexxa spotted the Beirut mall, she took a deep breath and patted Iliada's leg.

BEIRUT — OCTOBER 2, 2013, EVENING

Iliada plopped down on the bed, still clutching her purse. Nexxa took down her scarf that was still around her head; she motioned for Iliada to take hers down too. Nexxa stood by the dresser waiting for Iliada's response.

"I'm tired." Iliada put her purse down on the bed. She slipped off her shoes, moving her toes about. "And my feet smell," Iliada laughed. Nexxa watched as Iliada went to the bathroom. She heard the water running; Iliada was washing her tired, smelly feet. Nexxa pulled out her pendulum and turned to the end of the dresser where an advert for a local tourist company had been placed. Her pendulum spun vigorously in a circular motion. Nexxa moved the tourism brochure; Medan's business card was underneath. Iliada walked out of the bathroom. Nexxa grasped her pendulum, hiding it in her closed hand.

"Let's go have a drink."

"No! I don't want to leave the hotel again."

"Well, if you want to make it to the Ice Queen party," Nexxa started. "I meant the hotel bar anyway." Nexxa thought back to when she first discovered that she had been dubbed the Ice Queen. The staff, some of which were her friends from an upscale cigar club she frequented, had given her the moniker.

"Yeah." Iliada sat on the bed, looking down at her feet. "But were those men following us?"

"I don't know." Nexxa waved her hand, dismissing the notion. "It was probably nothing."

Iliada sifted through her purse. "I guess. I mean if we stay in the hotel for a drink." She carried her purse with her. "I'm going to freshen up," she announced as she walked back to the bathroom.

Nexxa opened her hand and held her pendulum out, moving the dangling crystal between her fingers. *Hmm, time to call our security director? Call him after work?* Nexxa's phone pinged. She tucked Medan's business card and her pendulum under her lingerie in a drawer in the dresser.

"Medan just sent me a text." Nexxa hollered to Iliada in the bathroom. "'Hi, how was your day? What are you doing tonight?'" *Hmm, okay, so not right after our date. Wonder what he's looking for?*

"Oh, well…" Iliada messed with her hair. "Zarian has texted me every day."

"Yeah, yeah." Nexxa reread Medan's text. "I'm not surprised." Nexxa sighed. "I'll tell him we are tired and that he can meet us here if he likes. Why don't we go for a swim?" Nexxa pulled off her clothes and typed a text to Medan: *Hi Medan, we are going to swim and then have drinks at the hotel bar. Join us?*

Nexxa and Iliada sat with their feet in the hotel's rooftop infinity pool, where the skyline gave a view of the country's mountains and sea.

"I'm going in." Nexxa lowered herself. "I want to swim a little."

"Okay." Iliada picked up her phone. "I'm going to text Zarian and see what he's up to."

Nexxa swam over to the other side of the pool. Reaching the edge, she sank in the water, leaning back and wetting her hair. With her hands, she parted the water, and Philip came to her mind. How he seemed jealous of her with her Russian tutor. But back to Medan, would she like to feel his hands on her wet body in the pool? Would *après* swim sex be good?

Something's just not right. Floating on her back, she couldn't drown out her thoughts nor the sound of a couple sitting in loungers by the pool. She laughed, hearing parts of their conversation, not all, but enough to know the woman was irritated with the man—naturally.

Nexxa swam back over to Iliada and waited in the pool until she put her phone down. The palm trees around the rooftop were red from the ambient lights, and when Nexxa emerged from the water, Iliada gave her a look.

"What?" asked Nexxa.

"The lights are accentuating your lavender."

"It's okay. You're the only one who can see it." Nexxa pushed up on the pool's edge sitting close to Iliada, exhaling, "Remember, unless I've been in a past life with someone, they won't be able to see my lavender."

"Only you have to worry about your lavender," Iliada laughed, "not like normal things like checking your hair or makeup."

"I need to see myself in a mirror." Nexxa knew she wouldn't literally look like she was a lavender glow stick, and that even if she encountered a soul from a past life, they would need to be an enlightened soul by this lifetime. Nexxa stood and said, "Let's go into the spa's lounge."

Nexxa dried off just enough to slip on the hotel slippers and walk into the hotel spa. The dressing area had a dark walnut wooden bench that ran the room's length, covered with a lush velvet cushion in imperial fuchsia. They placed their bags down and ran their hands over the plush seating. Iliada put on the silk kimono Nexxa had bought for her birthday over her bathing suit and pulled her hair into a low ponytail. Nexxa kept on her black one-piece bandeau top swimsuit with a notch detail at the top and sheer panels in the middle. She dried her hair, leaving it wavy, and put on her black layered wrap skirt by Chiara Boni La Petite Robe. Pool chic, she decided.

"How do I look?" asked Iliada as she was putting on her lip-gloss.

"Aw!" Nexxa touched Iliada's ponytail. "You're so pretty! I'm almost ready." Nexxa massaged on some of her shimmering body oil; the fragrance was described as "exuding luxury, and addictive"—she expected it to affect Medan.

While waiting for Medan to arrive, Iliada told Nexxa about her conversation with Zarian as they sat at their table drinking wine. Nexxa listened and nodded but managed to keep her mind on what had happened earlier that day. When Medan approached the table, Nexxa stood up to greet him. He gave her the traditional kiss on each cheek and said hello to Iliada. Instinctively, she knew he seemed off, that he was on the negative side of his polarity.

"Did you explore Beirut today?"

"Actually," Nexxa paused to taste her wine, "yes, we did."

"Well, we were in a lingerie—"

"We were surprised by how many lingerie shops there are here in Beirut," Nexxa spoke over Iliada.

"You were lingerie shopping?" Medan furrowed his brow.

"Apparently, when a woman gets married, she is supposed to choose some lingerie to wear for her husband." Nexxa made eye contact with Iliada and winked. "In bright colors." She knew she annoyed Iliada by cutting her off, but she needed to direct the conversation.

"So, what did you choose?"

"Well, something," Nexxa continued with a seductive smirk, "crotchless."

Medan sat back in his chair, putting his hand on his chin. He looked at Nexxa with his dark eyes. Hearing "crotchless" was a trigger to induce his hard-on for Nexxa. She was Pavlov, and Medan was the dog. The silence continued until the waiter approached. Medan ordered himself a drink. "Have you been busy with your work here?" he questioned after the waiter returned to serve his drink.

"No." Nexxa thought about Faroud, going to his house. "Not yet." Faroud hardly seemed like "work," more like visiting a friend. She took another sip of her wine. "Well, I do have a meeting coming up."

"You do?" Medan adjusted in his chair.

"Yeah. I do." Nexxa pushed her hair behind her ear. "So, what are you up to the rest of this week?"

"Your work," Medan started, taking the cocktail straw out of his drink before having a taste, "so you are meeting someone from here or from some other country?"

Nexxa heard his question; his voice sounded more profound, more intense. She motioned to the waiter, and he came over to their table; she ordered another glass of wine. Iliada ordered another glass too. Nexxa held Medan's attention by adjusting her bathing suit top; Iliada complied, smiling at them.

Iliada knew Nexxa wasn't giving Medan everything he wanted, answering his questions. She began re-orchestrating the day's events: the older man sitting in a chair by the shop, the women in hijabs leering at them, the *kind* woman from the lingerie shop, the begging boys, and finally, the men who looked to do them harm. She looked from Nexxa to Medan, wondering what would be said next. Did her sister have a reason to be elusive with Medan? Or could this just be Nexxa's way of being a little mysterious? (She had learned from being around Nexxa and listening to her that men don't need to know everything about you or everything about what you are doing. She remembered Nexxa saying, *You don't need to be deceptive, just fucking interesting.*) And then her thoughts were interrupted by the sound of her phone buzzing. She picked up her phone and walked away from the table.

Medan lifted his drink, shaking the ice. "So you are meeting with—"

Nexxa glided her hand along her décolletage. "Medan, you never elaborated on your import and export business. So, what is it that you import and export?"

Medan placed his drink down. "I told you," he said, shifting in his chair, "I had a business selling cars in the U.S."

Nexxa hadn't forgotten that detail. She simply didn't believe he imported or exported anything.

KLARIN

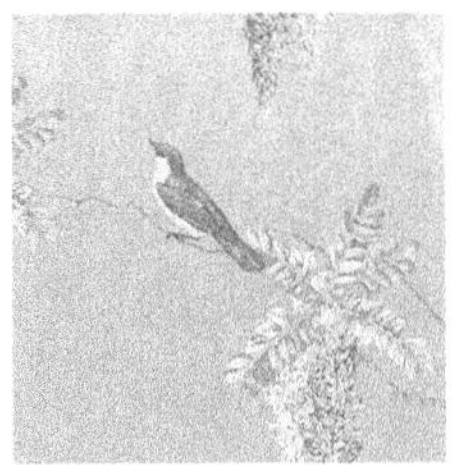

Her petite frame donned her sky-blue one-piece bathing suit under her black abaya. Her eyes wore round-framed tortoiseshell sunglasses by Alaïa for four hundred euros that she preemptively bought on Net-A-Porter before she departed Ireland for her second trip to Beirut. Seated on the farthest pool chaise from the bar, Klarin extended her fair skin legs underneath her abaya, estimating how many meters were between her and—not Nexxa—but Medan. She liked knowing that she knew about Medan. That several weeks ago, she had met with his cousin Sal at Sal's uncle's home with the fountain. She also liked that Medan wore a sky-blue button-down shirt this evening.

Irritated, Klarin ordered a white wine spritzer from the waiter when he came around to her; unknowingly, he had stepped in the way of her view. When her view was once again unobstructed, she saw the graceful blonde Nexxa touch her décolletage while the Middle East-Fuckable Medan shifted in his chair. She wondered if Nexxa had invited Medan to her room. If Nexxa would wear her Hanky Panky floral lace chemise for him. Klarin had been cautious upon her initial inspection of Nexxa's hotel room at Le Gray. Not a thing was moved out of place; she didn't leave any trace of the perfume that she wore, the same scent the dear old queen of England was reported to wear. (She knew Nexxa's travel details down to the time she checked in for her flight.) One minor annoyance kept her cautious, an assistant manager for the housekeeping staff—if you could call the eejit that—happened to be walking down the hall toward Klarin at the precise moment Klarin was approaching Nexxa's room. Her ankle twisted; she barely fumbled, but he was at her aid within moments. He offered to open her room door and escort her in—Klarin had on her sunglasses and hijab—but she politely declined his offer.

Klarin thought of when she was a young girl, most likely seven, when her father took her to the zoo that happened to have a train ride. The train was painted sky-blue; she loved it instantly. Then the conductor told her she couldn't bring on her ice cream. She hated him immediately, had visions of standing over him whilst he lay on the ground with blood pooling around his head.

BEIRUT — OCTOBER 3, 2013

Nexxa leaned on the railing where the air carried the aroma of fresh dirt from the racetrack. His voice was familiar, "The horses are beautiful creatures, a gift from Mother Earth." Would his face be? Nexxa slipped on her black Bvlgari sunglasses, trimmed in emerald green, and grasped her abdomen; she might have been nervous.

Wearing her white linen bootcut pants and a nude-colored tank top as she walked away, she questioned why she decided to wear the only non-black outfit she had packed for this trip. One day was all the time needed to pass before she would inevitably miss her black, she decided while heading to the outdoor café for a glass of prosecco. She also missed her grandmother, her nanny, which was the reason she went to the track. Thoughts of spending time with her nanny, staying up late with her, watching her study the positions of the planets for the day of the race to determine the winning horse rushed her mind.

The tables were quaint, placing her close to a table of women. Two brunettes and one with distinctively black, shiny hair took an apparent interest in Nexxa. She had hoped to people-watch, perhaps spot the man she heard speaking about the beautiful creatures, but the women were a distraction. One woman, the one with the envy-worthy shiny black hair, made eye contact with Nexxa. *Like, what is it? Change the scene, Nexxa; go to the ladies' room.* Nexxa lifted her prosecco, her nude and metallic stilettos gracefully making their way across the century-old stone beneath them.

Standing at the ladies' room vanity, the door opened briskly. Shiny black hair, diamonds adorning her hands, the woman entered the stall and closed the door. Nexxa silently counted to twenty. The woman flushed and exited the stall.

"Where did you get those stilettos?" She seemed determined to know, ready to buy.

"Oh." Nexxa set her glass on the vanity. "Well, from Barneys, in New York." Nexxa slipped off one of her stilettos and held the shoe up for the woman.

"I love the metallic strip going down the back of the heel."

"Yeah, they are Helmut Langs. I love this designer."

"I am here with my friends. And I am Yasmin."

"It's lovely to meet you." Nexxa smiled. "I'm Nexxa."

"You are here alone?" Yasmin adjusted her shiny black hair.

"Yes." Nexxa followed Yasmin's hand with the diamonds. "I am."

"Come." Yasmin reached for Nexxa's arm. They chatted as they walked back to the café, and Yasmin introduced Nexxa to her friends. Nexxa took a seat at their table; Yasmin summoned the waiter.

"It seems that man over there by the track keeps looking at you." Yasmin looked to Nexxa, then back across the grounds. "Do you *know* him?"

"No—no."

Yasmin's phone rang, and she apologized as she answered a call, leaving the table. Her friends chatted in Arabic. *Look occupied* came to Nexxa's mind. She tapped on an app, scrolling through the latest news. She heard cheering, several men clapping, giving pats on the back. One of them, the sexy one who carried himself in a powerful way, made his way toward the café.

Sergei took a seat at a table near the edge of the café. He placed his racetrack form on the table, laying his phone atop. A man walked by and patted him on the shoulder; Sergei spoke to him before the man continued on. Sitting back in his chair, he had a view of a lovely blonde woman. Unknowingly, he looked at Nexxa the same way his father looked at the only woman he had ever loved, Sergei's mom. Seeing her again, Sergei determined it was time to make a gesture by sending her a drink. He motioned for the waiter; his phone buzzed, and Sergei answered his call. When the waiter approached, Sergei held up his hand, letting him know he would need a minute.

With her new acquaintances still chatting and Yasmin occupied on a call, Nexxa took the last sip of her prosecco and requested her bill. As she waited, she watched Sergei as he talked on the phone. Each time he moved in his chair, she detected his essence. Nexxa slipped her phone into her purse and stood to leave. Her back now to Sergei as she walked away, she smiled at the thought of her grandmother. With Sergei's scent surrounding her, she knew she would encounter him again.

Nexxa stood at the Le Gray hotel bar and drank the glass of white wine she ordered like a shot. She needed it to go away— the feeling of wanting to be touched by the man from the track. Could the other patrons—the seductive-looking couple at the end of the bar, perhaps the bartender—know what she was thinking? Nexxa ordered another glass of wine and slipped out of the bar, making her way into the ladies' room in the hotel lobby.

Nexxa opened the two floor-to-ceiling stall doors. Empty, so she walked back to the main entrance and turned the lock. Careful to place her YSL handbag on the counter, she moved a gold pouf from the seating area. She pulled her top down, exposing a breast, and lifted her right foot upon the pouf. She dipped two fingers in her wine glass, putting her hand in her pants—she caressed her Cosabella thong. Cold, she maneuvered her fingers under her panties. She stopped, plopping her elbows on the counter, hiding her face in her hands. Nexxa looked in the mirror, pulling her top back over her breast. She lifted the wine glass, finishing what was left. She washed her hands and rinsed the wine glass, slipping it into her purse.

Leaving the ladies' room, she walked to the elevator where an impeccably dressed couple and their young daughter waited. She couldn't help noticing the rigidness of the parents on the ride up to her room. About six to seven years old, the girl was holding a baby doll. Nexxa smiled, watching her interact with the doll that had scribbles on the cheeks. When the elevator doors opened on her floor, Nexxa still had eyes on the girl and her doll.

"Is this for your room?" Her voice was sweet.

"Oh, yeah, yes." Nexxa looked to the opened elevator. "Sorry." She stepped off the elevator. The doors were slow to close; Nexxa turned, her hand barely lifting to wave goodbye, when a vision of herself holding a baby girl, rocking her to sleep, manifested.

BEIRUT — OCTOBER 4, 2013

Nexxa finished the last sip of her third cup of Earl Grey tea. "At least I am not getting ready for a date this morning," she said aloud, placing the cup on the saucer. "I don't have the energy to look extra pretty today since I couldn't sleep."

"Are you nervous about the meeting?" asked Iliada.

"No, I'm just tired from dreaming all night." She knew why she didn't sleep much. But for now, she would keep the man from the horse racetrack, who wouldn't leave her mind, a secret.

The hostess promptly greeted Nexxa; Nexxa asked if her guests had already arrived. She didn't have a clue he was in the restaurant. Following the hostess, she spotted the man from the track. He was casually dressed donning a black half-zip pullover, jeans, and black leather Chelsea boots. He was holding his phone, most likely reading something. *Fuck*, Nexxa looked down at her outfit. They smiled, all of them from China

Black Road, as she approached the table.

"Hello, I am Diane."

"I'm Nexxa." Nexxa extended her hand, feeling Diane's coffin-shaped nails. "Nice to meet you." Right away, there was something about Diane. She spoke English with an American accent. Did she remind Nexxa of an actress? There was that one time she stumbled upon Asian porn. No, that wasn't it, either.

"Diane is my sixth English name. Like Princess Diana. I liked it the best, so I still use it. My Chinese name is Qirong. I moved to the U.S. with my parents when I was eight. I had a hard time making friends. I wanted to be a cheerleader, but my dad insisted I play an instrument in the band. I earned a degree in economics from Princeton. My first job was with Alphabet, before I was recruited to return home to China to work for China Black Road." Diane smiled, twisting her feet in her black wedge sneakers that made her all of five foot four.

"Ooh," Nexxa exhaled, feeling like an overstuffed teddy bear. "Okay." She surmised the amount of "too much information" Diane had just divulged was probably on a dating profile somewhere on the internet.

"So, I'm here to provide advisory services to my client. As you are aware, we are handling the bond offering for the sovereign bank. At Faroud's request, we will offer our guidance in securing a contract with the general contractor they decide to work with." Nexxa was aware Faroud had already decided to use Diane's company, but she wasn't obliged to inform them.

"I am confident that we are the best contractor for the National Lebanese Bank," Diane recited, looking down at a page of notes in front of her. Nexxa looked to Diane when she lifted her face, then to each of her associates. They sat stoically, then one said something, and the three of them laughed. And they looked *exactly* the same, almost like they were triplets.

"Yes, I have done my due diligence and would expect to advise my client in your favor," Nexxa stated. Diane spoke to her associates in Mandarin; they seemed to agree, and she rose from her seat, motioning for Nexxa to join her. Nexxa looked across the restaurant before leaving the table, but she didn't see Sergei.

As Nexxa got closer to Diane, she watched as clouds appeared and moved in over the restaurant's terrace.

"Did you know that my emperor," Diane began, "Ch'ien-lung, told King George III that your people will never understand our culture?"

"Well…" Nexxa's eyes went around; she thought for a moment. "No, I didn't."

Diane stood closer to Nexxa, pressing against her side. "See him here." She held up her phone with an image.

"Okay."

"I can enlarge for you." Diane's hand with sky-blue coffin-shaped nails moved across her phone. Nexxa examined the photo. It could have been a photoshopped image of Diane's father. Or maybe just some old man in Cosplay? "My father is a scientist and has a proprietary invention of software-driven customizable magnets."

Nexxa stared blankly. "Your nails, the color is sky-blue, right?"

Diane held out a hand, moving her fingers and giggling. "A color I just discovered."

Nexxa exhaled. "So what about your father?" Cocking her head and squinting her eyes, she asked, "Is that him in the photo?"

"NO!" Diane pulled her chin in.

"I—" Nexxa's eyes widened.

"Oh, no, it's just that my people discovered that a piece of magnetized iron hanging freely will always turn north. So my father was destined to work with magnets."

"Interesting." Nexxa crossed her arms. "The only thing I know about magnets is that they have a north side and a south side, right?"

"Yes, so Polymagnets," Diane continued explaining, holding up another photo, "are fundamentally different from conventional magnets. They can latch, align, and spring."

Nexxa looked toward their table and back to Diane. Diane was staring at her.

"Well, I'm glad we've had a moment to talk." Nexxa motioned with her hand in the direction of their table. "We should probably get back to your associates."

While they had stepped away, Diane's associates had ordered pastries. One made a gesture for Nexxa to partake; she declined. Diane once again spoke to them in Mandarin, and her companions stood. They each stuffed a pastry in their pocket. Nexxa managed to hold in a laugh.

"It was a pleasure," Nexxa offered.

"Nexxa, we will be speaking soon," Diane announced before she glided away from the table with her trio following her in a choreographed manner.

Alone at the table, Nexxa gathered the pens and notepads with Diane's company name on them. Diane's associates each had a pen with a notepad placed perfectly and of equal distance between them. They opted to leave them, instead toting away pastries. Nexxa took a pen, doodled a heart, then a star, and then stuffed her purse with CBR paraphernalia before walking toward the restaurant exit. As she approached the hostess stand, she abruptly stopped. She blinked her eyes—her wolfness returned; she could smell him again. She smiled at the hostess and returned to the restaurant's terrace. Passing the table she shared with Diane and her associates, she realized she couldn't smell anything in Diane's presence. An emperor and magnets, what did this have to do with their meeting? Strange. Nexxa checked the time on her phone and set her purse on the ledge, looking out at the hotel grounds below.

"You like the thrill of the race?"

Nexxa halfway twisted her body. "My grandmother—"

"Used to take you to the track." Nexxa tilted her head; her eyes showed her curiosity. "Have you visited the Sursock Palace?" He stepped closer. "I think you should see it while you are here in Beirut."

Nexxa dropped her phone.

"I'm Sergei," he said as he picked up her phone, handing it to her.

"I'm Nexxa." She wanted to say something about seeing him at the track. *No, please let him say something.*

"I'm staying at the Four Seasons. I can send my driver to pick you up tomorrow."

Wow, very presumptuous—don't say that out loud. "I can

arrange for my *own* car."

"I'll have my driver pick you up." He flashed a confident smile. "How about four p.m.?"

Nexxa smiled. And inside, she howled at the moon with excitement.

BEIRUT — OCTOBER 5, 2013

Nexxa saw Sergei waiting in the garden area by the palace entrance when she arrived. Grasping her abdomen where white butterflies were surely fluttering around, she realized that lusting after him was not as difficult as she initially thought—going on an actual date was harder.

Sergei was standing with his hands in his pants' pockets, admiring the palace. He turned as Nexxa arrived, giving her a slight wave with a smile. Nexxa's stomach released her butterflies into the fresh Beirut air one by one as they walked toward each other. Taking the lead, Sergei directed them to the stone pathway as they strolled side by side to the palace's grand steps. He paused his step, pointing, and explained, "Sursock Palace remained staid during the Lebanese conflicts."

Nexxa took in the palace, noticing that there weren't any holes from heavy artillery on the palace's exterior before Sergei motioned for them to continue.

"Sergei! My friend, it's been a long time," a noticeable man eagerly greeted them moments after entering the building.

Sergei turned his body toward her. "This is Nexxa."

"Welcome to our palace!" He was theatrical.

"Thank you. It's lovely."

The man spoke to Sergei in Russian before laughing.

Nexxa understood that he said, "Whoa, she's something; good job, mate." She contemplated conversing in Russian but didn't want to embarrass him. She was relieved when a loud bang distracted the man, and he quickly turned, saying, "Must check that out," before he dashed off.

"Okay, well," Sergei motioned with his head and said, "let's walk then." When his hand grazed hers, Nexxa purposely kept her hand close to his.

"It looks like they are setting up," Sergei noticed as they passed a window, "for a wedding," he said, overlooking the grounds. "Maybe *we* will have a wedding someday."

Nexxa bit her bottom lip. He was forward, presumptuous; she found it exciting.

"Would you like to go out to the garden?"

Nexxa managed to smile, her way of saying yes.

The palace's grounds had a spread of tables adorned with white tablecloths and flower arrangements for the upcoming wedding reception. They strolled the perimeter. "I have the feeling of déjà vu." Nexxa grasped her forehead. Exhaling, she said, "I can't believe I said that out loud. I'm embarrassed; I thought that and it just came out."

"Why are you embarrassed?"

Nexxa shrugged her shoulders before bending over to smell the flowers on one of the tables. Sergei watched her. "The first time I saw you at the racetrack, I thought you had money." His face told her he had been waiting to say something.

"Oh." Nexxa drew her hand along her neck.

"You carry yourself in a certain way." Sergei looked directly at her then motioned for his driver. "Can I take you out for a drink?"

Nexxa didn't have time to accept his invitation. She barely had time to determine that she again liked his forwardness before the car was upon them and Sergei was holding open the door.

"The first law school was established here in 533," Sergei began, divulging his knowledge of Beirut while his driver drove them to an area of the city's corniche. Sergei tapped on the back of the driver's seat. "Thank you, Gage. We'll get out here."

"How are you familiar with Beirut's history?"

Sergei helped Nexxa exit the car. "Well, I studied architecture, namely structural engineering, and through that, completed studies of the Roman and Ottoman empires. Interestingly, the Sursock family is one of the Seven Families."

"I love history. But I work in finance."

Sergei reached for her hand. "Look at the buildings. I love the colors, like jewels. Ruby red and Tuscan yellow." As they approached a corner shop, Sergei stopped. "Just a moment," he said, stepping into the shop. "I need to get something." After what seemed like ten minutes or more but was only a few minutes, Nexxa delved into her what-ifs. *What could he be*

going in there to get? Stomach medicine, condoms, like what?
Sergei emerged with white roses.

"How did you know I like white roses?" Nexxa touched the top of the blooms.

"Well, red roses are so common." He smiled.

Sergei walked them a few paces more. "Let's stop here," he said, motioning with his head, "for a drink." He pulled out a chair for Nexxa. She thanked him as she took her seat at a perfectly placed table outside.

"I'm going to order a bottle of the Crios. Do you like white wine?"

"Sure, I like white wine."

"A bottle of the Crios," Sergei requested as a waiter approached the table. "I discovered this wine a few years ago. It's one of the whites that I like the best."

"My sister and I have a great wine store near our apartment. I've discovered *too* many wines I love," Nexxa laughed. The waiter returned with the wine, presented the bottle, and poured Sergei a taste; he drank and motioned to serve Nexxa.

Sergei took a large swallow of his wine and paused. His smile told her he was holding something back.

"What… what is it?" Nexxa asked.

"Well, I was thinking," he paused before continuing, "I don't want to—" Sergei cleared his throat and poured more wine into his glass.

Nexxa took a drink, then another. If he had confessed he wanted to take her to his hotel room, she would have admitted the same desire.

"So, tell me about this grandmother that you went to the races with." Sergei sat straight in his chair.

"My nanny, she was my mom's mother." Nexxa pushed some hair away from her face. "We were raised Catholic, but she studied astrology. She would read her metaphysical books at night, discreetly. She thought she needed to hide it, perhaps because of the church. My nanny was also intrigued by the Masons, how they founded America and their opposition to the Catholic Church."

"Well, my father was a spiritual man. He believed the forest was a place to clear your head and connect to Mother Earth. He used to collect things he found while taking walks in the forest. One time he found a gold griffin, and other times just some arrowheads."

Nexxa's mind immediately went to Thomas upon hearing Sergei mention arrowheads. She had always felt his presence with her and Iliada, even when she least expected it.

"Excuse me." Sergei stood and asked a waiter which way to the bathroom. "You'll be okay?"

"Oh, yes, I'll be right here." She was okay; she was holding on to the thought of Thomas.

Sergei knew it was a short drive to Nexxa's hotel. He managed to refrain from telling his driver there would be only one stop, not two. When they arrived at the first stop, his driver waited for Sergei as he walked Nexxa into the hotel lobby. Nexxa embraced Sergei for a hug. She didn't want to part. Before letting go, the Russian kissed her just the right amount. "Bye," she mouthed while walking away. Sergei remained, compelled to wait, to watch her walk to and get on the elevator.

On the way back to the Four Seasons, he realized he had a photo of them on his phone that the waiter had offered to take. Sergei stopped at the hotel bar, ordered a Scotch whisky, and looked at the photo. Watching a couple in the bar interact, he thought about Nexxa, wondering if he would miss her. Sergei had known since first watching her lips draw from the hookah pipe, sitting approximately twenty feet away just so he had a view of her—she not a view of him—when they both graced the same upscale hookah lounge Nexxa's first night in Beirut. He witnessed her endearing interaction with the young waiter and her playful yet adorable interaction with her blonde companion, her sister. When the Arab was crass enough to approach her, Sergei chuckled to himself. As the room filled more and more with lavender-colored smoke, Sergei inconspicuously leaned his upper body so he could continue watching Nexxa.

"I'm back," Nexxa announced as she walked into her hotel room. "Why don't we order some treats from room service? Iliiaada," Nexxa called, emphasizing the vowels in her name. "Iliada?" Nexxa looked in the bathroom, expecting—hoping—to see her. Nexxa's phone pinged, and she assumed as she collected it from her purse that it would be from Sergei.

Iliada: *Hey, I'm at Zarian's apartment now.* ☺ ♥♥

Nexxa stared at the happy face emoji with hearts that followed her words.

Nexxa: *Can you not stay out too late?*

Iliada: 😣

Nexxa: *Really?*

Nexxa tossed her phone on the bed then lay back and grabbed

a pillow, covering her face. She resolved to the idea that she would be alone, alone enough to think about Sergei all night. She was intrigued by him, making it seem unfair that she met him in Beirut.

The young man taking her order from room service was extremely kind on the phone. He delivered the date cups and tea she ordered himself. Nexxa signed the bill, thinking she could tell this stranger about her night with Sergei. Instead, she thanked him, smiling while laughing inside at her ridiculous thoughts. Nexxa ate her date cups, drank her tea, and realized Iliada for sure would stay out late. She examined herself, hating to look so pretty then having to take it all off, as she put her hair up in a ponytail and used a rose-scented cleanser to remove her makeup. She changed into her Hanky Panky floral lace chemise and looked out over the city.

Nexxa turned on the TV so there would be some white noise while she was alone. She heard her mind repeat, *No lucid dreams with the strange man, snake.* Taking the hotel stationery and a pen, she sat in bed. She wrote: Sergei, Russian, horses, structural engineering. She wondered what his last name was, what he did for a living. She surmised something white collar since he had excellent hands, was well-spoken and educated. She folded the paper into a square and put it in her purse. With the sound of Lebanese music on TV, she fell asleep.

The alarm on Nexxa's phone blended in with the music still emitting from the TV. The urge to go to the bathroom actually woke her better than her alarm. Sitting on the toilet as she reached for toilet paper, it occurred to her that she didn't have any lucid dreams. Washing her hands, she realized something else—Iliada had not returned.

BEIRUT — OCTOBER 6, 2013

Nexxa flipped through a folder with documents for her meeting with Faroud when she heard the hotel room door—Iliada had returned.

Nexxa stepped away from the desk. "Zarian, next time, don't keep my sister out so late." Nexxa did her best not to come across like Iliada's mother.

"I'm sorry," Zarian mustered as he kissed Iliada first on the cheek, then up her arm, making exaggerated kissy sounds. Nexxa rolled her eyes. Zarian left, saying, "I will call you my girlfriend!" Iliada beamed before her face clearly showed she was mad at Nexxa. For Nexxa, it was an acceptable loss in her effort to protect her sister. She could live with herself if Zarian just fucked off, but not if she failed to follow through on everything she had learned that was necessary for their safety.

"I have another meeting with Faroud this morning at ten

thirty," Nexxa spoke quickly. "Do you want to go to the spa when I get back?" she said with an apologetic face.

"You didn't have to be so rude to him!"

"Well, we don't know him that well." Nexxa reached for Iliada's hand. "Look, my meeting should be short today. Let's have the rest of the day just for us."

"Uh, I know him." Iliada kicked off her shoes, avoiding eye contact with Nexxa. "He is so sweet. I mean, he already told me all about his family."

"You're not going to be mad at me all day, right?" Nexxa asked as she primped in the mirror.

Iliada didn't respond, which told Nexxa that Iliada *would* be annoyed all day. Iliada lay down on the bed, looking at texts from Zarian. Nexxa bent over her and kissed her on the forehead. "I'll be quick, I promise."

Nexxa juggled her thoughts, Faroud first, as she pressed the down button for the elevator. Faroud was a handful but manageable, agreeing to meet at Nexxa's hotel this time. Going to his house again was a bad idea. Diane hadn't responded to Nexxa's last email. She thought about those sky-blue nails and the weird shit about her "emperor." Sergei, the Russian who gave her white roses and butterflies. Stepping off the elevator, she saw a dark-haired Arab man in the lobby who reminded her of Medan.

A woman was bouncing a baby in the lobby, an appreciated distraction, trying to get it to stop crying. The baby had black hair, but the mother had long blonde hair. She saw what must have been her friend taking photos of them. *Hmm, selfies for*

Instagram. Let me guess, hashtag Le Gray Hotel Beirut, baby-style, mom blogger, blah blah. Why do women do that? Nexxa entered the restaurant and detected Faroud's voice.

"Hello, Faroud."

"Ah, Nexxa, so lovely to see you again." Faroud moved his seat back, standing. "Come sit, sit."

"So, I have Dan's recommendations and our findings on the vetting process regarding a general contractor." Nexxa placed her folder on the table. "Burkina Faso and Senegal are two countries that have used China Black Road in their 'Africa Renewal' efforts," Nexxa spoke without taking a breath, hoping to launch right into business. Faroud stood again as the sound of two clamoring women and a baby came closer. Nexxa turned her head and discreetly sighed, realizing they were coming over to their table.

"Nexxa, I want you to meet my girlfriend, Oksana."

"Hiiee hiiee," Oksana screeched as she greeted Nexxa while taking her baby out of the stroller.

"Faroud, the highee chairs," Oksana demanded.

"Yes, yes." He motioned for a waiter. Oksana's friend eagerly took a seat at the table, and Oksana strapped the baby into the high chair that the waiter brought over.

"This highee chairs so old," Oksana said, giggling at her friend. "We make the baby with artificial." Her demeanor flipped from boisterous to cocky, then undefined.

"Oh." Nexxa smiled. "Okay." *Why would she tell me this the moment she meets me?* Nexxa took account of Oksana's age, her stylish accoutrement, and figured it was a dig meant for Faroud, given he was easily twenty years her senior.

"My son is ten months old!" Faroud slapped the table proudly.

"He's adorable."

Nexxa's phone pinged while she was talking with Faroud, but she chose to ignore it. Once again, Faroud ordered drinks, and Nexxa obliged.

"So, how did you meet?" Nexxa had already assumed that it was probably an international dating site.

"We meet in small city called Zadar. You know this place? I have my friend, Anna. We go there for her twenty-fifth birthday for girls' party time. Then I see Faroud in bar, and he asking me for a date."

"Ah, okay." Nexxa listened with her elbow on the table, resting her chin on her hand. "Yes, I know Zadar, in Croatia. I have a designer in Zagreb called Boudoir, which I commission to make a dress each year for my annual Ice Queen party in New York." And as she heard herself, Nexxa regretted her words.

"Oh, you have nice party!" Oksana said excitedly, looking at Faroud.

"Actually, I am still finalizing the details for the party. My friend offers his home in upstate New York for me to use. It's still months away, in December."

"We go to America." Faroud bobbed his head, confirming they would be able to attend the party.

"Yeah…" Nexxa glanced down at her phone. "Okay, sure." She tried to read a text from Iliada discreetly. All she noticed was the lack of happy emojis.

"So, would you like to go over the information now? The private placement options and the results on China Black Road?"

"Come, what is the matter?" Faroud motioned for Nexxa to move closer to him.

"Oh, sorry, it's just a text from my sister," Nexxa explained, bringing her phone up from her lap.

"Nexxa has a sister, Iliada." Faroud looked around. "She's so pretty, this girl."

Nexxa held her breath. *Why did Faroud say that Iliada was pretty in front of his girlfriend?* Oksana didn't budge. She drank her prosecco and chatted non-stop with her girlfriend.

"What does your sister say in this text that bothers you?"

"Well, she texted, 'I'm with Zarian and going to spend the day with him.'"

"So, what is the matter?" Faroud laughed, holding his hands up.

"Well—"

"Ah, come on." Faroud's forehead wrinkled. "She's young and has a boyfriend. Come," he advised, motioning to her glass, "drink."

"Day drinking." Nexxa smiled big, swallowing the last of her drink.

"What this?" Oksana asked.

"Well, it's when you drink, but during the day. You know, because it affects you differently."

"We have this too. Vodkatimee!" Oksana held up her glass, laughing, looking at her friend.

Nexxa took a sip from her glass of water and texted Iliada.

Nexxa: *When will you be back?*

She grasped her forehead and decided to put the sound of Faroud, Oksana, the baby, and the friend in the background.

They'll have to be my "backfill people" for now. Everyone that she had come in contact with recently flashed in her mind. She kept coming back to Medan. *I see two men who will approach you when you are together with Iliada. They intend to do you harm.* The warning from her mom—that's where her bad feeling rested. She needed her pendulum.

BEIRUT — OCTOBER 6, 2013

It was peeling away from the walls, wallpaper with bluish grapevines that was probably there since the '90s. Iliada bopped around, investigating the bedroom, wanting to snoop, wishing to have some fun while she was with Zarian waiting for Nexxa, who was in her meeting with Faroud. She slowly eased open a dresser drawer, unsure if it would squeak. Next, she was unsuccessful in opening what she thought was a closet door.

"I have something for us to eat." Zarian carried in a tray of food. "I have a *snack*." He continued making an exaggerated face.

"Do you have any wiiine?" Iliada asked, being that it was eleven thirty-ish.

"I, I go see." Zarian left the room and quietly put the key in the door, locking it behind him. Iliada played some music on her phone and looked at pictures from their trip until he returned.

"So, why are we eating in here?" Iliada pulled on the door that led to the terrace.

Zarian jumped up and said, "Drink," pouring her some wine. "I just thought we have some privacy." Zarian tried to convince himself *and* Iliada that nothing was wrong by dancing to the song playing. "You impressed with my uncle's house?" He licked his finger and stroked his eyebrow. Iliada wasn't impressed, not like she had been.

"Yeah, I mean," Iliada said, squinting her eyes, "I didn't get to see much. Can we go look around?"

"Okay, a little." Zarian put his finger over his lips. "Shh." Zarian walked Iliada around the second floor, showing her another bedroom before tugging her arm and guiding her to a sitting room. He would *like* to parade her around like a wealthy oil sheik's wife with her blonde hair and lovely fair skin, but circumstances didn't allow that.

"Can we go downstairs?" asked Iliada.

Three steps onto the staircase, a guard gave Zarian a stern look. "Come, let's go finish eating first." Zarian grabbed his blonde and moved them together in a playful, dancing way.

Iliada now had another indication that something wasn't right; she chose to ignore it.

"My uncle must want us to stay upstairs for some time so he can be with his girlfriend."

Iliada shifted her shoulders. "Oh, okay."

Zarian had told Iliada a story about his wealthy "uncle," that he was a player, and that he was taking her to his uncle's weekend home to hang out for the day. Iliada had no reason to mistrust Zarian and was annoyed with Nexxa because she had scolded him for keeping her out late. Why wouldn't she spend the day with Zarry? Upon arriving, she was initially intimidated by his supposed uncle's "security," armed with guns, but Zarian had a story for that: ex-military trained to protect dignitaries like the U.S. Secret Service protecting the president.

Back in the bedroom, Zarian picked up her phone, looking through her playlist, and before he could start a song, Iliada heard the sound of a door being locked. "Wait, is someone locking the door?" She got up from the bed and walked over to it. "Zarian, the door is locked," she continued while jiggling the handle, "from the outside, I think."

"Huh?" Zarian put on his dummy face. He took a scoop of hummus and returned to looking at her phone. Immediately, her nauseated stomach told her something was wrong. *What the fuck is going on? Maybe this was a bad idea. I thought he was like a hot Arab prince.*

Both of them were a bit naïve. Zarian thought that if he brought her there as ordered, it would only be temporary. "Take her to the house, entertain her, have fun with her," Sal had told him. Since Sal and Medan were cousins, he didn't question anything. He had been to Sal's uncle's house in the past with Medan but didn't remember much since he drank with Sal and had a low tolerance for alcohol. Although Zarian had no affiliation with Hezbollah, his involvement now was practically an induction.

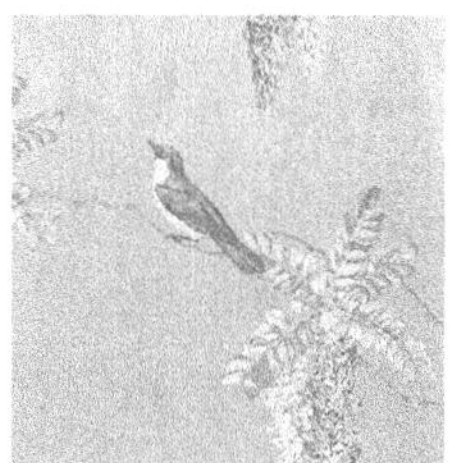

BEIRUT — OCTOBER 6, 2013

Opening her hotel room door, Nexxa saw a room that was somewhere else—a room with wallpaper that needed to be updated. She closed her eyes, holding her hands palms down. Her vibration was off; steadying herself, she realized that she had already had this experience.

Nexxa moved to the bedroom area. She looked to the bed, to the wardrobe, and to the desk. Opening the wardrobe, her hanging clothes were evenly spaced, and her suitcase was unzipped. The bed was made, but not by housekeeping. The pen that had been lying adjacent to the hotel stationery, where Nexxa last placed it, was now atop the stationery. She slid open the dresser's top drawer, where she noticed a perfectly placed long black hair across her lingerie. Who would so meticulously go through her belongings? Nexxa withdrew her black pouchette next to her lingerie. Her stones and pendulum were seemingly untouched.

Make a circle—light a white candle. Standing outside of a ring made from the white bathroom towels, holding a map of Beirut, Nexxa asked her spirit guide for protection. Then she stepped into the circle and used hotel matches to light a piece of hotel stationery, placing it in a glass, and withdrew her crystal pendulum. Nexxa asked for a blessing for her pendulum. Then, "Circle for yes, back and forth for no," she instructed. "Should I be concerned for my sister Iliada?" The pendulum circled. "Is my sister still with Zarian?" The pendulum circled. "Is my sister in Beirut?" The pendulum idled. Nexxa placed the map on the floor and pointed with her finger moving to various spots on the map, each time asking the pendulum if that was the area where Iliada was. Nexxa had a general location for Iliada, and she knew Iliada was in a room somewhere that had wallpaper with pieces pulling away from the walls.

Nexxa pressed in her code on the safe and took out the burner phone her security director Ezio had given her. One day, he approached her when she was working late, telling her, "Things are good until they're not." Nexxa powered on the phone and typed a text, then tapped the side of the phone before pressing the arrow, finally sending the text. He responded: *St. Dimitrios Cemetery.* Nexxa knew that she could go to the location, the cemetery, and a contact arranged by her security director would meet her there. If she were not to show, the contact would leave her another passport and some cash. Nexxa changed from her business attire to a pair of leggings and a sleeveless top. She put her pendulum, stones, and burner phone in her purse.

It only took Nexxa a second to determine that the woman sitting in the lobby resembled a woman she had met briefly in Paris. She donned a sky-blue jacket flanked by perfectly brushed black hair finished with a timid demeanor. *Look at me, let me see your face*, Nexxa thought, but the woman kept her head turned as she placed her teacup down, stood from her seat, and walked away, exiting the hotel through the restaurant.

Nexxa's phone vibrated; she exhaled and withdrew her phone from her purse, hoping for a text from Iliada.

Unknown*: Go to Nahil's Fashions*

Nexxa rubbed her temple before taking a few steps in the direction of the parking lot. A taxi driver pulled up, stopping abruptly. The driver motioned to Nexxa; she opened the back door and hurried in. "Nahil's Fashions." Nexxa typed in the name for an address. "Hold on, I'll get the address." The driver motioned with his hand indicating that he did not need the address.

He eyed her a few times in the mirror, paying more attention to her than driving. Nexxa distracted herself by checking her phone, deciding she would try to call Iliada once she reached her destination. Arriving on the street, he passed Nahil's Fashions, finally stopping at the corner.

"Out, here," he said sternly in his heavy accent.

Nexxa touched her hair, smoothing it against her head, wishing she had a scarf as she scanned the street, looking around for anyone she would recognize. Walking toward the shop, Nexxa dialed Iliada, with the call going straight to voicemail. She texted Ezio the name of the lingerie store.

The door was ajar. "Hello?" Nexxa pushed it open. "Nahil?" She looked around the shop, feeling a breeze blowing through, which slammed the door shut. Nexxa sprinted to the dressing room, closed the curtain behind her, and put her burner phone on the side of the cushion in the chair. She heard his footsteps and recognized his cologne. Nexxa slid open the dressing room curtain. Medan was standing there. He said nothing, reaching his arm toward her. Nexxa felt his tight grip upon her neck.

"Let's go." He pushed a gun into her abdomen and started walking her toward the door.

A car pulled up; he guided her in. "Is my sister with Zarian?" Shushing her, Medan tied a blindfold over her eyes. *Faroud in NYC, hookah, attractive Arab men, sky-blue heels, Diane, sky-blue nails, a Russian, and then back to Faroud in Beirut.* What didn't she see? Was this a plain vanilla abduction for ransom? Eventually, Nexxa could feel the road was smooth like they were on a highway. Would he be taking her out of the country? Did he or Zarian do something to Iliada like human trafficking?

The car pulled to a stop; Nexxa heard a fountain. "We're getting out." The air smelled sweet, and a sudden breeze lifted her hair as Medan guided her up some steps and into a house. Inside, Nexxa heard a woman with an Irish accent speaking on the phone.

"Who is the woman speaking on the phone, Medan?" Medan shushed her. "Is my sister here?"

Medan and a man spoke to each other in Arabic. "*Shu fi 'al gadha.*" Nexxa knew they were talking about eating.

The tile floor carried the sound of women's heels coming toward her. "Who are you?" Nexxa asked as she turned in the direction of the sound, feeling someone's presence. Medan tugged at Nexxa's arm. "Come." He walked her up two flights of stairs and into a bedroom.

Medan removed her blindfold. He stared at her for what felt like a few minutes, before tossing the cloth he had used to cover her eyes. "Would you like some tea?"

"Why am I here?"

Medan walked over to the windows. "There are towels in the bathroom," he said, closing the curtains. "I'll bring you some tea." Nexxa watched as Medan moved around the room, checking the dresser's drawers and moving a chair. As he left, she saw a broad man standing outside of the room. Sitting on the edge of the bed, she looked around the room. Just a few hours ago, she was at a meeting with Faroud, meeting his girlfriend and baby, and now she had no idea where she was or why. She figured it was a long shot that Nahil would find the burner phone she had left in the shop. She wondered if Iliada had her phone and would see that she had called.

Medan brought a tray into the room with tea as he said he would. Nexxa hadn't moved from the end of the bed. "Come sit." Medan motioned with his hand. Nexxa walked over, placing her hands on the table and lowering herself into the chair. Medan hovered over her as he poured the tea, grazing her breast when he handed her a glass. He stepped over to the dresser and leaned against it. His eyes burned into Nexxa. "How is your tea?"

"The tea is nice." Nexxa sipped her tea, wondering how many times his mood would shift, wondering what would happen when her glass was empty.

Medan walked over to the table. "Stand up."

Nexxa placed her glass on the table and stood. Medan put a hand on one of her breasts. Nexxa looked up to him, scanning his eyes for the man she thought she had first met. He pushed her back down onto the chair. "You are very good in your company."

"Uh, yeah." Nexxa adjusted her top. "I have worked there for about five years now."

Standing over her, he lifted her chin. Then he hastily pushed her face down.

A knock came at the door. Medan hollered for them to wait; he hurriedly put on the blindfold and bound Nexxa's hands. When the door opened, Nexxa heard a woman whispering to the guard. The woman's odor preceded her as she walked over to Nexxa and laid what sounded like a phone on the table. (The phone displayed a photo of Nexxa with Faroud outside his home.)

"It was a long time ago, I believe," she said in her thick Irish accent.

"Yes," Nexxa eagerly agreed, struggling to see through her covered eyes. She thought the voice was familiar—she wished she could hold her stones.

"How do you know Faroud Abboud?" asked Klarin.

"How," Nexxa said, pausing, "do *you* know him?"

"What is your purpose here in Beirut?"

"Why are you asking me about Faroud?"

"I'll ask the questions!" snarled the Irish woman wearing a sky-blue jacket.

Nexxa knew that were she to see the woman's face she would know for sure who she was. She could never forget the rigid Irish woman she met a decade ago with Quinn.

"Medan!" Nexxa turned her head. "Medan, what does she want?"

"You're working," Klarin spoke louder, "with China Black Road, yes?"

"My company is in a position to help Faroud, help Lebanon."

"Shut up, shut up!" shouted Medan. "You fucking Americans!"

"Your services are no longer needed." Klarin moved closer, leaning into Nexxa. "Are we clear?"

"Medan, I'm really just—"

"Ya fucking cunt, not all men want you," Klarin snapped.

"What men?"

Klarin bashed her cheekbone with the tea glass. It stung but startled her more because she hadn't expected it.

"Hey!" shouted Medan.

"Fuckin' cunt," Klarin mouthed in a huff while shifting her hair behind her shoulder as she hastily moved her heels across the room, leaving her stench behind.

"Medan!" Nexxa twisted her tied wrists. "Medan, what is—"

Medan nodded to the man standing outside, and the door was promptly shut. "Shh," Medan shushed as he went to the bathroom. He returned with a wet cloth and held it to Nexxa's face. She flinched, feeling the wetness and pressure from his hand. Medan laid the cloth on her lap before untying her hands and removing the blindfold. With her hands free, Nexxa touched her face, feeling blood on her left cheek. Medan lifted the towel from her lap and again held it to her cut. Nexxa raised her hand, placing her hand over his. Medan yanked his hand away. "Go to the bed."

"Medan," Nexxa said, her voice quivering, "it doesn't have to be this way."

He pulled her from the chair. "Shut up!" With his hand on the back of her neck, he moved her to the bed, pushed her down, and then unzipped his pants. Nexxa's chest moved up and down. He tugged at her pants. "Take them off."

Nexxa pulled down her leggings. Medan pushed her to a lying position and moved on top of her, pulling at her panties.

"Medan, don't do this, not this way."

Medan began to kiss her. Nexxa struggled to turn her face. He slapped her head and moved off of her. Standing up, Medan adjusted his jeans and tossed the blanket from the end of the bed onto Nexxa. Even though there wasn't any penetration, Nexxa felt violated. Saying nothing else, he left the room.

Zarian held up the bowl of hummus. Iliada shook her head that she wasn't interested. He wiped his mouth before putting her phone in his pocket. "I have something to do. I will be back soon."

Iliada didn't protest, at least initially. She had heard other women in the house, so with an open hand, she banged on the bedroom door and yanked on the door handle. Sprinting across the room, she re-checked the terrace door; it was still locked. Iliada plopped down on the bed with her face in her hands. *Okay, he is gone. For how long, who knows? And with my phone. Damn, and just like that, Nexxa was right.* She sighed and decided now was the time to ground her emotions and use what she had been taught: telepathy. As young girls, they learned to connect telepathically, using it into their young adulthood. Iliada slipped off her shoes and positioned her hair against the pillow as she lay down. Taking a deep breath, she mouthed, "Nexxa."

Nexxa remembered Thomas saying, *Since all has already happened, one can receive guidance from our dual dimension.* Nexxa encouraged Iliada to follow her thoughts.

Two figures appeared in Nexxa's mind. Nexxa directed her attention to the man she assumed represented Medan. The man was in a predicament, requiring him to choose a side; "I have to do as ordered," she heard. *But what is the purpose of me meeting Medan?* Nexxa sensed a man close to Medan, perhaps a relative involved with Hezbollah. Nexxa didn't know, but this man was Sal, and he had trained in Libya in a joint effort between the IRA and Hezbollah, to share tactics. Sal had met Kilmer, becoming close and remaining in contact for most of their adulthood. Nexxa did know, however, that Kilmer had a friend in Beirut. All of them had made choices in life based on their faith and loyalty to their organizations, which provided financial support in return for their services. Not all in the IRA or Hezbollah were financially successful in their independent ventures.

Next, Nexxa turned her attention to a feminine presence: a dark-haired lady wearing a sky-blue dress crying like an evil creature. With a knife, she was slicing an apple; she offered a piece to the militia leader. *Ahh, maybe she trained with the RIRA in Libya,* Nexxa determined. She sensed hatred and jealousy. Klarin, with her sky-blue accessories, was consumed with anger since her love, Seamus, had been killed in a counterattack in 2005 for a bombing in Northern Ireland. She not only lost her love but her influential role in the IRA.

So Nexxa had Medan and possibly Klarin, whom she met because of Charming Kilmer. And questions. What did all of this have to do with her? Had she and Iliada been followed the day they visited Faroud at his house? Money perhaps? She thought of how Kilmer had champagne taste and a desire to be like Quinn and others that had gone on within their organizations to become affluent. Her introduction to Klarin was through Quinn. Klarin had been working Quinn for information for years, posing as a Loyalist like him. Then along came Nexxa, and this angered her.

Zarian needed to clear his head. He decided he would try to sneak out of the house and go for a walk. Medan was leaning against a wall, fighting his urge to pace, when Zarian came downstairs. He reached out, putting his arm around Zarian as he walked by. A guard walked toward them; Medan gave Zarian a stern eye, pulling his phone out and holding it as if showing Zarian something.

"I do not feel this is right. When they make a deal with China Black Road," Medan spoke, lowering his voice some more, "I know that they don't want to let the girls go."

"We cannot do this!" Zarian's eyes bulged. Medan hushed him. "I bring her here. They said do this." Zarian thrust his hand in the air. "Nothing else." He pushed past Medan and left the house.

He walked briskly and without a destination. Eventually, he stopped in a local shop to buy a bottle of water. The shop had a menagerie of things and smelled like honeysuckle. When

Zarian stepped up to the counter to pay for his water, he found the source of the effervescent bouquet. He picked up a bottle of body wash.

"You have a girlfriend?" asked the lady behind the counter.

"Yeah."

"Why don't you try one for her?"

"Yes, I have one," Zarian said with confidence. "I have a girlfriend."

Randomly, the shop had a few silk dresses hanging on the wall. Zarian's eyes went to the one that was dark green. The lady noticed him looking at the dress and offered to take it down from the wall. His head down, he nodded yes, and she rang up his items. He rolled up the dress, shoved it into the pocket of his black leather jacket with the body wash, and started walking back to the house.

What would happen if someone went against them? Zarry's mind rushed for an idea, wondering if he could get her out without anyone noticing. When Zarian returned to the house, he could see the guards outside were halfway sitting, halfway slouching by the entrance. They looked satisfied, and mostly finished plates of food were on the ground. Walking up, he fumbled some excuses in his mind, but they didn't inquire as to where he had been. Zarian looked down at the plates, and one of the guards half-assedly lifted some scraps. "No, no," Zarian answered, holding up a hand.

Looking back down at the food, he had an idea. He went to the kitchen, put his hand behind the refrigerator, and unplugged it. Turning to leave the kitchen, a guard entered, sauntered past him to the sink, and clunked down his plate. Zarian stood with his hands by his side as he watched the guard walk away. He returned to the bedroom with a new fear but knew once he texted his friend, Zarry couldn't go back.

Zarian stood over Iliada, watching her, watching his blonde sleep. He wiped his eye, then wiped his hand on his jeans. He rolled out a prayer mat and knelt. Iliada turned on her side and opened her eyes.

"You look like an angel." Zarian jumped up from the mat.

Iliada smiled, moving upright in bed.

"I have some things for you. If you like, you can go into the bathroom and try them."

Iliada yawned. "Is my sister here?"

"Yes." Zarian lowered his head. "Yes, she is with Medan."

Iliada's eyes filled with tears.

"Here." He rushed to her. "Come to the bathroom." He withdrew the body wash from his jacket and unrolled the green dress. "Maybe try this."

"It's a body wash?" Iliada turned the bottle over and back.

"Yeah, I like the smell."

"But I showered this morning. In the hotel."

"Just try."

Iliada wanted to roll her eyes, but she resisted. Instead, she undressed in front of Zarry. He looked down; she went into the bathroom. The honeysuckle-scented body wash did smell good when she lathered it in her hands. Zarian opened the door, and Iliada turned to look over her shoulder. She expected he came in there to have sex with her.

"I can wash you." He took the bottle and squeezed some in

his hand. "I help take care of my mother. You know this." He moved his hands along her back. "I could go away with you."

Iliada leaned away. "I can finish myself."

Zarian heard the bedroom door open. "I have to see; they want something," he said, closing the bathroom door behind him. He had a knot in his stomach. One of the guards must have seen him unplug the fridge.

Medan pushed Zarian. "Quick, we do not have much time to talk," he said from the entrance to the other side of the bedroom.

"Why?" Zarian's eyes widened. "What, something?"

"Are you prepared to leave? Leave Beirut. For good."

"I have a plan, I—"

"Klarin!" Medan shouted, pressing his hands together, shaking them.

Zarian was thankful Medan cut him off. He had a plan that included now deleted text messages to a friend regarding an unplugged refrigerator, which would happen by nightfall if everything worked out.

"What are you doing?" he asked Medan.

Medan looked down; he didn't say it, but he felt Zarian should leave with Iliada. Leaving the room, he contemplated how he could stall for more time. Walking down the two long adjacent corridors to the bedroom where he held Nexxa, he unlocked the door, pushed on the handle, and opened it before closing the door again and locking it. He wiped the perspiration from his brow, walking around the house filled with an entourage of armed men. He looked at each of them, wondering how many were loyal to a fault. What would happen to him and his *family* if he were not to comply?

The conversation he had overheard conflicted him. Sure, Klarin was attractive; in different circumstances, maybe he would… Klarin was slick; she was more than what he observed when she was discussing matters with Sal's uncle. Never once had he experienced a woman, let alone a woman that wasn't Muslim, to have any influence. He assumed she had promised collaboration and support from the RIRA, known as the Real IRA, that broke away from the PIRA in 1997. The RIRA was envied, gaining substantial financial backing and political power.

Medan thought he had privacy when he was out on the terrace. He needed to fart; he did that when he was worried or before flying. Her perfume came ahead of her. It smelled *irritating*, if that was a fragrance.

"What is it that I can do for you?" Medan folded his arms, feeling his perspiration.

"Whatever you think about that woman," she moved closer to him, "you have no idea of her," she said. Medan exhaled deeply, saying nothing. Klarin turned her body to face him and, pushing up on her toes so her mouth was next to his ear, whispered, "You like her, *no*?"

Medan abruptly took a step away, bumping her without regard. *She's beneath me.*

NYC — 7 a.m.

Ezio stared at the steam coming out of the electric kettle. He made a cup of jasmine green tea and took it to the men's room.

He was concerned that Nexxa had not responded to his text message nor met her contact at the cemetery. Trimming his nose hairs with an electric trimmer, he concluded he had worked long enough with Nexxa to know her character, but hey, she was trained for this. He had counted precisely eleven minutes, then he returned to the trading desk.

Dan wasn't concerned. That changed when he received a call, an email, an instant message chat, and several text messages from Faroud wherein Faroud suggested that he was ready for the three of them to have a video call but couldn't reach Nexxa. Dan was half-joking when he leaned back in his chair to look at the security director, who sat at the end of the trading desk. "Should we send you to look for Nexxa if we don't hear from her by tomorrow?" He chuckled. Ezio raised his glasses over his bald head and contemplated whether he should track either of her phones using the PinME application developed by researchers from Princeton; he had an old friend that shared technological advances with him on the sly. He was the one who usually kept Dan in check, even more so than the company's dictator-esque compliance officer.

"She called in sick," snarled Nexxa's co-worker while she typed away on her computer.

"You spoke to her?" Dan sat up straight in his chair, seeming perplexed.

"I mean, she probably has a boyfriend over there. She's with him. She's young. Did you really think you could trust her with this new prospect?"

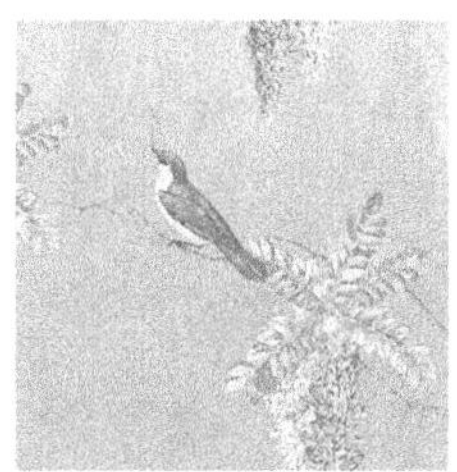

BEIRUT — OCTOBER 7, 2013, MORNING

Nahil turned the lock and opened the door to her shop; she was the first one on her street to open shop every morning, ready for a productive day. She liked that it was her business and did not belong to her husband. Inheriting a small sum of money when her mother passed away—she was an only child—she set up shop. Nahil had married Sal even though she didn't love him. They tried for children but hadn't been able to have any. She secretly dreamed of leaving Lebanon and living in the U.S. Wisely, she had never spoken of her wishes to her husband. Sal was faithful, so he told her. In his actual world, Sal was promiscuous with a side of Hezbollah. Nahil was older by almost a decade and, without a doubt, more mature. Occasionally, she encountered tourists and reveled in speaking English with them. She imagined what it would be like to have conversations in English but in a different country, perhaps even Europe. When

Nahil was a young girl, her mother told her stories of life in the Western world. She had wanted Nahil to know the side she had known, not what the media portrayed. Nahil's mother told her about a trip she had taken to Paris, wherein she visited the famous Moulin Rouge. *Oh, how the ladies wore brassieres and stockings for the show*, Nahil remembered her mother told her.

Nahil's mother's family had moderate wealth and were Druze, an Arabic-speaking, esoteric ethnoreligious group. The other side, Nahil's father's, was Sunni. Nahil had imagined what it would be like to be an entertainer, such as the cabaret dancers her mother described to her. She thought a lingerie shop would be an acceptable way to express her creative side.

Nahil had dropped her glass of tea, shattering it on the outdated tile floor. Picking up the pieces of glass, she wondered if something was about to change, and then later that morning, Nexxa and Iliada found their way into her shop. Sal had always teased Nahil, telling her that she seemed desperate when talking about tourists she met. So, when she encountered Nexxa and Iliada, she didn't mention it to him. Nahil had suspected that the men lingering across the street from her shop were there because of Nexxa and her sister, but at the time, she felt the situation resolved itself when they exited through the back and returned to their hotel. Medan used Nahil—he used her shop as a place to abduct Nexxa, with the plan being that Sal would send Nahil to check on his mom that morning, causing her to open the shop later than usual. And Nexxa used Nahil—she used her as a point of contact by leaving her phone in the dressing room, anticipating that Nahil would find the phone.

Noticing the chair and curtain for her dressing room were

not in their usual positions, Nahil proceeded to adjust them when she found the phone Nexxa had hidden in the armchair's cushion. At first thought, it seemed to her a case of lost and found. Maybe she would post a note in her shop window. After further thought, that didn't seem right, so she pressed the button to power on the phone, hoping it would have enough battery: no contacts or photos, only a few text messages. The first text: *St. Dimitrios Cemetery.* The next one: *Did you locate the grave? If not, get to the U.S. Embassy.* Then an outgoing text: *Nahil's Fashions.* She was instantly reminded that everything flows out and in and that all things rise and fall.

U.S. Embassy? Whose phone is this? Her mind went over the conversation between Sal and Tarek that she had eavesdropped on, hearing "two blondes from the West." Shaking her head in disbelief, she braced herself on the chair in the back room. If these women were in danger and never returned to the West, and her husband was to blame—how could she live with herself? How could she justify dreaming of a life different than her own? To help these women, Nahil would need to find her husband. Sal hadn't come home the night before. He might not share information with her, but she knew he was sloppy. Nahil stuffed some items in a shopping bag, turned her sign to closed, left her shop, and went to the apartment where the women with whom Sal was friends lived. (Sefa, which ironically means pleasure, was one of the women with which Sal had trysts.) Nahil knew she would talk to her in exchange for some lingerie from her store.

Sergei didn't need to "play the game" by waiting a few days to call a girl after a date. He liked Nexxa, and there was no way she didn't like him. Without a second thought, he had called Nexxa the morning after taking her to Sursock Palace. Now, another day in October had passed following his attempt to reach her, and Sergei knew they were both only in Beirut for a few more days—he hated this fact. Sergei lifted his phone, moving across his suite, wondering if he had unreliable mobile service—*no* new messages. Sergei plugged his phone into the wall, from seventy percent charged to full battery might make a difference, before pacing around his suite. Stopping, lifting his phone again, he sat down on the goldenrod sofa and hunched over with his elbows resting on his thighs. Standing again, he said, "Fuck," waving a hand in the air. "Why hasn't she called me back? This is too soon to end." Throwing on his jacket, he convinced himself, "Just go to her hotel!"

Sefa answered the door with a cigarette in hand and not much on. Failing to make eye contact, she examined Nahil, who was more reserved in her attire, wearing a long sleeve blouse tucked into a long khaki-colored skirt with a wide pink belt. "What is it? So early." Sefa stood, snarling.

Nahil flashed a fake smile, saying, "*Salam alaikum*," before politely gesturing that she wanted to enter the apartment. Sefa turned and shuffled away; Nahil followed her, glancing into the dirty kitchen, where two other women sat at a table smoking. Sefa crossed one skinny leg in front of the other toward the sofa, bending to put out her cigarette before slumping down.

Nahil brushed a spot on the adjacent sofa before sitting, holding a bag from her shop on her lap. Sefa's gaze was part drug-induced and part that of a stupid, heartless woman, Nahil decided. As part of the intent of her visit, Nahil took out a bra and a pair of panties, dangling them to show Sefa. Sefa reached out with her badly-in-need-of-a-manicure hand for the bra and panties. Nahil swiftly pulled them back, holding them against her body.

"What?" Sefa made a motion, dismissing Nahil. "What do you want?"

"Where has he gone?" asked Nahil.

"He likes my pussy, not your old one." Nahil knew the West was criticized for crude culture, yet women in her culture behaved just as badly. Sefa stood and sauntered into the kitchen. Nahil watched as she snorted a line of coke and lit another cigarette. She knew she was taking a risk by being there in Sefa's apartment. What if Sal or one of his men were to come over? What reason would she have for being there?

"For you." Nahil dangled the lingerie as she walked to the kitchen doorway. Sefa snatched the bra and panties, losing her grip on the bra. "And this." Nahil pulled the equivalent of one hundred U.S. dollars from her purse. Sefa bent and bent down some more for the bra; Nahil placed the money on the table.

"He is there, uncle house. The girls there for party." Nahil knew Sal was loyal to his uncle and had become focused on the raging war in neighboring Syria, whereas before, it was just Hezbollah business as usual. With the influx of refugees, many became sex workers, and drug use was rampant among them. Sal now had newfound interests, which became his weaknesses. Nahil was going to use this to her advantage. Sefa stripped off her ripped négligée, exposing her bushy crotch, and with an unstable stance, shimmied into the pair of panties.

The other women in the kitchen started teasing each other with obscene comments, saying they should all get new bras and panties to wear while fucking Sal and his friends. Nahil looked from one woman to the other and back to Sefa; they were oblivious that Nahil was still there. She pilfered around the living room, looking for anything Sal might have left behind, like a poorly scribbled note. Nahil found a magazine with a naked man on the cover. She plopped the magazine down on the rubbish-covered coffee table, which caused a bustle of air to lift a used napkin. Under the napkin was a pair of black Gucci sunglasses. Knockoffs probably. Nahil picked up the sunglasses.

I'm going to need a wig.

Nahil gently tugged at her black wig with layers framing her face and put on the Gucci sunglasses she swiped from Sefa's apartment before exiting the cab. Music emanated from the house, where women entertained Sal's uncle and his men. She had been told there would be partying there, so she came dressed to blend in with the other scantily clad women. Nahil knew a fake smile would not work this time, so when she approached the door, she flashed a *flirtatious* smile to gain entry. The armed guards showed their interest, making comments to each other. One said, "I'm going to fuck her later." Nahil heard, tilting her head and pushing out her breasts, wishing she hadn't.

Once inside, a guard hastily motioned in the direction of the music. In Arabic, she told him she needed to tend to girl problems first and asked which way to the bathroom. His nostrils widened as his eyes showed his disgust, shooing her in the direction of the bathroom. He took a step after her, but his lame intention was interrupted by the front door opening—only a man going outside for a smoke. Nahil recognized his voice as the men spoke to one another. She kept her glasses on, putting one foot in front of the other in sync with her beating heart as she made her way down the hall toward the bathroom. She knew that even if Sal saw her, he would not recognize her. It wasn't like he knew her, saw her—such an idiot.

Nahil pretended to enter the bathroom, pushing on the door and looking over her shoulder. No guard in sight. She let the door close quietly. She took off her knockoff Guccis and decided it was time to find what she came for.

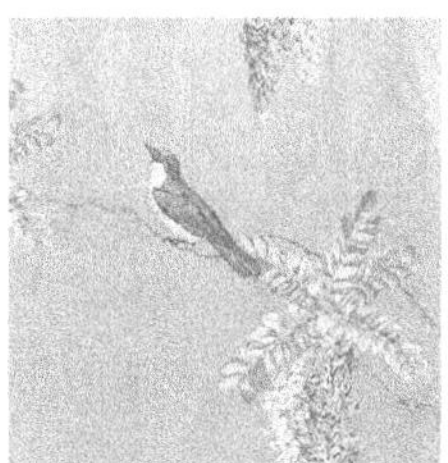

BEIRUT — OCTOBER 7, 2013

Medan rubbed his face, stood, and stretched, uncomfortable from sleeping in the chair in the bedroom, then walked to the window letting in cool air to close it. Standing by the window, he noticed how the bit of sun looked upon Nexxa's sleeping face as he tugged on the drapes. He approached the side of the bed, running a finger along her hair, gently lifting her chin, turning her face toward him.

Klarin slipped the key from a guard, deciding to see for herself where Medan had decided to spend the night. Medan heard the key and saw the handle move. Klarin emerged. Medan flashed a stern face. Klarin started with the top button on her blouse, then unzipped her skirt, letting it fall to the ground. Medan walked over to the chair, sat, and moved his legs apart. Bra, panties, barefoot, Klarin stepped toward Medan. She straddled him, and Medan felt her lips on his. Dry-humping, Klarin groped her breasts as Medan moved his hand, feeling her wet panties. Unzipping his jeans, he began to position himself inside her.

Nexxa awoke to see the old digital clock on the nightstand; the time was 9:51 a.m. She sat upright, gasping, covering her eyes.

"Get off!" Medan shoved Klarin. She fell like a cat, undaunted, breaking her landing with her hands. Nexxa felt around the bed for her phone, forgetting Medan had taken it away, catching Medan's eye as he stood, fumbling to zip his pants.

Klarin grabbed his gun from the side table by the chair. "*I'm in charge now!*" Nexxa plopped her legs off the bed, stood, and scanned the room. "You think they all want *you*," Klarin huffed, aiming the gun at Nexxa. Nexxa raised her hands, taking a deep breath.

"This is not for you to do. Put *down* the gun!" Medan ordered.

With her wicked cackle, Klarin turned, pointing the gun toward the desirable Arab before evil shaped her face as she returned her aim to the enviable blonde. Quinn's face flashed in her mind. She gripped the gun tighter, thinking about how Quinn was smitten with Nexxa. A young blonde who was able to waltz in and fuck up what Klarin had been trying to do for years. "You are nothing but a cunt."

A commotion could be heard; the bedroom door opened, and in strolled a wigged woman. "Anybody for morning party?" Nahil suggested with a slutty giggle.

"Get out!" Klarin kept her eyes on Nexxa. "For fuck's sake, you whore!"

Medan used the distraction, ripping the gun from Klarin's grasp. He threw his arm in front of the wigged woman to dissuade her from entering the room further. Nexxa recognized the kind woman from the lingerie shop. She also recognized the jealous woman from her time in Paris. Klarin withdrew the knife strapped to her thigh, lunging at Medan. Nahil took the small pocketknife from her bra, opened it, and threw it at Klarin, striking her in her temple. Klarin slumped over. Medan's eyes bulged. He knelt and put his fingers on her neck, feeling for a pulse.

Standing, Medan glared at Nexxa. "I have to get rid of you now."

"I have a girl you might be interested in."

"What kind of girl?" asked Olek.

"I have a girl, an *American*," Medan indicated.

"Text me."

Medan pushed the button to end the call and leered at Nexxa.

"Fix your hair, and put on some lipstick," Medan barked at Nexxa as he tossed her purse to her. "Look sexy." Medan took a picture of Nexxa and texted it to Olek. His phone pinged immediately with a text. His eyes gave a surprised look. Nexxa assumed he was pleased. He was making decisions now that Klarin was out of the picture. But how was he going to explain her death? Her body was light, considering she was dead. With the pocketknife removed from her temple, she was now slumped over in the armchair where Medan had slept.

He knew Klarin had been contracted by someone else. The only way to find out *who* that someone else was, was to talk to Tarek or maybe Sal, if they even knew. *No time for that now*, he told himself. Nexxa would benefit him and Hezbollah if he could convince Sal's uncle this was a better alternative, a *lucrative* alternative, to killing her and her sister. She would be out of the way, allowing Tarek to execute a deal for financing and general contracting with China Black Road to build infrastructure in Beirut. Tarek and Sal could handle Faroud, let him know *they* would be working with the Chinese.

"You need to get out of here." Medan tucked his gun into the back of his jeans. Nahil turned her head, looking at Nexxa. She said nothing, but her slight smile said it all. Nahil believed Nexxa would have a better chance now, at least escaping what she was sure was death.

Medan's grasp was tight on Nahil's arm as he walked her toward the bedroom door. He opened the door to see no one was there guarding the room, so he pulled her with him, locking the door behind him. Laughing, watching a YouTube video on his phone, a guard walked toward them from down the hallway. Medan nudged Nahil; she smiled and moved his arm around her shoulders, pulling her to him as if they were kissing. The guard looked up with one eye, preoccupied with his video. Medan let his arm slide down, touchy-feely-like along Nahil's backside. Nahil threw up a bit in her mouth, not because she didn't find him attractive, but because she imagined this was what her husband probably did with other women. Keeping his arm around Nahil, Medan reached for his phone and dialed a local taxi company as they exited the house. He walked her to the fountain in the driveway and waited with her. Medan flipped a piece of her wig; Nahil turned her face.

"Why?" Nahil demanded.

"I did not want this." Medan furrowed his brow.

"What will you do now?" Nahil gestured with her hand, then

clarified, "With the woman?"

The taxi pulled into the driveway, coming to a stop beside them.

"Go." Medan motioned to the taxi. "You can go now."

Nahil opened the car door; she slipped on her Gucci sunglasses, the pair she swiped from Sefa's. "Sal?" Nahil asked.

Medan gave her a look. Nahil knew she didn't have to worry.

BEIRUT — OCTOBER 7, 2013

By noon Sergei, with a growing growl in his stomach, went with the intent of having the reception at the Le Gray hotel call her room to confirm she was still a guest, but when there wasn't an answer in her room, he gave the concierge a generous tip in exchange for Nexxa's room number.

Standing in the middle of room 168, his intentions took over. His eyes went to a pair of shoes on the floor with some clothes strewn about. Sergei picked up the stilettos and garments, placing them on the bed. He thought about the way she looked at the racetrack, the way she spoke at Sursock Palace, the way she smelled in the hookah lounge. Nexxa wasn't the type that would leave her clothes on the floor. A blush pink shopping bag—Nahil's Fashions—rested in the armchair. Sergei lifted the bag—some tissue paper, no receipt. Sergei folded the bag, tucking it under an arm.

There was a teacup with a slight tea residue and red lip marks on one nightstand and on the other was a champagne flute with a trickle of champagne. Sliding open a dresser drawer, he saw an array of intimate garments. Shutting the drawer, Sergei looked to the white wardrobe. His eyes went right to left and back to the right. He moved his hand across Nexxa's hanging clothes; Sergei cupped his nose and mouth, inhaling the aroma. With the lingerie shop bag in his possession and Nexxa's essence on him, he left her room.

In the Russian's mind, he imagined seeing her again for another date and possibly taking her back to Moscow. She would meet his babushka and niece. And they would have an enormous amount of sex, naturally. Instead, he was now trying to find her. He was familiar with *how* and *why* people went missing from past experiences in Russia, but as he left the hotel, he thought about the Arab men Nexxa and her sister had been sitting with in the upscale hookah lounge; sure her intoxicating aroma was what compelled him to stay longer, watch her that night. This predicament, his gut told him it *was* a predicament, would be different in Russia; he would have his associates to help him.

He kept a poker face on the drive to the Haret Hreik, but secretly, he had a pit in his stomach. The driver took the exit for Old Saida Rd., heading south past the Beirut Horse Track, and right about that time, Sergei accepted his feelings. His hand to his jaw in thought, he could smell Nexxa again, and with an exhale, he succumbed to the fact that he cared. And as if no time had passed, the driver rounded the last turn, and they were in front of Nahil's Fashions. He glided from the back seat; *What would she have been doing in this neighborhood?* As he stood on the footpath looking through the shop window, his eyes met Nahil's; he knew that the woman in the shop would know something about where to find Nexxa.

He carried the shopping bag he found in Nexxa's hotel room into the shop. He laid it atop the counter and patted it with his left hand, keeping his phone in his right hand.

"A blonde American woman."

Nahil stopped folding some scarves and motioned with her hand for the good-looking stranger to follow her. "Come." She looked outside, scanning the street, then grabbed ahold of his arm and walked him to the back of her shop.

"She was here," Sergei stated confidently, "now she is missing."

Nahil looked down. "He wants to sell her now."

"Who? Your husband? He traffics women?"

"No, no, it is *something else* with her. With the American woman. I tried to help her." Nahil thought of her pocketknife. "I was at the house, my uncle's house. I'm sorry, my husband, *his* uncle's house. That is where Medan has her."

"When were you there?"

"I found a phone this morning in my shop." Nahil looked toward the dressing room. "And I was there today." Nahil touched the watch on her wrist. "I was there at ten a.m."

"Why?" Sergei noticed Nahil's watch; it looked like an antique. "Why were you helping her?"

"My mother told me stories of the West when I was younger. About how the girls from the West lived. The opportunities, the independence they had. We all need to believe in stories, fairy tales." Nahil reached out, touching a picture of her mom on the wall. Sergei had heard enough; he pulled up Mikhail on his phone.

"Find out who is moving girls in Lebanon."

"I'll call you back."

"What can you do?" Nahil put a hand to her chest.

"I'm going to offer more." Sergei's confidence filled the space between them. He swiped a few times on his phone. "I will compensate you."

"I'll make some tea." Nahil turned on her small electric kettle and prepared two glasses for tea as Sergei looked at Nahil's family pictures on the wall. Her back turned to Sergei, she said, "I am not expecting anything in return."

Sergei cleared his throat. "She should never have been here." He did it again. "In this country."

"My mom once told me our steps, our path is already laid out for us. This is something she only said to me. Perhaps this was just part of her path. I knew she came into my shop that day for a reason."

When Mikhail called Sergei back, he had a name—Olek.

"Right, okay," Sergei acknowledged as he took a sip of his tea and ended the call. "I need to speak to them." Nahil reached into her purse and pulled out her phone. She dialed Medan's number and handed the phone to Sergei.

"What do you want?"

"I understand you have something in your possession that you intend to sell."

"Who is this?"

"I know of two horses," Sergei responded.

"Two—horses?" Medan asked.

"Let's say a series of unfortunate events—in your favor. The blonde."

"Do you want to buy her?" Medan straightened his stance.

"Meet me at the Beirut Horse Track, by the finish line. One hour," instructed Sergei.

And just like that, the Arab was intrigued.

"What will you do?" Nahil's mind raced, thinking about Sal, Medan, and Nexxa.

"I have to get two horses down."

"I don't understand this." Nahil waved a hand in the air. "Horses?"

Sergei gave Nahil a comforting smile and handed the phone back to her. She gave him a slight embrace. "Thank you." And just as he arrived, the good-looking Russian left Nahil's shop.

Sergei had been following races while he was in Beirut. His driver, Gage, inquired as to where his next destination was. Sergei heard Gage but gave no response. His thoughts were coming together.

"Sir?"

"The track."

The driver maneuvered away from the curb down the street.

If the top two horses are out, then the long shot will most likely win. Put up ten thousand for the bet, and Medan can make triple or more than what he would get if he sold her. Sergei motioned to his driver; they had a good rapport, but he still needed to put in his earbuds.

"Hooli, Hoolihane."

"*Salut mec! Quoi de neuf?*"

"*Très bon.* Alright, man, I know you are on holiday in France, but my French sucks."

"*Nema problema.*"

"Fuck, Croatian now?" Sergei shifted his body. "I need something done in an hour."

"Let's go, man," Hoolihane enthusiastically echoed as he stepped in from the terrace of the Airbnb apartment he was renting in Nice. He placed his neatly manicured hand two inches above his PalmSecure mouse. Capturing an infrared image of his unique palm vein pattern, he securely signed-in to his laptop and then inserted his USB drive to run Tails. His vigor preceded his words as he asked, "What are we doin', man?"

"Eli Kattan, jockey for Barbys Ken, racing today at three p.m. here in Beirut one hour ahead of you. Minister of Foreign Affairs for Azerbaijan—"

"Monacoian," quipped Hoolihane.

"Yeah," Sergei responded.

Hooli commenced his new task with his uncontrollable shoulder jerk, followed by a long breathy exhale to calm himself. Hooli had been homeschooled, which lent to self-learning. Traveling as a child built his interest in international workings. He tirelessly people-watched on his trips, teaching himself about human nature, namely human weaknesses. This launched his interest in becoming a hacker. Initially, he did things such as moving his parents' funds around between their various accounts to irritate them when they limited his junk food intake. Then he moved on to creating shell corporations and changing friends' grades in their private schools—all for a fee, obviously. From a young age, his mom told him he needed to be an entrepreneur—so he became one.

Hooli was in his early twenties when he caught Sergei's attention in a restaurant in London. Sergei noticed how he commanded the restaurant's servers with poise, yet he looked like a punk dressed in a black hoodie and what Sergei considered "pajama pants." Hooli observed the Russian watching him, which annoyed him, so he requested to pay for Sergei's meal if he agreed to leave. Sergei, humored by Hooli's brazen offer, instead approached his table. He first explained to Hooli that a change in his attire might be helpful going forward before they began to work together. Hooli acted tempestuously, but once the Russian suggested it was apparent he was a hacker, a novice one, but that he had permanent employment for him for an outrageous compensation, he calmed down and ordered ice cream—vanilla—for the both of them.

"Got it, I'm on it, man." Hooli already had the information for the pending horse race pulled up on his laptop. His protégé back in Moscow, whom he was chatting with via a secure proprietary messaging app, was getting the details on the Minister of Foreign Affairs for Azerbaijan.

"You don't even—"

"Man, c'moooon."

"So, I need Barbys Ken to have a positive drug test and the Minister to have a scandal. A disqualifying scandal." Sergei silently counted to sixty over and over until more than five minutes had passed.

"Done. Bam, baby! We got it goin'."

"How...?"

"Ok, so we've got, we have a positive drug test, and the online chatter has already started about the Minister's embezzlement of government funds." Hooli sat back in his chair and tapped the screen on his phone. "So, I'm guessing you need Hard Candy Kristmas to come in first?"

On the grounds of the horse track, Sergei's driver came to a stop at the entrance. The phone to his ear, Sergei scratched his nose before nodding to Gage and reaching for the handle opening the car door. He stood with eyes looking up to the sky, thinking the imposing dark clouds moved like celestial beings. "Yes, that's right."

Hooli slapped his hand down on his desk. "So, you gonna make a good one on this, man."

"Mm, it's not quite like that this time. Mikhail will take care of you; I have something to do. You're the best, man."

"Alright, later, man."

Sergei took his phone down from his ear and watched the call end. What he just did would set in motion his karmic debt. His babushka constantly reminded him about karma and its universal law, interjecting her wisdom upon him at times like a mother scolding her child.

Sergei returned his phone to his pocket and contemplated their conversation. *How does he get into their systems? To be able to do all this in an hour. Disseminate fake news so his horse is eliminated.* Sergei's phone pinged with a text message. It was a link to tweets with articles about the Minister of Foreign Affairs.

"Azerbaijan's Minister of Foreign Affair's Horse is not the only Monacoian! Minister Becomes a Monacoian with Government Funds."

"Azerbaijan Government Freezes Minister of Foreign Affair's Bank Accounts! Minister Pulls Horse, Monacoian, from Pending Race, so his Anticipated Winnings Can't Be Confiscated."

"Barbys Ken Tested Positive for Corticosteroid Betamethasone, Banned from the Race!"

Sergei smirked. "He's the best, fucking good," he whispered to himself.

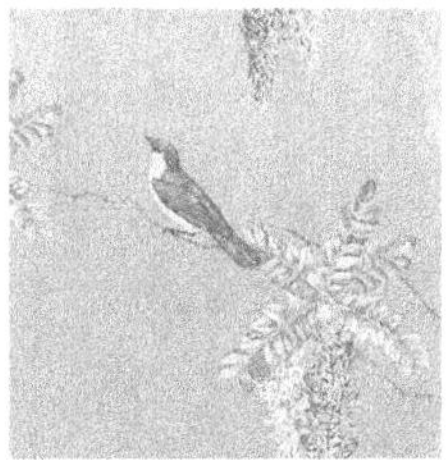

BEIRUT — OCTOBER 7, 2013, AFTERNOON

It was easy for Medan to spot Sergei. He was, however, an agent within the General Directorate of State Security Missions, Lebanon's version of the CIA. It mattered not to him that Russia's president had been an ally of Syria, the sister nation of Hezbollah.

Sergei handed Medan a race form with a horse circled.

"Hard Candy Kristmas?" Medan questioned.

Sergei nodded before indicating with his eyes that they should go to the window where bets were placed. As they walked, Sergei handed Medan an envelope of cash.

"It's just under ten thousand U.S., for win," Sergei told him.

Medan peeked in the envelope; his eyes widened. "To win?" Medan looked back to Sergei.

"Win, place, show. For *win*."

Standing at the window while the clerk counted the money,

Medan turned toward Sergei and sarcastically muttered under his breath, "Christmas." Sergei kept his stance, legs apart, arms crossed. He watched as a smug Medan reluctantly took the ticket from the clerk.

"Let's have a drink." The Russian walked toward the bar, and the Arab followed his lead. At the bar, Sergei ordered two Beluga vodkas. They stood a stubborn distance from each other as Medan eagerly tasted his drink. Medan finished his vodka first, holding his glass in the air waving "hello, hello" to order another round. Sergei observed, *He has no couth, like a beast.*

Sergei continued watching as Medan sipped his second drink, shifting his manner. "Beirut is my city. No, you see, with this money, I can show payment from the sheik and contribute to my city, my friend's cause—Beirut is my City."

Medan rambled on and on, and Sergei finally met his tolerance level. He took the last sip of his Beluga vodka, put the glass down, wiped his mouth, and leered at Medan. "Continue to amuse yourself," he said, walking away.

Sergei pulled up the picture he had of him and Nexxa. He dialed his grandmother; it had been a long time since he sought reassurance. "Babushka, I need—"

"I see," she interrupted, moving her hand over a piece of cloth.

"I've never, I'm..." Sergei moved the phone down from his ear. (He had mentioned meeting a woman, Nexxa, to his babushka during a call back home to check on her and his niece.) Sighing, he returned the phone to his ear. "I may have made a bad mistake."

"My *vnuchok*, there are no mistakes."

"Right." Sergei rubbed his hand over his head. "No mistakes."

"When you have her back, go to Turkey." Ankica knew the borders of Lebanon. "My cousin Rosha can help you."

Sergei looked up in the sky. "It's been a while since you've talked to Rosha."

"I see his energy, his soul." Ankica saw a horse. "Christmas will win."

Sergei told his babushka goodbye and to kiss his baby niece for him.

Medan had remained at the bar, downing another drink and checking his watch every few minutes. As the time for the race approached, he moved across the grounds toward the track with his prayer beads moving between his fingers, reciting a Muslim prayer.

Sergei heard his babushka's voice, *There are no mistakes*, and Medan shouting, "Go, go!" as the race commenced. The horses rounded the curve of the track toward the finish line. Hard Candy Kristmas was in the lead. Then just like that, the horse Old Moon passed him up. Sergei thought of Nexxa as the horses surged past them, and he could smell the dirt from the track. Medan delighted. Hard Candy Kristmas won—he was a *Win*. Old Moon trailed him in second, for Place. Medan shouted, "Yes, yes!" turning to Sergei with a smirk. Sergei knew this face. He recognized Medan felt in control; one party always does. Sergei had been there before—the first time you feel in charge, that empowering feeling, that rush. Now Sergei would need to commandeer Nexxa's captor.

"Make the call," Sergei demanded.

"Let me collect," Medan barked.

Sergei walked a few paces behind Medan, watching him as he

pushed past people to the front of the cashier's window, thinking, *You would have already been killed if this were anywhere in Eastern Europe.* Medan cashed out his winning ticket, then plopped the cash in a plastic shopping bag and folded the issued check, stuffing it in his front pocket. He tilted his head from side to side, popping his neck as he approached Sergei.

Medan stood close to Sergei. "I didn't fuck her yet. Tell me, Sergei, have you fucked her?" Sergei stood, arms folded. He had to restrain himself from murdering Medan right there in the middle of the Beirut Horse Track.

He cleared his throat. "Now, *make* the call."

"I have her." Medan smiled.

"Take me then."

He was prematurely confident and *greedy*, so without time to speak with Sal's uncle, Medan bravely decided to take Nexxa to Sefa's apartment before meeting Sergei at the track. So with the guards preoccupied with debauchery, Medan made his move with a suggestion from Nexxa. At times in their presence, Klarin wore a hijab and exaggerated eye makeup. So did Nexxa, along with Klarin's signature sky-blue jacket and skirt, as she strode out of Sal's uncle's house.

Sergei's driver had both doors open as they approached the car. Medan plopped in and forcefully closed the door. Sergei, the one with couth, greeted his driver, thanking him for his patience. It was annoying listening to Medan's ringtone as he took his time to answer his incoming call.

"Where is the girls?" the voice on the other end asked.

"Meet me at Sefa's."

"Why Sefa's? Zarian is gone." Sal coughed. "His girl is gone."

Medan hung up on Sal. Laughing, he said, "I can't believe Zarian left with the sister."

Arriving at Sefa's apartment, the door was ajar; Medan pushed it open. Sergei followed, looking back over his shoulder. Medan told Sergei to "stay," like commanding a dog, in the living room before he went into the bathroom. The blonde American was in the bedroom with Sefa. Sefa was to keep watch over her per Medan's instructions, having been promised a significant sum of money. As if she would have anything to spend it on other than cigarettes, drugs, and tacky frocks. While Medan was at the track, Nexxa was able to convince Sefa to untie her hands. She offered her the sky-blue jacket and matching skirt she had on, which was a cashmere wool blend. She had managed to leave with her leggings and sneakers, stuffing them in her purse, and couldn't get out of Klarin's clothes fast enough.

Sal needed another line of coke to function, so he chain-smoked on the taxi ride to Sefa's apartment. When he entered her apartment, he saw a handsome Russian man. "Ah, she's one hundred," Sal garbled to Sergei, thinking he was there for a prostitute, on the way into the tiny kitchen where the coke awaited. Sal bent, snorted, then motioned with both hands and a pelvis movement mimicking doggy-style sex. "You can try before you buy."

Sergei stood an equal distance between the rooms, with no signs of stimulation toward the prostitute in the living room or the prostitutes in the kitchen.

Sal walked over to him. "Maybe you want something else." With his hand over his crotch, rubbing his penis, he said,

"Maybe you like me suck your dick. C'mon," Sal continued as he reached for Sergei's crotch. Sergei grabbed his hand and squeezed until Sal winced.

Medan was one step out of the bathroom when he first heard Sal, then saw Sal reach for Sergei's crotch. "Fuck!" Medan shouted, lunging toward Sal, grabbing ahold of him. "You disgrace Allah," he said while choking Sal, causing them to crash onto the coffee table, crushing it. The prostitute in the living room started screaming. Sefa came running. She shouted something in Arabic about her broken coffee table.

Nexxa heard a man calling her name; she moved from looking out of the bedroom window, following the familiar scent. She lifted her purse, which Sefa had thrown on the floor, and pushed open the poorly locked door. Sergei was in the middle of the hallway. He grabbed her hand. "Let's go." Sefa was screaming at Medan while picking up pieces of glass from the floor; Medan was shaking Sal, still shouting about Allah. Sergei swiftly lifted the forgotten plastic bag of money that Medan had so carelessly let go of in his rage. They ran out of the apartment; Nexxa didn't even feel her feet on the stairs.

Sergei led them about two blocks and turned a corner before he stopped running. Nexxa ran a few more paces, looking back at him, then looking past him for anyone after them. Sergei jogged after her and threw his arms around her. "You're okay; you're okay." A black sedan sped toward them. Sergei opened the car door for Nexxa. "Get into the car." Nexxa hesitated, searching Sergei's eyes before entering the car. Sergei had requested his driver to drop him and Medan off a few blocks from Sefa's apartment, not trusting the situation, feeling it was unwise to have his driver parked outside the apartment like a sitting duck.

"How?" Nexxa asked, shrugging her shoulders.

"I went to your room, the bag from the lingerie store."

"I *have* to find my sister." Nexxa couldn't fathom leaving without her.

"She left with a guy, Zarian, Medan said."

"Okay?" Nexxa squinted her eyes. "That is Medan's friend. My sister thought he was, I mean. We met them, and she liked him."

"We have to leave Beirut," Sergei asserted.

"St. Dimitrios Cemetery." Nexxa leaned closer to the front seat.

"Cemetery?"

"I left something there."

Sergei nodded to his driver. Gage made a turn and headed north. Nexxa looked at the bag Sergei held on his lap. *Don't even ask*, she told herself. When they arrived at the cemetery, Sergei stepped out of the car, tucking the bag of money in the back of his pants. His driver rolled down the window. "Wait here for us," Sergei instructed.

The grounds of the St. Dimitrios Cemetery were damp. Nexxa walked, with Sergei by her side, over to a tomb, bent down, and dug into a potted plant. She pulled out a plastic bag. It contained an EU passport and some cash. Kneeling, she put her hands over her face. She thought about the tiff she and Iliada had over Zarian. She knew she couldn't leave Beirut without her sister. Sergei reached for her hand. "We should go." Nexxa stood and exhaled. Sergei caressed her cheek, wiping a tear away.

"Are you sure?" Nexxa started to ask when she felt Iliada in a place, a place with a different language, happy.

"We need to get out of Lebanon. We need to get a car. They'll be looking for us."

While riding in the car, Nexxa separated the cash from the passport. She leaned forward, handing Gage the money. "Can you give this to Nahil? She has her shop—Nahil's Fashions." Gage agreed. Sergei pulled up a car dealership on his phone and gave the address to his driver.

Sergei held open the grandiose glass door. Walking in, he embraced Nexxa, turning her into his body. "I'll get us a car," he said.

So, we're fake car shopping, Nexxa guessed. Sergei eyed a white Jaguar F-Pace. Nexxa shook her head in approval. *Yep, this is the car; this is the car from my dream that we traveled in with me holding my passport.*

Sergei convinced the dealership to let him test drive the car for a day by handing over the equivalent of ten thousand euros in Lebanese pounds as a deposit instead of his passport. He let the salesman know he didn't need a rundown on how the car operated. Sergei pushed the button to start the engine and then configured the ambient lighting. "We're going to Turkey. I have a relative—Rosha."

BEIRUT — OCTOBER 6, LATE EVENING COME MORNING, OCTOBER 7, 2013

After being waved on by the port authority, the truck drove onto the ferry. Zarian's first instinct was to check on Iliada in the back, but it wasn't safe yet. It was night, and he could still see the lights from beach clubs as they moved away in the Mediterranean Sea. The only time he had been on a boat was to clean it when he worked for the Dbayeh Fishing Club as a teenager. Now, every wave reminded him of the risk he had taken.

"Are you cold?" Zarian touched Iliada's arm.

"I'm fine." Iliada's smile was brief. She had been rescued, which she expected to seem romantic, but it wasn't.

Zarian had contacted his friend, who worked at the ports. He told his friend he needed to move something and arranged for him to make a bogus delivery to Sal's uncle's house. Zarian knew that Sal's uncle frequently bought the newest televisions, appliances, and other electronics. He bet on the fact that the men guarding the house would not question a delivery. They had agreed that a box for a refrigerator, albeit an empty box, would be a good choice. Zarian's friend wheeled in the box on a dolly, and as predicted, the men on guard directed him straight to the back of the house where the kitchen was. He had stuffed packing foam on top of another box inside the box to disguise that the box was empty. Having concocted the plan, Zarian confidently laughed to himself, thinking, *Seems so simple, maybe stupid.* Zarian's friend didn't want anything in return since Zarian had helped him get his first job when they worked together at the Dbayeh Fishing Club.

In the late afternoon, the day of their escape, Zarian's phone pinged with a text from his friend telling him the delivery truck was in transit. At this point, the other men in the house had become complacent, making it too easy for Zarian to sneak Iliada down to the kitchen. Zarian lingered by the entrance of the house, smoking with the guards, and when the delivery arrived, he made out like the uncle had informed him that a new refrigerator was coming, saying, "Yeah, yeah, I was told this was coming today."

The box had been wheeled to the kitchen. Nobody was around so Iliada went in, and his friend wheeled her out in the box on a dolly. "Wrong refrigerator," he told the guards. Zarian offered to help load the box back onto the truck; his friend slammed down the door and hopped behind the wheel, driving off. Not a single Hezbollah guard noticed that Zarian remained in the back of the truck.

"I'll get you to the airport once we get to Cyprus."

"Okay." Iliada took a drink from her water bottle.

"I don't know like where you can go." Zarian had his hands in his pockets as he shrugged his shoulders.

"I just…" Iliada sat, putting her head in her hands. "I'm worried about my sister."

"Hey." Zarian sat next to Iliada, putting his arm around her. "I know Medan. He's a good guy."

"What?" Iliada flinched. "You, like, what the fuck? No, he's not!" A man who worked on the boat walked by, eyeing them. Zarian grasped Iliada's hand and smiled.

"Look, you're safe now, here."

Iliada looked to Zarian. She thought about the night they met, how sweet he seemed—Zarry, how sweet Zarry seemed calling her his girlfriend.

Zarian had been careful to ensure Iliada left Beirut with her black-on-black YSL handbag. When Zarian walked away, Iliada searched through her purse. She found her phone. Taking it out, she tried to turn it on. Unfortunately, it was dead. At the bottom, she discovered her emerald ring.

A bar that was only detectable because two older men sat outside drinking marked the beginning of the quaint town on the island of Cyprus. One older man rumbled to another old man as they turned, watching the passersby.

"Uh, airport." Zarian waited for the driver's response. He nodded.

Iliada got into the back of the car, pulling the door closed. She leaned back, clutching her purse in her lap and closing her eyes. Zarian opened the door; she sat up. "What?" she asked.

"I want, I thought I go with you. Make sure you, you're safe."

"I'm safe. Right?"

"Yeah, yeah," Zarian assured her.

The taxi driver looked at Iliada in the rearview mirror. Iliada looked to him, then back to Zarry, reaching her hand out for the door. Zarian's friend, who arranged the phony delivery and box escape, was standing on the other side of the street. He called out to Zarian in Arabic. Zarian told him to wait.

"Okay." Zarian paced in the space between the open door and Iliada. "I guess you can text me." Iliada closed the door.

Iliada boarded her flight, and a few hours later she landed in Rome. A stylish girl was screaming at an Italian lady in really American English. Iliada passed by, noticing her Prada purse in a dull shade of beige, a waste of a designer purse. Iliada stood in the taxi line, reminding her of New York. She rechecked her phone; it still wouldn't turn on. She had never traveled alone except from Canada to New York City to live with Nexxa, but Nexxa had made the arrangements for her and even greeted her at the airport.

The stylish American made her way to the taxi line. She practically pushed past some dudes who were goofing around, placing her next in line behind Iliada. Iliada told her it was her first time in Europe. The girl squealed. She told Iliada she was there to shop for her twenty-first birthday. Then she told her she was really twenty-three but that her dad had forgotten her twenty-first birthday; he is rich and always away for work, so he agreed to pay for a trip to Italy. Iliada took her phone out again like it would magically be charged. Her new friend suggested they share a taxi into the city centre.

Iliada started to cry in the taxi. The stylish girl asked her why, offering her some candy. Iliada laughed, taking the candy. She explained to the stylish girl that she didn't know where her sister was, saying only that they got separated and that her wallet had been stolen on the plane from her purse. Really what had happened was that Zarian used the cash she had to pay for the ferry. She had just enough in her bank account to use her debit card for her flight, maybe sell her emerald ring to pay for a stay in a basic hotel. She was both surprised and not surprised that Zarian had taken her Amex card.

"Really?" she inquired. "Like, that's awful. I have my dad's credit card. Why don't you come back to my room, and we can call your sister?"

BritNay called her dad, and he suggested that her friend speak to American Express' concierge. With the help of BritNay's dad, Iliada got a replacement card for the Amex account she shared with Nexxa. BritNay unpacked and offered to share her clothes with Iliada. Iliada thanked her, crying again, saying she missed her sister. BritNay told her not to worry, that after they went to eat, her treat, they could call her dad again to see if he could help. Iliada told her not to bother, that once her phone was charged, she was sure she would be able to reach her.

A late lunch happened, followed by BritNay browsing some shops. Iliada's feet were tired; she thought about how her feet had been tired after she and Nexxa walked around the Haret Hreik. She wished she had listened to her sister that day when she asked her to stay at the hotel. While BritNay tried on some clothes in Versace, Iliada plopped herself on the sofa outside the dressing room. She breathed, "Nexxa," trying to connect with her.

LEBANON — OCTOBER 7, 2013, EARLY EVENING

"You know what I like about you?" Sergei looked over at Nexxa. "Your smile."

Moving fast along the coastal highway to Tripoli, the road shimmered like gold, and every time he spoke, Nexxa knew she was safe. She wanted to compliment him, but she couldn't help but smile about what came to mind—that Sergei would have a gentle roughness with her when they would first sleep together.

"Voicemail again." Nexxa laid the phone in her lap.

"You didn't leave a message?"

"No, I guess I should." Nexxa twisted her torso. "So, Medan told you, I mean, he was certain that my sister left the country, right?"

"Right. Call back and leave a message."

"I don't want to keep using your phone. This is expensive."

Sergei gave her a look of insistence. Nexxa called again.

Her voice cracked, and the hand she held Sergei's phone with shook as she left a brief message for Iliada. Nexxa put down the phone and folded the small piece of paper she had with Iliada's cell number written on it.

"What is that?"

"Oh, someone once told me to write things down like addresses and phone numbers in case you lose your phone or… your way. Since Medan took my phone, I don't know Iliada's number by heart. I had this stuffed in a pocket in my purse."

"You'll always know your way with me." Sergei shifted into sixth, then reached for her hand. "Stick with me," Sergei grinned before continuing, "and you'll see the world."

When they arrived in Tripoli, Sergei parked the car close to the area where you catch the ferry and left the key fob on the driver's seat. Sergei had gotten them this far; now, all they needed to do was board the MedStar ferry. Nexxa was queasy standing before the passport control officers in uniform as her eyes moved from one to the other. She thought the officers seemed intimidating, like Hezbollah, but calmed her thoughts by reminding herself that they were all only souls, all cloaked in their own disguises.

"This is not how I expected to spend the night with you." Sergei inspected the bed and peeked his head in the bathroom once in the ferry's passenger cabin.

"It's…" Nexxa tilted her head and laughed. "… okay."

"Come." Sergei took her hand, holding it tightly as they walked to the main deck in search of something to eat. "I feel terrible that we can't even have dinner together. Well, it looks like some Fantasia potato chips and Flippies cheese balls for tonight." Nexxa looked to Sergei and shrugged one shoulder with a smile. Sergei paid for the snacks and opened a bag for Nexxa before they strolled back to their passenger cabin, eating a few chips on the way.

"When will we get to Turkey?" Nexxa asked, yawning.

"It will take us overnight to get to Turkey." Sergei stood by the window, looking out over the sea. Nexxa couldn't stop yawning as she took off her shoes. Sitting on the lower bunk, she pulled her legs onto the bed, and with one last yawn, she placed her elbow on her knee and rested her head. Sergei closed the shabby curtain on the window and sat down beside her. He pulled her into him, and she leaned her head on his shoulder.

Nexxa slowly moved her head down to his lap. His body was warm. She felt his breathing as she closed her eyes. Sergei stroked her arm, and Nexxa moved a finger along his hand resting on his thigh. "I have…" Sergei said, leaning his head back, "a baby girl. She is my *brother's* baby, but I take care of her with my babushka. Her mother died when she was only a few months old."

"A baby girl," Nexxa said softly.

"How do you feel about that?"

"I can tell you that women are here to provide a way for the souls that want to incarnate. We have this opportunity that men do not." Nexxa yawned one last time.

Sergei pushed Nexxa's hair from her face. "I provide for her, I love her, but I want to have my own child someday."

"Yeah…" Nexxa thought about the girl she saw in the elevator of her hotel. "That would be sweet."

Sergei maneuvered his legs onto the bed and positioned himself so Nexxa could lie with plenty of room, plenty close to him. Deep into their voyage, Nexxa awoke to Sergei's hand on her breast; she fell back asleep to the sound of his breathing.

In the mid-morning, the ferry was finally pulling into Tasucu, Turkey.

"I feel disgusting." Nexxa tried to wash her face and swish out her mouth in the ferry's tiny cabin bathroom.

"Don't worry; we will get somewhere to get cleaned up soon."

Nexxa examined her face in the corroded mirror. *Well, if he can see me like this and still like me, then that means something.* "I've had the same lace thong on for over two days."

"Take them off."

Nexxa stood in the bathroom a moment, tapping her fingers on the sink. Was he challenging her? Why had she blurted that out? Emerging, she took off her leggings, tossed them on the bed, and then looking him in the eyes, took off her thong and folded it.

Sergei kept his eyes on her face, reached for her lace underwear, and stuffed it into the back pocket of his jeans. Then he said, "Let's go buy you some new lace thongs."

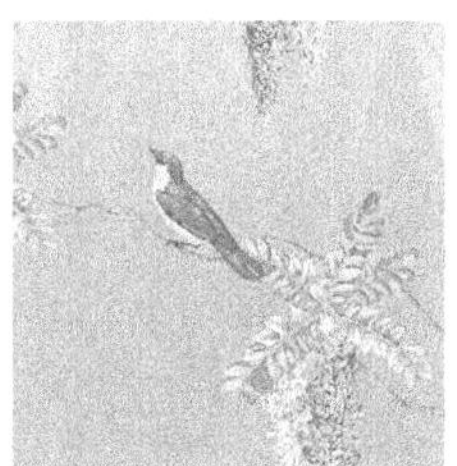

TASUCU, TURKEY — OCTOBER 8, 2013

"After we get you some clothes, you can freshen up at Rosha's, my grandmother's cousin. She will meet us dockside." Looking down at his watch, Sergei heard a recognizable squealing on the dock.

"Ooooh!" She was pushing through the crowd of people to greet Sergei and Nexxa. "Eeee!"

Sergei had an intense look. "That is my grandmother's cousin."

"Sergei, Sergei!" she shouted, enthusiastically waving her hand in the air. She at first looked about sixty-five years old with short, rolled, bright blonde hair. Barely five feet tall, evenly round throughout her body, and naturally bombastic, Rosha didn't seem like an eighty-year-old woman.

"Come." Sergei motioned with his head. "Let's go meet Rosha."

Rosha squealed with bulging eyes, reaching up to grab Sergei's face. He leaned over, and she kissed him on each cheek. "Ooooh, and who is the pretty girl?" She looked to Nexxa.

Nexxa sniffled, touching the corner of her eye. Rosha took ahold of Nexxa's hand, smiling up at her and leading them away. Rosha spoke in Russian; Nexxa could hear Sergei laughing as he walked behind them.

"Don't worry. She is complimenting you by having a go at me." Rosha was saying that she was certain Nexxa was the prettiest girl Sergei had dated. Nexxa understood that much. And that the rest had been whores. Older-looking whores, she added. Nexxa understood most of that. Rosha knew this from recently talking with Sergei's grandmother. But then, how could she have known what the women were like that Sergei had been dating? Sergei figured that Rosha had probably been calling Ankica, his babushka, but his babushka hadn't let on. "I speak to Ankica little here—" Rosha flipped her hand, "—little there." Sergei determined they had settled their bad feelings.

"We need to go to a women's clothing store."

"Okay, I show you now. My friend has a store."

Sergei motioned to a waiting taxi driver. Rosha sat in the front and told him their destination. About ten minutes later, they arrived at a boutique called Frida Butikk.

"I'll be quick," Nexxa said as she moved around the boutique. Sergei chatted with Rosha and the owner, Rosha's friend, as Nexxa picked out some clothes.

"Okay, I'm done."

"That was quick." Sergei looked surprised.

The shop owner moved from behind the counter, saying Nexxa should try on the garments she selected. She was insistent, walking toward the dressing room. Nexxa didn't follow.

"I am fine." Nexxa gave a look of assurance. "I'm fine. Thank you," she managed. Inside she was thinking about when Medan was outside the dressing room, ready to abduct her in Nahil's lingerie shop.

"Okay, we'll take these." Sergei handed the store owner cash to pay for the clothes. The owner bagged the items and gave the shopping bag to Nexxa.

"Thank you," Nexxa told the shop owner. She looked to Sergei. "Thank you."

"You don't have to thank me."

"Well, I would never ask for anything. You know, he, Medan, took my wallet."

Sergei took Nexxa's hand in his, rubbing the top of her hand with his thumb. "I am happy to do this for you." Keeping ahold of her hand, they walked together like a couple that had been together for years.

"I hate to mention it, but I really need to go to a drug store too."

Rosha led them to a pharmacy, and Sergei handed Nexxa some cash. "Let me know if you need more." Nexxa nodded. A few minutes after she was in the store, Sergei came in and found her. He reached for the basket she was carrying; Nexxa smiled, mouthing the Russian word for thank you. They moved around the store together until Nexxa found what she needed. Sergei placed the items on the check-out counter, requested a bag from the cashier, and bagged the items.

Rosha was stopped several times on the street by friends wanting to chat, but she had a mission. With each friend that tried to stop and chat with her, she said in English, "I have to go; I have important business." It was apparent she was eager to bring her *important business* back to her apartment. Sergei had made it clear they would stay in a hotel, but she insisted they come to her apartment first.

The apartment had the odor of velvet furniture from the seventies soaked in cigarette smoke. The breeze from outside picked up the smell of Rosha's perfume and wafted it around the apartment. She showed Nexxa the bathroom. While Nexxa showered, Rosha gave Sergei some cake and pulled out pictures to show him. He had a good laugh looking at photos of his grandmother and Rosha when they were teenagers. She even managed to find a photo of Sergei and his high-school girlfriend. Sergei made sure to put that picture at the bottom of the box that held her photos.

Nexxa slipped into a new thong, stepped into a new dress, and ripped the tag off. She sprayed herself with a body spray she bought and put on a dab of her lip-stain from her purse. Lastly, she hung the towel she used over the shower and wiped some water off the floor. She curiously peeked into Rosha's bedroom before she walked into the kitchen to join them.

"Thank you, Rosha."

Rosha kept her grin.

Sergei stood and motioned for Nexxa to sit. Rosha plated her some cake. Sergei placed his hand on Nexxa's shoulder, feeling her wet, towel-dried hair. He noticed how her skin looked with drops of water. He didn't notice the butterflies in her stomach. Rosha jumped up from the table and went to the apartment door like she was being lifted in the air.

"What is that all about?" Sergei looked over his shoulder as Rosha left the kitchen. Alone, he pushed Nexxa's hair aside and moved his right hand onto her décolletage while slowly kissing her neck. Nexxa placed her hand on his, pushing it down into her dress onto her breast. They heard squealing; they laughed, and Sergei removed his hand.

"Eee, haha," came from the living room, from Rosha's friend Yana who came over to see Sergei. Nexxa stood up, holding her hand over her chest. Sergei grasped her other hand, leading her to the palpable excitement coming from the two women in the living room. Rosha had called her friend over because she was anxious to show her what a grown man Sergei was now and, obviously, his new girlfriend. Yana looked like Rosha's twin. They had the same hairdo, the same height, and even the same outfit. She bombastically greeted each of them with a kiss-kiss on the cheeks. She, like Rosha, also reached up to stroke Sergei's head.

Sergei did his best to suppress his sexual urges, hoping to conclude their visit soon after meeting Yana. Not even a chance.

Rosha and Yana lit cigarettes and motioned for Nexxa and Sergei to sit in the armchairs across from them while they settled on the sofa—speaking, laughing; speaking, laughing, mainly in their native tongue, Russian. Nexxa's cheeks hurt as she smiled, looking from Rosha to Yana to Rosha to Yana. She understood most of what they said, wishing she couldn't, only because she was so tired and wanted to turn off her brain.

Sergei stood after a few minutes and asked Rosha what liquor she had. He needed a drink. Sergei made himself a Scotch and poured Nexxa a glass of wine. They sipped their drinks while

Sergei chatted with Rosha and Yana. Nexxa's guilt and worry about Iliada mounted as she observed what happy friends Rosha and Yana were. When there was a pause in the conversation, Nexxa leaned toward Sergei. "I need to try to call my sister again."

"Rosha, we need to get some rest." Sergei stood. "I think we are going to go to a hotel now." Rosha's bombastic eyes drooped. Nexxa finished her wine and stood to take the glass to the kitchen. Rosha motioned for her to put the glass back down on the table. She moved over to Nexxa, hugging her before kissing each cheek. Yana hugged Sergei and then motioned for Nexxa to come to her for a hug. She hugged Nexxa so tightly that Nexxa wondered, *Is this like when a kid latches onto your leg and won't let go?* Rosha hurried to the kitchen and returned with a small bag with some cookies inside. She handed it to Nexxa and hugged her again.

"Eat cookies; you feel better, yes."

The woman at the front desk handed Sergei a key, an actual key, and told him they would have a view of the sea. The hotel was basic yet quaint, operated by a local family. Nexxa had been running on adrenaline, but now her eyes were heavy as they made it into their hotel room. She didn't care to check out the view; she needed to think aloud about what had happened to her in Beirut.

"I was supposed to meet with Faroud." Nexxa tried not to let her eyes close while sitting with her hands under her thighs. "And then Diane."

"What is that about?" Sergei asked as he took off his shoes.

"Who is Faroud?" he continued, sitting in the chair.

"I met him in New York."

"Someone that you work with in finance? You told me you work in finance, right?"

"Yes, Faroud, I met him in New York, and we were supposed to work together. I do, yes, I work in finance for a broker-dealer."

"Nahil said that it was "something else" with you? What did she mean by that?"

"I met Medan in the hookah lounge; we—"

"You were…" Sergei furrowed his brow as he said, "involved with him?"

"No, no." Nexxa noticed Sergei sounded irritated, jealous. "Nothing happened between us. They kept asking me about Faroud and how I knew him."

"You were taken by Hezbollah. Why would they want you unless they intended to traffic you?"

Sergei stood and stepped out onto the balcony. He pushed his sleeves up and stretched his arms out on the railing. He looked out over the sea as the sun cast an amber glow as it turned toward evening. *She's involved in something, but what and how deep does it go?*

Nexxa sat down on the bed, gliding a finger back and forth across her bottom lip. She thought about Klarin, why she was there. And Diane, why she couldn't smell when in her presence. With Sergei on the balcony, Nexxa's thoughts jumped all over. *Okay, rest for a few minutes, then try to call Iliada. Maybe try to call my office too. They're probably worried. Aw, fuck, what about Faroud?*

Sergei turned, facing the room. Nexxa was sitting on the bed, and her tired eyes closed. Seeing her, he walked back into the room and caressed the side of her face. "You should sleep." Sergei pulled back the duvet, and Nexxa slipped under to lie down.

"I'll sleep on the pull-out."

"Okay." Nexxa covered her mouth as she yawned. All she wanted was for Sergei to lie down next to her. Nexxa drifted asleep, thinking about being on the ferryboat and Sergei carrying the basket for her in the pharmacy. Hours later, she awoke to a dark room with only a peek of moonlight shining in. She got up and went to the toilet to pee and brush her teeth. When she returned from the bathroom, she lay beside Sergei on the pull-out bed. Half asleep, he put his arm around her, pulling her closer to him. Nexxa slept through the night, but only because a Russian held her.

"I booked us flights to Moscow."

She opened her eyes, still lying in bed. "To Moscow?"

"I want you to come with me." Sergei handed Nexxa his phone. "I know you need to find your sister first. I'll go get us some coffee and something to eat."

Nexxa sat up. "I do, I do," she said, covering her mouth to stifle a yawn. "I meant to try to call her last night, and my office."

With Sergei out for breakfast, Nexxa went to the bathroom, brushed her teeth, washed her face, and inspected her hair. *Great, my stomach is rumbling. It's now or never; better go while he is out.* Nexxa used the toilet, showered, and the stress released from her body. She wrapped herself in a towel and dialed Iliada's number. The call was ringing. Nexxa held her breath while she watched lines of water drip down the foggy bathroom mirror. In her mind, there was no way she could go away to Moscow until she knew where Iliada was.

"Hello."

"Iliada!"

"Nexxa!"

"Are you okay? Where are you?" Nexxa swallowed, trying not to cry. "I'm so sorry. I was so worried."

"I'm in Italy." Iliada looked at a tourist brochure on the table. "Well, Rome."

"Rome, okay, that makes sense." Nexxa thought back to when she was in the cemetery, how she sensed Iliada was somewhere else.

"We took a boat, me and Zarian. I was in a refrigerator box. We were in the house together. They had you there too. Are you okay? Are you still with Medan?"

"No, I'm, no, I'm *definitely* not with Medan. I'm with Turkey in Sergei. I mean with *Sergei* in Turkey." Nexxa wiped the mirror with her hand. "A box? Okay, okay. I'm trying to envision that. I wanted to connect with you again. But I couldn't; I just sensed you were somewhere with… well anyway."

"Yeah, his friend drove us to the port and onto the boat!"

"Zarian helped you?"

"Ummm." Iliada thought about how icky she felt about Zarian ever kissing her. "Yes."

"So, how are you? I mean, do you have your Amex?"

"I'm staying here, like in this hotel, with BritNay. I met her, and she was like, so, so nice to me." Iliada started crying. "Her dad," Iliada explained, pausing to wipe her eyes, "helped me.

So I don't have a card yet. I mean—"

"Iliada, Iliada." Nexxa held her forehead. "It's okay, it's okay. So you have somewhere to stay?"

"Yeah, I'm staying in her room," Iliada spoke through tears.

"Okay, okay." Nexxa shook her head. "That's good. So I assume that Zarian took your wallet and her dad helped you call American Express, right?"

Iliada nodded.

"Iliada, right?" Nexxa asked.

"Yeah, yeah." Iliada put the phone on speaker and walked to the bathroom, using toilet paper to wipe her eyes and nose. "So, Sergei?"

"Yes." Nexxa smiled. "He came for me. I mean, he found me, found Nahil's shop."

"He's the one you had the date with, right?"

"Yes, there's so much to tell." Nexxa placed the phone down and put the call on speaker. "Jesus, I'm just so glad you are okay. Medan had told Sergei that the guy you were with, that you both had left. So, I knew." Nexxa wiped a tear. "I went to the cemetery—"

"Cemetery?"

"Yeah, part of procedure for… Anyway, I'll explain that later. A feeling came to me of you in a hotel room, speaking a different language. Not literally, but around a different language."

"I know, I'm sorry. Zarry, Zarian turned out to be an asshole." Iliada sat between shopping bags on the end of the bed. "But now I'm staying in this cool hotel."

"Okay, so I think," Nexxa started saying, trying to process the thought of Iliada being without her in another country, "I think

I will go to Moscow for a few days with Sergei. I mean, with everything that has gone on, I need some time to figure out what happened. I'm going to call my office now. Let them know I'm okay."

"Okay, yeah, I mean, me and BritNay are going wine tasting today."

"Oh…" Nexxa started assessing everything they just discussed. "Or, maybe I should come there to you."

"Nexxa, go with Sergei."

"Okay." Nexxa managed to smile. "Yeah, I'll listen to my little sister. Okay, we are leaving this morning." Nexxa tapped on the speaker button. She lifted the phone to her ear. "I will call you from Moscow. Do you need money?"

"No, I should have my Amex card in a few days, and she is paying for things. I mean, we really get along. I like her a lot. Her dad was so sweet. He told me not to worry, that he could tell I would be a good friend to her, like, that she is not alone in Rome."

Nexxa nodded her head. "Okay, good. Oh, and you can call me on this number. It's Sergei's phone."

"Okay, I love you."

"I love you too!"

Sergei returned to the room with coffee and some fresh bread. He paused, looking in the bathroom at Nexxa. "That was your sister?"

"Yes, she is okay. She is in Rome."

"So, you are going with me to Moscow?"

Nexxa came out of the bathroom and picked up the shopping bag with the new clothes in it. "I still need to call my office."

Sergei walked over to Nexxa, as she sorted the clothes on the bed, and took her hand.

"These events have been extenuating. Come with me. It will all work out."

Nexxa turned to Sergei. "You're right," she said and repositioned the towel around her body. "You're right."

Sergei picked up a dress. "This one." Nexxa took the dress and returned to the bathroom. When she came out, Sergei handed her a coffee and a piece of bread.

"You'll feel better after you eat."

"So, where will I stay—"

"You'll stay with me if that's okay with you. Or I can arrange a room for you in a hotel."

"Oh, yes, that's okay. *To stay with you.*"

"See, it's all working out." Sergei couldn't have looked happier.

MOSCOW — OCTOBER 9, 2013

Sergei pulled the small carry-on, the only luggage they had. He had been presumptuous about Nexxa joining him. Her few belongings, at this time, deserved something more than shopping bags, he decided. Sergei showed their boarding passes, they were wished an enjoyable flight, and they walked outside. Nexxa put her arm through his as they walked on the tarmac. Sergei offered Nexxa the window seat. She hesitated. His look told her to take it. Once in flight, Sergei ordered a vodka; Nexxa requested sparkling water.

"Have you been to Russia before?"

"No, but I've always wanted to go."

"You will meet my babushka and my niece, Natina."

"I feel I shouldn't. I mean, what happened in Beirut was completely crazy."

"Are you afraid?"

"No." In truth, Nexxa was. "It's just—"

"You are safe with me. Moscow is my home." His grip was always tight but comfortable. It reminded her of holding hands with Thomas when she was a little girl, comforting.

Moments after they exited Sheremetyevo International Airport, a white Jaguar F-Pace pulled up to them. A man swiftly left the driver's seat. He took the luggage from Sergei. He made eye contact with Nexxa and then looked back to Sergei.

"Okay, let's go." Sergei held open the passenger door for Nexxa.

"He's not coming with us?"

"No."

The traffic was terrible. Whenever they slowed to a stop, Sergei would lean on the center console and grasp his jaw while looking at Nexxa; she could feel his confident eyes piercing through her. Their ride was quiet and they spoke very little, yet since arriving at the airport, Nexxa was impressed even more.

Sergei lifted his phone from the console, tapped it a few times, and the gates opened.

Nexxa examined the exterior of Sergei's home. *Okay, so this seems fitting. This definitely looks like a house fit for Sergei, like a modern French château.* Stepping out of the car, she said, "Your home is nice, looks… like a home for a *family.*"

Sergei closed the driver's door. He took the carry-on bag from the back, came around to Nexxa, and took her hand.

"Promise me," Nexxa started to let go of his hand and said, "you're not married."

"Not yet," he responded with a grin.

Nexxa managed to smile.

Sergei used a touchscreen keypad to unlock the front door and motioned for Nexxa to enter. Nexxa could see into the kitchen from the foyer and through the kitchen windows into the backyard. His home was modern yet had cozy elements blended in. Nexxa saw an older woman in the kitchen moving pots around on a vast range. It was messy in the kitchen but smelled so good. Sergei set the luggage by the staircase and walked into the kitchen.

"Babushkaaa!"

"I am happy you are home. I see this beautiful lady." Sergei's babushka, Ankica, gave each of them a kiss-kiss on the cheeks. Ankica looked up at Nexxa, smiling just as Rosha had. Her smile was big, and her eyes twinkled. Without a pause in her grin, she took ahold of Nexxa's arm below her elbow, leading her to a seat. "Come, sit, have something to eat." It was unmistakable how good her English was, like Sergei's. Sergei pulled out a leather barstool and motioned for her to sit. Ankica handed each of them a plate and left the kitchen.

"She knows I like to sit here, to eat at the island."

"Is she going to eat with us?"

"She usually eats a big meal during the day."

"That's your niece?" Nexxa acknowledged the baby she heard crying from the baby monitor on the counter.

"Yes, she will bring her here now."

Ankica had a cute waddle to her, almost looking like she was carrying a heavy sack of potatoes when she returned to the kitchen carrying the baby. She held her out to Sergei. "I need to make her the bottle." Sergei stood and took the baby in his arms.

He set her on his knee, bouncing her and kissing her on the back of her head. Nexxa wasn't interested in eating or drinking; she was only interested in watching him hold and soothe his baby niece.

"Oh, she's so sweet."

"You want to hold her?"

"Yeah." Nexxa stood up.

Sergei handed her the baby. "This is Natina."

Nexxa held her against her chest. Ankica brought the bottle and gave it to Nexxa as she swayed Natina to soothe her. "You can feed her." Nexxa took the bottle and turned Natina around to feed her. She fussed some, looking up at Nexxa until she took the bottle in her mouth. After a few suckles, Natina calmed down. "She's so sweet," Nexxa gushed, never imagining that she would be in Russia holding a baby. Sergei watched, noting Nexxa's affection, how she naturally held the baby, how she naturally cared for her.

"It is a lot of work." Sergei stood with his arms folded. "I never knew how much you had to do for babies."

"Do you change diapers?"

"I actually do." Sergei sounded believable, as he looked over at his babushka, who shook her head no.

"Well, I have maybe once or twice."

Baby Natina reached for Nexxa's hair as she drank. She started to coo when she finished her bottle, letting the bottle nipple slip from her mouth.

"Okay. Time to burp now." Ankica announced like it was time

for recess to end.

"Oh, okay." Nexxa put Natina upright and patted her back gently, looking back and forth between Sergei and Ankica for confirmation of her method. They both watched with gratitude.

"Can I see the nursery?"

"I'll show you." Sergei had picked up his phone, looking at the home security app. "Hang on a minute." Nexxa didn't resist her urge to kiss the baby in her arms.

"Okay," Sergei said as he slipped his phone into his pocket, "let's go upstairs."

While holding the baby, Nexxa took off her shoes before walking to the staircase. Sergei looked amazed. "I work out," Nexxa offered as an explanation of her coordination and balance.

Natina's nursery had a round crib flanked with a pale peach sheer canopy that twinkled with silver and gold stars. A white wooden cabinet with glass doors held toys. The best part was the white armoire that was illuminated from behind. In one corner of the nursery was another floor-length canopy with star-shaped pillows, a plethora of stuffed animals and dolls and wooden toys dispersed on the rug beneath.

"Wow, this is impressive! Did you pick all this out?"

Shaking his head, Sergei said, "No, no. I paid a designer."

"You are a great uncle then." Nexxa kissed the baby and put her down on the rug to crawl around.

"Her father, my brother, he can't be here all that much. So, I wanted to do the best for her."

"It's lovely." Nexxa ran her hand across the railing of the crib. "So serene." Ankica entered the nursery carrying a laundry basket and put away some of baby Natina's clothes.

"Babushka, I am going to show Nexxa the room." Sergei bent down and handed baby Natina a stuffed doll and then put his arm on Nexxa's lower back as they left the room. Ankica looked over her shoulder; she was hopeful.

"You can stay in here, the guest room. My room," Sergei motioned with his head, noting, "is on the other side down there."

"Okay." Nexxa had her hand on the doorframe as she leaned in the room and looked around. She stood back and grinned at him. Silence, and more silence. "Can you show me *your* room?"

"Yeah!" Sergei grasped her hand. "Yeah." He walked her through the second-floor sitting area to a short staircase. The door to his bedroom was obscure, almost undetectable. She expected he would open it with a keypad lock of some sort. *It smells like him in here*, Nexxa observed. "So, I'm close by if you need me." Nexxa's dirty mind wandered, *Mmm, definitely need you.*

Sergei walked to his closet, took a few items out, and walked toward the ensuite bathroom. "I'm just going to change quickly." After changing into a pair of tracksuit pants and a long sleeve t-shirt, he poured himself a Scotch.

"Would you like some wine? I can go downstairs and get you a glass."

Nexxa grasped her neck. "I would like to get changed as well. Shower too."

"Sure." Sergei took a sip of his Scotch and set the glass down on the table by the mid-century leather chairs in his room. They walked back to the guest bedroom. Sergei turned on the bathroom light.

"Everything you need is in here."

"Do you have anything for women?"

"Tampons?" Sergei questioned as he started to open a vanity drawer.

"Oh, no." Nexxa laughed. "Like face cream."

"I see something in here." He pulled out a tube of cream. "This?"

"Oh, yeah, thank you."

"Would you like to go out for a drink later?"

"Well, I don't really have like heels or anything."

"Why don't we go shopping?"

Nexxa fidgeted with the cap to the cream. "I can't have you buy anything else."

Sergei smirked with a laugh. "Here." Sergei took a towel from the linen closet. "Why don't you shower? Then we are going shopping."

"Will anything still be open?"

"Don't worry. I'm going to get cleaned up myself." Sergei pulled the bathroom door ajar. "Then we'll go."

Nexxa told herself that her hesitation would go away after she showered. A shower always does you good. The water was different, possibly a little dirty, but the shampoo smelled good. *Baby Natina, it's awful that she doesn't have a mother. She's so sweet; you could just hold her forever. His babushka is so amazing to be able to take care of a baby at her age. Can only imagine what Sergei's brother is like.* Nexxa turned off the shower, and her thoughts subsided.

She wrapped her hair in a towel and dabbed on some of the face cream Sergei had found for her. *Just a little*, she told herself as she lined her eyes with black eyeliner and brushed on some mascara. She opened another drawer where she found some body lotion and took it into the bedroom. Sitting on the bed in just a thong and the towel on her head, Nexxa carefully squeezed some lotion in her palm and rubbed up and down her legs.

Feeling hot from showering, Nexxa took the towel off her head, walked to the terrace doors covered with curtains, and drew the curtains back. *Wow, this is beautiful!* She unlocked the door and stepped onto the terrace. She could see the light from Sergei's bedroom when she walked to the edge of the terrace but didn't think he would be able to see her. "Look at these beautiful trees," she spoke to them as she looked out over the vast wooded lot. *This breeze feels so good,* she thought as she ran her fingers through her hair before covering her breasts again with her hands.

"Nexxa," Sergei called out as he knocked on her bedroom door. Nexxa tiptoed into the bedroom. Sergei opened the door a crack.

"Can I come in?"

"Oh, I was just outside; I was hot," Nexxa was apologetic while trying to grab the towel from the bed to cover her body.

"You opened the door?"

"I… yes."

Sergei walked to the terrace doors and opened them. He stepped outside and looked around before coming back inside. Nexxa stood still as her heart raced, wondering why he seemed upset. She thought of Medan holding her hostage as she watched him lock the door and close the curtains.

"Hey." He stepped toward her. "I don't want you upset." Nexxa wiped a tear that fell and tried to readjust her towel. "The alarm wasn't triggered." Sergei helped her adjust her towel. "I don't understand why." Nexxa heard the baby as she was crawling down the hall, cooing. Ankica did her best to keep up with the eleven-month-old, but she was quick. Nexxa picked up a dress lying on the bed. Sergei turned as she took off her towel and slipped it on.

Natina crawled into the guest room where Nexxa and Sergei were; Nexxa bent down to pick her up. Baby Natina reached up, touching Nexxa's face. Another tear fell down Nexxa's cheek, and Sergei wiped it away, putting his hand with the wiped tear up to his mouth. "Your tears are mine." He kissed his closed hand.

"She's just so sweet," Nexxa said as she bounced her.

An exhausted Ankica said, "Ah baby, you are getting too fast," as she entered the room.

Nexxa carried the baby, following Ankica to the nursery. Nexxa kissed Natina on the forehead, and Sergei did the same before Nexxa placed her down on the rug next to her toys.

"Okay, baby, we are going out now," Nexxa spoke in baby talk.

"Babushka," Sergei said, once again looking down at his phone checking his home security app, "we will be out for the evening." He kissed his babushka on each cheek, and Nexxa did the same before they left the nursery. Taking Nexxa's hand as they walked down the hallway, he gave his phone a voice command to "call Hoolihane."

"Hooli, I need you to check something for me on the security system."

"Yeah, man, give me a sec."

Sergei smiled at Nexxa and motioned for them to enter his room before they went downstairs.

"Okay." Hoolihane fell silent while accessing the backend. "I'm in, looking around."

"I think the system was down for some time," Sergei indicated as he tapped on his tablet on his nightstand.

"No unknown IPs; no jamming alerts."

"Probably nothing, just needed to check."

"Alright, man, I'm going to dig deeper, and I'll get back to you."

"Let me know." Sergei tapped on the tablet, signing out.

Sergei looked to Nexxa with a huge grin. "Okay, you ready?"

"Yes."

"Take a deep breath; it's all good."

The lights from the city dashed in through the windows and around the Jaguar. They were the same colors as where Nexxa lived, but not the same; these were Moscow lights.

Sergei pulled up to the valet for Moscow's premier luxury department store. Nexxa stepped out, and a shiver rippled through her body. Sergei didn't hesitate to take off his jacket. In one motion, he wrapped it around her shoulders, kissing her on the cheek.

"Okay, let's shop."

"How do you pronounce the name of this store?"

"It's pronounced gum, like gum you chew."

They rode the escalator to the women's floor and walked over to the shoe department. Right away, Sergei picked up a heel. "These are nice."

"Yeah, I like those a lot."

"Size eight," Sergei said to the attendant, guessing the correct size. Nexxa tried on the shoes the attendant brought her and walked over to a mirror.

"They look good. I like watching you walk in them."

Nexxa turned from the mirror; she liked watching him too.

"Good, okay?"

"Yes, these are perfect," Nexxa confirmed.

"Okay, that was quick."

"Well, I usually know right away what I want." Nexxa looked down at the heels on her feet.

Sergei thought the same as he scanned Nexxa up and down.

"Now, let's get you something to go with these."

Sergei paid for the shoes, and they walked around to the women's clothing. Nexxa looked around, she found a dress, the price tag, she did the math in her head, rubles to dollars, then another dress, the tag, the math. Sergei moved behind her, his hand on hers as she looked at another price on a dress and pushed the tag away. "Just find what you like."

Nexxa grasped his hand. "Okay."

Sergei held out a dress. "I like this."

"I do too. I've always wanted a Hervé Léger dress."

"Let's try it."

"Sergei, these dresses start at like a thousand—"

"Try the dress on."

The sales attendant came to Nexxa, took the dress, and showed her to a nearby dressing room. Sergei lingered around the dressing area, waiting. He knew that she would feel more comfortable with him nearby; she had told him brief details on their flight from Turkey about how Medan had abducted her. Nexxa slipped on the dress sans bra and came out to show him how it looked. He nodded. She put the dress back on that she had worn into the store and told the attendant she would take the Hervé Léger dress.

"Why didn't you keep the dress on?"

"I kind of need a different pair of panties to wear with it. A bra too," Nexxa explained, resting her hand on her décolletage.

"Okay, let's go get it."

"Which way to women's lingerie?"

"Yes." The sales attendant was on hand to assist them. "I'll show you."

In the lingerie section, Nexxa picked out two different bras and a seamless thong. Unexpectedly, Sergei also picked out some things, including a white chemise with lace.

"I think that is *bridal* lingerie," Nexxa informed him, tilting her head.

"Good, you will need it," Sergei asserted. "Now, come, try these on, and change into the dress."

Nexxa quickly tried on the bras and thong she picked, deciding which would look best underneath the dress. When she came out of the dressing room, Sergei had the shoebox open and handed her the heels he had bought for her. Nexxa stood, bending each leg back at a time, and slipped on the heels with grace.

"Looks okay?"

"Beautiful."

He handed the sales attendant his credit card, and she rang up the dress and lingerie. She handed Nexxa the shopping bag with the bridal lingerie and the clothing she acquired from Turkey. Nexxa thanked her several times.

Sergei clapped his hands together with a feeling of accomplishment. "Let's go have a drink now." He took the shopping bag from Nexxa. "Can you walk in those? The restaurant is just across the street."

"Oh yeah, sure."

Crossing the street, Sergei huddled Nexxa close to him. His cologne rolled around her senses. *Damn, he smells so good. And damn, I'm in Moscow in a Hervé Léger dress.*

"This is Vogue. My restaurant with my partner."

"Oh, wow."

The doorman opened the door, and they stepped into the lounge area. Nexxa let her eyes go around the room. The hostess approached Sergei and asked if she could take his jacket.

"Are you cold?" asked Sergei. Nexxa had just positioned herself, her Hervé Léger dress, and her new stilettos in the restaurant. "Nexxa, are you cold?"

"Sorry?"

"Are you cold?"

"No, no." Nexxa stopped counting heads. "I'm fine. Sorry, I got distracted."

Following the hostess through the vibrant, trendy lounge, several pairs of eyes latched onto Nexxa. The hostess presented them with the table reserved for Sergei. The chairs were smoky gray tufted suede, which contrasted nicely with the shimmering silver-painted walls. A mix of medieval and modern light fixtures and sconces in contrasting gold flanked the restaurant.

"This place is beautifully designed."

"Just like…" Sergei pulled out the chair for her. "You," he whispered in her ear.

"Hervé Léger sends his gratitude. He likes the restaurant."

Sergei laughed. He took Nexxa's hand. "Where have you been all my life?"

"In Canada," she laughed. "And the States."

"You belong in—"

Sergei was interrupted; he turned to the waiter who approached the table. He didn't hand them menus, only stood stoically waiting for Sergei to order.

"Would you like champagne tonight?" Sergei offered.

"Yes, that would be nice."

Sergei instructed the waiter to bring a bottle of champagne. Before he could initiate another compliment or premeditated sexual innuendo, his phone pinged with a text from Hoolihane: *You were right; looks like an hour or so of time is missing. You've had a breach.*

Sergei pushed the button to turn his screen off. He motioned for the waiter. "Scotch," he requested as he approached. Sergei leaned back in his chair. He leaned forward. He placed a hand on the table near Nexxa's. "I loved watching you with my niece. I imagined you being pregnant when you were holding her."

"Oh… so…" Nexxa balanced his forward comment while taking notice of each woman, *all the women,* that emitted evil eyes through their false lashes. "Sergei, I feel like people are watching us."

The champagne and Sergei's Mortlach Scotch whisky were served. Sergei took a sip of his Scotch, then lifted his glass of champagne, "*Na zdorovye!*" They clanked glasses. Nexxa took a large mouthful. She had two more glasses of champagne. Sergei told her a joke, maybe something a dad would tell someone. Nexxa told Sergei she needed to go to the ladies' room. He caught the attention of their waiter; he escorted her. When she returned, Sergei stood as she approached the table. It was time; she just knew.

Nexxa put her hand on his chest and moved her body into his. "I didn't come to Russia to go shopping, and you didn't invite me to Russia to go shopping."

Sergei reached for his Scotch and took one more sip.

"Let's go."

MOSCOW — OCTOBER 9, 2013, EVENING

Sergei went to take a piss—his words—while Nexxa looked out over Moscow from the balcony of their Ararat Park Hotel suite. She took off her heels. "No," Nexxa whispered to herself, putting them back on. She knew what Sergei wanted from her. But, the Hervé Léger dress had to come off; the *Sin of Lust* said so.

His penis was bulging through his jeans. She tingled as she straddled him on the velvet bench in the ensuite. If the Russian continued to kiss her like that, she was going to faint. Sergei unzipped his jeans; his penis stood erect. Nexxa positioned over the Russian's erection. Then, Nexxa detected a familiar scent— pounding on the suite door ensued. She raised herself off of Sergei. Sergei stood, pulling up his jeans. He grasped the back of Nexxa's head, kissing her on the forehead as he moved out of the bathroom. Sergei lifted his phone from the bedside table and withdrew his gun from the nightstand drawer.

Sergei spoke in Russian as he stood at the door. He turned the lock; a bottle of champagne on ice was wheeled into the room by the room service attendant. Sergei reached in his pocket for a tip. He stared at the bottle. Not his taste; he knew something was off since he hadn't ordered the champagne.

Nexxa was certain an hour had gone by while Sergei was investigating the noise. Her breasts were cold, and her nipples were firm. She had goosebumps all over, so she grabbed a towel; too bad it was a hand towel. She stood with a shiver every few seconds, hearing Sergei and another man's voice. When she heard the door shut, she walked out to the bed.

Sergei locked the suite door. With the *Sin of Lust* in his eyes, he walked toward Nexxa. Placing his gun and phone on the nightstand, he pulled off his shirt, jeans, and underwear. He took the towel she held in front of her and tossed it, running his fingers over her erect nipples. Lifting her chin, Sergei moved his lips along the side of her neck to her collarbone. With a gentle roughness, the Russian spun her around.

Kissing her back, he said, "I want to fuck you like this," gliding his hand along her butt. Nexxa bent over on the bed; he inserted his penis, thrusting slowly. Gradually, gracefully, Nexxa moved, positioning on her knees; Sergei withdrew his penis, moving onto the bed behind her. He wanted to go deep, thinking about what she said in Vogue, how she hadn't come to Moscow to go shopping. Nexxa was so wet, and he was almost deep until she lay flat on her stomach. Sergei was forced to slow his thrust, withdrawing his penis, rubbing it back and forth against her butt. Bending over her, he kissed her neck.

"Is it too much?"

"No." Nexxa's chest moved up and down. "No, I don't want it to stop." Turning over, she commanded, "Come here." While sitting up on her knees, Nexxa took his penis in her hand, stroking him before licking the tip of his penis.

Sergei leaned his head back, "Ahh, ahh." He grabbed her head, pushing his throbbing penis further into her mouth.

"I don't want to cum like this." He pulled his penis out of her mouth. "Lie back."

Nexxa told him it was okay, and as she lay down, he moved his penis once between her breasts.

Kissing her, he said, "You make me so fucking hard!" He moved Nexxa's thighs apart, inserting himself again. Nexxa closed her eyes briefly before reaching to touch his muscular shoulders. Sergei pounded her before he climaxed.

Pushing up, he put his hand on her left breast. "I just came in you."

"I'm not on birth control," Nexxa exhaled.

"Okay, maybe we made a baby."

Still catching her breath, Nexxa grasped her forehead. "Is that a good or bad thing?"

"I would assume good." Sergei lifted himself off of her and walked to the bathroom. He splashed water on his face. From the bathroom, he said, "I can take care of you," as he wiped the tip of his penis with a tissue.

"Take care of me?" Nexxa sat up in bed and pulled the duvet over her. "But I've always taken care of myself."

Sergei returned with a wiped-off penis and pulled the covers back, lying beside her. "Stay with me here in Russia."

Nexxa turned to lie on her side to face him. "Really?"

"My mother and father were ten years apart like us. I have been to many countries, but I've lived in Russia my whole life except when I was away for racing school in Canada. Now I have finally found you." Nexxa scooted closer to him and laid her head on his chest.

"What about…"

"Huh?"

"Well, what about…?"

She wanted to ask him so many things. What about my job, my sister? But she didn't want to ruin the most blissful moment she had ever had in her life. Nexxa began to say something else but stopped herself. She heard Sergei breathing; he was already asleep.

Nexxa didn't wake up through the night to pee as she usually did. Great sex like that will put you to sleep as well as the incredibly comfortable mattress in their suite. She did, however, wake before Sergei, for which she was glad, cautiously slipping out of bed without waking him. The thought of him seeing her in the morning again—oh, the horror. Peeing first, she wondered if she had made any sounds in her sleep, realizing she hadn't ever slept that well in bed with a man. A bustle came from the bed. Nexxa quickly wiped, washed her hands, and grabbed one of the complimentary toothbrushes to brush her teeth. In a hurry to freshen up before he might see her, she reminded herself that he had already seen her in the morning on the ferry and he was still around.

"Nexxa?" Sergei knocked on the bathroom door.

"You can come in."

"I can wait."

"No, it's okay. I'm finished." Nexxa tied the belt of the robe around her waist. Sergei waited outside of the bathroom. When Nexxa came out, he put his arms around her. "I won't subject you to my morning breath."

With Sergei in the bathroom, Nexxa inspected herself in the sizable trifold mirror atop the vanity by the bed. Her makeup was mainly still on, and her lips were a little pouty and stained red from her lipstick. Honestly, she was glowing. *This will have to do*, she realized since she didn't have a brush.

Sergei walked through the bedroom; he thought she looked cute sitting at the vanity, messing with her hair. He walked over to the window and stood holding his hands up, rubbing his palms together.

"Today is going to be a good day."

"Well, but first, I guess I have to do the walk of shame." Nexxa stood holding the tie to the robe.

Sergei grinned, moving his eyes over to the Tsum shopping bag on the armchair. "I think you have something else to wear."

"No, no." Nexxa laughed.

He walked over to the chair and picked up the bag. "Maybe you can wear it tonight for me," he suggested while pulling out the white lace chemise he had bought for her.

Nexxa rubbed her lips together before grinning. She loved that he was playful.

"I know, I know," he continued, putting the chemise back in the bag. "My babushka will make breakfast for us. She likes you."

"I like her too."

Sergei picked up Nexxa's dress lying across the top of the armchair and walked over to her. He draped the dress over the chair to the vanity and pulled her into him. He ran his finger down into her cleavage and untied the robe she was wearing.

Sergei put his hand between her thighs. "Tonight."

MOSCOW — OCTOBER 10, 2013

"*Dobra jutro.*"

"Oh, you speak some Russian?"

"Oh, well, a little." Nexxa tilted her head. "Just a bit of Croatian mostly. I've been there a few times. And I knew a few words were similar."

"Sorry about the gates; I put them up when I cook. The baby wants to go go," Ankica explained while she was busy in the kitchen, pushing some sausages around and tending to baby Natina. She had the news on, switching her attention from that to the baby, who was crawling around the kitchen.

Sergei leaned into his babushka and kissed her on the cheek. "*Dobroye utro.*"

Ankica smiled before announcing, "Okay, it is ready." Sergei bent down to baby Natina and gave her a piece of bread he tore apart. "Not too big piece, Sergei."

Sergei patted Natina on the head. He kept his "I'm very happy" face while looking up at Nexxa, then said, "Let's eat!"

"You are so happy," Ankica spoke with a big dollop of her Russian accent.

"I am. I spent the night with my lovely Nexxa."

"Um, Sergei." Nexxa pulled at the top of her dress.

"Guess what we did?"

"I know you are going to tell me. But I already know."

Nexxa tilted her head down with her hand slightly covering her face. She moved her finger gently across her eyebrow. Sergei made two plates of food, asking, "Kolbasa?" as he held a plate over the pan on the stove with the sausages.

"Yeah, yeah," Nexxa responded, thinking about how she told him she didn't come to Russia to shop, how the *Sin of Lust* took over.

"We went to Tsum and then to the restaurant."

"It's all very nice." Nexxa smiled at his babushka.

"And then we went," Sergei paused to grin at Nexxa, "and spent the night together at the Ararat."

"Dear, I sleep like the Russian brown bear."

"She does," piped in Sergei.

"You don't have to worry about me. You can sleep in the room with Sergei."

"Oh, no, I couldn't." Nexxa looked from Sergei to Ankica. "I mean, I understand, we aren't married."

"Except when I get up with baby Natina." Ankica winked.

"See, she likes you. She made a joke," Sergei commented, wiping up his plate with a piece of bread. Nexxa wasn't hungry; she only pushed her food with her fork.

"Eat more." Ankica handed Nexxa a platter with kolbasa and fried eggs on it. "Here, put more."

"Okay." Nexxa imagined—she tried not to—Sergei's penis. She told herself to eat so her head was clear, so she could call her office and check on Iliada again.

Sergei stood from his barstool, moving behind Nexxa, rubbing her shoulders. He leaned into her, telling her to relax. Nexxa wanted to relax. Not now, she couldn't.

There was a thud, and the baby started to cry from bumping her head on a lower cabinet. Ankica was washing pans. "I can get her." Nexxa leapt out of her barstool and hurried to baby Natina, picking her up. She hushed her, kissing her forehead.

Sergei walked over to Nexxa. "I need to go to make a call," he said and kissed her on the mouth. Nexxa nodded with acknowledgment and started to bounce the baby.

"Maybe I could take her to her nursery and rock her if that's okay?"

Ankica agreed. "I will make her bottle."

With baby Natina and her bottle, Nexxa headed to her nursery. She passed by Sergei's office, hearing him on the phone. The stairs were easy to walk, easy to carry the baby she kept ending up with in her arms. She thought about what Sergei had said about staying with him in Russia. She liked being there with his family, but she had a life in New York and her sister.

"Hoolihane, tell me something."

"Man, I sent you the missing footage I found."

"And?"

"Well, you tell me. Did you get my email?"

"Watching now."

Sergei watched the video Hoolihane emailed him. He could see a man in his backyard. His first inclination was that it was a daring punk of a thief. The video ended with the unidentified prowler disappearing off into the woods. But then he thought about his conversation with Nahil, the owner of the lingerie boutique in Beirut. Her comment, *It is something else with her*, regarding Nexxa's abduction. The champagne delivered to his hotel suite last night, which he did not order nor was complimentary, was even more bothersome now.

"You there, man?" asked Hoolihane.

"Yeah, yeah. Hoolihane, I need something else."

"I thought you would."

"Nexxa Davoren. From New York. Works in finance. I want the usual."

"I'll get back to you."

Nexxa sat rocking the baby in her nursery. Natina sucked down her bottle quickly. "Sweet, sweet baby girl, sweet, sweet baby girl," she sang, soothing her to sleep. Nexxa took the bottle out of her mouth and placed it on the table by the rocking chair. Resting her eyes, she continued to rock, holding baby Natina.

"Nexxa," Sergei wasn't quiet.

Nexxa opened her eyes and saw Sergei standing in the doorway. Nexxa held a finger close to her mouth, shushing. He motioned with his eyes to the crib. She carefully stood, cautious not to wake the baby, laying her in her bed. Sergei came behind Nexxa as she stood by the crib, covering Natina with a blanket. Putting one hand on her abdomen, he pulled her toward him. Nexxa leaned her head onto his shoulder; he kissed her neck, spinning her around. Sergei took Nexxa's hand, saying nothing, and led her to the sitting area between the bedrooms. Sergei told her to sit. Nexxa sat in an armchair, her hands together between her crossed legs.

"I have a surprise for you tonight."

MERCEDES BENZ FASHION WEEK

MOSCOW — OCTOBER 10, 2013

With a nod, they breezed past security, and Nexxa knew this was her type of affair. "This is for you," Sergei said as he stopped and embraced her with a kiss. A glare came from a dark-skinned show attendant clad in a leopard print dress, but Nexxa brushed it off. Sergei declined the request for photos from local paparazzi and led Nexxa by hand to the lounge. They seated themselves, and with enthusiasm, Sergei insisted that Nexxa try an infused vodka shot. She initially said no, immediately changing her mind. As Nexxa drank the shot, *pickle-flavored*, she laughed, thinking about how her sister would like that flavor.

"Now, I'll have pickle breath."

"Let me see."

"No, no, I'm not—" Nexxa tried to cover her mouth.

Sergei gave her a peck on the lips. Nexxa felt relieved; it was only a peck. He smiled at her, then he overpoweringly kissed her.

"Just a tad." He looked even sexier when he was flirtatious. "Did I tell you, you look beautiful tonight?"

"Thank you. I can't believe how great it fits." Nexxa ran her hand over her lap, feeling the black metallic jacquard A-line dress she borrowed from Sergei's babushka. Ankica had overheard Nexxa tell Sergei that she couldn't allow him to buy her anything else. "Come, come, you try. I have something. I've had it since the fifties," she had demanded. She even insisted Nexxa use her red nail polish. Nexxa wore a vintage dress amongst many modern, sexily clad women, but her borrowed dress was momentous, a cherished memory made in Nexxa's new Russian history.

Sergei leaned into Nexxa, holding her hand. He had a way of looking at her like he was going to propose. "Ready for some champagne?"

"Absolutely," Nexxa affirmed.

"Be right back."

Nexxa looked around the lounge, creating a profile for each person she saw. Her innate propensity was never gone. Nexxa forcefully blinked her eyes; she told herself to stop. *Stop and enjoy yourself.* Sergei returned with two glasses of champagne.

They had front-row seats for Nexxa's first experience attending a fashion show. It was easy to feel lifted by the music. Sergei kept his arm around her, kissing her occasionally on her neck. The collection worn by the runway models was enchanting, depending on what your mind believed. *Kikimora*, Nexxa concluded, as a sheer black dress exposing breasts flanked with

French white lace draping from the shoulders made its debut on the runway.

"Torturing them with desire," Nexxa whispered to herself.

"What's that?"

"Oh, nothing."

When the finale came with a wedding dress, Sergei took his arm away from Nexxa and grasped her hand. Turning her hand, he ran his finger along her ring finger. In her mind she heard Sergei's voice—from the first time at the Beirut Horse Track.

Backstage Sergei introduced Nexxa to Ella, the designer of the collection they had just viewed. Ella reminded Nexxa of Sergei's babushka, maybe how his grandmother might have been in her younger years. Their encounter with Ella was brief since reporters were biding for Ella's time. Leaving the venue, Nexxa told Sergei she needed to use the ladies' room.

"Do you blow him? Oh yeah, I bet you suck his dick." Nexxa wiped, flushed, and quickly adjusted her dress. She assumed the woman in the next stall was on the phone with a friend—having an outlandish conversation. The first pump she tried didn't have soap. Nexxa ran her hands under the faucet. The water almost burned her hands. More vulgarities were accompanied by banging on the stall door. Nexxa reached for a paper towel. She noticed what looked like a blonde hair extension on the counter. Then, when a hair extension flew over the stall door, Nexxa decided her hands were clean enough. She left, shaking her hands dry.

MOSCOW — OCTOBER 10, 2013

"You ready for bed?" Sergei asked with *I'm going to fuck you* eyes.

"Sure, I'll just go to my room." Nexxa twirled her hand, pointing toward the guest room.

"You fucking... turn me on." Sergei grabbed Nexxa and lifted her onto his dresser. He reached behind her, unzipped her dress, and pulled the top of it down. Caressing her breasts, he pressed his face against her body, quivering in her essence. Nexxa lifted his head, pulling him up to her mouth to kiss him as Sergei glided his hand down her inner thigh, gently stroking.

"I'm going to shower now." She heard Sergei speak, but her mind wandered to something someone once told her about staying balanced, all things in moderation. Sergei stood back from Nexxa and took off his top, then unzipped his jeans, taking them off. His black boxer briefs brandished his penis.

"Mmm." Nexxa forgot about staying balanced, all things in moderation, as he took off his briefs. He stepped up to her and put his hands on her breasts while he overpoweringly kissed her, pushing her against the wall. With the gentle force of his muscular arms, he pulled her back to him, seductively biting the side of her neck. He held out her arm; Nexxa slipped off the dresser and let her dress fall off her, and he led her to his ensuite.

Sergei stepped into the shower, turned on the water, and extended his arm to Nexxa. She stepped in, and he pulled her into the water next to him. Nexxa turned her back to him, taking out the hairpin she had holding her hair in a French twist. Sergei gently moved his hands through her blonde locks as she leaned back, wetting her hair. Nexxa faced him and knelt on the tile. With the water falling on her, she kissed his right foot, then his left. Moving up on her knees, she kissed along his thigh while moving one hand onto his testicles, massaging them.

Nexxa moved her mouth further, water still falling upon her face until she reached, licking the underside of his penis. She positioned her lips around his engorged penis, sucking the ridge first, then sucking deep.

"Mmm," Sergei breathed. *God, yes, God,* he thought, bending his knees. Before climaxing, he withdrew his penis from her mouth and positioned her on the tiled bench, wiping water from her face. Now, the Russian propped a leg beside her, moving his erection between her breasts. Sergei moved his leg down, wiping the shower water on his face. Kneeling before her, he lifted each of her feet one at a time, kissing them, saying, "*I ya tebya lyublyu.*" And kissing each thigh, he said, "*I ya tebya lyublyu,*" and kissing each of her breasts, he said, "*I ya tebya lyublyu.*"

Sergei stood and turned off the water. He took ahold of Nexxa's hands. "I want to take you to my bed." He stepped out of the shower and grabbed a towel. His penis still erect, he wiped his face and then gently patted Nexxa's face. Sergei lifted her in his arms like a husband carries his wife over the threshold and brought her to his bed.

Nexxa watched as he poured himself a Scotch whisky. He took a sip and set his glass down on the nightstand. "Let me have a sip." Sergei lifted his glass and handed it to Nexxa. She took a sip; some Scotch dripped between her breasts and trickled down to her stomach.

Sergei pushed Nexxa back and licked the Scotch from her breasts to her stomach. "I want to taste you so bad," he moaned down to her vagina as he parted her labia, licking.

"I want you to sit on my face," he breathed. Sergei moved to the top of the bed, lying down. Nexxa turned over and positioned herself over his face. "Don't hold back," he said as Nexxa rested her hands on the headboard. "Mmm, mmm," Sergei moaned. His cologne wafted with a feeling that it was inside her body as she felt the stubble on his face against her thighs.

"Oh, god! Sergei." Nexxa breathed heavily, moving off of his face. She wanted to ask him if she tasted okay, but Sergei reached for his glass, had a taste of his Scotch, and moved her back onto his face. His tongue and the warmth from the Scotch brought her to an orgasm. "Sergei," she said, breathless. "Sergei, I can't anymore," she cried as she moved off of him. Nexxa lay beside him; she held her chest. Sergei moved on top of her, and his erect penis grazed her thigh. She whispered his name—he inserted himself into her. He tenderly kissed her between thrusts, eventually moving his hand under her body, pushing his penis deeper.

Sergei climaxed, ejaculating inside her, and kissed her on her forehead. He rested on top of her, breathing deeply into her neck. Nexxa glided her hand across his back as she tried to catch her breath, wondering what would happen with them.

"I want you to stay with me," Sergei breathed before turning to lie on his back. Nexxa turned on her side, kissing Sergei on his chest and then on his lips before lying back again.

Sergei grabbed the TV remote and changed the channel to a football game, lowering the volume to almost mute. Nexxa lay pretending to be asleep. The house was quiet, she was warm, and there wasn't anything else she wanted. When she heard Sergei snoring lightly, she let herself go to sleep.

Without warning, the daytime was there, and she remembered her responsibilities. They were seven hours ahead of New York. Yet her new normal had become the time where she was now, in Moscow with the Russian. Sergei rolled over and put his arm over her.

"Sergei, I need to call my office today."

Sergei turned over to his nightstand and looked at the time on his phone. "It's about three a.m. there."

"I don't even know what to say."

"Well, you have about three to four hours to think about it." He repositioned in bed, pulling Nexxa tight under his grasp. She didn't even mind that the sports channel was still on TV.

His touch eased her worry, convincing her to stay in bed. After sleeping another few hours, Nexxa moved Sergei's arm from her, trying to sneak out of bed.

"Where are you going?"

"I've reached my max with how long I can go without brushing my teeth."

He took a breath and rolled over on his back. Nexxa found her panties and slipped them on. She lifted the dress his babushka had lent her; she slipped that on too. Sergei lay seemingly content, so she left his room. Kind of a trek to get to the guest room, but Nexxa liked having her *own* bathroom. She brushed her teeth, flossed, then rolled her stiff neck around. Looking in the bathroom mirror, Nexxa recalled the vulgar woman she heard in the ladies' room at Mercedes Benz Fashion Week. Her mind was stopped as though by a directive when she heard Sergei knock on the bedroom door.

"Nexxa, come with me," Sergei hollered from the doorway.

Sergei walked Nexxa downstairs to his office. When he opened the door, Nexxa saw several computer monitors. "Come over here," Sergei insisted as Nexxa stood at the entrance of his office. Nexxa walked over to his desk; her eyes widened, seeing he had a Bloomberg Terminal, the leading platform used in the financial industry for traders, analysts, and more.

"You're on Bloomberg?" Nexxa questioned.

"Yes, I have a few financial ventures. Here, you can use mine to contact your company. Smarter than calling."

"Whooo is Carlos Finch?"

"He's standing in front of you," Sergei stated, pointing to himself.

Nexxa agreed, better to be cautious and send a message under his username. Also, she didn't have the device she needed to log in as herself into Bloomberg. So, she initiated an instant Bloomberg message with her boss Dan. It was mid-morning in New York. She typed: My mom has a new book she suggested I read. Perhaps I can tell you about it over dinner. Any new sushi restaurants you would recommend? Nexxa saw that Dan was typing a reply.

"What's that about?" asked Sergei.

"My boss and I sometimes have dinner, discuss what I read."

Sergei nodded his head.

Dan wrote: Oh, that's great to hear. I enjoyed our last discussion. We could check out Satsuki.

Nexxa sighed. "We are good. I'm done."

Sergei's phone was on his desk when it pinged with another text from Hoolihane. He swiped to open the message and then abruptly picked up his phone. He looked up from his phone and smiled at Nexxa.

Hoolihane had investigated Nexxa using her current employer as a start. He enlightened Sergei on the new normal that vulnerabilities were built into devices and that while Nexxa's firm used a Bare Metal Server, it was hackable. Sergei was most surprised by one discovery Hoolihane had made regarding Nexxa. But now wasn't the time to confront her about it.

"I think I will go shower now." Nexxa stepped toward the door.

Sergei grinned.

"*No*, not that kind of shower." Nexxa smiled.

Sergei signed out of his Bloomberg and turned off his

computer monitors. They headed up the stairs, and Nexxa went to the guest room. To her surprise, her leggings, tank top, the thong she handed Sergei which he kept in his jeans on the ferry, and even her socks had been washed and were folded on the bed in the guest room. She undressed and went into the bathroom to shower, where clean towels had been placed on the bathroom vanity. *A beautiful home, financial ventures, a baby niece, a babushka.* Nexxa took account of what she had been experiencing with Sergei, the man who wanted her to stay with him in Russia. She thought about Beirut, China Black Road, Diane, and how events had led her to Sergei. She smiled, but right about when she rinsed the conditioner from her hair, the thought about *how things are good until they're not* came to her mind. Perhaps if she knew more about Sergei, what his financial ventures entailed…

MOSCOW — OCTOBER 11, 2013

Rochelle promised her she would wait in the car. She was very convincing, always believable. "I'll only carry clothes to the front door and straight back to the car." No one understood why Ella remained friends with her, not even Ella herself.

Sergei watched as the white Range Rover emerged in the driveway after he tapped on his security app to open the gate. He failed to notice the woman in the passenger seat; she ducked down, hiding in the boxes she held in her lap. Sergei had Ella, the fashion designer he had introduced Nexxa to, lay out the clothes on his bed. One caught his eye immediately: a white beaded floor-length dress with spaghetti straps in red crystals and a chandelier pattern draping across the exposed back. Ella went downstairs, returned to her Range Rover to get a dress form, and saw that Rochelle wasn't in her car. A billow of smoke greeted Ella from a crouched Rochelle as she approached the back of the SUV.

"What are you doing? You promised to stay in the car. If he sees—"

"What is he doing? What does she look like up close?" quizzed Rochelle.

"No, no, no." Ella exhaled. "You *promised* to be good, Rochelle."

Rochelle flicked her still-lit cigarette and strutted back to the passenger seat of the car. Ella pressed the button on the back and lifted out the dress form, placing it on the ground.

At only five feet tall but over five foot five with her black suede over-the-knee Gianvinto Rossi boots, she teetered across the stone driveway to the front door. Ella plopped the dress form down in the foyer; Sergei told her to leave it there. She could hear Ankica in the kitchen, so she decided to visit with her.

Sergei determined he had time to rinse off in the shower since he hadn't cleaned up before Ella arrived, but before he showered, he sprinted downstairs and grabbed the dress form. "Quick shower," he shouted into the kitchen, looking in the direction of Ella. She nodded in acknowledgment as she was in mid-conversation with Ankica about the drama around the seamstresses that worked with her on her collections. With the dress form, he sprinted up the stairs to his bedroom. Sergei initiated the camera on his security app, showing Nexxa sitting on the bed in the guest room. He smiled, looking at her as he ripped off his tracksuit pants and t-shirt and took a much-needed toilet break before getting into the shower. He didn't want to wash Nexxa off of him but wanted to be presentable when he surprised Nexxa with Ella's couture.

"I'll be out in a minute." He assumed she heard him, but she didn't respond. He reached for one of his Abyss & Habidecor Egyptian bath sheets, a fresh one in deep blue was always waiting for him. Only this time, it was not there. A hand towel was in eyesight and closer than the linen closet. *Can dry my dick with this*, he figured, as he grabbed the hand towel. "Ella, I have to come out. I'm not dressed," Sergei hollered.

The luxury hand towel was held over his sizeable penis as he stepped out of his ensuite to his bedroom. Ella was like a sister, and he couldn't care less if she saw his ass. This moment was one of those situations when he regretted not having his closet connected to his bathroom. Sergei remembered his architect saying, *A small wardrobe to hold a bathrobe*. He didn't see her as he walked to his dresser, so he figured she had left his bedroom.

Nexxa was sure she heard a woman, someone else, in the house. She put down the advert she was looking at from the fashion show and looked toward the bedroom door. Did she smell something familiar? Was she losing it? She exhaled and took her purse from the nightstand, reaching in for her phone to call Iliada again. *Right, no phone*, she realized, knowing she would need to use Sergei's phone again.

Making her way toward Sergei's bedroom, Nexxa heard the woman's voice again, whiny in tone, and Sergei talking in a low decibel to her. She stopped in the sitting room that separated the bedrooms upstairs, standing, silencing her breathing. *He's not talking to his babushka. He has a sister? He is married or has a girlfriend? Well, he brought me here, and if things don't work out...* Nexxa knew she would figure it out even though she didn't have her credit cards, her phone, and that little thing, the finger scanner, that she needed to sign in to Bloomberg; she remembered yet again that she didn't have that. Hair extensions flying over the bathroom stall door from the fashion show came to her mind. Nexxa was never physically intrusive to get answers. She didn't need to be. She just needed a whiff.

Her coffin-shaped nails scratched his testicles as she groped him from behind while he was in the midst of pulling on his underwear. It didn't feel right, yet he expected to see Nexxa's face when he turned around.

"Fucking Rochelle!"

"Can you tell me you love her?" Rochelle's face begged. "Tell me in my eyes."

"How did you get in here?" Sergei's chest swelled. "You know," he lowered his voice, saying, "you are not allowed around me." Sergei pushed her annoying bony body from him and reached for his phone on his bed. Rochelle swiftly plopped down on top of his mobile phone and almost his hand.

Nexxa reached the doorway. Standing with her hand on the lever of the ajar door, she leaned her head back. The scent was the same, the same from the fashion show. Nexxa pushed open the door, and bless her, Rochelle, she was trying to smile playfully, but her wicked long Yalorde lashes made her look like a drag queen.

"I love you, Sergei." Rochelle continued in her *fake* needy voice, "Why did you push me away?" Nexxa played spectator, smelling, at an unaware Sergei and an unaware Rochelle.

"Get off my phone." Sergei's voice was calm with a hint of sternness.

"Tell me you still love me!" insisted Rochelle as she wriggled on Sergei's bed.

"Rochelle, I *can't* say that since I *never* loved you!"

Sergei stood in a pair of black boxer briefs before a still-sitting Rochelle. She reached for his groin. Nexxa gasped. Sergei turned. "Nexxa," he called to her.

Suddenly, as if she were no longer trying to hatch an egg, Rochelle lifted off Sergei's phone. "This is her?" she asked, stroking her dark purple nails through her disastrous blonde hair extensions. Rochelle strode her lanky body toward Nexxa with her exaggerated puffy lips and spider eyes. "Let me tell you the truth about him."

Nexxa was eager to hear from the woman standing before her, from the woman she encountered in the bathroom at the fashion show talking about sucking a dick and pulling her hair out. Looking past Rochelle, Nexxa saw Sergei pulling on his tracksuit pants and doing something on his phone. She wondered what his next move was going to be. Nexxa wanted to leave, but she kind of wanted to play with crazy.

"Maybe we should have some wine."

Nexxa's suggestion elicited a smile—if you could call it that—from Rochelle. Nexxa had seen her type before, different looking. Rochelle was well over six feet tall with her heels on, but the same kind of schizo.

Sergei motioned with his head toward Rochelle as Bogdan, who looked like the first human ever created, not very tall but stocky, entered his bedroom. Rochelle started shaking her head like a toddler as Bogdan approached her. He didn't even put a hand on her body before she began stomping toward the bedroom entrance. Sergei held his eyes on Nexxa, concerned about her reaction. Nexxa kept her eyes on Rochelle, noticing the "Sergei" tattoo on her abdomen, visible because she was wearing a crop top. They both remained still as they listened to Rochelle forcing a cry, repeating, "Sergei's mine," while she was escorted down the stairs.

"I have something for you," Sergei said as he pulled on a shirt.

"What?" Nexxa muttered just as an uncontrollable rush of emotion hit her. "Okay," she swallowed, trying to hold back from crying.

Sergei walked over to Nexxa. "I hope you're not worried about anything," he said, embracing her. "She's followed me a few times."

"Who was that man?"

"He works for me."

Nexxa pulled back from Sergei's grasp. "Where did he come from? Where did that *woman* come from?" Sergei gave no further explanation. With his eyes, he looked over at the dress on the dress form. Nexxa moved her gaze to it as well.

He smiled. "I was going to surprise you."

Nexxa didn't respond.

"Try it on," Sergei insisted.

"I don't—" Nexxa stood, grasping her hands together then letting them go. The image of the woman reaching for his groin flashed in her mind. "I'm not in the mood."

"You want to go for a walk?"

"Well…" Nexxa finally let out a breath. "Okay."

"I feel like I need to be in the forest, see my trees."

CRYPT CHIC

MOSCOW — OCTOBER 11, 2013

The very tips of the trees held up the overcast sky moving in as they walked further. "So, are these *your* trees?" Nexxa teased Sergei. He gave a half-smile, half chuckle.

"*Actually*, they are."

"Literally?" Nexxa looked up, noticing the tops of the trees. "This is your land too?"

"Yes."

Sergei chose the left at the prominent divide in the path, leading them to a traditional old-style izba painted grass green. The windows were decorated with white wood carvings, and a satellite dish was mounted on the front of the cottage by the door. Bogdan emerged with a smile that was only just big enough to show he had teeth on top of teeth. He still looked to Nexxa like our Creator's rough draft of the human species. With his mangled smile, he motioned for them to come inside. Nexxa took one step and stopped. *Is this where he took that woman with the Sergei tattoo and bad hair extensions?* Sergei put his hand on her lower back. "He wants to give you something," he assured her. Nexxa looked at Sergei and then back to Bogdan. She might have taken a whiff before deciding to step inside the quaint Russian home.

Inside, a football game was playing on the flat-screen TV. After he closed the door, she watched as Bogdan pried something from overhead. Nexxa wanted to ask Sergei what in the world Bogdan was doing, but Sergei was already involved in the game on the television, and then he handed her something. It was a gold Mezuzah case with glass covering the hand-painted scene of a windmill by a river. Three stars were at the bottom and the Hebrew letter Shin adorned the top. His weathered hands spoke for him, motioning for her to turn it over. Bogdan pulled the back off and took out the paper that was folded inside it. The Traveler's Prayer was inscribed on it. "For keep you safe. Safe travel." Nexxa shook her head as she let a few tears flow to the edge of her high cheekbones. She held the gift with one hand and wiped her tears with the other before another awkward smile came from Bogdan when he grasped her hands. She knew she would never forsake his kind gesture.

Sergei took his gaze from the game on the TV and looked over to Bogdan, giving him a nod. With excitement, Bogdan pointed to the corner across the room, "Ah, the Hi-Fi work!" he said.

"The Wi-Fi," Sergei corrected him with a connotation reminiscent of a proper Brit, while keeping his eyes on the game.

"Hi-Fi," Nexxa laughed, looking to Sergei when Bogdan

walked across the room. Sergei smirked, looking down, shaking his head side to side.

"Alright, Bogdan, we are going to head out."

Bogdan let out a gruff as he stood up from putting another piece of firewood into the Russian stove. He fumbled around with something, then, saying nothing, stretched out his short but muscular arms; each held a tattered woven bag.

"Oh, okay." Nexxa reluctantly reached for the bags. "*Spasiba.*"

The aspen trees had already begun to change from green to shades of golden. Nexxa opened her hand and ran her fingers over the Mezuzah.

"I have something to show you."

"Will I feel pleasantly or unpleasantly surprised?" Nexxa flashed her flirtatious smile.

"Miss Ballou," Sergei addressed her by her maiden name.

Nexxa paused her step. Impressed. A little scared.

"Come." Sergei reached his hand out. Nexxa relaxed her shoulders as he took hold of her left hand, her right still holding the kind offering from Bogdan. They walked further down the path into a mix of larch, aspen, and spruce trees. A clearing in the woods exposed walled hedges connected with a tall, black, ornate wrought iron gate. Sergei once again used his phone, and the gate opened, revealing a quaint cemetery. Sergei placed the bags Bogdan gave them on the stone bench and knelt by a tombstone. Nexxa read the names: Kristoff Kozlov and Vera Markoff Kozlov. She realized that at one time, there were these great people who came together and created Sergei.

Sergei made the sign of the cross and kissed his thumb on his closed hand. He took out a corked bottle from the first bag and set it down on the bench and took some wrapped food from the other.

"He bakes too," remarked Sergei as he pulled out two treats. "It's a Russian tradition to visit the graveside of our ancestors, usually on the holidays." He handed the bottle to Nexxa. "And you drink and have some food. These are Russian—"

"I know. I mean, they are Russian tea cakes." Nexxa took a bite and held her other hand under to catch any crumbs. "My mom used to make these at Christmastime."

"She did?" Sergei gave a look of surprise.

"Yeah, I always looked forward to them, more than other holiday treats." Nexxa glanced over at the crypt that looked to be modeled after Sergei's home. The crypt was set off to the side with a pathway leading there from where they were sitting in front of Sergei's parents' grave. The crypt pulled, and Nexxa turned.

"You want to see?"

"Yeah." Nexxa felt the pull. "Yes, I would like to."

Sergei stood, motioning for her to follow. Nexxa laughed when, once again, he used his phone to open the crypt's door.

"Just a sec," Sergei tapped on his phone, continuing, "lights!" Fascinatingly, the bronze vintage candelabra sconces behind the romantic burgundy velvet couch illuminated. Two black round tables flanked the sofa.

"Crypt chic," Nexxa said under her breath.

"What was that?"

Nexxa touched her hair, repeating herself, "Crypt chic."

"So, you like it?"

"Of course." Nexxa's eyes showed her Vampy approval.

"I designed it after this hotel in Paris."

"Oh." Nexxa tilted her head.

"Hôtel Costes. Have you heard of it?"

"Uh-huh." Nexxa nodded. Quinn was right there, in her mind. What *could* have been. She remembered how good Quinn smelled and how nervous she had been when she went to his house in Dublin. If Kilmer had not blown their operation in Paris in Hôtel Costes, would she still know Quinn all these years later?

"The furniture is from the Golden Age—Louis the Fifteenth, I believe."

Nexxa could hear Sergei talking. Her eyes moved around the crypt, but she was lost in thought. Sergei lifted a box from the ledge under the window and struck a match. Nexxa was brought back to her new time in Moscow. Sergei lit the candles on the tables. Nexxa leaned over and blew. The match was out.

"Have a seat."

Nexxa sat. She shivered and held out her hands to the flame of a candle.

"You cold?" Sergei asked while opening a chest on the buffet-style table that was in the place of a coffin.

"A little."

Sergei blew into each of the two chalices, then wiped them out with the hem of his long sleeve marled grey t-shirt. "This should warm you up from the inside." He poured some of the homemade wine into the red chalices. He turned, smiling. "Until something else is inside you." He sat beside Nexxa on the Louis the Fifteenth-era sofa, handing her a glass. Nexxa took a sip, then another. She rubbed her lips together, moving around what was left of her lip gloss.

"I wish I had my lip gloss. My lips feel dry."

Sergei placed his glass on the table in front of them. He licked his finger and ran it over her bottom lip, which triggered her reflex to close her eyes. The wind blew, moving the black lace curtain over the only window in the crypt. The sound his phone made when a text came through startled her from the moment.

"What now?" Sergei sighed as he pulled his phone from the pocket of his tracksuit pants and entered his passcode. He looked at the message.

Ella: *Sorry, I told Rochelle to stay in the car.*

Sergei: *She needs psychiatric help!*

Sergei returned the phone to his pocket.

"Everything okay?"

"Yeah."

Nexxa looked down at Sergei's crotch. She cupped his groin and then slowly moved her hand under his waistband. Warm, and his penis was becoming hard. She maneuvered her hand underneath his boxer briefs and slithered her fingers along his penis for a few seconds before taking her hand back. "Thank you." She dabbed her top lip. "All better now." Sergei grabbed her hand, letting her finger slide down, holding her bottom lip, then gliding down her chin.

"Your pre-ejaculate is moisturizing," Nexxa said. "*Spasiba.*"

His grip was tight on her wrist; it didn't hurt but was uncomfortable as the Russian moved her hand in his pants to his growing erection. At first, she stroked him as he pleased. When she abruptly let go, standing up, Sergei stood and held her face, breathing heavily as he kissed her and muttered, "I'm sorry, sorry, my love." Nexxa pulled out of his grip, out of his kiss. Sergei looked her in the eyes as he pulled down her tank top, exposing her breasts. She wanted his gentle roughness; her eyes told him yes.

Nexxa shivered as his sultry mouth moved along her breasts. Quivering, Sergei took a few deep breaths. Nexxa caressed his head asking, "What are we doing?" He pulled his tracksuit pants down and stroked his penis. Nexxa bent over and untied her sneakers. She slipped them off along with her leggings while Sergei positioned himself on the sofa.

Sitting, with wide legs, he said, "Nexxa, come sit on me." Nexxa stepped toward him and lifted her right leg, propping her foot on the sofa. She slipped her hand into her panties. So… the Russian pulled Nexxa onto his lap, moving her thong to the side and inserting his well-endowed dick. He gripped her hips, moving her up and down.

Sergei's foot bumped the table; a candle wobbled before falling over. It was extinguished. Nexxa leaned her head down into Sergei while still holding onto his shoulders, kissing him on his neck. "Sergei," she breathed.

He stopped thrusting. "Mmm, mmm," he moaned. Nexxa lifted off of him, moving onto the sofa. When she pulled her thong back over, she felt wetness. She stood from the sofa, looking at her fingers moving closer to the still-flaming candle on the other table.

"Is that blood?"

"Oh. Yeah, it's—"

"Was it too much?" asked Sergei.

"You mean too hard?"

"Yeah."

"Sergei…" Nexxa turned, looking at him. "I guess it's that time of the month." Looking down, Nexxa wiped the blood from her hand on her thigh.

Sergei licked his fingers and rubbed the spot on her leg where she wiped the blood. That one gesture, that moment, she had no feeling to describe it.

Nexxa resisted, lying back on the sofa before she felt his stubble on her thigh. "Sergei, no, you can't."

"I'm only—lie back."

She gave in and did as his voice spoke. His tongue twirled her clitoris. Nexxa caressed his head. So… *once in a crypt*, Sergei earned his Red Wings.

Nexxa dressed and drank the rest of the wine in her chalice. It was Sergei's chalice, but that was okay. She swallowed the wine in the other one too.

"I guess we should get back," Nexxa told Sergei.

"Yeah?"

"Yeah," Nexxa responded with her sexy humor, "we're out of wine."

Grinning, Sergei agreed, "Then I guess we better."

MOSCOW — OCTOBER 11, 2013

Sergei pulled the door to the crypt. "He recruited you," he said and the door closed firmly.

"What?" Nexxa looked to Sergei while he locked the crypt using the app on his phone.

"Patrick. You trained in Ireland. Before this, though, there was the Indian, whom you trained with."

Nexxa noticed a cloud vigorously move away just as her chest tightened.

"You immigrated to New York," he continued as he looked her straight on, took her hand, and proceeded to lead them out of the cemetery. "Your career in finance began with Van Bauer." Another cloud moved away, making room for the next grim-hued puff in the sky. "Kilmer," Sergei paused, looking at his phone to lock the gate, "the one you married, and you left."

Nexxa felt her body temperature drop. She gave one more

look over her shoulder to his parents' grave. *Where is he going with this information? Why and how does he know all this about me? No one knows this.* "What is this?" she asked as she let go of the Russian's hand.

"I don't mind you were married," continued Sergei as they walked.

The loneliness she believed she had chased away in Brooklyn with a Santería love potion came to the surface. *It does sound like he minds. Is it time for an exit plan? No, why would I leave Sergei?*

"So, then, what is it that you are doing?" Nexxa reached to her temple; the pain was sharp as her words came out. The walk back was a blur.

Sergei stopped as they approached the back of his house. "I asked you to stay with me here in Russia."

With her hands on her hips, Nexxa exhaled, "Yeah."

Sergei's phone vibrated. Then again. And again. He looked at his messages, then looked up at Nexxa. "Let's go inside." She heard the seriousness in his voice. She thought about what happened in the crypt as she followed him up the stairs that led to the terrace connected to his bedroom.

"I need to make a call." Sergei walked over to his leather armchairs.

"Sergei, I need to go to a drugstore. I need to—" She saw he was already on a call. Nexxa lowered her head, touching her brow. "—Get tampons." Sergei turned back, nodding at her.

Nexxa didn't hear a word of his phone call since she was obsessing over the conversation they had on the walk back from the cemetery. Him going down on her, mmm, that was great, and bam, now asking him to take her to get tampons. Nexxa felt dirty—she felt exposed. Why had he looked into her past? Now embarrassed, the idea of leaving Moscow crossed her mind.

After ending his call, Sergei returned his phone to his pocket and asked, "Are those the ones that go inside or stick to your panties? I can go to the store for you."

Nexxa was jolted from her mind rolling. She closed her eyes and put her hand over her forehead. She took a breath before looking at him. "Tampons go *into* the vagina. So, the ones that go… inside."

"Okay, anything else?"

Yeah, a blanket to hide under. No, don't say that. "No, I just need to go clean up again." Nexxa thanked Sergei, and he smiled.

She heard plastic bags rustling but hadn't heard the bathroom door open.

"I'm back," announced Sergei as he placed the bags on the vanity.

"Okay."

"I got what you needed from the store."

"Okay." Nexxa stood in the shower with her back to Sergei. "Thank you."

"I got you," Sergei stalled, looking in one of the bags, "some that are organic and some other things too," he explained.

"That's nice, thank you."

"You know you could have showered in my room," Sergei announced while leaving the bathroom.

Nexxa practiced what she would say as she opened the glass

door from the shower, stepping onto the plush bathmat. "Sergei, how do you know those things about me? Or say, like, did you do a background check on me?" She lifted the box of tampons he had left on the bathroom vanity; reading the label, she determined they were the right size.

"Oh." Nexxa stopped suddenly as she walked into the bedroom, seeing Sergei in her room sitting on the bed. "You are here." She stood there in just a towel and a thing that you "stick inside."

Sergei had checked the lock on the bedroom terrace door, ensuring the locking mechanism was working and that the room was secure. He had determined that the prowler that had been snooping around on his property wearing a black mask and clad in all black with blonde hair was likely Rochelle by zooming in on the video footage; her coffin-shaped nails with tacky jewels gave off a glare. Rochelle knew his car and the places he frequented from her days stalking him. Given that, he assumed Rochelle was the one who sent him champagne the evening he spent with Nexxa at the Ararat.

"Sergei, so I have to ask. I mean, what is this?"

"What is what?"

"You know about my marriage?" Nexxa motioned with her right hand, palm up. "About Thomas?"

"Yes." Sergei stood from the bed. "I know."

"You know what exactly? That I was in an awful marriage?" Nexxa adjusted the towel around her. "That, that Thomas helped raise my sister and me? Since, like, our dad wasn't around? Is that what you know?" She really didn't want him to answer. Saying parts, significant parts, of her life out loud seemed awful.

At that moment, she missed Thomas and her sister, doubting why she was there with Sergei.

"I need to call my sister."

Sergei maneuvered his hand in his pocket.

"Can I have your phone to call her?" Nexxa asked.

"I—" Sergei held out his phone.

"What?" Nexxa interrupted him. "What is it now?"

"The other thing." He could tell she was irritated. He didn't want her worrying. But there was more.

"What *other* thing?" Nexxa let her towel fall. "Something else you know about me?" Worked up, she forgot the little white string hanging between her toned thighs. She walked over to the dresser, opened a drawer, and chose a pair of panties from the few that she had. She slipped them on.

Sergei placed his phone on the dresser. "It is okay." He pulled her into him, rubbing her arms. "You will see; it will all work out."

That was all it took for Nexxa, feeling her breasts next to his chest and inhaling his skin. She heard more of his Russian accent at that moment. Perhaps she had ignored it before. He kissed her on her forehead, and she smiled. Nexxa pulled on a tank top, no bra, and Sergei ran his finger over her nipple through her shirt. She wondered if he knew he could invoke her desire to fuck that easy.

"Here." Sergei pulled a box out of his other pocket. "I have something for you." Nexxa opened the worn leather box. She tried the ring on her right hand. He shook his head, indicating no. "It would turn pale under light if you were in the wrong place." Keeping a solemn face, he removed the ring and put it on her left-hand ring finger. Nexxa stared at the ring on her finger, an oval-shaped ruby in an antique rose gold setting.

"I want you to have it."

"I don't understand." Nexxa looked down, fidgeting with the ring.

"It belonged to my mother." Sergei had always planned, hoped, to give the ring to someone he cared for one day. Sergei lifted her chin. "This is the *other* thing."

Nexxa didn't know whether to cry or kiss him. On tippy-toes, Nexxa kissed Sergei.

"My brother, Demo, he is in Rome. Yeah, he texted me that he is there now. Doing some play."

Nexxa pulled on her leggings. Her stomach growled. "Wow," she said as she held her stomach.

"Hungry for Roman food?"

"Maybe," she laughed, allowing her shoulders to slouch; it had been an intense day.

"Let's see what we've got. You know I can cook."

Nexxa nodded and said, "Uh-huh," but she didn't believe him.

It was past sundown and just the light over the sink was on in the kitchen. Sergei opened a cabinet or two, then pulled out a pot. Filling it with water, he started to hum. "I'm going to make you the best pasta you've had all day." He grinned.

Nexxa looked around the kitchen. It was spotless. She felt terrible that they were, well, that Sergei would more than likely make a big mess.

"How does your grandmother, babushka, do it all?" Nexxa looked at the baby bottles on the drying rack. "I mean, take care of the baby," she continued while pointing at the baby's formula on the counter.

"She's a very strong woman. My babushka."

"Yeah, but this house is huge, and cooking, laundry, the *baby*."

"I offered to get a nanny. A housekeeper full time."

Nexxa nodded her head looking, thinking, *Yeah, a housekeeper for sure.*

The water in the large stockpot reached a rapid boil, and Sergei dropped in the spaghetti. He popped open a jar of sauce and poured it into a saucepan. Nexxa's stomach growled again when Sergei poured some red wine for her. She took a sip and looked at the ruby on her finger. Then Rochelle came to her mind.

"Sergei, that woman. Rochelle. So why was she even here today?"

"I don't want to talk about that."

"No, really, I want to know. We just kind of rushed off. For a walk."

He stirred the sauce, tasting it. "You wanna taste?"

"No, I, I want to know who she is. She said something about loving you."

"She followed me a few times. After we dated."

"You *dated* her? Like as in *girlfriend*?"

"No, girlfriend, no. I took her to an event once. Ella, the designer I sponsor, she is her friend."

"So, she stalks you? Should I be worried?"

"No, it's not a problem." Sergei drained the pasta and plated them each some. "Let's eat!"

They could hear baby Natina whining on the baby monitor

in the kitchen. After a few minutes, they heard the sound of shushing from his babushka.

"So, your brother is in Rome?"

"Uh-huh." Sergei was really into his pasta and didn't elaborate.

Nexxa watched Sergei, how he slurped a few times. Perhaps, no, she knew this was the only bad thing about him. She forced herself to take one bite after another. What was he thinking? What wasn't he telling her? Her sister was in Rome, and now she knew his brother was in Rome. They were in Russia with a Carlos Finch and a Rochelle. A Bogdan too. The Beirut crew, most importantly Faroud. How did all this fit together? Nexxa dabbed her mouth with a napkin and took their plates. "I'll wash these."

Sergei leaned back in his barstool, turning the barstool next to him to put his legs up.

Nexxa washed the pots they used as well. She couldn't bear the idea of leaving dirty dishes in the kitchen. When she finished, she saw Sergei had closed his eyes. *Finally, the Russian bear sleeps*, she told herself.

"Sergei," Nexxa tenderly said while caressing his back. He opened his eyes and, one leg at a time, put his feet down from the barstool and stood. He stretched and yawned. His eyes locked onto Nexxa. His facial scruff pressed against her neck as he taunted her with each bite. Her blonde locks pulled on his stubble as he made his way to kissing her slightly wine-stained lips. She hated to, but she reminded him it was her time of the month.

"Okay, okay," Sergei said through another yawn.

"Come on, let's go to bed."

Nexxa had the hand adorned by the ruby ring on Sergei's back while she leaned into his shoulder, walking to his bedroom. He sat on his bed, rubbing his head. Nexxa came to him and kneeled, slipping off his socks. Then she motioned for him to lie down, and she pulled his tracksuit pants off. He wasn't too tired to smile.

MOSCOW — OCTOBER 12, 2013

The day before was extraordinary. It seemed like a propaganda-inspired dream from watching several intense streamed TV series. Firstly, Rochelle and a man with overly abundant teeth. Then a Judaic gift, a crypt, a background check, and a ruby ring followed by pasta.

The brightness woke her. She sat straight in bed. *It's probably time to get ready for work*, she told herself, but it seemed too dark for the morning, and then she realized where she was. It was the tablet on the nightstand that was emitting the bright light. Nexxa pushed the covers off her and walked over to Sergei's side of the bed. She swiped her finger across the tablet in different directions, trying to turn it off. He was facing the opposite way, so it failed to wake him. Nexxa realized that the tablet must have run an update, and when it came back, the prompt to "set up a passcode" was visible. She selected to bypass. She could feel her heart constricting as she did it, but she just needed to know something, anything that perhaps Sergei wasn't telling her. She saw a shortcut for a video. Tapping on it, she leaned in closer, peering at the screen then glancing at Sergei.

What played was distressing. She saw what made her cover her mouth and gasp; well, if she hadn't gasped, he wouldn't have woken up. But the volume was unintentionally turned up, so, well, that woke him too.

"What?" Sergei muttered, half asleep as he rolled over toward his nightstand. He opened his eyes and reached his hand out toward Nexxa. When she didn't reach for his hand because she felt aghast, Sergei sat up and realized she was watching something on his tablet. He touched the bedside switch to turn on a light. He tapped on the video to stop it. Sergei rubbed his hand over his face, across his head. Nexxa stood from her crouch.

"What the fuck?" That was all she could think to say.

He lowered his head and reached his arms out for her.

"Sergei!"

He knew he had to tell her something; he wasn't going to lose her. Sergei looked up at Nexxa. "I have a thorough security system. A camera in every room."

Nexxa shook her head, saying, "No, no," under her breath.

"Come back to bed."

She tugged at her hair that was pulled back in a ponytail and held her forehead with both hands. She stared at the wall. Then she looked at the other wall. It suddenly hit her that cameras were most likely all over the house.

"Show me footage from my—from the guest room. The guest

bathroom."

Sergei stood up and walked over to the table in the middle of his room that housed his Scotch. He poured, sipped, and set the glass down. Poured, sipped, and placed the glass down again. He poured one last time and carried the glass to the only woman he had ever loved.

"Well, Sergei," Nexxa demanded.

"Take a drink," he insisted.

"If I do, will you show me?"

Sergei nodded. "I was waiting to..." he sighed.

"Waiting to what? I feel like I need to brace myself."

"I want to take you to Rome."

"Rome?" Nexxa took the glass of Scotch and took a sip. "What? Why?" She let out a cough. "Okay, show me now."

Sergei lifted the tablet out of the stand from where it rested on his nightstand. "Sit."

Nexxa watched as Sergei stood in front of her and tapped on his tablet. He held it; she looked up at him, he looked at her, then handed her the tablet. She felt relieved as she watched herself on video. When Sergei showed her around the guest room and bathroom, she fast-forwarded the part of her showering to the part where she walked out onto the terrace. Changing into the dress his babushka lent her to attend the fashion show. Standing with her blonde hair pulled back in a low ponytail, smelling the bouquet in the vase on the dresser. At first look, she thought, *That's me*, then she paused the video and looked at the time and date. She pinched the screen to zoom in—the nails, coffin-shaped with tacky jeweled accents.

Faint, she lowered the tablet to her lap. She could hear Sergei speaking to her but only heard, "One, two, three, four, five, six, and seven." The voice repeated, "One, two, three, four, five." You could hear a bam, then the woman said, "Six!" Nexxa looked down to the video. She saw the woman re-arranging the floral arrangement given to her by Ankica, three pink peonies mixed with four pale peach roses. The woman removed a rose, smashed the bloom with her fist, and left through the terrace door, taking the smashed bloom with her. Sergei understood the Russian superstition behind gifting an even number of flowers, an omen of back luck, or even death.

"Your name won't go on the passenger manifest. I'll arrange a place for you and your sister to stay. My brother Demo, you will stay with him in a villa."

"How could you let me stay here after this?"

Sergei walked to his nightstand. He removed a pack of cigarettes, lighting one. He took a drag. "You think I wouldn't do everything to protect you!"

Nexxa looked down at her nails; a few were already chipping. Sergei's anger blindsided her. She wanted to know what to believe.

"I had a dream recently. I was walking down the hall, and a snake was waiting before your doorway," he said, taking another drag. "The guest bedroom's doorway."

Nexxa placed the tablet on the bed, then she turned to look over at Sergei. A snake, Medan, *two men that intend to do you harm* came to mind. She realized there was so much she still didn't know about the Russian.

He looked angry. "I have men in and around the perimeter of the house," he assured, moving his hand with the cigarette.

Holding her hands out, she said, "But I never saw anyone."

"You're not supposed to."

"Then who is the woman in the video?" Nexxa cleared her throat. "I mean, if you have security, men, how did she get in?"

"She must have..." he stopped, taking another draw from the cigarette. "I have to… I'll find out."

"You have to," Nexxa said. "Is that Rochelle in the video?" Nexxa stood, and with her fingers extended, she grasped the sides of her face. "This is crazy!"

"I told you!" Sergei shouted. Nexxa lowered her face in her hands. Sergei moved closer to Nexxa, extending his arms. "Hey, I'm sorry. Sorry. I told you I'd protect you."

Nexxa sat down on the bed. "My sister," she sighed, gesturing with her hand. "She's already in Rome, so yeah, I guess."

Sergei stood before Nexxa. He leaned his head back and took a deep breath. When he looked down at her, Nexxa reached for his cigarette. She took a drag and handed it back to him. The smoke made her dizzy.

"I'm taking the baby. Your grandmother is tired." Reasons for taking baby Natina flooded her mind. Standing, she explained, "It's, maybe it's not safe now, here, for her."

"Okay." Sergei rubbed his palms together, shifting his weight from leg to leg. He knew where Rochelle was *now*, Psylab; he knew it could have been her that invaded his home—he also knew that the woman's voice in the video seemed odd, something about her muddled Russian accent. "You'll need some baby gear." He smiled.

ROME — OCTOBER 13, 2013

Natina looked good in lavender. She also looked like Nexxa, so told by anyone they encountered.

"Oh my god, this is so good." Iliada smiled like Nexxa remembered as she took a sip from her martini glass.

"Yeah, I never would have thought about using juiced watermelon in a cocktail."

"Oh, she's beautiful; has your eyes," the sophisticated Roman from the next table remarked as she stood from her table and pulled her leashed dog along.

Nexxa and Iliada looked at each other. Nexxa smiled at the lady standing over them, thanking her. Oozing Italian charm, the woman kept smiling at Natina as she walked away, joining a dapper male friend who was walking by.

"Tomorrow, let's do some shopping."

"Okay, yeah." Iliada swiped on her phone. "I went to this street that has a lot of shops, H&M, Puma, and some baby boutiques."

"Yeah, I want to get Natina something. I really want to put her in something sweet, an outfit from Italy, when we bring her to Demo's play. Well, her dad's play." Nexxa lifted Natina out of her stroller.

Nexxa had explained to Iliada the situation regarding baby Natina and how Demo was her dad but Sergei provided for her. How Sergei's grandmother took care of her but was getting older and wanted to travel to see her cousin in Turkey before she wasn't physically able to. She fibbed a bit about why she had brought the baby with her to Rome, only mentioning the stalker ex-girlfriend in vague detail and about the ruby ring Sergei gave her.

ROME — OCTOBER 14th

Natina fussed a lot, but each time Nexxa took her out of her stroller, she stopped. Iliada eventually took over, pushing the stroller and putting their shopping bags in the baby seat. The black Babyzen Yoyo stroller looked sleek even without a baby. Sergei had insisted Nexxa have a new "pushchair" for the baby on their trip.

"I need some tea." Nexxa shielded Natina's face from the sun and adjusted her on her hip. "Shopping with a baby is a lot of work."

"Which way should we go?" Iliada asked, pausing her step.

Nexxa turned a corner and fixed her eyes on signage for a café.

"Nexxa?" Iliada walked after her. "Do you know where you're

going?" she huffed.

Nexxa was good on foot, with an innate sense of discovering the places she would enjoy, even with a baby on her hip.

Iliada pushed the stroller over the threshold. "It's medieval in here," she declared with her eyes fixed on the wall lined with some home apothecary. "But modern too," she added, while pushing the chic pushchair. "If I ever had a shop, I would like it to look like this, and have a bakery in it just like this one."

"Yeah, I love it. I would add a few more Vampy and black touches, then call it Modern Medieval Vampy. Or something like that." Nexxa bounced Natina, continuing to smile at the baby she held.

The café had a fountain in the center with flowing water and a conveniently placed counter with a perfect tablescape of Italian-made jewelry.

A waiter seated them, asking if they would require a baby chair, and took their order. Nexxa requested two green teas and a donut for the baby. Nexxa watched through the arched doorway as the waiters, like they had taken a vow of silence, prepared their order.

"Mmm, even green tea is amazing in Rome." Nexxa sipped her tea while tearing a small piece of the donut to give to the baby.

"How are we the only people in this café?" asked Iliada.

"It is only new place," came from the eavesdropping waiter.

"Oh." Nexxa moved her suspicious eyes around the café. "Okay." Natina mouthed a few more bites while they continued sipping their tea. Nexxa felt warmth coming from the baby on her lap. "I need to change Natina's diaper."

"Okay, I'll go with you. I need to pee anyway."

"The ladies' room is downstairs," directed the waiter who, moments ago, was across the café but managed to have vampire*ish* speed to now be tableside.

A petite older man was sitting on a bench between the doors labeled Signora and Uomo. His face was benevolent. There wasn't a changing table, so Iliada sat in the ladies' room chair and held Natina on her lap so Nexxa could change her diaper. "This is silly," Nexxa said, laughing while she struggled to put a new diaper on a wriggling baby. The door was a little jammed when they tried to open it to leave. Iliada managed it open, laughing, almost bumping the older man with the door. He was standing in their way and most likely unaware, from the look on his face, that he could have been knocked toward the wall from the force of the ladies' room door. Spryly, he lifted his cane, pointing down the hall. Iliada let out a giggle. Nexxa looked to Iliada. "I think he's serious."

Nexxa adjusted Natina on her hip, Iliada took the diaper bag from her, and they started to walk down the hall. Iliada looked back. "He's gone. And wait, what about the stroller?"

"I'm sure the attentive Italian waiters will mind it for us."

The hallway seemed to narrow after about twenty feet, and the stone walls were covered with moss. The best part was the sconces which had actual flames. Nexxa lifted her hand to a sconce, feeling the heat. Iliada couldn't resist either. A welcoming smell of lavender mixed with cigar smoke permeated the hall. A steep wooden curved staircase was at the end of the corridor. Nexxa tried to hold onto the wall, slipping slightly, but Iliada caught her. The room at the bottom of the stairs had a cathedral ceiling with natural light coming from above and apothecary bottles resting between wooden beams in the walls.

"*Amor, mors. Bellus.*"

"What do those mean?" asked Iliada as she twirled her head around the room.

"Well, love, death, and beautiful!"

Cigar smoke began to travel toward them. An arched doorway revealed a man sitting in a winged chair with a cigarette table beside him. He rose from his seat; they turned their attention toward the man in the alcove.

"Hi," Nexxa and Iliada spoke simultaneously.

"I'm Alano," the Spanish-looking man with kind eyes spoke. "I'm happy to see you both." Baby Natina cooed. Nexxa kissed her, and Iliada caressed the baby's arm. Alano placed his cigar down before stepping away from his chair. He moved over to a nook in the wall, taking down a small figurine. "I believe you could use this," he said, holding out his hands toward Nexxa.

A look of confusion swept across her face. Iliada leaned in for a closer look.

Alano insisted, "Keep the Gargowl by a window in your home."

Nexxa extended her hand; Alano placed the figurine in her palm. She juggled, holding Natina, managing to move a finger across the head carefully. "It's—" Natina reached for it. "No baby, you can't hold this."

Iliada held her hands out so Nexxa could hand off the figurine before Natina's little hand could get ahold. "Oh," she muttered in surprise as she grasped it, for the figurine had an almost feathery feel and was making a raspy breathing sound.

Alano motioned, "Come sit with me." Nexxa looked around, thinking about their brief yet insistent encounter with the older man by the bathroom. She held Natina on her lap, keeping her occupied with a toy from her diaper bag.

With the Gargowl, the creature in her hand that had stolen her interest, Iliada moved about the apothecary room.

"There have been a few lunar eclipses this year."

Nexxa listened, trying to prevent her eyes from wandering around the dimly lit alcove.

"Your sister is very special to you."

She looked over her shoulder at Iliada. "Yes, yes, she definitely is." Nexxa laughed, thinking how cute her sister was, hearing her say, "Aw, you're so sweet," to the adorable creature.

"Your strengths are different yet complement each other. You are more complex; you can sense things. She can sweeten people who have evil intentions."

"Yes, that sounds about right."

"This is your baby, no?"

"No, no, she's not." Nexxa looked to the baby on her lap.

"I see a man."

Nexxa laughed, leaning her head to the side.

"You saw him when you were in your kitchen," Alano continued, making the motion for stirring, "stirring a pot."

"Yes." Nexxa heavily sighed before kissing baby Natina on the head.

"She is very beautiful. What is her name?"

"This is Natina."

"The boyfriend, his baby?"

"No, not really."

Alano took a puff from his cigar. "Her mother, she used drugs, yes?" he said, scrunching his forehead.

"I think something like that."

"She's gone." Alano waved his hand in the air, mimicking something floating away.

"Yes, I was told she died, well passed away."

"Hmm. You love this man?"

Nexxa looked to Natina, avoiding the question.

"You have to be careful. Not from this man. This man is good. Loves you a lot."

"Okay, well." Nexxa rubbed her finger along her temple.

"I see something else. Did you have a problem with a colleague?"

"Well, maybe."

"You have a problem with a woman." He narrowed his eyes. "Two women. One you just met. And one that is gone now. But somebody else around her, he hasn't forgotten you." Alano put down his cigar. It was sincere when Alano made eye contact with Nexxa. Holding his gaze, he said, "He wants to harm you."

Nexxa did an on-the-spot assessment: *Klarin is dead. What other woman could he be seeing? Rochelle is in a treatment center, Psylab or something, according to Sergei. Medan should no longer be a threat. So, what man then?*

Alano dabbed his cigar into the ashtray. Nexxa focused on the smoke still billowing. "Do you have any questions?" Nexxa looked up as she thought, then back to Alano. When Natina sneezed, she realized the smoke was obviously bad for the baby. Alano handed Nexxa his business card and stood from his chair. Iliada approached Nexxa, helping her with the diaper bag. Alano handed Iliada a shopping bag; the Gargowl was placed inside. Nexxa embraced Alano. It felt great to hug him, a stranger in a hidden room in Rome. She was thankful yet had a new sense of dread.

BEIRUT — OCTOBER 14, 2013

Faroud repeated the phrase his father had said to him in the mornings before school, "Learned objects teach you universal qualities." As he wiped his forehead with a handkerchief, he realized *he* was the father now. *Keep moving forward; maybe we will be compared to the UAE one day*, he told himself in the men's room as he sat down on the toilet. When *it* was done, he flushed, buckled his belt, and after washing his hands, pushed a nose hair back in his nostril. Faroud let out a silent fart as he returned to his office. He was expecting Tarek's visit, albeit in thirty minutes. *Why did Tarek bring his baboon?* Faroud questioned as he opened the door to his office with trepidation.

"She's beautiful." Tarek stood by the window, holding a picture of Oksana. Sal slumped in a chair in front of Faroud's desk. "She went missing," Tarek said.

"Who? What are you talking about?" Faroud questioned as

he looked down at Sal's legs stretched out before him. "My girlfriend?"

"Your Miss America."

Faroud tugged at his suit jacket. "My associate with Kuretz Investments?"

Tarek set down the framed photo, turning to see the expression he had expected from Faroud. Faroud scratched his forehead. Tarek walked over, standing in front of Faroud's old-world walnut burl desk. Faroud had opted to pay for it himself, over four thousand dollars, since the bank would not spring for it. Tarek spun the globe that displayed an off-white ocean color with a walnut base to match the desk. He swiped a finger over the desk; a thin layer of dust was visible with the glare from the sun. He revealed the mess on his finger to Faroud before he leaned over.

"*Where*," he asked with a hostile tone to match his best intimidating face before calming, "is she?"

"Did you take her?" Faroud couldn't fake his confused face even if he tried. "I don't know who you are saying."

Sal stood up. "*We* are going to work with the *siniyeen*."

"*You* are?" a taken aback Faroud responded, shaking his head. "You will never get permits." Faroud's desk phone rang. He looked at the telephone, opting not to answer the call. "We've already worked out a deal," he fluttered his hands about in the air before finishing, "with the American broker-dealer for a private placement; this is the bank's decision." In actuality, he was trying to firm up details with Nexxa but hadn't been able to reach her. "And China Black Road—"

"You will withdraw your permit requests!" Tarek shouted

over Faroud.

Faroud slowly moved his hand toward his desk phone. With one touch, he could call the National Lebanese Bank's security office located on the lower level of the building.

"Such a shame. The American. She *was* so pretty," Tarek said before motioning for Sal to get up. Sal cupped his hand under his mouth, letting some saliva fall. He sauntered over to a framed copy of *The Ambassadors* that hung on the wall, smearing his spit across the picture. Faroud's eyes widened in shock as he adjusted his stance.

Sal made the gesture of slitting someone's throat as he strolled out of Faroud's office.

Faroud closed his door—he shit himself.

Oksana, Faroud's girlfriend, walked by the "I love Beirut" sign, pushing her baby in a red Uppa baby stroller. Sal waited until she moved further along.

"You have a baby." He was cheery as he approached, putting his arm around her.

"What?" she barked, stepping out of his touch.

"Shh." With his foot blocking her way, he stopped her from pushing the stroller further. "I need something; you will do."

Oksana fumbled in her purse, pulling out her iPhone with a sparkly charm dangling from the phone cover. He yanked it out of her hand.

"I need to know. Where is she?"

"Who?" Oksana stomped her foot. "Who!"

"The woman. Faroud is working with her. Find where she is." Sal pulled his cigarettes from his jacket and lit one. "You love your mother." He blew toward Oksana and continued, "Nina, and would be sad if anything happened to her," he said. He bent over with the cigarette in his mouth and attempted to unclip the stroller harness. The baby started to fuss.

"Leave him alone!" Oksana tugged at Sal's jacket.

"Shh." Sal was calm as he stood from his crouch. "Or I break him."

"What about my mother?" Oksana pushed to position herself in front of the baby. "Who are you?"

He handed her a flip phone. "Call this number in the phone. You have twenty-four hours." Sal had a personal reason for ensuring Nexxa could no longer execute a deal between her broker-deal in New York and the National Lebanese Bank. His personal vendetta aside, Hezbollah was not just a militant group; the organization needed ways to thrive financially. Which was why Tarek would need to execute a deal with China Black Road, expecting to receive preferential access to building permits from the Lebanese government. Otherwise, without a contract, permits, and Faroud and Nexxa out of the way, there would be no cut, no financial gain.

Oksana looked at the phone she was holding. "Ick." She unzipped her Prada diaper bag with red rosebuds and dropped the phone in. She wasn't sure yet if she had been threatened. He seemed like a bumbling fool. When the baby started to cry and cry, she looked around to see that he was still nearby watching her; it *felt* like a threat. She got into a taxi quicker than ever, barely folding down the stroller properly. She called her mom back in Belarus; she was okay. So, what could he have been talking about? *What this about a woman?*

"Faroud, Faroud!" Oksana managed to screech louder than the click-clack of her six-inch platform heels as she crossed the foyer in Faroud's home. She could hear him in his office on the phone. He sounded distressed. Of course, he was; he had left work early needing to change his underpants after Sal graced him with his presence. After handing the baby to the housekeeper, she barged into his office. He waved his hand, letting her know he was busy. She stepped outside the door and paced around until the sound of her heels prompted Faroud to get up and close the door. She pushed her ear to the wall. She didn't understand much since she hadn't bothered to learn Arabic, using a translation app instead. Faroud ended his call and came out. He kissed Oksana on each cheek and walked off, calling his housekeeper's name.

Oksana leaned into Faroud's office and noticed his mobile phone on his desk. Click, clack, her heels were loud. "Shh," she shushed herself as she tried to tiptoe into his office. She knew the code to unlock his phone; she had insisted, and Faroud always gave in. Scanning his text messages, one stood out from a contact labeled "Nexxa NY Kuretz Investments."

Nexxa: *Hello Faroud, this is Nexxa and this is my new number. I'm going to Rome with my sister.*

Nexxa: *I didn't disappear on purpose. I know you spoke to my boss, Dan.*

Nexxa: *We should talk, not over text, though.*

Faroud: *Are you in trouble?*

Nexxa: *No. I will contact you.*

Faroud: *Ok* ☺

Oksana went to her stroller, where her diaper bag rested over the handle and withdrew the "ick" phone. "Pretend terrorist," she laughed as she texted—*rome*—not even bothering to capitalize it, to the number programmed in the phone. She waited for a second or two. No response. "Hmm," she said, shrugging before going into the powder room and dropping the phone into the trash. She had lost interest. *Boring,* she told herself. Oksana was more self-centered than, say, a Good Samaritan.

MOSCOW — OCTOBER 14th

Sergei stood looking out over his front garden while on the phone with Hoolihane. Hooli informed him that he found recent calls and texts between Nexxa and Kilmer before she had left for Beirut. Sergei didn't like that Nexxa's past included someone like Kilmer and that he was still in her present. Kilmer also had calls and text messages, starting before Nexxa went to Beirut, with a cell number based in Lebanon. A string of online chats, some flirtatious, with a contact SalKiss4U, with a Lebanese IP address.

"That's what I needed, Hooli."

"I got you, man."

"Keep tracking him," Sergei insisted.

"Yep, on it."

Sergei lowered the phone from his ear, about to end the call, when he heard Hoolihane say, "Hmm."

Swiftly lifting the phone back to his ear, he said, "What's that? Hooli! You there?"

"Yeah, yeah, he just booked a flight to Rome," Hoolihane explained.

Sergei pulled open a desk drawer. He removed his pistol. Knowing now that Nexxa's ex-husband had been texting her, messaging someone in Medan's circle, all of this didn't add up.

"You good?" asked Hoolihane.

Sergei wondered if the universe was mad; maybe Mother Earth was punishing him for cutting down a dead tree on his property. "I cut down that tree."

"What man?"

"Nothing." Sergei leaned his head back. "Nothing. When does he arrive?"

"Seven a.m. tomorrow. I just sent you everything."

Sergei ended the call.

ROME — OCTOBER 15, 2013

Inevitable. Nexxa believed that she would run into somebody she knew, maybe a colleague from another firm. He was there, on Via del Corso, looking in the window of a boutique. Her first instinct was to cross the street and push baby Natina away. But *la via* was busy, and so fate had its wicked way. Leery, she glided the pushchair straight on. Kilmer turned on cue like an actor in a movie.

"Look who it is." Kilmer grinned. "Whoa, imagine this!"

"Hiii." Nexxa couldn't hide her skepticism.

"*Iliada*," Kilmer addressed her, "Nexxa's sister. And who is this *wee* one?"

Nexxa turned the stroller to the side slightly and, with her foot, put the brake on.

"So, like, *what* are you doing here?" she asked as she put her hands up toward him, forming a barrier for her personal space.

"What?" He pretended as he let out his distinct cunning laugh. "What happened?"

"Really?" Nexxa insisted, looking him directly in his Irish eyes.

"What?" With a shocked face, Kilmer continued, "You're not happy to see me?"

"The last time, I mean in New York—"

"Give us a kiss." Kilmer leaned in to kiss Nexxa on the cheek. Then Iliada. Baby Natina fussed and turned her head as he bent down to her. Kilmer did a body shimmy with arms open waist-side and a cheeky smile. "Fancy running into yous here."

"Yeah, *fancy* that." Nexxa gave Kilmer a look of disapproval.

Iliada shook her head, rolling her eyes. "This is awkward."

"Come on; I'm here for work." He put his arm on Nexxa's shoulder; she flinched. "Hey, I'm sorry about that night in the bar. Don't stay mad at me. Let me buy yous a drink."

Nexxa looked at Iliada—she rolled her eyes again. "Whatever, let's go."

"Where'd you get the baby? Babies 'R' Us? Haha." And again, the cunning and very annoying laugh followed his idiotic joke.

But somehow, Nexxa felt sorry for him. She never understood why she sometimes gave in and agreed to meet him. This chance meeting seemed like the story of Hades in his excursion to kidnap Persephone and make her his wife. And so, at an outdoor café, Nexxa mostly attended to the baby, trying to survive an uncomfortable hour of her time while she, Kilmer, and Iliada pretended.

"Did your sister ever tell you how we got to New York?"

Nexxa was leaning down to Natina in the stroller. She couldn't believe what Kilmer, all on his own, decided to bring up. She remembered well the exhilaration of their first operation in Paris with Quinn and the *shock* when it abruptly ended, bringing her back to Canada.

"We rode in the trunk of a car from Canada." Kilmer had a look of accomplishment.

Nexxa wished to keep all of this in the past. *Come on, why is he bringing this up?* Looking up from baby Natina, Nexxa apologetically tried to explain herself to Iliada. "Yeah, I never told you any of this since it was so long ago, and you were a lot younger at the time."

"What?" Iliada leaned in over the table. "Did you guys really do that?"

"Yes." Nexxa knew if she didn't finish the story, Kilmer would. "Once we were over the border, we were given a car to drive to New York City. It was scary because the car that had been arranged for us to drive was registered to our temporary aliases, and we were stopped by police in upstate New York for a taillight or something. I talked our way out of getting a ticket. I was a natural. Who knew? Kilmer was impressed with me." Nexxa looked over at Kilmer. "Right, Kilmer?"

"You didn't let on anything when they were questioning you," Kilmer added.

"We stopped on the drive to the city for an early lunch at an Irish pub owned by one of Kilmer's contacts. Of course, he said, 'Let's have a pint.' While Kilmer was having a drink, I decided to walk around the quaint town. I saw a church and felt compelled to go in, wondering what it would be like to be married."

Kilmer grinned. Nexxa was stroking his ego. "Married to you," she continued, tilting her head and smiling at him. He took a drag from his cigarette and, with his free hand, reached for her hand. She obliged.

"I waited for him on a bench in front of the church. And you know me, I joked with him that we should get married. 'You're my brown-eyed girl,' he said as he kissed me. Once we were in Brooklyn, I found a black dress with white lace on the top. Kilmer bought rose gold wedding bands. And then I was his."

Iliada rolled her eyes. Nexxa wished she hadn't, for she was only trying to keep the dragon amused.

"Where are yous staying?" Kilmer abruptly adjusted his legs, crossing one over the other.

"We're staying at The St. Regis." They weren't, but he didn't need to know they were staying in a villa somewhere in Rome.

"Let's go have one for the road." Kilmer extinguished his cigarette in the ashtray.

"Let's go where?"

Kilmer looked to his brown-eyed girl. "The St. Regis."

THE ST. REGIS HOTEL BAR

"Did I tell you I got a pet snake?"

And that was it—that's how Nexxa knew. Thank goodness the baby started to fuss. Nexxa had already given her a bottle; she drank most of it in the stroller on the walk to the hotel. She had quickly learned the different cries a baby makes.

"We have to go, Kilmer." Nexxa swallowed more wine than

she wanted. "She needs a nap," she said, placing her empty*ish* wine glass down.

"You never did tell me whose baby?" Kilmer motioned with his head.

"I didn't?"

Kilmer squinted his eyes. "No, actually, you didn't."

"Well, it's my friend's baby. She's in a play here in Rome."

"Ah." He didn't look convinced when he peered down at the baby in her stroller.

Nexxa lifted Natina out; Iliada put the diaper bag back in the stroller. "Come on," Iliada insisted as she took the brake off and started maneuvering the posh pushchair.

Kilmer stood. "I'll walk yous to your room."

Nexxa felt it, that same old lousy feeling. Tough when pushed, Iliada blurted, "No! No, Kilmer, we're fine."

The bartender looked up. Nexxa made eye contact with him; his expression indicated he knew there was a problem. She hadn't paid much notice to him; however, his presence was known once he stepped from behind the bar. Kilmer eased back down on his barstool. Nexxa walked toward the elevator, and Iliada followed. Kilmer took the last sip of his beer and placed some cash on the bar. The bartender waited while Kilmer exited the hotel before returning to his post behind the bar.

Nexxa pushed the up button again. Still, no elevator. She looked over her shoulder and saw her ex-husband had left. "Let's just go get a taxi now. He's gone."

"Don't you think we should wait some more?" Iliada persisted as she pushed the elevator button a few times.

"No, it's okay. We'll get straight into a taxi. Besides, there are hotel doormen outside, and she needs a nap, like now."

Nexxa had baby brain. When they arrived at the villa, she rummaged in her bag for her phone. Demo hadn't left for his rehearsal for the evening yet, so he was able to let them in. After he held his baby girl, kissing her relentlessly, Nexxa took her to their bedroom for a nap. She lay down on the bed with Natina and changed her into a clean onesie. Demo reminded Nexxa to set the alarm after he left. Nexxa nodded at him as he stood in her bedroom doorway. She dozed off a bit, snuggling the baby. Nexxa had a dream where she was on the phone with someone. She woke, tired, and decided to look in the diaper bag Sergei bought to find the mobile that Sergei had set up before leaving Moscow. Nexxa remembered checking the time on her phone when they were at the bar. And, she remembered placing her empty*ish* wine glass on the bar so Kilmer would get the hint she was ready to leave.

Iliada had decided to take a bath and eat some chocolate. And, naturally, check out Instagram. Nexxa's hand hadn't tapped on the bathroom door yet when she heard someone knocking on the main entrance. She looked in on the baby, leaving the door ajar before she headed to see who was there. *Demo must have forgotten something.* "Coming," she said under her breath with a yawn.

Opening the door, she gasped. "Kilmer?"

He held out Nexxa's new mobile. "You forgot this."

"How did—"

"I asked at the hotel; they said you weren't staying there."

Nexxa touched her brow. Why did she lie, like really? It was just Kilmer, not, like, Hezbollah.

"Yeah, I mean, my friend offered us to stay with her. You know, easier to help watch her baby."

Kilmer shivered, showing he was *obviously* cold. Nexxa pushed the door open more. He stepped in. Not wanting to, she let him pass, realizing it wasn't *that* chilly outside.

"Tea?" Nexxa asked from habit.

"I'd love a cup of tea." Kilmer's voice was cheery.

Nexxa knew Iliada would be furious when she realized Kilmer was there. But then she could say how nice it was that he found her phone and brought it to her. After his cup of tea, he would surely be on his way.

"So," Nexxa turned on the faucet, filling up the electric kettle with water, "how did you find where we were staying?" she asked.

"You have a screenshot of the Airbnb listing."

"Ah." For a moment, Nexxa thought that Kilmer probably went through her phone, photos, and contacts.

"Nice phone you have," Kilmer offered before letting out a cough.

"Uh-huh." Nexxa placed the full kettle on the base and turned it on. She realized all of her photos wouldn't be on there. Anything she wouldn't want him to see, especially her contact for China Black Road, was on her old phone, the one Medan confiscated.

Kilmer annoyingly moved his spoon around in his teacup. He glared at her with *I want to fuck you* eyes. Looking at Nexxa, he thought he would like to put a cock ring on and *her* thong before penetrating her. One last time, one for the road, he wanted.

Nexxa took a deep breath, then lifted her cup of tea, blowing on it. Taking a sip, she tried to hide that it burned her mouth.

He looked around the kitchen. "Have yous had dinner?" As he stood, the barstool screeched along the floor.

"Um, what?" Nexxa placed her teacup down.

Kilmer opened the refrigerator. Nexxa desperately searched her mind for a reason for him to leave—and for what his ulterior motive might be.

"What did you say you were in Rome for?"

"Yeah," he grumbled, his head in the fridge, "I'm in Rome."

"No, really, Kilmer. Why are you in Rome?"

Kilmer shut the fridge. He placed some cheese on the counter. "Have a cutting board?"

"Um yeah, okay." Nexxa opened a cabinet, then a drawer. "Here."

"A knife."

Nexxa heard Natina cry. Kilmer looked toward the sound.

"I'll be—"

"I know me way around a kitchen."

Nexxa only heard "kitchen" as she dashed to the bedroom. Natina was sitting up and reaching her arms out. Nexxa crawled onto the bed, hushing her as she picked her up.

"Hey, I'm going to meet BritNay and her friend at the bar nearby." Iliada was scrolling through her Instagram feed. "Like, he's from New York too."

"Oh, okay." Nexxa motioned with her head for Iliada to come into the bedroom, since she was wrapped in a towel standing in the hallway. "So, Kilmer is here."

"Kilmer?" Iliada's eyes widened.

Nexxa tried to get Natina to take a pacifier. "Yeah. I know. He brought my phone. I guess I must have left it on the table or bar. I don't know."

"Nexxa," Iliada huffed, pressing the button on her phone to display the time, "this is crazy."

"Yeah, I know." Nexxa looked out of the bedroom toward the kitchen. "I will tell him he has to leave."

"Um yeah!" Iliada returned to the bathroom to get ready.

Nexxa carried the baby into the kitchen and took a bottle from the fridge. She bent down with Natina on her hip and tried to take a pan out from the cabinet. Kilmer jumped from his barstool, putting a piece of cheese in his mouth, and took the pan out for her. He put it on the cooktop.

"Um, you have to put water in it," Nexxa laughed.

He took the pot, filled it with water, and placed it back on the cooktop.

"Thank you."

"What is it for?"

"Oh." Nexxa placed the bottle in the pot. "To warm the bottle."

"Hey. It's *Kilmer* again," Iliada huffed, walking into the kitchen.

"Look at you," Kilmer responded without turning his head.

"Yeah, look at me," Iliada remarked before turning to look at Nexxa. "So, I can stay."

"No, no, it's okay. After I give her this bottle, she'll go back to sleep." Nexxa turned toward Kilmer. "Yeah, so I'll have to go to sleep. Early night for me." She made a sad smile.

Inside, she knew it was a lame attempt to make Kilmer realize it was time to go. Nexxa situated Natina on her hip, catching a glimpse of the ruby ring Sergei had given her; the color was lighter. He had told her it would change if she were in the wrong place, which meant danger.

Thirty minutes had passed with Kilmer offering to make dinner, helping with the baby, bringing up things he liked about his "brown-eyed girl" and good times they had had; all this distracted Nexxa's awareness. Demo would be back shortly, she told herself. The worst, she feared, would be explaining to Sergei's brother what her ex-husband was doing there. And she had her phone back; she could text Iliada too. That ulterior motive that she was searching for wasn't at the forefront of her mind. Like, Kilmer was eating cheese and sipping tea in the kitchen. Now trying to get Natina to settle down and sleep was on her mind, and the irony of whom she had run into in Rome.

Nexxa heard the TV. She leaned up some as she sat on the bed, holding Natina with her bottle. *What is he doing? Did he turn it on and can't figure out how to turn it down?* Nexxa found him in the living room, sitting and smoking.

Iliada spotted BritNay right away. Her new bestie was wearing oversized sunglasses pushed up on her head and had her new LV bag on the table that she had been showing off on her Instagram. WiL.L, his Insta name, had a mess of curly hair you couldn't miss—and you could hear him talking ad nauseam even over BritNay talking about her new handbag. They gushed when Iliada approached, quickly complimenting her hair. BritNay demanded to know which brand of blush Iliada was wearing, and Iliada informed her it was a highlighting powder in gilded gold by an Italian start-up brand that she and her sister had come across. As BritNay used her phone to search for the brand's website, WiL.L chatted non-stop about some guy he met on the flight while simultaneously summoning over the waiter for another round of Aperol and Prosecco cocktails. Iliada sat smiling, looking from BritNay to WiL.L. Drinks were served. Without a breath, WiL.L sipped his, continuing, and BritNay sipped hers without looking up from her phone. Iliada twirled the straw in her drink, looking from table to table. Lounge music played softly in the background. Iliada released her drink, grasping her abdomen.

Then—it was *loud*.

"Where's the remote?"

Kilmer had a piece of his perfectly coiffed dark hair dangling down his forehead. His eyes super squinted as he sat in the armchair, lifting his cigarette. Nexxa shifted Natina on her hip and set the bottle on the coffee table.

"Kilmer!"

No response. Nexxa looked around the room, lifting shopping bags, jackets, and take-out menus, expecting to find the remote. Shushing Natina, she started to feel frantic. If she could only turn down the volume, she could figure out what had happened with him. Maybe just call Demo and Iliada, she rationalized. That's when she turned and saw he was holding up her phone.

Now the Bluetooth speaker was emitting voices. It was strange, someone talking. The sound was competing with the TV. Nexxa stepped slowly toward Kilmer, starting to shake but trying to cover that up by bouncing Natina. She hoped he would hand her back her phone. Natina was now crying; Nexxa was choking up.

"You always thought you were something special."

Nexxa looked toward the same door she had let him in through. Could she make it? Would he grab her before she did? She was hesitant; she had a baby in her arms, and she was sure he knew he had the advantage over her. Nexxa paused her panic, closed her eyes briefly. *Iliada, Iliada,* she said in her mind. She found a baby blanket in the still open stroller and draped it over Natina. Kilmer stood. She knew he was going to say, "I'm going to kill you and the baby."

Nexxa saw out of the corner of her eye the knife he had used to cut some cheese *wasn't* on the cutting board on the kitchen island. *Does he have the knife, or is it in the sink?* Natina squirmed to the extent that she slid down from Nexxa's hip. Nexxa called to her as she crawled over to the dining room table. It felt like that moment had happened before when she looked to Kilmer. He smirked at her and turned his evil self toward the baby crying beneath the mid-century table. He took one step toward the baby, then, with an unexpected rush, turned his stance and, like a rapist, dragged Nexxa by her hair to the first bedroom down the hall. He slapped her and, pleased with himself, cackled. Pushed down by his hand over her face, she lay on the bed, comforted by the sound of Natina still alive, now crying through the loudness of the TV and music playing.

The angry ex-husband ordered her to roll over. As Kilmer bent over her from behind, he noticed her ruby ring, now pale. He ran his palm back and forth over it as if he were trying to slice his hand. Nexxa felt his hand between her legs as his other hand was back on her head, pushing her face into the bed. She heard him moaning as he pressed up against her backside. Kilmer screamed, "Your panties!" Nexxa pointed toward the dresser. Kilmer slipped on a white lace thong—they were new from a Russian department store—over his pants. An angry Kilmer thrust against his once-upon-a-time bride.

"Kilmer, I saw that woman," Nexxa cried.

Kilmer moaned, his coif shifting with his thrusting.

"Klarin," Nexxa managed as she fought him forcing her face down.

Kilmer's eyes widened.

It was so fast, the whack against his head, him slumping next to Nexxa. *Get up*, *get up*, she encouraged herself. Nexxa turned over, expecting to see her love's brother, Demo. Kilmer winced, causing Iliada to whack him again.

Sergei had made progress working with Hoolihane to discover who had delivered champagne to his hotel suite and breached his home security; the thing about the muddled Russian accent counting the flowers, he couldn't let that go. Hoolihane did a deep dive on Nexxa's colleagues and the business associates she was meeting with in Beirut. Sergei had intentions of going back to Beirut, using another identity. He believed the person responsible was still there. But with an Irishman from Nexxa's past on his way to Rome, Sergei boarded a flight to Italy. He didn't want to wait for his jet share to arrive back from London, so he was at the mercy of flying commercial. His flight to Rome was canceled due to a mechanical problem, so he was rebooked to fly into Milan. To his advantage, it was customary to go through red lights in Italy; however, his six-hour drive put him in Rome after Nexxa's ex-husband Kilmer.

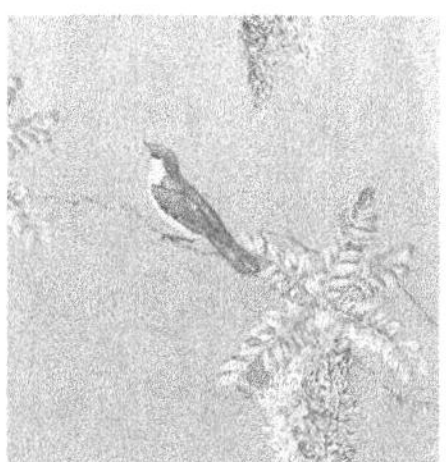

ROME — OCTOBER 15, 2013, EVENING

Time blurred between the whack and her running to the baby, who had finally stopped crying, still in her hideaway. As Nexxa held her, kissing the side of her head, she noticed the TV remote on the floor under the sofa. Nexxa only pointed to it, and a disheveled Demo bent down to pick it up. "What happened? What happened?!" he asked as he turned off the television blaring Italian music videos.

"Um, guys." Iliada stood in the bedroom doorway, where the dragon was lying.

Nexxa was worried about how she would explain what had just transpired when she and Demo heard, "No, you stay, no, no!" Nexxa ran toward the bedroom, and Demo followed.

"Oh my!" Demo shrieked as he leaned on the doorframe. "I'm guessing this is… Who?"

"This," Nexxa looked at Iliada before saying, "is my ex-husband."

"This fucking asshole was trying to—"

Nexxa shook her head, hoping Iliada would shush, say no more.

"Saint George," Demo spoke without explanation. Nexxa turned her body, shielding the baby, when she heard Kilmer moan. Iliada hovered over Kilmer, putting her knee on his back. Demo swiftly moved to the other side of the bed, where he saw Nexxa's bag on a chair. He unclipped the strap from the diaper bag and clipped it to a belt loop on Kilmer's jeans. "*Scarf*," Demo demanded. "Get me a scarf!"

Iliada motioned for Nexxa to go to the living room. Nexxa rushed, which caused Natina to jiggle and giggle, dissipating her sad baby face. Nexxa found Iliada's bag by the door and her wrap on the floor by it. She brought it to Demo, who tied it around Kilmer's neck. With Iliada's help, they dragged him to a closet in the kitchen. Before the door was latched, Demo dashed off to his bedroom. He returned with a blonde wig he had among his theater attire and put it on Kilmer's head, securing it with some Spirit gum adhesive around the face. Nobody asked about the white lace thong Kilmer had over his pants.

The three of them packed quickly and left for The St. Regis. Demo called his brother from the Metropolitan suite. Nexxa sat with her sister holding baby Natina, anticipating what she would hear from Sergei. How would she explain what had happened? As she listened to Demo speak, primarily in Russian, she was able to piece together a story: *A mercenary who traveled to a land where a dragon was terrorizing the women. Offerings appeased the dragon temporarily until the maiden, Sergei's love, was in danger. The beast was wounded and bound with feminine attire, and like the animal he was, was dragged away.*

Sergei listened to his brother's story. He was, in fact, standing outside of the villa they had fled, looking through the living room window. He had arrived about two hours after they left.

ROME — OCTOBER 15, 2013, EVENING

Diane arrived carrying a small crumpled brown paper bag and wearing a ball cap, part of KitchenGod's guise. Inside the bag was Chinese soup, half-eaten. The door was unlocked, so she opened it, stopping when it made a creaking sound. She was petite, her steps more like levitating than walking. She never carried weapons since she had trained in the martial art Wing Chun with a master since her early childhood.

 "Delively, delively." That was enough playing *delivery* guy, Diane decided and placed the bag on the counter. A thud came, and she just happened to see the closet door budge with the sound. "Haha," she laughed with happy eyes. The latch was simple, and when she slid the lock over to the right to open, "she" fell out of the closet. Small but freakishly strong, Diane half-lifted the body and dragged it over to the chair in the living room. She had brought one more thing with her, some wire, which she withdrew from her pocket. Tightly bound now to the chair, she could admire her game, pushing back her blonde hair. She removed her phone from her pocket and found the image she had saved of Nexxa. Tilting her head side to side, she decided Western women were manly, similar to the women of the hinterland in China. Kilmer was, after all, wearing a black V-neck t-shirt, and skinny red jeans with a white thong. Diane lifted on her toes, leaning into Kilmer; she moved her nose across Kilmer's shirt and then to his groin. She confirmed the scent she had tracked: Nexxa.

Kilmer's speech was slurred since Iliada managed to stuff a few Xanax in his mouth before he had been locked in the closet. KitchenGod found it arousing, spooning soup in Kilmer's mouth and unsuccessfully wiping his chin. This neglect wasn't intentional as she had drippings of soup on her face, shirt, and hands as part of her character disguise. What a mess, anyone else would think. She deemed it essential to feed Kilmer before he was to go. *This will make better sense*, she thought. Next, she removed his shoes. "Oh so manly," she said under her breath as she tugged at the socks. She tickled each foot with a spork, laughing each time her victim's foot jerked before scraping the dirt from under his toenails.

Diane propped up her phone and tapped on the QQ music app to play a music video, then she disappeared to the kitchen. She danced around with her arms flopping like limp noodles to the K-pop band, waiting for the water to boil in the kettle. This time, the spoon *didn't* clank in the teacup when it stirred, as the spork was doing the stirring. In the cup, she dipped her finger, which had a coffin-shaped nail, and tasted the prepared drink of dirt from under the toenails. Kilmer would need to drink—to establish honor—before KitchenGod could resume. She had intentions of finishing what Klarin had been paid a nice sum to do but failed to accomplish. When Diane didn't receive a confirmation from Klarin, a photo of a deceased Nexxa, she took it upon herself to find Nexxa. She did find her, using her wolfness, in Moscow, but Jupiter was in retrograde. Now she found something even better—a man in a blonde wig in a villa in Rome.

UPPER EAST SIDE, NYC — OCTOBER 2013

Nexxa struggled to keep up with Iliada; her stride was longer, and Nexxa moved her head around, noticing all the new moms out pushing strollers. She had noticed Upper East Side moms, nannies, and babies before, but never like this. Now that she and Iliada were back in New York—Sergei had arranged for their return from Rome—she wanted to keep her mind busy until she would see Sergei and baby Natina again. Rounding back onto Fifth Avenue, where it happened to be cloudy and the air became thicker, Nexxa caught a whiff of something that she wanted to follow. A scent she thought she had smelled in Moscow. She just started to stray from their route home when an Asian mom, with coffin-shaped nails adorned with tacky jewels pushing a stroller while on the phone, bumped her, causing her to fumble. Nexxa regained her balance, ready to apologize, but the woman hurried off, and Nexxa heard Kilmer's voice. He was on the southwest corner ahead of her, and when he ended his call, he gave Nexxa a look that said he was happy to see her. Nexxa looked him directly on, and as he took a step from the curb toward her, he dissipated. Nexxa twisted, looking down 63rd Street—Iliada turned back to see that Nexxa wasn't behind her. Iliada determined from Nexxa's face that she had seen another apparition.

Iliada had a way of surprising Nexxa. She effortlessly turned the key to unlock the main entrance and kindly held open each door for Nexxa. They were exhausted after their run, but Nexxa was something else as well. Nexxa struggled; her side-tie-wrapped tank clung to her breasts as she undressed. In the shower, she tried to remember if they had locked the apartment door behind them.

Nexxa's mind twirled from eleven p.m. until fourish when she finally woke. Standing by the bedroom window, she wondered, *What if it snowed?* It was too early for it, but New York looked peaceful when snow was on the ground. Nexxa held her obsidian stone, waiting for it to warm. With her hand emanating heat, the thought of a dark-haired man in a struggle came to mind. Nexxa lifted her pendulum from where she had hung it on her mirror upon returning from Rome. The pendulum swung vigorously, then idled. She just wanted any indication if her feeling was of Medan or Kilmer. She couldn't raise her vibration; something was blocking her from seeing through the filter. Nexxa looked to Natina's pacifier on her dressing table, the only baby item that made it back to New York among Nexxa's things.

"Iliada, Iliada," Nexxa whispered.

Iliada rose. "Yeah," she said, rubbing an eye with a finger.

"I just need to think about something." Nexxa picked up Natina's pacifier.

"Huh?"

"Well, I realized when I was with Diane—"

"Who?" asked Iliada.

"The lady, the woman I was working with from China Black Road. You remember I told you about her, with the scientist father. She had sky-blue nails."

Iliada sat listening. She looked at the Gargowl on her nightstand, reaching a finger to touch it to see if it would come to life again.

"Well, anyway, when I was around her that day, I don't know." Nexxa looked up, thinking. "I couldn't smell, like I didn't smell Sergei, and he was in the restaurant the day I had the meeting with Diane and her colleagues. I mean, obviously, I saw him there that morning."

"Sooo, what do you think?" Iliada got out of bed and shuffled to the bathroom.

"Well, and you know, when Kilmer showed up in Rome, I should have seen something about him, but I didn't." Nexxa lifted her pendulum again; it spun vigorously. "I just assumed it was because I had the baby."

Nexxa closed the blinds tightly on the bedroom window, and Iliada came back to the bedroom. From the bathroom, as Nexxa used her Fairy Wheel electric toothbrush, emitting the sound of a European ambulance on the massage feature, she said, "I don't... you can't go back home."

"Huh?"

Nexxa swished her mouth. "I just don't think things can be the same anymore." Iliada and Nexxa switched places so Iliada could fit into the bathroom to brush her teeth. Nexxa entered the kitchen and put the kettle on the old white stove. She prepared two mugs for Earl Grey tea, honey in each. Popping her head around to see when Iliada was in sight, she continued to explain. "Well, the opportunity with Faroud, you know how that ended. And now." Nexxa blew on her tea, sipped, and then twisted her hair up. She brought Iliada her mug of tea, placing it on the dressing table. "I think it's not the best for us to stay here, stay in the city. I'll find a way to work something out."

"I still have my job," Iliada assured her while she examined her work wardrobe in the closet.

"Yeah, I have other ways I can work, make money," Nexxa responded as she watched Iliada looking through her clothes. She wanted to say that it wasn't safe for them to stay in Nexxa's apartment long-term and that she was going to talk to Dan, her boss, and depending on how that went, Nexxa would make her decision.

Iliada was sluggish on her walk to work. Not her usual adopted pace. She looked back to see if she could still see Nexxa, but she had her phone to her ear. If it weren't for that, she might have called out to her; she assumed Nexxa was on the phone with Sergei. So, she crossed the avenue and picked up the pace. She was wearing the right clothes, she reminded herself, black with more black that had borne pricey tags, more money than she would have ever imagined spending, but for Nexxa, and now for Iliada, this was the norm. So why did she feel everyone eyeing her? Even the man selling coffee from his street cart, Middle Eastern looking, seemed to have eyes on her. Seeing him reminded Iliada of Zarian. She had mixed feelings about Zarry now and what had happened with him. Then—a man, slender, in shades of city wear, looked at her, and when she returned the look, he had already started crossing the street toward her. He ran right into her. Her bag caught the brunt of his force. Iliada turned to scold him. Kilmer? It could have been him. Beautifully coiffed black hair. Arrogant walk. Suddenly she lost count of the streets and passed her office building, the Namaguto building on 56th Street.

Later that evening, Nexxa stood with her welcome glass of champagne, listening to the blasé chatter of her co-workers dispersed about Dan's living room. Eyeing a few of her socially inept colleagues, she muttered to herself and partly to Maria as she took Nexxa's jacket from her, "It is impossible to make progress without a sense of humor." Maria understood a little English. She laughed.

Going back to when he established his firm, Dan held a holiday party at his Upper West Side apartment each year. Nexxa attended alone every year; this year, she brought her black Max Mara jacket since her plus one was back in Russia. Dan liked, he more than liked, making time to discuss spiritual wonderings with Nexxa. His props consisted of aged red wine for sipping and homemade ginger snap cookies for biting. He would rather bite Nexxa while she canvassed the Archangels explaining their divine responsibilities. Dan would make his move by simply asking her, "How is your mom?" And as before and now, Nexxa would tell him what she and her mom had recently discussed and quote tidbits from the latest book she had read. You wouldn't know that he was the type to delve into the supernatural from looking at him.

Dan was tall with wavy salt and pepper hair and had an actor-esque look. But, Nexxa knew him well, probably better than his wife. What she knew was that they were lovers in a past life together, as *William* and *Naomi*. Nexxa kept this to herself. For one, would he believe her? And secondly, she wasn't daft. He would be turned on—more aroused than any porn or swipe on a pretty girl's pic on Tinder. But he was unsuccessful and lost Naomi in that past life. So, he reincarnated into quite a different life, this time as Dan. Married, wealthy, could have any woman he desired, all at about fourteen years older than Nexxa in this lifetime. He imagined fucking her; he did. Nexxa—she secretly sought his approval. The only intimacy this time around was the mental kind. She knew him immediately when he hired her in their firm, recognizing something in the small details.

"Let's go onto the terrace." Dan motioned with his salt and pepper head of hair toward the door. "It's too noisy in here," he continued.

Nexxa leaned on the terrace ledge. "You and I have an affection between egos, not just merely between personalities." Lifting on her tiptoes, she said, "It's what makes our relationship strong and permanent." Nexxa had more confidence speaking while looking out over New York City.

Dan rubbed his hands together. "I feel like I can tell you anything." And that was it, what she needed. Nexxa turned to

Dan and embraced him.

"Aw," she said as he hugged her. "I love hearing what you have to say. I'll always be here or somewhere," Nexxa continued with a playful smile. Dan lifted a pack of Marlboros from a side table, lit a cigarette, took a puff, and gave it to Nexxa. She took a drag and handed it back to him.

"That was something, huh, Beirut. I really thought we were going to need to start that GoFundMe page." Dan lifted his chin as he blew, fitting a smile in.

Nexxa caught her co-worker staring at her from inside the apartment.

Dan continued, "You are wonderful. I'm just glad you're back. Faroud, he's something, huh?"

Nexxa looked back at Dan. "Yeah, Faroud, he's great."

Dan hugged her, almost squeezing her; Nexxa felt her breasts pushing against him. "Ah, this feels good. And don't worry, we'll make sure your ex can't enter the building."

Nexxa wanted to say so much more. She was dying inside, like having a major crush on a guy, wanting to discuss the possibility of putting together another private placement. "You and I can still work together, your personal interests?" Nexxa had been testing her intuitive thoughts, providing insight for her boss on CPIs, Companies and Persons of Interest. Real estate in Central America, a girlfriend or two, but, primarily trading the firm's capital for which Dan signed off on all significant positions.

Dan took a sip of his wine. "Let's see what happens."

Out of the corner of her eye, Nexxa noticed Philip watching them from inside the apartment. He was standing there, wine in hand, with a solemn face. He could have been looking at the view of the city.

"Isn't Philip great?" Dan saw Philip watching them as well.

"He's entertaining to hang out with."

"I have to go check on things in the kitchen," Dan said, sipping the last of his wine as Philip stepped out onto the terrace, joining them.

"What are you up to?" Philip cocked his head to the side.

"Oh, just chatting about," Nexxa paused and closed her eyes, exhaling, "nothing."

"Ah," he said, shaking his head up and down, making a face. He knew Nexxa and Dan were close but couldn't understand why. He hated to admit that it bothered him. Nexxa was *Philip's* little pleasure. Things were just as he wanted them. He had made it clear he couldn't give her more; therefore, he didn't have to worry about disappointing her.

"Would you like me to come to your apartment after the party?"

"Why?" Nexxa turned away from him. "Are you too tired to make it home?"

Dan liked to keep one eye on Nexxa whenever she was around Philip. She noticed that he was already back from the kitchen, now having his turn standing with a glass of wine in hand, looking out at them through the glass terrace doors.

"Don't you want me to come over?" Philip leaned against the ledge facing Nexxa, reaching out for her hand. She walked away, and Philip promptly followed her. He put his arms around her, pushing himself, with a rising erection, against her back. "I've missed you."

"What?" Nexxa turned her head to the side. "Well, what

happened in Beirut, I feel like it changed everything," Nexxa continued.

"Okay," he said as he swiftly moved his hand down the front of her pants into her panties. Kissing the back of her neck, Philip inserted his fingers in her. Nexxa flinched. She thought of Sergei. Philip began to finger her.

"Stop!" Nexxa pulled his hand out of her pants.

"I should come over later," Philip whispered into her neck. Philip pushed his hand down into her pants again, holding her tighter.

Nexxa twisted out of his grasp. "We have to go in now."

"What's wrong?" Philip leaned against the ledge with folded arms, his therapist stance. "Nexxa?"

"I—" Nexxa adjusted the waist of her bootcut leggings. "I met someone." Nexxa's eyes started to fill with tears. "And fuck!" Nexxa grasped her hair, lifting it from her shoulders. "You didn't even seem, or ask me like, what happened in Beirut."

Philip moved in closer. "I thought you were okay."

"No." Nexxa exhaled, letting go of her hair.

Philip reached for her hand. "Why don't I come over later? We could talk." Philip moved intimately close. "I could probably stay over." Philip had never been able to stay the night.

Nexxa closed her eyes, exhaling again. "I don't know. I don't think it's a good idea."

Philip returned to his stance, leaning against the ledge. "Doesn't it feel good that I'm chasing you?"

"No, it's just too little too late."

"Right then, that's settled." Philip hid his emotion. "Let's go have another drink."

Philip always seemed confident; that was what had attracted Nexxa the most. She watched as he was able to return to the party full of their colleagues and project a jolly, carefree disposition. Philip retrieved himself and Nexxa each a glass of wine, and with the same hand he fingered her with, took a ginger snap cookie Dan offered him, ate it, and licked his fingers.

Cheeky. He's a cheeky bastard, Nexxa thought as she managed to elicit a smile with her lovely red lips.

UPPER EAST SIDE, NYC — OCTOBER 2013

Nexxa was friends with the doorman, he looked more like a bouncer, of the cigar lounge next door to a coveted Manhattan hotel for celebrities. He assured her he wouldn't allow a particular Irishman to gain entry, should he try, into the establishment. She didn't mention that she had other adversaries or what had transpired on her business trip, only that her ex-husband had taken up stalking her. It was the weekend, and Nexxa wanted to see Mr. Albert, the Asian proprietor, who was in his mid-sixties and Nexxa's confidant. She was safe with him. But then, she always traveled with the protection of angels.

"Look who just walked in, the *Ice Queen*," the hostess snarled to the waiter next to her while she used her newly manicured nails, tips and all, to gather up two menus.

"Oooooo do you think *this* time, if you are nice to her, you will get invited to her Ice Queen party?" The attractive young waiter bobbled his head, batting his accentuated eyelashes. His culture didn't allow for sass, but then again, he wasn't at home with his Bangladeshi parents; he was at work.

Nexxa stood before the hostess, who just happened to be wearing a seemingly new jacket. Sky-blue, one button, peplum style. Nexxa wasn't fond of that color now.

"Follow me," she instructed with her pretentious smile. "Your table is in the lounge."

Nexxa took account of the people at the two-tops, the bar, and all the table and couch seating in the lounge area as they walked to their table. She knew the bartender was new and that Mr. Albert was not on the floor yet. Spotting the usual suspects, executives entertaining clients, it was too bad she brought her Fuckability with her; it would encourage one of them to hit on her or her sister.

"Thank you." Nexxa made direct eye contact with the auburn-haired hostess. "I think it is important to have a table reserved," Nexxa began as she sat. Adjusting her posture, she continued, "It seems proper for women to have a reserved table when not accompanied by men. It is more respectable, classy if you will." Now eyeing the table of executives, she said, "You don't want to be standing around *holding up the wall.*" Maybe a wink and *I want to fuck you* eyes were directed toward the blondes.

With Nexxa's first lesson over, she silently counted. And then, as if summoned from a genie bottle, the sassy young waiter, she liked him the best, was ready to take their order. Nexxa ordered some rosé. "This will be our appetizer wine." Club Montecristo, a cigar bar self-described as an elegant oasis in NYC, was directly across the street from Nexxa and Iliada's apartment. Nexxa liked watching men in suits smoke cigars in a place with wooden walls that looked like one giant study for affluent men. Now, a glass of wine each, Iliada took out a box of the Fantasia Nat Shermans, lighting a red one for Nexxa and then a pink one for herself. Nexxa, taking another sip to moisten her palette, announced, "He's here," leaning into Iliada.

Mr. Albert, with fastidiousness, made his way to their table. While he was composed, the music became more intense, and smoke billowed around him as he whispered into Nexxa's ear. With precision, he placed a box on the table; he adjusted it, so it was squared, and motioned for Nexxa to take it. A moment passed. Nexxa pushed her hair behind her shoulder and rested her hand on her collarbone. She liked the part of the song playing, so before she reached for the discreetly dressed box, she allowed herself to reminisce about Sergei, Sergei licking the Scotch that dribbled down her abdomen.

Iliada ping-ponged her eyes from Mr. Albert to Nexxa. She wondered if either of them were about to taste each other's blood. Or maybe she had watched too many vampire series. One glance around, and she caught the eye of the sassy waiter and motioned him over. She had become friendly with him during her first visits to Club Montecristo. Watching her sister, Iliada also knew it would not be long before a man would attempt to hit on Nexxa since she had a permanently seductive look. Or a high Fuckability score, as Nexxa had self-described.

"The usual," which meant caviar, Nexxa instructed the sassy waiter.

"We don't have caviar tonight." The waiter smiled with his white-white teeth. And just as the waiter spoke, Mr. Albert gave him a look. The waiter withdrew his two-way radio, speaking to the kitchen manager.

"It will be here shortly," Mr. Albert stated, correcting the waiter. Nexxa looked up at Mr. Albert, and he motioned with his eyes to the box he had placed.

"What was that all about?"

"He does not desire to disappoint me." Nexxa held a straight face, before she grasped Iliada's hand and laughed. She was serious but always with some playfulness.

Iliada shrugged her shoulders and turned to the sassy waiter, who smiled at her like a sweet baby. Auburn hair and manicured nail tips, the hostess walked another group of gentlemen to the lounge. Nexxa made eye contact with good intentions. The hostess acted aloof, but secretly she envied Nexxa. Nexxa withdrew a hundred-dollar bill from her purse and stood before she could walk past their table.

"Thank you for taking our bags to our apartment." Nexxa extended her hand with the folded money.

"I didn't." She popped her hip out with her hand on it. "I had Mila do it."

Nexxa smiled. "Thank you," she insisted. The money was withdrawn from her hand. She felt the fake nail tips. Nexxa always tipped well, part of why she was known as the Ice Queen, and she didn't mind choosing to incorporate the title into the theme for her annual brunch party.

"You see, Iliada, giving to charity is great, but giving to people that are working hard, I believe, is more beneficial." Nexxa took a breath, deciding she had said enough. Iliada would learn from watching her.

"Yeah, I get that. I feel you."

The sassy waiter was around again, this time with the caviar and condiments Nexxa requested. He leaned on the table, showing his white-white teeth, crafty, utilizing the time he served them to tell her something inconspicuously. Nexxa took in his words. He spoke of a man. If she were to look around, she would need one more swallow of wine. She swallowed, then checked her lips in the grand mirror on the wall. An apparition might have appeared and smiled at her. Nexxa didn't mention it to Iliada. Her hands caressed the top of the box. "I should open this box from Mr. Albert at home."

"Is it a gift?" asked Iliada.

"I wouldn't say that." Nexxa grinned. "It's a potion. He insisted I take it, drink it before the Ice Queen party. And we might not be—" Nexxa withdrew her hands from the box; she hadn't decided what to tell Iliada yet. The band began a familiar Latin song—intense but not too loud. Iliada topped off their glasses, holding up her glass to cheers. Their glasses clanked, and the man the waiter spoke of, from the sound, turned toward Nexxa's table. She could feel him, his ready-to-go desire from across the room. She looked in his direction. He smiled at her. Nexxa imagined him carrying her to his lair. From his looks, she discerned he was from Cyprus. He would be a challenge; she just knew. The little detail that she was to remember was his mustache.

Nexxa leaned closer to Iliada. "So, our waiter was asked by a gentleman if I would be interested in meeting him."

Iliada smiled. "So, are you going to meet him?" She was

curious, looking around. Nexxa reached for her hand. There was so much she still needed to teach her. Nexxa knew this moment had happened before, but this time, she would choose not to. It wouldn't work out well, and now she had Sergei.

An instinctive sensation propelled time forward, and Nexxa abruptly stood from her seat. Several men, including Mr. Mustache, noticed, expecting her to approach them before she walked toward a back door labeled Private. Mr. Albert and Nexxa sat across from each other in his office as a teacher and a student would. She divulged more details of her abduction in Beirut, the mysterious woman who breached Sergei's home security, and the unfortunate incident with Kilmer. Mr. Albert used his radio to summon the waiter to Nexxa's table to watch over Iliada. He reminded Nexxa about her *Smeared Lavender*, her precious lavender glow desirable for a student to practice defending themself. Nexxa thanked Teacher, Mr. Albert. She now had the encouragement she needed to work on something other than her career, her supernatural abilities.

UPSTATE NEW YORK — WINTER 2013

Nexxa leaned on the balcony, feeling the cold on her bare arms, wearing only her floral lace string bodysuit in a color called *Cloud*. It was dusk, and the woods started to twinkle from the evening lights.

"You want to play ball snow?" he asked in an East Indian accent. Nexxa looked to the balcony to the left, where a dark-skinned man with a top of curly hair sat in a hot tub.

"Well, I suppose if it snows more."

"You want to come in?" He looked down to the water.

Nexxa adjusted her pose. "Oh, well, so what do you mean by *ball* snow?"

"Hey." His accent emphasized his excitement. "You want to play too?" he asked when he saw Iliada emerge onto the balcony in a vivid claret silk kimono with nothing else on but her *Immoral Hibiscus* color painted toes.

"*Oh*, who is this?" Iliada asked, leaning around Nexxa.

The Indian man's snowflake-covered eyelashes batted as he continued his attempt to charm the lovely blondes. In his mind, he was already in bed with the *blonde hairs*, "I like your hairs," draping over him. He envisioned himself lying down while she would sit with her back to him, holding a mirror, all the while watching him twist her hairs with his brown fingers.

Nexxa tilted her head to the left, making a fist with her hand; she placed the palm of her other hand over it. Iliada acknowledged and tapped her music app on her phone, playing the playlist she curated for this time of year. With care, Nexxa retrieved the wooden box Mr. Albert had given her while in the city from the side table; inhaling the crisp air, she lifted the lid. Nexxa took a sip of the elixir, winked at Iliada, and handed her the vial. Nexxa gracefully moved to the sound of "Deceive" by Trentemøller as the sky swirled into a violaceous scene.

Iliada followed her elixir taste with a glass of champagne, placing her empty glass on the ledge before unzipping her bag, which looked to be for an art school teacher. The Gargowl squirmed a bit, then hopped out. Iliada patted her thigh. "Come on, come on," she encouraged him. He dashed up her leg and rested in her palm. Then he fluttered to the railing. Snow accumulated on his body, and a burgundy cloak formed. Nexxa put her hand to her heart; she had worried the Gargowl wouldn't come to life again as he had in Rome after their trans-Atlantic trip. As it dashed around on the balcony, Nexxa decided on his name, *Flash*.

"Hey, what is that you have?" The Indian man stood in the hot tub, Speedo and all, to follow his curiosity. Flash folded in and hardened like a statue. Nexxa held out her hand and caught a snowflake that fell in the pattern of medieval lace. Iliada pushed more flakes toward Nexxa. Nexxa collected the snowflakes and formed round balls, one larger than the next, like Russian stacking dolls. Nexxa placed the snowflake formations on the ledge.

Iliada whispered, "Lavender," while pouring more champagne, handing two glasses to Nexxa. Iliada was worried the evening sky would illuminate Nexxa's lavender glow.

Nexxa mouthed, "Don't worry," to Iliada before she turned to the hot tub man and extended her arm to him, holding a drink. "Would you like some champagne?"

He couldn't hide his astonishment; even his head of black curly showed his disbelief as he reached for the glass with a slow-moving arm. Iliada opened the stacking of snowflake balls and tossed one, hitting him in the face.

"Easy, Iliada, be careful with Mr. Albert's guest," Nexxa teased, winking at her admirer before he slumped down with a pouty face then smiled again, sipping his champagne.

"Well…" Iliada extended her arm for Flash to crawl up, "at least now he'll be quiet," she said, laughing while looking to Flash as he emitted a creature chuckle.

Nexxa sat on the fur-covered chaise lounge, extending her legs out. She swallowed her glass of champagne before lifting her phone from the side table. *One more night*, she reminded herself while contemplating sending Sergei a message. She missed him, having had mixed feelings over leaving him and baby Natina when they were in Rome. Sergei wanted Nexxa to return with him to Moscow; she knew she had to return to New

York.

Nexxa looked through her contacts in her new iPhone; her original contacts were downloaded from the cloud, as she noticed Kilmer's and Medan's names. She assumed Kilmer would always manage to be a threat, especially after what had happened in Rome. And Medan, the attractive Arab turned abductor she once shared a hookah with, she wondered if he was still a threat. Her boss Dan had been optimistic that the private placement they were putting in place with Faroud would still go through. But upon returning to New York, the disappointment from no deal led to disenchantment. Dan re-assured Nexxa Kilmer would not be permitted entry to the building, but that was a mild appeasement in Nexxa's mind.

With winter coming and after her conversation with Mr. Albert in his club, Nexxa accepted his invitation for her and Iliada to stay with him at his home in upstate New York. His upstate residence was different than his apartment in the city, divided into two structures. The main house was for his personal use and the other for his butler and a dedicated staff that had been the caretakers for a long time. Nexxa had informed Iliada that she had worked it out with her boss Dan to work remotely for a few weeks during the holidays. Iliada didn't question anything because her company, Namaguto, offered ample vacation time, which she thought they were having.

Iliada rose from her lounger, offering to summon the attendants for more champagne. Nexxa stepped inside from the balcony and returned with a deck of Tarot cards. Flash hopped atop the Magician card, which fell from the stack and pranced around before resting. Iliada emerged. "Oh wow!" she exclaimed as she hurried onto the balcony, placing the champagne on the ice.

"I thought this might be fun." Nexxa took another sip of the elixir, extending her arm to Iliada. "Here, have the last taste."

ICE QUEEN I

UPSTATE NEW YORK — WINTER 2013

The sound of shattering glass came down through the fireplace as Nexxa dashed through Mr. Albert's expansive modern home located atop Kalelarga Mountain. Standing in her one shoulder white lamé gown, Iliada lifted an invitation from the kitchen island while she sipped her appetizer wine. The translucent pentacle hanging in the see-through fireplace illuminated when she read aloud the invite.

"United Souls have bright glowing chakras

You are advised to smell as decadent as you look

Ice Queen Party"

"Hmm, presh," Iliada hissed as she took a bite of a Russian tea cake dusted in white powdered sugar, licking her mouth. Shining white was the color for the party, with white orchids and tiered trays of white Russian tea cakes.

"You like them?" Nexxa asked Iliada about the white Christian Louboutin heels she slipped on.

The guest list for the party Nexxa was hosting consisted of Nexxa's chosen few: Viraj, her Russian tutor, a few fortunate girlfriends, and Mr. Albert's guests. This year Sergei was added to the list. The affable Chinese man, Mr. Albert, entered the kitchen requesting an attendant to pour him a drink before informing Nexxa there would be one more invitee, someone special he had recently met, who would be attending as his guest for Nexxa's party.

Guests were snacking on white caviar and sipping Veuve Clicquot Champagne while he was furious, watching her laugh. He knew he wanted her. That *he* should have her, never to let her go again. Watching the equally attractive, strong-looking man with dark salt and pepper hair hover around Nexxa ignited Sergei's emotions. Nexxa hadn't realized Sergei had arrived at the party. He was outside the kitchen entrance being patted down by security when he witnessed her brief conversation with Quinn before they walked out of sight. He, like Quinn, preferred the Colt Close Quarter Battle Pistol.

Quinn, the special guest, had met Mr. Albert on holiday to New York City, taking his wife of ten years shopping. Upon making Mr. Albert's acquaintance in Club Montecristo, he saw a picture of Mr. Albert and Nexxa on the wall, albeit a small photo behind the bar. Quinn had married, expecting to produce an heir for himself. The most exciting thing that had happened in a long time had been watching squirrels play under the

Portaloo on his land while his château was under renovation. His wife kept herself busy with his money since she couldn't have children. *He* kept himself busy reminiscing about Nexxa.

Nexxa was in the foyer—stone walls and cathedral ceilings—when introduced to Mr. Albert's special guest. She gracefully lowered the drink in her hand, giving way to her shock. Ten years faded away the moment he embraced her, and she remembered his scent. She expected the special guest to be a woman. Mr. Albert dated, never a serious girlfriend, but ironically kept them separate from his personal life. Quinn leaned into Nexxa and told her something that caused her to laugh. His energy was lighter now than when their paths had crossed a decade earlier with Kilmer and Klarin. Nexxa looked down the expansive corridor filled with white orchids flanked by white candles, trying to find a reason to excuse herself. *Don't cry, just don't cry*, she thought.

"Excuse me; I need to check on something." Mr. Albert stepped aside, making way for Nexxa. Quinn momentarily held his position.

"I'll join you," Quinn said, swiftly handing his champagne flute to the person standing to his left. He went after Nexxa.

Nexxa had always looked forward to perusing Mr. Albert's library. He added to his collection weekly with books in different languages, many of them about European history. She turned to see Quinn behind her and, extending her hand, allowed him to join her away from the guests. "This is quite a home," Quinn acknowledged as they made their way to the library, passing several modern, well-appointed rooms, each emulating the "Residence" on Etihad Airways. Mr. Albert's alter ego existed, thrived in this home. He once told Nexxa he liked to make a mess and have someone apologize to *him* while they cleaned it up. Quinn assumed Mr. Albert let Nexxa use his home for her brunch party because he was fucking her. Quite the contrary, as Mr. Albert and Nexxa had become friends early on when Nexxa moved to New York. It was unknown to her or anyone if he had any family, yet he was unsparing when it came to Nexxa.

Nexxa removed a book from a shelf in the library. With a book in hand, she turned, seeing Quinn had the same look he had a decade earlier in his home—when he had watched her while she admired his artwork during his party before he approached her. Nexxa took a deep breath as she looked past him through the window at the falling snow. She ran a finger along her bottom lip. *The last time my lips were dry, well, Sergei's pre-jack worked,* she remembered. Nexxa looked down at the book she held, opening the cover and closing the cover, and one more time with the cover. She could sense Quinn was nervous. Nexxa hadn't felt a man's vulnerabilities in a long time, if ever.

Quinn looked around the room. Was there any Scotch? He needed a Scotch. He smiled and walked toward her. Quinn removed the book from her hands, placing it down on the table. He grasped her, running his hands down her arms. He spoke softly at first, then with more directness, confidence. Their bodies were close, yet they had the past, present, and maybe a future between them. Quinn ran his hand across her collarbone; Nexxa grazed his other hand with hers.

Nexxa and Quinn, the "special guest," walked especially close, leaving the library to join the party again. Without any explanation, Nexxa's eight-hundred-dollar heels stopped her.

She looked to Quinn before darting away from him into the first entrance to the kitchen from the corridor. She missed Sergei; she smelled Sergei and perhaps didn't trust herself. Nexxa picked up a bottle of champagne sitting on the fifteen-foot-long stone countertop and poured herself a glass, then another. She hated Quinn for what he had told her when they were alone in the library. Quinn confessed something he had held in for a decade.

Nexxa stepped over to the wine fridge between the kitchen and the dining room; she saw the pentacle in the fireplace twist. "No, no," she whispered as she removed a bottle of red wine. Nexxa had a craving, and it needed tending to.

"Can I open that for you?" Nexxa turned to see Mr. Ball Snow. She watched, impressed that he could open a bottle of wine and surprised that he was still *trying*, pursuing her. He handed her his business card, naturally.

While watching Quinn, Sergei was conversing with Mr. Albert. He noticed how Quinn kept cupping his mouth with his hand, taking a sneaky whiff. What was he so eager to keep smelling? The leftover smell of hand soap? He had seen Nexxa walk away with him; he hadn't had a chance to find her.

Followed by an attendant with a tray that held a bottle of Beaujolais, Nexxa approached her sister. She stood over Iliada, seated on the semi-dark velvet bench under cathedral ceilings flanked with fire bowls. Nexxa could hear footsteps on the stone tile coming toward them—she felt her nipples harden, exposing slightly through her shimmering white dress—she could smell him coming for her. Nexxa glanced at the business card in her hand before placing the card on the tray beside her sister. Iliada looked at the card, smirking.

Nexxa crossed her ankles, enjoying the fragrance of the orchids on the basin where he had propped her. He pushed her dress up, exposing her panties. With his hand, he moved her thong over. Nexxa grasped his head with one hand and braced herself with her other. His tongue was warm, gentle, and assertive. She wondered who had waited more for this moment before she orgasmed. Thoughtful, he pulled her shimmering dress back down for her. She watched as he took a piss, purposely missing the white orchid petals in the toilet, replaced after each guest. *Mr. Albert is thorough*, she determined. He zipped his pants, and she kissed him, moving his hand onto her breast before he washed his hands. He moved his other hand onto her face. "It's how it should be," he muttered between kissing her lips.

Iliada was waiting outside of the powder room when Nexxa opened the door. "Here, put some on." She handed Nexxa a lip gloss.

"I'll be down there." Sergei motioned with his head toward the gathered guests at the other end of the expansive home.

Iliada pulled Nexxa by the arm into the bathroom. "He is so hot," she giggled while primping in the mirror. "I wonder if you have a baby with him if the baby will have dark hair like him." Nexxa froze. She wondered if she was mixing up the *little things*, the clues for this lifetime, which in this case would lead her to another choice, which might not be so good.

Stoically, she said, "Come on; it's time for the game."

Mr. Albert had an attendant pour him a glass of Greek ice wine and follow him outside into the snow with the bottle. He stepped upon his dais overlooking the sloped terrain. His attendant brought him a wooden box about a laptop's size, which he opened and took out three faux dragon eggs. "I need dragon eggs," he'd said, so his assistant had found some on Etsy. Before the guests were directed outside, he had his attendants hide the three colorful eggs as he watched.

Nexxa slipped off her heels as she made her way toward the party and twisted her hair up in a knot. She intended to follow her sister into the kitchen and slip out the side door to the outside. But he was there. Mr. Ball Snow handed Nexxa a flower, an orchid he took from one of the arrangements. Given the circumstances, she graciously accepted the borrowed orchid, pulling back when he moved in to embrace her. Mr. Ball Snow motioned with a cheesy shoulder movement and a hand gesture that he would be going outside. Nexxa looked over at the gentleman sitting at the other end of the island sipping Scotch; he winked at her.

As instructed, they removed their shoes and were ready to play "ball snow." Mr. Albert had a hidden sense of humor but was still very much in control as the Master of Ceremonies. Wooden signs had been erected on the lighted trees in the lower level area of the grounds with the game's name, "Winter Tag," as a nod to Laser Tag. He came up with the idea from watching movie clips from the '80s on YouTube, although he would never let on. The game was simple: throw a few snowballs at each other and look around for a dragon egg before your feet go numb. The game attendant ensured the curated music flowed in sync with their movements.

Nexxa took her place beside Mr. Albert, and his assistant draped her with a wool shawl covered with fresh flower buds in a mix of white and pastel pink. Together they watched as the game commenced. The event presented an appropriate time for Mr. Albert. With silence, he placed his left hand on the middle of Nexxa's arm. She looked to him; she looked out over the guests elatedly running about in the snow. He extended his right arm toward the guests; with the backdrop of a forest, he cast a glittering black over them and the land. A scattering of trees glowed. Nexxa sipped a glass of ice wine as she watched her sister blissfully play. Mr. Albert withdrew his A. Lange & Söhne pocket watch, held it for three minutes, then he nodded toward one man, the one emitting a *white glow* once the black began diminishing. Nexxa lowered her head; she lowered her hand holding the glass. She stepped down from the dais and, on her toes, quickly made her way back inside.

Poached pears topped with crème fraîche and an assortment of flavored Croatian brandies were served to each guest as they returned inside to warm up by the fire. There was no reward for finding a dragon egg. Sergei embraced Nexxa from behind. "Keep me warm," he said, hugging her as he shivered. Quinn entered the house carrying all three dragon eggs while conversing with Mr. Albert, managing a stoic face glancing at the Russian embracing Nexxa. Nexxa maneuvered in Sergei's arms, turning to face him, leading him to the fireplace where the party attendants were dispersing wool socks. He sat in an armchair in the dining room, pulling on the socks, and without Nexxa realizing it, he caught her looking toward Quinn in the kitchen. Quinn rested the eggs on the kitchen island and thanked a server as he poured more Scotch before joining the rest by the fire. Sergei stood, and Nexxa introduced him to Quinn. Their handshake was wintry. They made small talk, gruffing, as Nexxa would call it. Nexxa caught Viraj's eye and ever so slightly nodded him over.

"Hello, I'm Viraj, Nexxa's friend from the spa," he gabbed in his unmistakable way. She heard "Scotch," Sergei's voice, then Quinn's Irish accent, and Viraj's sweetness; her wolfness filled her head like smoke inhalation. *You just need to talk to him, smell him alone, once more; there's something you don't know.* She wanted the thoughts to stop—then crash, someone dropped their glass, and jeers erupted in the room. Nexxa looked down at her hand; *she* had dropped her glass and had cut her hand in the process. Quinn swiftly handed his drink to Viraj and reached for her hand, putting his cocktail napkin over the blood. An attendant rushed to Nexxa's aid. Seeing her hand dripping blood, he ran off, saying he would get a bandage.

Quinn walked Nexxa to the powder room, holding her hand, applying pressure. The attendant returned, following them to the bathroom.

"Do you have any iodine?" Quinn asked.

With an unsure face, he said, "I will find out."

"Can you tell me where my luggage is?"

"It's been deposited in your room," the attendant answered.

"Can you show me?" pressed Quinn.

The attendant cleared his throat and tugged at his white jacket before motioning for Quinn and Nexxa to follow him. They took the staircase in the back of the house, which led them directly into a bedroom. The attendants had taken the liberty of unpacking for Quinn.

"Toiletry bag?" Quinn looked around the bedroom. The attendant had left, closing the room door behind him.

"Maybe here," Nexxa suggested as she walked into the ensuite. Quinn followed her. It was quiet; they couldn't hear the party down below.

He unzipped his leather bag by the sink and withdrew a small bottle. She wanted to tell him about Kilmer. But she didn't want to talk about Kilmer either. He squeezed some iodine on her hand and reached for a tissue to catch the drips. She noticed a wedding ring in his bag. Something about him was comforting. Or maybe he was a conquest she needed. Quinn opened a bandage and applied it to the cut on her hand. His body was close to hers. She was able to smell. Nexxa's hair fell out of her makeshift knot; Quinn pushed a piece from her face.

"Tonight—seeing you again—has been great."

Nexxa exhaled, "Yes."

"In the loo with you," he whispered as he held her face and kissed her. Nexxa's mind flashed to earlier that night in the powder room. She couldn't catch herself. Quinn lifted her onto the basin. He looked her in her eyes before his mouth moved down her neck. Nexxa searched for the white. The white glow.

"Mmm," Quinn muttered, shaking his head with a naughty but happy look.

"I need to pee."

"And I need me Scotch." Quinn helped her off the vanity and kissed her on the cheek. He stepped out of the bathroom. Nexxa closed the door and sat on the toilet. *Don't hear me pee; just turn the water on a wee bit.* Sitting back down to pee, she only had to tinkle. Through the sound of the toilet flushing, she heard the sound of the hammer being pulled back on a gun. Then a knock on the bedroom door. "Nexxa, are you in there?"

Quinn placed his gun back into his carry-on and plopped it on the floor by the dresser.

What the fuck? Is that what it sounds like? Don't they keep the weapons in a safe in the garage? Shimmying her panties up, Nexxa rinsed her hands, and when she got her bandage wet, she pried open his toiletry bag to look for another one. The bag shifted, and Nexxa saw the cover of the magazine the bag had been placed atop.

It was a current issue of Forbes Middle East magazine. The heading for an article caught her eye. She flipped to page thirty-eight. "I spend most of my time away from being VP of Project Management for China Black Road in Cosplay character. I like to wear blonde wigs with my costume in The International Cosplay Competition. My country is close to Russia, so naturally, I am interested in their customs and traditions. Well, maybe just the morbid ones, which I draw upon for creating my evil twin." The woman had coffin-shaped nails adorned with gaudy jewels and a long blonde wig in a ponytail. She was also Asian. Nexxa read the caption under the picture. Diane Soo Hoo was the name.

Nexxa abruptly left Quinn's room, only saying that she needed to borrow the magazine that she waved as she dashed out of his bedroom. She ran down the staircase and passed by the guests. She saw Sergei in mid-conversation with Viraj; her eyes met his concerned eyes.

"Excuse me." He patted Viraj on the shoulder and walked briskly, trying to catch up to her. Nexxa was already sitting on her bed close to the nightstand lamp, reading the article.

"You okay?"

Nexxa wasn't sure either way.

"Nexxa?" Sergei was louder. She looked up from the magazine and held it out for him. Sergei stepped from the doorway and set down his Scotch. He held the magazine. "What is it?" He scanned the article, then closed it, laying it down by her on the bed. "Where did you get this?"

Nexxa's mind went to Quinn, the sound of brass sliding into a steel chamber, the magazine, and coffin-shaped nails in the video footage of the blonde woman in the guest room in Sergei's home. Sergei sat beside her and lifted her hand, kissing it. "My love." He pulled Nexxa into him, and they lay back on the bed. Sergei pulled the blanket draped over the end of the bed, covering them. He didn't ask Nexxa what happened when she was alone with Quinn, an *old friend*, as Nexxa had introduced him.

Sergei didn't pay any attention to why Nexxa was upset. His mind was on yet another proposition he had for her. But first, selfishly, Sergei hadn't fucked her in over two months. He ran his hand under her dress up her thigh. Nexxa was tense, guilty, and yes, she wanted to feel him inside her. He unzipped his pants and moved on top of her. Nexxa's phone buzzed; she assumed it was Iliada or Mr. Albert looking for her. Sergei fumbled around, feeling for the phone.

The way she looked, their intimacy, that turned him on. But seeing her in her environment, seeing more of who she was, more of her essence, rendered him senseless. Sergei wanted to say it; instead, he pulled out of her and stood up. Nexxa sat up, and Sergei pulled her to the edge of the bed and, stroking his penis, moved toward her. "Get on your knees," he directed, more like demanded. Nexxa knelt on the floor. "How deep can you take it?" He pushed the back of her head; she liked it. Nexxa's phone vibrated again. Sergei pulled his penis out of her mouth and huffed. Nexxa stood; he grabbed her and kissed her.

"Slow down," Nexxa whispered as they kissed. Sergei couldn't get it out of his mind—Nexxa, in the bathroom, from earlier that night. Nexxa told Sergei to lie down on the bed and positioned herself over him.

Each time her phone vibrated throughout the night, Sergei would move an arm over Nexxa, and once a leg over her. Nexxa was mainly awake; she never really slept. She wondered why Sergei was the way he was. Nexxa slipped on her white kimono-style robe then lifted her phone from the nightstand, on Sergei's side of the bed, where he had placed it. She looked down at him then left the room.

It continued, in the string of telling events with a message in Italian. She almost pushed to delete the voicemail when she heard, "Kilmer Davoren." A pain zigzagged down her chest. "He was—" Nexxa replayed the message. "He was… No," she said, shaking her head. She braced herself with her hand along the back of the sofa. "He, he's not supposed to be."

"He's not what?" Quinn asked, walking toward Nexxa. He grasped the hand that was holding her phone, putting it down on the sofa.

She expected to be alone in Mr. Albert's library. Nexxa looked to her extended fingers, moving to their own emotions. Shaking, she said, "Kilmer."

Quinn caressed her face. "Nexxa, what is it?"

With Quinn close to her again, Nexxa's zigzagging pain was close to freezing now. What was he doing there, with her, at Mr. Albert's house after all these years? She dashed, darted out of his reach—leaving him and down the corridor to a side door. Nexxa heard Quinn calling her name as she pushed in the security code, opening the door and running outside. She didn't feel the snow beneath her feet, like when she ran down the stairs with Sergei fleeing Medan in Beirut.

She felt his hand on her shoulder. Then on the front of her neck. When she fell, Quinn went down with her. That's because she intended him to. What she didn't expect was his hand to still be on her neck. This time was different; she didn't want Sergei to save her.

Nexxa lay still, eyes closed. She held onto Quinn's scent; it was more defined. She heard his voice.

"Nexxa, Nexxa." Quinn lifted her body from the snow-covered ground. He carried her to his room and put her on his bed. Her skin was cold, and her white robe was wet, exposing her breasts. Quinn stood over Nexxa's body; his feelings felt sorted, almost. He retrieved a towel from his bathroom. Quinn removed her robe. He laid the towel over her body. Quinn sat in the armchair by the window and looked to his bag on the floor, the one with his gun.

DIANE

Diane sat at her desk in her apartment in Shanghai, staring at the dead roses in the vase. Some of the blooms were drooping; some were simply dried up. She screamed, lifting the vase and throwing it against the wall. She had asked her friend to replace them before she returned, and weekly; there were supposed to be seven roses alive in the vase. Diane was tired; she had been traveling, disguising, smelling.

Diane slipped on a pair of clear latex gloves. She meticulously picked up the glass from the floor. A shard penetrated her left glove. She looked to the dusty framed photo on her desk. Wiping the glass, blood smeared across. Diane tore off the glove and, using her saliva, vigorously rubbed the frame until the blood was gone. She slammed the frame, breaking the glass and removing the photo. The same height as Diane, she was the only Uighur with fair skin and red hair Diane had *loved*, still loved.

Opening her wardrobe, she removed a brand-new suitcase. Opening a drawer, she removed a brand-new blonde wig. Sliding open a drawer to her vanity, she removed a brand-new bottle of nail polish, a new color, *Lavender Gliss.* Diane packed her suitcase. She rolled it out to the living room. Sitting down at her desk again, she re-read the last email from Nexxa. She printed it off, and with a knife, she sliced the printed email into tiny even slivers.

Sitting in her car in the parking garage of her building, she remembered how her love taught her how to drive. Diane played their favorite song, by a K-pop singer with a popular beat, "shake it, shake it," on repeat. She wanted one last drive in the car they had shared, only driving herself in circles in the garage, having never really learned how to drive out amongst the bustling city. Diane parked.

Wheeling her suitcase back inside, she wiped a tear. With only a few words describing her apartment and a few clicks, she listed her Shanghai apartment for sale on the start-up app, Lianjia. She typed up her resignation letter requesting approval to resign from her position with China Black Road. Once her resignation was approved, Diane would be free to leave China. But before leaving she would need to properly tend to the matter of her heart by visiting the grave of her beloved to burn more joss paper, giving her red-haired love money for her future travels.

Diane removed her top and bra. She licked her finger, drawing it down her décolletage and circling her finger just above her breast before wiping her finger dry and using it to unlock her phone. She scrolled through to the picture she had of Nexxa.

She scratched a coffin-shaped nail along the screen, lifted the phone to her nose and sniffed the image on the screen, and finally she licked the picture of Nexxa. Now she was ready. She was ready to accept that Nexxa had the wolfness like her. Diane plopped the phone down on the rug. She stepped over it, then did a backbend. She inhaled and exhaled; the phone vibrated, pulsed a lavender light.

Nexxa had something else Diane deemed envy worthy… her lavender glow.

ICE QUEEN II

The ceiling was painted the same as the walls—no detectable difference in color, which was Penthaus White. This was visible from lying on the bed. Her cheeks had become flush, and her nose was still rosy. Quinn wanted to kiss her, revive her.

Nexxa shivered, and Quinn stood. "Thank you," she said as she assessed the dry towel over her.

"What were you running for?"

Nexxa had many thoughts rolling around. Each one felt like a sharp icicle falling off. There was so much she wanted to say, to ask.

Quinn came to the bedside, pulling the duvet over her. "I'll only be a minute."

"Okay," Nexxa breathed.

Quinn left the room, closing the door behind him. In the library, he found Nexxa's mobile still on the sofa. He picked up the phone and saw the phone app still open. He pressed the play button on the voicemail Nexxa last listened to. Quinn knew something as well about Kilmer.

When she saw the chrome door lever move, Nexxa pushed herself up in Quinn's bed. She looked to her wet robe lying on the end. She stood, holding the towel in front of her cold body. Nexxa flashed a bashful smile. Quinn scanned the room and spotted the bathrobe he had brought. He held the robe out toward her. Nexxa held the towel with one hand, reaching with the other. Quinn laid the robe by her, turning around. "Let's have a cup of tea," he suggested.

Sitting at the kitchen island, Nexxa watched as Quinn managed to find the coffee mugs and the drawer with flatware. Nexxa motioned to the pantry where the tea was kept. Naturally, Quinn was familiar with the built-in Miele coffee system, knowing how to dispense hot water. He recently had one installed in his remodeled kitchen back in Ireland.

"So, you want to tell me what this is about? Kilmer—" he asked before Nexxa knew where to start. "You married that bloke?"

Nexxa indicated yes, then promptly clarified, "We're divorced."

"You're with?" Quinn moved his head and eyes, suggesting the man upstairs.

"I, well—"

"The message on your phone said they couldn't locate any other relatives to contact."

"Yeah, Kilmer didn't have any family."

Quinn cocked his head, running a hand over the top.

"Yeah, he told me he was an only child and that he never knew his father. I don't know what happened to his mother. He never would tell me."

"Many years ago, that night in Paris." Quinn shook his head with a look of disgust.

Nexxa felt the zagging chest pain; she remembered that night. Bits of it always managed their way into her lucid dreams. She knew what Quinn would say. He would say he was furious. She was sure he was furious with her for deceiving him when she was with Kilmer.

"Klarin," Quinn paused, leaning on the kitchen island with both hands, "was, is Kilmer's *sister*." Quinn said it sternly before continuing. "The woman I introduced you to, with Seamus, in the restaurant."

Nexxa's soft brown eyes were in shock. "What?"

"After what happened, that time in Paris," Quinn stopped to take a quick sip of his tea, "I learned of it," he said.

"No." Nexxa stood from her barstool. "No." She put her hand over her mouth. "He didn't have any family. I mean, that's what he told me. Fuck, she wanted, tried to kill me."

"Tried to kill you," Quinn repeated. "For fuck's sake. What do you mean?"

Nexxa took an exhaustive breath, looking down at her hands. "In Beirut, I was there for work."

Quinn set down his coffee mug, rushed to the other side of the island, and embraced her. Quinn was warm; he smelled of power. Nexxa hated the thoughts she was having while in Quinn's arms.

"I was expecting you to say how angry you were with me."

Quinn looked at Nexxa. "My dear, I was *never* angry with you." He kissed her on the forehead. Nexxa ran her hands through her hair, and her robe came untied. Quinn looked down at her body; he took his time, gently closing the robe and retying the belt.

"You're married?" Nexxa asked.

"I am."

"So...?"

"She, my wife, is back in Dublin." Quinn moved over to the refrigerator and took out the milk. "This man you are with. You met here?"

"He helped me. We met in Beirut."

"He's Russian," Quinn stated, thinking with his eyes.

"So, how long have you been married? Kids?"

Quinn cleared his throat. "No." He kept his eye contact with Nexxa. "No kids." Quinn leaned back, crossing his arms. He smiled.

"What?" Nexxa couldn't help but return the smile. "What is it, Quinn?" She thought she knew what he was thinking. She wanted to know if what he told her in the library during the party was real—truly how he felt.

"Nexxa?"

Nexxa looked toward the doorway of the kitchen. Sergei was standing there. "Sergei." Nexxa adjusted the robe she was wearing and walked toward him.

"What's going on?"

"I couldn't sleep. My phone. I just wanted to check it."

"Morning." Quinn looked to Sergei.

Sergei put his arms around Nexxa. "My love, you okay?"

"Uh-huh."

Sergei stood back from Nexxa. "Q. O. K?" he questioned, looking at the embroidered initials on the robe Nexxa donned.

Quinn kept his stance, arms folded. Nexxa felt him watching her and Sergei.

"I should go change." Nexxa looked over at Quinn. He conspicuously winked at her. Sergei noticed.

Upstairs, Nexxa stood before Sergei, wearing only the ruby ring Sergei had given her and Quinn's robe. She felt guilty and somewhat delirious.

"I woke, and you weren't in bed."

Nexxa was about to explain, gathering her thoughts, some not so good, when Sergei approached her and moved the collar of the robe. "What is this?" He saw she had nothing on under it. "You're naked?"

"I had a call, a voicemail." Nexxa looked around the room for her phone. She forgot she didn't have it with her. Sergei pulled the belt to the robe. Her shoulders were exposed, and then it fell to the floor. "I'm freezing."

He lifted her hand that donned the ruby ring and pulled her body to his. Nexxa moved away from his touch and picked up her chemise from the bench by the end of the bed. She slipped it on, went to the dresser, and pulled out a pair of panties. Sergei watched her. Nexxa walked over to him and picked up the robe from the floor. She placed it on the bed.

"I got a voicemail—this police officer from Rome. My ex-husband is *dead*." Sergei's face bore no emotion. "I thought all this time he was here, in the city, following me or watching me."

"Why did you have this man's robe on?" Sergei lifted the robe and plopped it on the chair.

"What? I, I was scared and in shock. I ran outside. He, he came after me."

"He came after you?" Sergei furrowed his brow.

Nexxa shook her head, saying, "No, not like that."

"Are you coming with me to Moscow?"

"What?" Nexxa questioned, gesturing with one arm bent at her hip. "Sergei, I need—why wouldn't you tell me why you came to Rome?"

"You haven't answered me," Sergei insisted.

Nexxa lowered her arm. She looked to Sergei, meeting his eyes.

"And now," Sergei motioned with his head toward Quinn's robe, saying, "this man."

"Did you know my ex-husband was going to be there? In Rome?"

Sergei moved his hand along his jaw. The thought of losing Nexxa crossed his mind. He wanted her back on his soil.

"I have to know what happened. That woman that was with Medan. I mean, I didn't know why she was there. Now I know. Kilmer had a sister, Klarin."

Sergei tugged at her hand. Nexxa conceded. Still tired since it was only five a.m., she got back into bed and fell on the pillow next to Sergei's warm body. She wanted to say something about the woman, Diane Soo Hoo, from China Black Road, about her blonde wig and coffin-shaped nails. She wanted to believe that nothing else mattered when she was with Sergei. Instead, Nexxa muttered, "I have to go to Rome to collect his ashes."

It was sunny when Nexxa awoke around seven-thirty a.m. She heard the water running in the bathroom. She waited for Sergei to come out, but it seemed like forever. She glimpsed at herself in the square mirrored vase on the nightstand. Sergei didn't answer her when she tapped on the bathroom door. When she opened the door, he wasn't in the bathroom, but the faucet was on just a little. She yawned while on the toilet, and while washing her face and brushing her teeth, she noticed his toiletries weren't on the sink vanity. *Wasn't his stuff in here last night?*

Nexxa saw Quinn's robe still in the bedroom. She figured she would find Sergei first, then return the robe to Quinn. Opening a drawer for a pair of socks, she saw that Sergei's bag wasn't on the floor by the dresser. She ran back to the bathroom. After becoming sick, spitting up some, Nexxa's instinct was to call him—she remembered her phone was either with Quinn or somewhere in the house.

Downstairs she didn't see anyone in the kitchen. She ran to the library and opened the door, hoping to see her phone in there. As she stood disappointed, she heard Iliada and Viraj coming down the hall; they sounded happy. Nexxa put on a smile. She greeted them as she walked past them toward the stairs leading to the guest room that was for Quinn.

"He left," Iliada blurted.

"He did?" Nexxa stopped on the first step.

"Yeah, he gave me something to give to you."

Nexxa turned back to Iliada. "He gave you something?"

"Yeah, he said," Iliada's tone was calm, "he wished you would come with him."

"Would come with him?" Nexxa repeated. As she heard

herself, her eyes widened. Iliada was talking about Sergei. "Where?" Nexxa eagerly stepped off of the staircase. "Where is it?"

"It's in your room." Nexxa dashed past Iliada and Viraj. "I just brought it to you!" Iliada shouted to Nexxa as she was running down the corridor.

Nexxa had the urge to spit up again. In her room, she scanned with her eyes. It didn't occur to her to ask exactly what was left for her. Then she saw a white envelope on the nightstand by Sergei's side of the bed. Her hands were worried as she opened it. Money fell on the floor.

She unfolded the letter. Scanning it, she saw her name then looked to the bottom to see an address and a number written down. *What? Dublin?* Wiping a tear, she saw it was signed *Quinn*. She laid the letter down. The money, several thousand dollars, was on the floor. Nexxa quickly bent, picking up the money. She folded the letter and started to tear it. Then she opened the letter again, looking at the bottom, at Quinn's signature. She refolded the letter and placed it in the zipper pocket of her purse, along with the money.

Mr. Albert was laughing. He looked younger when he laughed. Nexxa walked down the hall, following the voices. The door for Mr. Albert's private study was ajar; Sergei looked over at her. Nexxa's eyes spoke her surprise. He smiled, and Nexxa became flush. Sergei excused himself. Mr. Albert turned, looking outside over his property. Sergei seemed happy. Did Mr. Albert tell him something?

Nexxa had light perspiration on her face. "You didn't leave." Nexxa's relief was in her voice.

Sergei approached her and wiped her brow. "Leave?"

"Your stuff, bag, it's gone."

"I thought we could go to the city." Sergei caressed her face. "See where you live."

"See where I *lived*." Nexxa smirked.

"Mr. Albert was just telling me about his business in the city."

"Yeah, uh-huh, his club."

"His club?" Sergei cocked his head. "He said he is an architect."

"Yeah, that too."

"Well, I was thinking…" Sergei paused.

Nexxa turned her face slightly with her smile. "Okay?"

"I will need to do some modifications to my house." Sergei grasped her hand. "You know, when you move in."

Iliada came down the hall. "Did you get what he left for you?" she asked innocently.

"Who left for you?" Sergei searched her face. "Nexxa?"

Nexxa looked back toward the bedroom. The money, the letter, Quinn, came to her mind.

Iliada made a face showing she was perplexed. She walked past them and into their bedroom. Sergei followed her. Nexxa looked to her hands, extending her fingers. Mr. Albert emerged from his private study. She knew his face was meant to encourage her, to inspire her belief in the white glow, which singled out her fated soulmate across lifetimes. She walked briskly toward her bedroom. Iliada was already leaving, and she started to say something to Nexxa when Nexxa put a finger up, shushing her. Iliada mouthed, "Oh."

There was an arrangement of flowers in a glass vase on the dresser. Sergei was standing in the middle of the bedroom.

"The head attendant brought flowers to the guests' rooms." He motioned with his head toward the flowers.

"Ah, okay." Nexxa's eyes looked to some money she had missed on the floor under the bed.

Sergei noticed. "What's that?" he asked as he moved over, reaching for the cash peeking out from the bed.

"I really have to go to Rome," blurted Nexxa.

Sergei stepped toward her, cocking his head. "I can take you."

"Sergei." Nexxa looked at the money in his hand. "When, or like, why did you come to Rome?"

Nexxa had drops of moisture above her top lip and along her hairline. She held her forehead—wondered if it mattered why he came to Rome, how Kilmer died.

Sergei came intimately close. "You're…" he started as he wiped above her lip. "You look…" Sergei lifted a piece of her hair. "There's purple around you."

Nexxa rested her head against Sergei's chest. "It's just the lighting in here." Sergei wrapped his arms around her, tightly but comfortably. Looking to the dresser, Nexxa admired the flowers. She counted the flowers. Six. There were *six* flowers, a perfectly even number aligning with the Russian superstition of a bad omen. Nexxa had knowledge of the seven spirits before the throne of God, the seven planetary beings, and now through research, she was aware of the meaning behind the seventh flower being smashed on the video in Sergei's home.

Sergei had told Nexxa that Rochelle was in Psylab. Klarin died before her in Beirut. Diane was the only one left.

Sergei had just seen her lavender, her *Smeared Lavender*, and she had seen his *white glow*.

Epilogue

Mors Tristis

ROME — JANUARY 5, 2014

The frost that delicately covered Rome carried a scent of religious faith. Iliada stopped pushing the luggage cart and retrieved perfectly rolled cashmere blends from her black leather Tumi carry-on. She shivered as she helped Nexxa maneuver her arms in her sweater. Nexxa paused, and simultaneously they pulled their hoods over their tied-back blonde hair while standing in the passenger pickup area of Leonardo da Vinci-Rome Fiumicino Airport.

"Can you smell that?" Nexxa asked, detecting the smell of death. Iliada shook her head to indicate no. But… she *could* smell something. All the devout Catholics not far away in the Vatican.

"St. Regis," confirmed the driver.

"Yes," Nexxa nodded. This time, Nexxa and Iliada *were* staying at The St. Regis, courtesy of Sergei.

She purposely hadn't eaten much on the flight from New York, hoping to ward off any nauseating feelings upon her return. After she fastened her seatbelt Nexxa pulled her phone from her handbag, searching for the mobile number of the Italian police officer that had called her in December. She scrolled through the contact info looking at the address of the crematorium: *Via dei Reti*, 1/A. The *Carabinieri*, Italian police, hadn't had any luck locating Kilmer's relatives. Nexxa's number was still in his phone as Wife My Brown Eyed Girl. Nexxa remembered feeling like she was going to throw up when the Italian police officer inquired if she was "Wife, my brown-eyed girl."

Now she was going to have to answer "only a few questions," Carabiniere Vice Brigadiere Giardini had explained to her over the phone a few weeks ago in his thick Italian accent. She knew about a blonde wig and some Xanax, a cup of tea she made Kilmer, and him lying on top of her—ick, she remembered how his erection felt against her backside. But nothing more really. She knew she had had questions for Sergei. "Don't mention me," Sergei had told her before further explaining: saying the least is always best when dealing with law enforcement. So, Nexxa assured him that she would not mention him, expecting to find out more about how Kilmer died when she spoke to the police officer. Maybe knowing would give her the feeling she was searching for about Kilmer.

Arriving at the hotel, Nexxa began her usual: assessing the environment and taking count of patrons and staff. Looking in the direction of the hotel bar Nexxa visualized the afternoon when she, Iliada, and baby Natina, upon Kilmer's insistence, had a round of drinks.

"Nexxa," Iliada said while rummaging through the carry-on they shared. "Nexxa!"

"Oh, sorry." Nexxa pointed to an inside pocket where she had placed their passports.

Iliada took charge, handing the front desk lady their passports and confirming the length of their stay. Iliada hadn't a worry; she was different this time. Time spent at Mr. Albert's estate had been good for her. She listened more, taking in Nexxa's interactions with Teacher. Flash, their Gargowl, had become her confidant, teaching her Latin and critiquing her yoga poses. She also discovered her interest in alchemy when one evening Mr. Albert bumped his glass of wine, knocking it over. Iliada quickly handed Mr. Albert the napkin she had just used to blot her lip glossimer with. She watched as he used the cloth to wipe the wine—how a powdery substance formed on the table where the spill had happened. On a supernatural high, she decided that if they never returned to live in NYC, she could still be happy.

Nexxa stared at her clothes, hanging in the armoire of their hotel room. Iliada motioned to a top and a pair of bootcut pants. When Nexxa remained motionless, Iliada withdrew the recently hung clothes and handed them to Nexxa. Properly dressed for the deceased, they left The St. Regis.

Mr. Dragonetti warmly greeted them outside of *Cremazione Roma* and Nexxa returned his smile. She told herself that this was the last good deed for Kilmer. Inside Vice Brigadiere Giardini introduced himself. Nexxa detected a scent in the hallway as Mr. Dragonetti escorted the three of them to his office. Vice Brigadiere Giardini positioned himself behind the desk. Nexxa heard his questions; she answered. An urn was placed on the desk. Nexxa and Iliada stood. Iliada asked for a bag. They left.

On the drive back to the hotel, Nexxa's phone buzzed with a call from Sergei. She pushed the button to decline. The first time ever. She had just answered questions about Kilmer to an Italian police officer, and she still had unanswered questions from Sergei. However, one thing seemed strange. They asked if Kilmer would have been in Rome with a woman. It seemed a strand of long black hair was found on his body, on his shirt. Suppose Nexxa had been told about a strand of blonde hair—hers, the wig—that would have made sense. But a strand of long black hair?

"Yay, that's done now! Let's go for drinks to celebrate," Iliada cheered.

"Well, would it be okay if we just got some wine and took it back to the hotel room?" Nexxa asked.

"Okay… how about we go for at least one drink in the hotel bar?" Iliada countered.

"Hmm." Nexxa leaned her head back, thinking.

"And yeah, Kilmer wouldn't be here this time to make it fucking weird!" Iliada reminded her sister.

When they arrived back at The St. Regis hotel, they promptly made their way to the bar. It did feel lighter this time. Holiday decorations, lights, and fresh green garlands were still strewn, giving an ambiance quite different than when they had been there months ago. A similar-looking bartender was behind the bar. He was tall and medium build with long dark hair tied back—Iliada's observation, not Nexxa's. A table by the fireplace was available and drinks were promptly served while Nexxa was preoccupied with assessing the patrons. Iliada loved when Nexxa would sum up a couple. "That man is obviously only with that woman because her parents are wealthy Italian aristocrats," Nexxa said, looking with her discerning eyes toward the table by the window. "And… that man is here on a business trip and hoping to have a taste of another woman, while his wife is at home in America assuming he is *mostly* faithful."

Iliada laughed, "Really?"

"I'm going to the ladies' room." Nexxa stood abruptly.

"Are you okay?" asked Iliada, not wanting the fun to end.

"Yeah, I just need to pee."

Nexxa grasped her neck, feeling her tense muscles matching her tired eyes as she walked out of the bar. A gaggle of ladies giggling breezed past her as she made her way down the corridor. All but one of them had British accents, one of them being Irish. She smiled with the thought of their innocent adventure. *Probably on a girl's holiday trip*, she thought. The end of the corridor was dim, only wall sconces flanking a mirror. Nexxa stopped. She examined the skin under her eyes. Moving her head to the right she spotted something—rather, someone. A woman was walking toward her, sky-blue coat, dark hair. The woman narrowly passed by Nexxa entering the ladies' room.

Iliada ordered another drink. One for Nexxa too. The waiter placed her glass down. "This Language" by Stateless began playing; a patron bumped the waiter and Iliada watched as Nexxa's glass toppled over as the waiter was placing it down, wine spreading on the table. Iliada rose and dashed out of the hotel bar.

Standing in front of the mirror by the bathroom, Nexxa

retrieved her lipstick from her purse and applied some. When the woman exited the ladies' room, Nexxa waited a few seconds then followed her down the corridor and out of the hotel. A Bentley Bentayga in Dragon Red emerged, and the woman with black hair wearing the sky-blue cashmere coat entered the passenger side. Standing on the steps of the hotel entrance as the vehicle pulled away, Nexxa saw the woman's profile. *Attractive, but no one I know.*

Iliada pushed through the hotel's entrance. She gave Nexxa a big *little* sister look thinking, *What the fuck?* Nexxa shrugged her shoulders and mouthed, "I don't know."

Jetlagged the next day and with the euro to U.S. dollar not in their favor, Iliada decided to see what else was happening on the scene during a frosty Italian January. She found a gaggle of British ladies there for a discounted winter dating excursion called "Single Women Looking for Amore in Italy." Iliada happily accepted the group's invitation to join their table for drinks before their afternoon walking tour began.

Nexxa sat at the desk in their suite looking at the pamphlet that came with the urn which explained about "care and storage suggestions." Her phone vibrated.

"Be careful while you're there," Sergei spoke when she answered.

Nexxa sighed. "We don't have any plans for the day." Sighing again. "Nothing planned."

"What's wrong, Nexxa?"

Nexxa tossed the cremation pamphlet in the trash then placed something from the waste bin over it. "I'm fine."

"I miss you. I'm ready to see you."

"Yeah me too. I—"

"I have to take this call. Call you back," Sergei responded quickly.

Nexxa plopped her phone down on the desk. She thought back to when she had declined his call the day before. Nexxa stood and walked to the window. She watched a couple and their toddler walking down the street. She picked up her phone and typed out a text: *I miss you too! I can't wait to be there with you.♥* Nexxa deleted the heart emoji before sending the text then plugged her phone in to charge. She put on her hooded cashmere wrap and left their room.

Standing for a moment outside of the hotel bar she watched Iliada. She was smiling—laughing. Nexxa joined Iliada, and the ladies insisted on buying them a bottle of wine. It was a nice red blend. One glass down, Nexxa summed up the women. The night before they had looked younger, at least to Nexxa's tired eyes. Only one in the group seemed eager, more like desperate, to find a love connection in Italy. Three of them were in their late forties and only interested in traveling. And the last one was a very mature virgin.

The Italian woman who arranged the single ladies love group arrived and the women invited Nexxa and Iliada to tag along on their venture. Nexxa listened to the woman telling them about the history of Vatican City. "In full—State of the Vatican City, Italian—*Stato della Città del Vaticano.* Vatican City is the world's smallest fully independent nation state. The medieval and Renaissance walls form its boundaries except on the southeast at St. Peter's Square, *Piazza San Pietro,*" the lady said in one full breath. The guide and the women, along with Iliada, continued down the street. Nexxa lagged, watching as two tourists, tipsy, were gawking at the Pontifical Swiss Guards commenting on their traditional dress, mustard yellow and blue boots peeking out from under the black capes they wore for winter.

A guard called out to Nexxa. She pulled her hood down. Nexxa's eyes met his. They were gleaming a shade of lavender. His tone was sincere. Without looking around Nexxa knew she was alone—she was the only incarnated soul who could hear him. Nexxa mouthed, "Iliada, Iliada."

Engaged by their British accents and their light cavorting, Iliada moved along with the group of women and their guide. The lights from St. Peter's Basilica pulsed. Iliada froze. One of the women inquired if she was okay. Iliada shook her head yes… then, she ran.

The two of them stared at the guard who was not allowed to move or leave his post. Iliada clenched Nexxa's hand. A man in a gray hooded cloak emerged standing in the space behind the two guards. The guards turned and left walking toward the medieval gates that guarded Vatican City.

The cloaked man, Drakos, motioned gently with his hand saying, "Come here. Come closer."

Nexxa turned to Iliada and said, "Stay behind me."

"I'm walking with you!" Iliada asserted, squeezing Nexxa's hand. They reached the man in gray feeling the barrier of impenetrable air that separated their bodies.

Drakos whispered to Nexxa, *"Tua lavandula a lupo desideratur."* Nexxa grasped her throat. The scent she had detected in the crematorium hovered above them—which meant Nexxa's wolfness wasn't alone. She either had an admirer or someone that felt she was trespassing…

LIST OF INTERESTING TERMS

Appetizer Wine
Wine such as white or rosé consumed before red wine or a cocktail

Backfill People
Author Dolores Canon's description for people other than your immediate family

Bloomberg
Live trading system used in finance

Cash and Prizes
Obviously cash, gifts, and other monetary compensation

Dlisted
Michael K's gossip site

Fuckability
High on the desirability scale; deemed fuckable by potential suitors

Gargowl
Mixed species of an Elf Owl and Gargoyle. Feathery exterior approximately ten inches high. Face of a snowy owl without a bill. Petite bodies with petite wings, arms, and legs.

Gruffing
A dialect of growling from man to man in conversation

Holding up the Wall
Lingering in an upscale lounge or restaurant without a reserved table, especially for women

Izba
Traditional Russian forest house

Kikimora
A dark spirit that takes a form of a beautiful woman and then visits men in their dreams, torturing them with desire and dragging life out of them

Little Things
Clues before we incarnate, from the book *Journey of Souls*

Loku Notch, Russian
English—Good night

Long Island Lolito
Middle-aged man from Long Island, NY

Luxury Import
Women with blonde hair in NYC that are not from the tri-state area

Masterly Humanness
Exhibiting skillful traits lending to unmasked supernatural abilities

Modern Medieval Vampy
Modernized decorum reflective of centuries ago, including an element of black

Rigout, Irish
English—Outfit

Russian Tea Cakes
Petite ball-shaped cookies doused in powdered sugar
Recipe derived from Eastern European shortbread cookies

Smeared Lavender
A lavender glow, specific to Nexxa Davoren. One of many possible glows around an enlightened soul providing protection from spiritual attacks, visible to other enlightened souls and sinister entities with supernatural powers.

Teacher
Also known as Master, a respectful way to address a teacher in China

Vampy
A life less ordinary filled with all things black

Vnuchok, Russian
English—Grandson

Wolfness
Gifted sense of smell; the ability to track scents on a higher level similar to the Canis lupus species

Aut habet ille gustum meliorem quam meum?, Latin
Ily na vkus ona luchshe menya?, Russian
English—Or does she taste better than me?

Cogito ergo sum, sed ante futuis me., Latin
Ya dumayu, poetomu ya est. No snachala trahny menya.,
Russian
English—I think therefore I am but first fuck me.

I ya tebya lyublyu., Russian
English—And I love you.

Stalk Natalie Rucando, founder of Smeared Vampire

If you liked my first novel please leave a review!